BELINDA JONES

The California Club

arrow books

Published by Arrow Books in 2003

3 5 7 9 10 8 6 4 2

Copyright © Belinda Jones 2003

First published in the United Kingdom in 2003 by Century

Arrow Books Limited
Random House UK Ltd
20 Vauxhall Bridge Road, London, SW1V 2SA

Random House Australia (Pty) Limited
20 Alfred Street, Milsons Point, Sydney, New South Wales 2061, Australia

Random House New Zealand Limited
18 Poland Road, Glenfield
Auckland 10, New Zealand

Random House South Africa (Pty) Limited
Endulini, 5a Jubilee Road, Parktown 2193, South Africa

The Random House Group Limited Reg. No. 954009

www.randomhouse.co.uk

A CIP catalogue record for this book is avilable from the British Library

Papers used by Random House UK Limited are natural, recyclable
products made from wood grown in sustainable forests. The
manufacturing processes conform to the environmental regulations of the
country of origin

ISBN 0 09 944548 4

Type by SX Composing DTP, Rayleigh, Essex
Printed and bound in
Bookmarque Ltd, Croydon, Surrey

For Tony Horkins

(for showing me just how fabulous
unrequited love can be)

Acknowledgements

First thank you to Kate Elton, my awesome editor, who has guided me with such expertise throughout the writing and development of this book; I really feel she deserves a co-author credit. (It is beyond me how you manage to remain so patient while unscrambling my brain but I am most grateful for your superhuman powers!)

Abundant appreciation as ever to the gems at Random House – Ron, Mark, Georgina, Tiffany, Kate, Lisa (even now you're gone!), Sarah and Cassie. I couldn't wish for a lovelier or more supportive team.

Supertini toast to my agent Lizzy Kremer, accountants Hitesh and Athos (who happens to be a black belt in karate!), the ultimate Surf Diva Izzy Tihanyi and my beloved Belles Sarah and Sammy.

Hi to my fly guy Richard Bartlett-May who continues to amaze me with his lightening-quick research skills – you're the best in the business and you're not even in the business!

Gracious thank-yous to Lauren at the Hotel Del Coronado, Wendy at The Beverly Hills Hotel and to the creators of Madonna Inn – Phyllis & Alex, you are an inspiration!

To the hard-working animal lovers at Shambala,

Tiger Rescue and Bobbie at Lions, Tigers & Bears in California – thank you for your insights and the cub-cuddling privileges.

To my exquisite ma, Pamela. Thank you for not understanding what the heck was going on in the original Chapter One – it's so much better now!

California sunshine to all the family Joneses, Gwythers, Johnsons and Lamberts (especially Julie and William) and my faux-husband James and kitty Cabbage who accommodate my anti-social tapping so blithely.

To Donald Short for the 'kissing M&Ms' concept.

Finally, to Lara, my heroine's namesake – this book is in honour of our twenty-year friendship. (Even if I am hopeless at keeping in touch I've thought of you on every page!)

1

Elliot.

I've been carrying a torch for him so long people mistake me for the Statue of Liberty. In fact just last month I celebrated a whole decade of unrequited love. But now look at me – standing at Heathrow airport about to jet off with His Sexiness for two weeks of swaying palms, candy-coloured convertibles and air-brushed skies.

Shame he's bringing his girlfriend.

Elise. That's right – Elliot and Elise. The two Es. Shouldn't be allowed.

It would all be fairly unbearable were it not for the fact that I am to be joined by two fabulous allies – Sasha and Zoë. They got me through the first meeting with Elise and they can get me through this. Not that this was supposed to be an ordeal. The original plan was a two-week romp over to California to visit our beloved friend Helen and stage a grand sandy reunion of our old gang: the Brighton Beau-Belles. For the record, we comprise one beau (Elliot) and four belles (Helen, Sasha, Zoë and me – Lara). Categorically no Elises.

1

The five of us were drawn together one brow-moppingly hot summer by The Seaflower – Brighton's most wincingly chintzy B&B. I'm allowed to say that because it belonged to my mother. Belonged. Past tense. As of a week ago it belonged to me. But I may as well continue using the past tense because, before I can so much as change a lace doily, I am about to lose it. That's got to be the ultimate definition of carelessness – losing a six-guest-room building. And I got off to such a great start – inheriting it without my mother even having to die and just at a time when I fancied a career change. (I'm a Home Stylist which sounds bogus, I know, but in reality I make a decent living shopping with other people's money and providing the finishing touches once the interior decorators have done their darndest. Whether you're after a Regency mud-scraper of Warhol original, an antique Venetian mirror or functioning Sodastream to ruin the look of your Tikki Bar, I'm your woman.)

The thought of getting my hands on the B&B – ripping out every carpet and cornice – thrilled me, as for nearly twenty-two years I've been planning a stunning re-design from the depths of my ever-metamorphosing bedroom. Every year since I was eight, my mum has given me a birthday present of a Room Makeover Kit (pot of paint and a new duvet cover in the lean, younger years, hard cash ever since I was big enough and ugly enough to haggle at flea markets). Each spring I'd create a whole new environment for myself – running the gamut from space-age tinfoil to Zen bamboo. But not this year. This year I'm going to be thousands of miles from home, staying in someone else's hotel, assessing their knick-knacks.

I was hoping we'd be checking in to the hotel where Helen works as head pastry chef – the legendary Hotel Del Coronado, set on a tiny island across the bay from San Diego. It's where *Some Like It Hot* was filmed and still attracts big movie stars today – in fact the day Helen called to say Russell Crowe had just checked in was the day we finally quit our assorted procrastinations and booked our flights.

I don't know why she's got us staying elsewhere (she wouldn't say why or where) as I'm sure she could have wangled us a reasonable room rate with her keen negotiating skills. That's how she got out to America in the first place, on a business exchange with a tech company in Arizona. But how she ended up fluffing meringues by the seaside is beyond us all.

Helen was always the executive among us, even at the age of nineteen when she decided to use the B&B as a case study for her Business Studies degree course. That's how we met. It was an auspicious start within a matter of months she'd taken over from our accountant, neatly trimming back our overheads and plumping up our profits. She was a natural – so smart, so quick, so ambitious – and as the rest of the group began to form Helen easily filled the role of Mother Hen, but never in a clucky, fussy way. It was more that she's the hyper-organized one. At times she can come off a little bossy but she always has our best interests at heart, chivvying us along, intent on us reaching our full potential. Mrs Motivator, we used to call her.

I stepped out the way of an out-size family struggling with an over-stacked trolley (which will almost certainly topple over and flatten at least one of their three tots before they reach the lifts) and survey the airport concourse for signs of Zoë. I arranged to meet her half an hour early so I could break the news about the B&B to her first. For all her in-yer-face bravado she's going to be the most devastated about losing it. It was her home for seven years, after all.

Zoë turned up at The Seaflower just shy of midnight one Tuesday in June with a face snogged free of make-up and the man responsible for her stubble rash lurching behind her. He was much older – twenty-five, I think. Doesn't sound that old until you consider that she was fifteen at the time. They were both drunk and not the least bit interested in hearing about the coffee-making facilities. The next morning she woke to find him gone, leaving a soggy condom (actually a blessing – teenage pregnancy runs in her family) and an unpaid bill. As a schoolgirl with only a Betty Boop purseful of coins to her name, this presented her with something of a dilemma.

My mum threatened to call her parents but the look on Zoë's face made me intervene. Mum was late for the hairdresser's anyway so she left the situation in my inexperienced hands. I'd seen enough soaps to know that all problem-solving began with a nice cup of tea and so I took her through to our private living area, away from the other guests. I even made use of the teacosy – the kind now the favoured headwear of

Enrique Iglesias – and something about the general clichéd homeliness of our kitchen caused Zoë to spill her heart out.

She told me all about her volatile, racist stepfather (who seemed permanently furious with Zoë that her real father was black) and her cowering, in-denial mother. She had no one to stand in her corner and I could only imagine what her stepfather would do if he found out what she'd been doing last night, and with whom. (Not that Zoë knew – she never even got the stubbly chin's name.)

Being five years older than her and having always hankered after a younger sister, I adopted her on the spot. And then my mum did the same for real a year later. The three of us lived in giggly, girlie companion-ship until the day Zoë decided her destiny lay in Hemel Hempstead. Not an obvious relocation destination for someone hoping to be discovered, but at the time she had a more valid reason for moving – her youngest cousin on her father's side was diagnosed with dyspraxia (formerly known as the clumsy child syndrome) and in her efforts to gather every scrap of information on the subject she so impressed the MD of the Dyspraxia Foundation that they offered her a job at their HQ in HH. It was just answering enquiries and general office admin but considering Zoë had barely attended school she felt this was her big break.

It was a real wrench for me, not least because I felt like she didn't need me any more, but I understood that she had something to prove to herself – her mother and stepfather barely set a skanky toe outside

Brighton's notorious Whitehawk Estate and she has always felt a keen need to not be like them. I reckon the 'Have a Beautiful Day!' mentality of California has got to be the ultimate leap away – must remind her to send them a postcard.

'Lara!' A clattering of mule heels and a jangle of charms announces Zoë's arrival. Since I saw her last, her springy brown curls have been ironed straight and interlaced with multi-coloured extensions hanging in chunky layers past her shoulders like a carwash brush. Gotta love her – she's full-on drag queen glamour 24/7.

'Did you see him?' she yelps, releasing me from an overexcited embrace.

I take a moment to recover – Zoë's hugs always put me in mind of those junkyard compressor machines that can turn a tank into a battered metal sheet in one crunch.

'Did I see who?' I ask, setting my shoulder back in its socket.

'Ian McShane – you know, Lovejoy! – he's over there at first class check-in.'

That's way beyond my viewing range so I have to take her word for it. (Not that we normally give any credence to Zoë's star-spotting – to her every man in a tuxedo is Pierce Brosnan, every grey-haired gent drinking red wine is Anthony Hopkins and every petite brunette eyeing the security cameras is Winona Ryder. Even if we're at the Harlequin Shopping Centre in Watford.)

'He's still a hottie, isn't he?' she continues, leering over at the bushy-browed grin.

I roll my eyes – considering she's only twenty-five, Zoë is partial to a strange array of retro crushes. I blame the repeats on Living TV.

'I think it's a sign!' she decides.

'Of what?' I laugh.

'That I'm going to shag a celebrity!'

'Well, law of averages, it's going to happen sooner or later.'

'I'll have you know I've been very restrained lately,' she sniffs.

'No more single fathers, child psychologists or male nurses?' I check.

'No, I've cut right back!' Zoë looks pious.

'Conserving your energy for this trip?'

She nods eagerly. Men of America beware.

'So what did you want to talk about?' she tilts her head expectantly.

Suddenly I can't do it. The timing is all out. She's hyped up about the holiday and I don't want to see the work-of-art that is her eye make-up streaking on my account. Maybe it's best I tell the Beau-Belles about the B&B when we're all together?

'Lara?' Zoë tries to prompt a response.

'I just wanted to make sure you'd get here before Elliot and Elise – you know how I feel about seeing him with her . . .' It's only half a lie – I am genuinely queasy at the prospect.

She gives me an understanding squeeze. 'Vile creature. I don't know why he had to bring her,' Zoë grumbles. 'Why can't it just be our gang like the good old days?'

'Like she was going to leave him alone with four women,' I huff.

'Yeah but he's known us for years, if he was going to get it on with any of us it would've happened by now. Oh!' Zoë clamps her hand over her mouth. 'Sorry Lara, I—'

'It's okay,' I mumble.

'Obviously he wouldn't *you know* with the rest of us. But you . . . you he could shag any minute!' Zoë gives me an earnest smile.

I'll be lucky if he can hold himself back!' I try to play along. 'We might have to do it right here on the suitcase scanner.'

Nervous laughter.

I wish I could convince the Belles that I'm over Elliot so they wouldn't have to constantly feel bad on my behalf, but it's tricky. First I'd have to convince myself.

'At least we can count on Helen to be single!' Zoë takes a different tack. 'Maybe she can hook us up with some naked chefs!'

I chuckle. She may well have some spare – Helen has always found men too disobedient and lax with their promises to take seriously. She once totted up how many hours her sister wasted waiting for the phone to ring or sobbing into her pillow over some skateboarding schmuck and – other than the occasional accidental summer romance – decided she had more productive things to do with her time. Zoë's

8

relationships rarely lasted either, but that's more down to her 'variety is the spice of life' motto.

As for Sasha, she gets more offers than all of us put together but never seems particularly keen on any of the poor blighters. She only goes on dates to prove she isn't aloof and out of fear of seeming ungrateful, because she's heard so many girls complaining they never got asked out. Whereas I long to inspire eternal devotion, she actually finds that infatuated puppy-dog look the biggest turn-off. She once told me it makes her want to give the guy a good slap and screech, *'Stop looking at me!'* Well, if she acted on that impulse today she would have already assaulted half the men in Terminal 4 – as she walks towards us they gawp after her slinky bod and swishy hair like she's hooked their noses with an invisible fishing line.

I look at my watch. 1 p.m. on the dot. Sasha never did learn the diva ways of a supermodel despite nine years in the business and a cereal ad campaign that made her a household bottom. She's given it all up now and is currently between careers, though the first word that springs to mind when you see her will always be 'model'. (Fractionally ahead of 'vain cow' – not that she is, but you can't help wishing, can you?)

'Belles!' she breathes, gliding into our arms and staying there for a full minute.

'It's so good to see you!' I smile and inhale her Scandi-fresh scent.

'You too,' she sighs, still holding life-raft-tight. 'I'm sorry I've been such a recluse lately.'

Sasha's normally the best at keeping in touch but

over the past few months she's been uncharacteristically 'absent'. I presumed she just wanted to take some time to de-program herself now that she's an *ex*-model – you know, let her cuticles grow ragged and maybe cultivate a baby pot belly – but it'll never work, she's beautiful to the core.

'I've been thinking about you all so much.' She's misty with sentiment as her eyes flick between us. 'We've had some good times, haven't we?' she adds with perfect death-bed delivery.

'We're about to have a whole lot more.' Zoë reminds her with a playful nudge.

'Yeah!' I grin to excess in the hope that it proves contagious, but all Sasha can manage is a slight 'let's hope so' smile. She never was exactly a raver but today her meek streak seems more apparent than ever.

'So, how are you?' I probe, feeling the first twitches of concern. 'How's life without the lens?'

'Fine,' she looks uncomfortable but quickly brightens. 'You know how the last time we spoke I said I wished I'd never gone into modeling in the first place?'

I nod. She had a point – there is a certain class to being that exquisite and not doing the obvious thing.

'Have you changed your mind?' I ask.

'Oh no! It just occurred to me that if I hadn't gone down that path we might never have met!'

Beautiful, languid Sasha slipped into the B&B one afternoon in July on a fashion shoot for *New Woman* magazine. I would have stared longer but the photographer distracted me with his rapturous tizzy on seeing my mother's décor: 'This is exactly the level of naff we were going for!' he cheered as I showed him to our flouncey four-poster suite. 'I mean, it looked cheesy in your brochure but all these ornamental bells and cross-stitched cushions – it's perfect!'

I thanked him through gritted teeth and left them to it, but within twenty minutes the make-up artist came dinging on the reception bell asking me to call a doctor – Sasha was being violently ill. I thought she'd looked a bit pale on arrival but this was back in the days where all models were supposed to look eerily pallid so I hadn't taken much notice. Turns out she had gastroenteritis and couldn't move from the bathroom. Not even back to the luxury of The Grand Hotel where the rest of them were holed up for the night.

She ended up staying with us for a week, sweating and vomiting and writhing until 'can't take any more' tears slipped down her poreless face. No family swooped in to look after her – they live in Monaco – so Zoë and I took it in turns checking on her. Then Helen became matron to our nurses and by the following Wednesday we were all having a Babycham slumber party in Sasha's four-poster, getting her to regale us with stories of who she'd modeled with and where – from Yasmin Le Bon to a bikini shoot in Peru. Zoë was particularly entranced. 'You've got the perfect life!' she used to tell her. 'All pampering and pandering, *darlings!* and champagne!'

Sasha told us repeatedly that it wasn't nearly as glamorous or as fun as it sounded but we didn't believe

11

a word of it. Proof positive that Sasha led a charmed life came when she was well enough to eat again and we discovered she could indulge her profoundly sweet tooth with no repercussions, whereas Zoë in particular has to watch every Revel. Not that Zoë begrudged Sasha her speedy metabolism, just like I don't begrudge her the fact that Elliot had a brief crush when they first met. Anyone would. Everyone does.

'Maybe we should be feeling sorry for Elise,' Sasha takes a rather controversial stance as we re-congregate by the telephones to avoid further clashes with the stream of harassed holidaymakers. 'Going away with three girls she hardly knows, to visit a fourth she's never met – she must be worrying about being the odd one out.'

Zoë and I give her a stern 'whose side are you on?' look.

'Sorry,' Sasha demurs.

'Here they come now!' Zoë sounds the alert.

'Oh God!' I take a breath.

'Don't worry, we know what to do,' Zoë reassures me.

In one hand I feel Sasha's long cool fingers interlacing with mine, the other becomes comfortingly indented with Zoë's chunky, nubby rings. I have every confidence in their support. The ability to decimate a love rival is one of the most crucial qualities in a best friend, and they do it so well. The first time Elliot arranged to introduce Elise to me, I begged them to come too and they were swift to oblige. We arrived early at the chosen bar and positioned ourselves strategically at the back, standing united as though Elliot was a hostage about to be marched towards us by his evil captor. Being irritatingly short-sighted, I was relying 100 per cent on their vision and bitching expertise to get me over this first hurdle.

'She's orange!' Zoë got off to a good start as soon as they stepped through the door. 'Badly applied St Tropez, probably didn't exfoliate before application.'

'What's she wearing?' I asked, heart pounding.

'All black,' Sasha jumped in.

'Audrey classic or cop-out?' I had to have specifics.

'Cop-out, and they're mismatched blacks: trousers washed-out cotton – you know when it gets that greenish undertone?'

I nodded fervently.

'Next to purplish-black acrylic cardi.'

'Figure?'

'Hmmm . . .' Zoë and Sasha seemed stumped for adjectives.

'What? Oh no, it's good, isn't it?' I cried.

'Hard to tell,' Sasha did the diplomatic thing.

'Hair!' I barked, moving on. They were getting closer and I needed to end on a negative.

'Looks like she's growing out highlights,' Sasha squinted.

'No, it's split ends,' Zoë whooped in triumph. 'Inch-long fray!'

I could hear Elliot's voice. My stomach gurned a response. 'Anything else?' I hurried them, just seconds to go.

13

'Needs a pedicure,' was Zoë's last word on the subject.

Today Elise's trotters come encased in a pair of spike-heeled boots, a long black coat shrouds what did indeed turn out to be an annoyingly good bod and her neck is entwined with a rash-inducing mohair scarf. Welcome to March in the UK.

'What's with the leather Gestapo gloves?' Zoë hisses.

'They must be new because she's constantly adjusting them,' Sasha deduces.

'They're giving me the creeps,' Zoë shudders. 'She looks like she's about to strangle someone.'

'Preferably herself,' I mutter before realizing that's not actually possible.

Come on, force out a smile, I encourage myself.

'Elise! So nice to see you!' I beam. It turns out my pleasure is entirely genuine – she's still bright orange.

I press my cheek against her Flash Bronzer but blow my kiss directly at Elliot.

'Lara!' he grins as our matching indigo eyes meet. 'Come here!' and he pulls me into a hug.

Every time. He gets me every time.

Though he was the last to join our group, I'd known of Elliot the longest. We were at the same university, but with little likelihood of overlapping, what with him head down in computer science, and me swanning round the Art Department in vintage Pucci. I actually caught my first glimpse of him at a gig, drumming for some hopeless student band. I only looked over to see

14

what was making such an ear-tweaking noise but was instantly mesmerized. His tawny hair had a 'just got out of bed' look that made me want to get right back in. (Ironic, really. Now I know that when he does get out of bed his hair is flat to his head and he looks like an owl.)

While the rest of the band floundered round posturing and twanging inappropriate chords he kept a steady rhythm and just looked so laid back. From time to time he'd catch someone's eye, a grin would light up his face and these dimples would appear – ones that made you smile just looking at them. I was smitten. From then on my day was incomplete if I didn't have a sighting of him. I used to loiter in the coffee bar watching him with his mates, wondering what his voice sounded like, what he was saying . . . I'd will him to look over and when he did I'd send him telepathic messages of love. Though he never sent any back, he would occasionally smile. And when he did you'd never seen anyone bound to Mrs Montgomery's art history class with such exuberance.

I thought of a million excuses to speak to him, but in a way I didn't want to. I wanted to keep this perfect state of adoration as it was.

Then one Saturday in mid-August he walked into the B&B. I was just on my way to meet Sasha at the station, but immediately darted behind the reception desk, joining my mother.

'Oh, hi!' he smiled recognition. 'You're . . .'

'From Brighton University. We both go there.' Thank you, Einstein.

'That's right!' he smiled. 'I'm just here to pick up my parents, they checked in last night. Harvey?'

'Ah yes, room 5, would you like me to call them for you?' My mother dealt with the business in hand.

'Thanks,' Elliot nodded.

'This is my mum,' I whispered while she was on the phone.

'And here's mine—' he motioned to a grey-haired lady coming down the stairs. She was at least twenty years older than my own mother. 'And my dad.'

He was even older, but both of them had transparently sweet dispositions.

'Pleased to meet you!' they twinkled at me, revealing strong Mancunian accents that had somehow eluded their son.

'This is . . .' Elliot went to introduce me but faltered, realizing he didn't know my name.

'Lara!' I leapt in.

'Pretty name, that!' the dad noted.

I flushed with delight and gave my mum's elbow a squeeze for making such an excellent choice.

'Is this your first time in Brighton?' I asked, sounding ridiculously prim.

'Ooh, yes, dear and we're loving it!' Mama Harvey cooed.

'Elliot's taking us on the pier today.' Papa Harvey puffed up.

'You watch yourselves on that helter-skelter!' my mother teased.

They chuckled delightedly and tootled on their way.

16

I couldn't believe it. Elliot and I had gone from never having spoken to meeting each other's parents in a matter of minutes. (My mum is both parents to me, Dad being long gone.) This boded well.

'Do you want to do a bit of dusting while you're up there?' my mum said, nudging me when they'd gone.

I looked at her, still fizzing as if I had Alka-Seltzer swirling through my veins. 'What?' I squeaked.

She raised her eyes to the ceiling then winked. 'Let me know when you're ready to be scraped down!'

I grinned back at her then ran out the door, yelling, 'I've got to go and meet Sasha!'

I couldn't wait to tell her my news. Better yet, I got to relive it all again an hour later when we met up with Zoë. She seemed even more excited than me – if such a thing were possible – and she's been my number one *Elliot 4 Lara* cheerleader ever since. Sometimes I think I can't give up on him till Zoë does.

Anyway, when Elliot came back to drop his parents off that evening, he left a message about a gig he was playing Sunday night and all four of us girls went along. He loved that, having his own personal harem, and over too many bottles of K cider we decided he could be the one Beau to our exclusive collection of Brighton Belles. His girlfriend of the time didn't approve so he finished with her. I was in heaven. Until he got another. And then another.

I soon learned that his girlfriends would come and go but his Belles could never be replaced. We'd claimed the best part of his heart, I used to tell myself.

17

It was us he introduced to his parents, not any of these dippy two-month flings.

Mr and Mrs Harvey became regulars after their first successful visit and I'd grill Elliot to find out all the little treats they were into at the time, then plant them in their room so that they'd coo, 'Oh, Lara, you do spoil us!'

I loved it. They felt like the grandparents I'd never had.

So it was utterly devastating when Elliot's dad passed away, aged eighty-three, just two years ago. I don't ever remember feeling that sad before. Convinced his mother would die of a broken heart, Elliot moved back to Manchester to be closer to her. But within a year she was gone too.

At first I spoke to him every day and went up to stay whenever I could but pretty soon Elise was dominating the scene. I didn't feel I could put my arms around him in front of her. I never felt comfortable when she was in the room – she always seemed to be watching me, willing me to leave, I could feel it. Elliot was withdrawn at the time anyway, and with her blocking my every move I couldn't really reach him. What could I do? She was there in Manchester, I wasn't. So I stepped back and ached for his pain from the sidelines.

We've been speaking a little more since this trip was confirmed but it's not the same. I wonder if it ever will be again.

*

'Are we waiting for something?' Elise queries.

We look blankly at each other. Someone to take charge, apparently.

'God, isn't it weird not having Helen here to organize us?' Sasha shakes her head.

'Elliot, you'll have to be Dad!' Zoë nominates him.

'You're joking!' Elise titters. 'He hasn't even changed up his money yet *and* we missed out on an Apex train fare because he forgot to book a week in advance – hopeless!'

I hate it when couples make sideswipes in public. Is she trying to prove that she knows him better than us?

'This way, troops!' Elliot deliberately points away from the ticket desks.

We laugh and drag him into position in the cordoned-off line.

It's funny, most of the people around us are also about to go on the trip of a lifetime and yet they couldn't look more wretched if they tried. It's the queuing that does it – knocks the holiday spirit right out of you.

Whereas the rest of us shuffle forward in an absent-minded fashion, Elise appears to be one of life's tailgaters, nudging Elliot every time he lets more than an inch elapse between him and the man in front. 'Mickey, I don't know where you are half the time!' she tweaks his chin.

I close my eyes. I'd forgotten their pet names for each other – Mickey and Minnie, because their first snog was at a work outing to EuroDisney. Can you stand it?

Sasha and Zoë are talking but I switch back to my eavesdropping on the Es.

'And you won't like the bacon out there, it's just the streaky bit – all dark and crispy,' she fusses. 'But the good thing is that if you order a Coke or Sprite they'll keep topping it up for free. And sometimes you won't have to order a drink at all because they bring iced water to your table automatically. Mostly I just drink that.'

'Have you been to America before?' I find myself asking, even though she wasn't talking to me.

Elise nods in a smug fashion.

Great. That's all we need: someone to go, 'I know!' every time we pip with excitement at a new discovery.

'Yeah, I lived out in California for a while,' she breezes.

'Really?' I try not to look too impressed. I didn't know that. But then I know very little about this woman. Probably because I never asked – I didn't want the precious space in my head filled with details about her.

'How come?' Zoë's now joined the conversation.

'How come what?' Elise plays hard to get.

'How come you lived in California?'

She opens her mouth and then closes it. It seems there's no simple answer to that.

'Oh, it was just something I wanted to try. Mickey – we're moving again!'

Elise links arms with Elliot and turns her back on us. Subject closed apparently.

The girls and I exchange a suspicious glance. We so

should have hired a private detective when she first came on the scene. All we'd have to do now is flick through her dossier and we'd know exactly what she'd got up to.

'Let's see your passport photo.' Zoë reaches forward and taps Elise on the shoulder. 'Airport ritual.'

Good ruse. There could be a clue within!

Elise looks reluctant.

'Don't be shy.' Zoë extends a palm. 'I've seen all the others.'

Clamping her hand over her typed information, Elise holds the passport open at the photo page, keeping it well out of snatching distance. Definitely hiding something. Her age, for one thing. Elliot said she was older than him but I don't know by how much. I study her face a little closer desperate for her to squawk, 'They're not crow's feet, they're laughter lines!' so I can give her a sour look and reply: *Nothing's that funny.*

'Next!'

That's us. We scuttle forward to the desk.

'Hi, I'm Brendan!' The pupils of the chap behind the counter dilate wildly at the sight of The Model. 'We do have some space available in first . . .' he addresses (or should that be undresses?) Sasha, mentally booking her on a flight to Temptation Island.

'I'm with my friends – there's five of us altogether,' Sasha informs him.

His face falls.

'Unless you can upgrade us all, I'd rather just stick with economy,' she says, simply.

21

Brendan is clearly crushed that she won't now be beholden to him.

'Well, if you're sure. Let's see if we can at least get you by the exit – that way you'll be able to stretch out those lovely long legs of yours.'

'Can I get the seat next to her?' Zoë pips. 'I have unusually large boobs.'

Brendan looks up with a start.

'It's like wearing an airbag,' Zoë continues. 'Nobody can get by me if I'm in a normal row. I mean, these seats have 32-inch leg room but I've got 36D boobs. You try getting your tray table down—'

'Yes, yes, madam. I'll see what I can do,' Brendan scrabbles to regain his composure.

'Me and Mickey don't mind where we sit, as long as we're together.' Elise morphs into her girlie-whirlie alter ego, snaking her arm around Elliot's.

Urgh, get a toilet cubicle, I cringe, silently praying I'm not seated next to the Es. I don't think I could take eleven hours of passive nuzzling.

Brendan looks up from his clicking. 'We have a band of four with the extra leg room and I can seat one of you in the row directly behind.'

'You don't mind, do you, Lara?' Elise gives me a look, equal parts patronizing and dismissive.

'Oh, can't she sit with us?' Zoë wheedles, craning to peer at Brendan's screen.

'It's a very busy flight!' he snaps, shooing her away.

'It's fine,' I mumble, nudging Zoë. 'If you recline your seat back you'll practically be in my lap anyway.'

'Are you sure?' Sasha checks.

'Honestly. I'll be watching the movies most of the time.' As I squeeze a smile I get a horrible sinking feeling. It's going to be me that's the odd-one-out.

Round One to Elise.

Brendan hands us our boarding passes.

'OK, all set and that's two vegetarians: Sasha Williams and Zoë Harriott.'

'I didn't realize you'd gone veggie, Zo,' Elliot queries.

'I haven't. I'm not lacto-intolerant, kosher or vegan either, but those people always get their food served first so I thought, for a change . . .' Zoë shrugs.

'Did you know there are more vegetarians in Brighton than any other place in Europe?' I announce.

'Really?' Sasha coos. We love a fascinating fact.

But Elise has no interest in our smalltalk. 'Shall we meet up again at the gate in an hour?' she cries.

Unbelievable – she's trying to get rid of us already!

'What's everyone doing?' Elliot takes the more sociable approach.

'Well, you'll make a beeline for Dixons,' Zoë makes the obvious prediction for The Gadget King. 'Sasha will be in W.H. Smith, looking for a book for the flight.'

I know, a model who reads: shocking isn't it?

'And Lara and I will be in Duty Free!' she cheers, then remembers she's got a letter to send before we get airside.

'It's actually a job application,' Zoë confides as we two go off in search of a postbox. 'The closing date is while we're away.'

'I didn't realize you wanted to leave the Dyspraxia Foundation.' I frown.

'I don't, but with this new job there's a chance I could go on to become a celebrity PA!'

It's ironic really, Zoë has by far the most worthy job of all of us and yet she's the one who deep down always yearned to be a finger-clicking, hair-swishing diva. Lately she's modified this wish to fit the current celebrity-ravaging climate, deciding that working *alongside* a star would mean a good deal of the perks without any of the wild accusations in *heat* magazine that she's losing her hair/man/mind etc. Not a bad plan in theory, but I've a feeling the reality would be a nasty wake up call, and then what dreams would she be left with?

'Do you know where this new company is based?' I ask, hoping she'll move back to Brighton.

'West London, so at least I'd be more in the swing of things,' she notes. 'Of course it's irrelevant, really . . .'

'Why's that?'

'Well, seeing as I'm about to get discovered by Hollywood!' She does a little twirl and I giggle back at her.

Zoë stops short of the queue at Passport Control and turns to face me.

'It could happen, couldn't it?' There's genuine hankering in her voice.

I look into her maxi-lashed eyes and smile. 'Why not?'

Why is it so hot in airports? I can't believe Elise stayed wrapped up the whole time we were queuing – I guess it's not just her eyes that are made of flint. I juggle my

24

bags and coat and bottle of water as we approach the security check.

'You go first, Zo,' I nod ahead, still in a tangle.

Zoë steps forward through the archway, instantly setting off the bleeper.

'Bugger!'

Retreating, she clunks her charm bracelet and fake Gucci watch into the plastic tray then tries again.

It bleeps again.

'Do you think it's my belt buckle?' She rattles her midriff.

'Worth a try,' I shrug.

She tugs her belt through the loops of her Earl jeans and coils it into the tray.

Still she bleeps.

The security man beckons her over and, starting at her heels, strokes her aura with his bleeper-wand, mentally eliminating possible causes as he goes – no steel toecaps, no ankle chains, no pins holding her knees in place following a serious netball injury, no bellybutton ornamentation and definitely no nipple rings – he lingers a while to make absolutely sure and moves on with visible disappointment. As soon as the wand reaches ear level it bleats frantically.

Zoë raises her hand to her scalp in confusion, then blanches and looks back to me with an, 'Oh God!' expression.

I frown back a 'What?'

She's already removed her earrings and unless she's had a ton of Goldie-style caps since I saw her last I can't imagine what it could be.

She leans forward and whispers to the security man. Behind me the line gets impatient. The security man shakes his head and sends her back through to my side of the arch.

'I can't believe it!' Zoë hisses. 'Is he looking?'

'Who?'

'The stud.'

I turn back to check on the one good-looking guy in the queue. Everyone's looking.

'No,' I lie. 'What's wrong?'

'I got these new hair extensions, you just clip them in place at your roots . . .' Discreetly she lifts a flap of hair and reveals one of the troublesome metal grips.

'He's not making you take them out?' I gasp.

She nods again.

'No!' I cry, giving the security man a stern look but he remains resolute.

As the next person in line is summoned, I help Zoë moult.

'Just bend the clips back on themselves and they'll pop open,' she instructs me.

Poor Zoë. She's no stranger to striptease but this is humiliating in the extreme.

I sneak a peek at the stud. He's making no attempt to disguise his disgust. Pig. I wish him halitosis and a lifetime of uncomfortable shoes. As he reaches for a dish to offload his pocketful of coins, one of the grips catches on his sleeve. I go to grab it back but he's too quick for me and strides on through the arch.

Beep-beep-beep!

The security man points to the cause and the stud freaks, batting it off like a hairy caterpillar and stamping it into the carpet. Then, instead of doing the decent thing and picking it up and returning it to Zoë, he simply grabs his rucksack off the conveyor belt and heads straight for Boots.

Zoë looks crushed.

'I thought you were saving yourself for Will Smith,' I remind her.

Zoë brightens. 'He'd laugh at this, wouldn't he?'

I nod. 'He'd just give you a big grin and say, "You'd make bald look good!"'

'Yeah!' she high-fives me.

'That's the last one.' I hand Zoë a scarlet streak last seen on the Little Mermaid.

She fluffs her remaining hair, now shrunk up to her jaw, and sighs. 'I feel like one of those dolls with hair that grows, only in reverse.'

I take her arm and whisper, 'You still look discoverable!'

'Thanks!' she smiles, bravely.

For someone who dresses so audaciously, Zoë can be surprisingly insecure about her looks. A couple of times we've tried to convince her to tone down the pantomime make-up and poke-your-eye-out outfits and let her natural beauty shine through but she's still convinced that her sex appeal needs to be flagged up with bright colours. One day she'll realize that she could be wearing a muumuu and still get an X-rating.

'Bureau de Change,' Zoë alerts me.

We're just pooling our money so as not to incur a

double exchange fee when Zoë flinches. 'It's that guy again!'

The stud is just one person ahead of us, taking his turn at the counter.

'Let's go to Thomas Cook,' Zoë pleads, turning to leave.

'No, wait – have you got a spare extension?'

'Why?'

I make a just-hand-it-over motion.

'This one is too blonde for me really . . .' She pulls a flaxen wisp from her bag.

I take it, pretend to be leaning forward to check the exchange rates – 'Would you look at that – 14 South African Rand to the pound!' – and gently clip it to the end of his jumper.

Zoë's eyes widen.

'Pin the tale on the donkey!' I snicker.

Zoë muffles a guffaw. 'Pin the tale on the honky, more like!'

We grip each other, convulsed with mirth as he walks off counting his Euros, oblivious to the peroxide tail swishing from his bum.

'What an ass!' I shake my head as we head for Duty Free.

While Zoë swithers between mandarin and kiwi flavoured vodka, I give myself a surreptitious squirt with Elliot's aftershave: Happy for Men by Clinique. The smell alone makes my heart and stomach entwine.

'We have the female version . . .' The assistant swoops.

'I'm fine!' I blush, backing off.

'Would you like to try it?' She follows me with a sample that she must have been hiding under her cuff.

'Oh, I wear that!' Elise announces as I collide with her. 'In fact I've just run out.'

'Well, there you go.' I try and palm her off on the assistant.

'I wish I could, but it's too much of an extravagance.'

'It's £23.50,' I frown.

Not that Elise should ever wear a perfume called Happy, she could get done under the Trades Descriptions Act. Poison would be far more appropriate.

'Perfume should be a gift,' Elise simpers. 'It feels kind of unfeminine buying it for myself. Am I being silly?'

I think the word you're looking for is manipulative, I mutter to myself as I watch Elliot reach for his wallet.

'My treat!' he offers.

'Oh no! I don't want you to feel obliged.'

Yeah, you do. I shake my head. Some women just have a knack for getting men to do these things. Maybe it makes them feel more of a man if she plays the little woman. Either way, *yuk*.

I catch up with Zoë (who's decided to get both vodkas) and we go clanking swiftly to the gate.

'I need a snifter now!' I stop suddenly.

Zoë unscrews the kiwi cap without comment. I take a glug.

'Strewth!' I husk.

'Better?'

I nod and cough.

Boarding is uncharacteristically free of aisle-ditherers
and no sooner are we in our seats than the stewardess
greets the five of us with complimentary glasses of
champagne. Must be Brendan's doing, I decide, about
to take a gulp. The vodka's worn off already.

'Wait!' Elliot stops me. 'I'd like to say a few words.'

I scoot forward, trying to feel a part of their row and
block out the stares of my neighbours.

I raise my glass, ready to toast Helen! California!
The sun-kissed adventures that lie ahead! But instead
Elliot puts his arm around Elise and punctures my
parachute with the words, 'We're engaged!'

Slowly Elise removes her glove and flaunts her
sparkling ring finger.

I fall back into my seat with shock.

Why do I get the feeling it should be her middle
finger jutting forth?

2

So far I've come up with three ways I might dispose of Elise on the flight:

1. As she goes to retrieve her bag from the overhead bin, Zoë's vodka bottles roll out and zonk her on the head.
2. I replace her anti-Deep Vein Thrombosis flight socks with a pair that cut off her circulation altogether.
3. During dinner she chokes on a chicken bone and no one can give her the Heimlich manœuvre because the captain has switched on the Fasten Seatbelts sign.

Engaged!

If only she were a toilet door and I could simply slot her back to Vacant.

Am I numb? I must be. Otherwise I'd be screaming. Not that I'd have room for much of a tantrum at the moment. I can't even cross my legs – Zoë is so far reclined I feel I should make myself useful and give her a scalp massage. And who'd listen to my wailing anyway? Sasha is buried in her book (one of those geisha sagas) and Elliot and Elise are engrossed in each other. With the emphasis on gross.

Fighting back the swell of tears, I try to focus on the movie but the sweeping battle scenes in *Lord of the Rings* aren't ideally suited to my Post-it note sized screen. Dinner comes as a welcome distraction, aside from the eating part. When I decline the steward's offer of a chilled bread roll Elise leans back and asks if she can have it. Sure! I feel like adding, first the man I love, now my bread roll, go ahead and take it all.

I take another gulp of wine. Perhaps the second bottle of Pinot Grigio was a mistake. It's making me all sentimental for the good old days, when we were young and fiancé-free.

I always relished the times when Elliot was between girlfriends – then I could tousle his hair and lean on him and be fairly open in my adoration, passing it off as a tactile friendship. Like now, if She wasn't here, we could watch a movie on entwined headphones, pick at each other's pretzels and get cricked necks trying to fall asleep on each other's shoulders and no one would necessarily be any the wiser to the divine bliss I'd be experiencing internally. But when there's a girlfriend – or worse still, future wife – at large there are all these no-go areas and unspoken rules. I'm obliged to tiptoe, speaking with a few seconds' delay to censor anything that could be misconstrued or give the game away. It makes me feel as though there's a little man in a white coat monitoring my behaviour and giving me a running commentary – 'You wouldn't do that unless you loved him . . . Don't touch him there! . . . You shouldn't have said that in front of her . . . Quick, turn to her and smile and make her feel included.'

And so I end up wildly over-compensating, often ignoring Elliot in a bid to ingratiate myself with the girlfriend. 'Who, me? In love with your fella? Get outta here!' And sometimes, in the name of *faux* girlie-bonding, we gang up on him. But it's just a defence mechanism: two women sussing each other out, both with something to prove – her that she's good for him but not lovestruck to the point of losing her identity, me that I'm a girl's girl and thus not about to jump in bed with him the second her back is turned. (Chance would be a fine thing!)

If the girlfriend is nice, which hasn't actually been too much of a problem to date, I feel guilty about having such strong feelings for him and live in fear that they might guess my dirty secret. I daren't even look directly at him in front of them because I'm afraid the love pouring from my eyes will be all luminous and glowy like something from *Ghost*. But really, why should I feel so ashamed for adoring him? Sometimes I get indignant, feeling like I'm cow-tailing to someone who'll only be around for a few months instead of being true to myself. His girlfriends cling so tight but he always gives them the slip in the end. That is my consolation. At the risk of sounding like a psycho-stalker – I've outlasted them all! But then, he's never asked any of them to marry him before.

I feel a sickening twist in my stomach. And it's not just the lukewarm burrito I wish the flight attendant would remove from my tray.

I know it sounds silly but I always thought it would be me he'd marry. In the end. I never much minded when my feeble attempts at relationships floundered because I always felt that their ending brought me one step closer to a beginning with him. Surely now the time is right? I'd think. Surely I've endured enough duds that now I get my prince?

Not that he fits some fanciful notion of a knight in shining armour. He just hits home with me: I get this warm sense of satisfaction when he's around. He makes me laugh in that way that makes me feel all helpless and dizzy. And he really listens. If I phone him I never feel he's cleaning out his microwave at the same time. Other men seem to wait for me to finish my sentence and then change the subject. Not Elliot, he never cuts to the chase. He lies down and gives himself over to the conversation, prepared to follow any meandering tangents wherever they may lead. He's always there for advice (especially if you're considering purchasing anything technology-related), general trivia and playfulness (he's basically a big kid). And he gossips like a girl. What could be better?

On the downside . . . Well, if you were nitpicking you might mention his tummy – you know those tiny paunches on an otherwise slim physique? But I'm so fond of his I look upon it as a portable puppy. And you should see him in his glasses when he's concentrating. And he has this thing about reading last thing at night

– he's always so determined to finish whatever magazine article he's into that he refuses to set it aside, even after he's fallen asleep so it's quite normal for him to wake up and find himself still clutching it. But these are the kinds of foibles I can live with. The only really bad thing about him, the thing that really gets my goat, is that he's not in love with me.

I sigh and flick through the channels. There's a George Clooney sex scene on one but the man next to me is watching the same writhing bods so I can't possibly stay on that channel – it'd be like sidling up beside someone at a peep show. I move on to the kids' channel: yet another shambolic sports team about to be transformed into champions by a Hollywood has-been. Suddenly a hand reaches back and wriggles its fingers at me. Elise would call it stretching, I call it shoving her engagement ring in my face. I hadn't even noticed the solitaire diamond until now. Solitaire, how ironic. I'm the one who's alone.

I scoot forward and reach my hand over the seat to snaffle a chocolate Brazil from Sasha's pick'n'mix but find Elise's other hand in the bag. It's like one of those amusement arcade grabbers, only her claw has actually secured a great cluster of booty. I sit back in my seat and watch her feeding Elliot – one pink prawn for every five fizzy cola bottles she gobbles down. I find all this relationship stuff bewildering. He's known her less than a year and she gets all these great perks – the whole intimate/physical/sexual side to him that I can only fantasize about – and if she marries him (hark at me clinging to 'if', not yet ready for 'when') she goes

35

one step further and gets official ownership. I think of the way Victoria Beckham can look at David and say so confidently: 'He's mine!' How nice to be that sure, to be able to stake that claim and feel you belong to each other. Elliot's my friend but he's not *mine*. And if he marries Elise he never will be.

Awash with self-pity, I decide it would be wise to dilute the alcohol with some water, so I dip into the galley to help myself to a plastic cupful. Sipping slowly, I stare out the window at the everlasting expanse of rusty peaked earth and the tiny improbable villages set in various crooks in the river. Other worlds. Other populations. Other men.

I have thought about trying to find someone else I can call my own but the thing that seems to be holding me back is that I don't know how to un-love Elliot. If I don't see him for a while I still get a flutter at the first sight of him. Still? People say to me, 'you're *still* in love with Elliot?' And I just pull a 'Wh'dathunkit?' face but what I want to say is, 'Why do you think it's going to go away? This is true love. It's everlasting, Goddam-mit!' So the upshot is that I've settled into an accept-ance of the situation – I know he doesn't feel the same way but I'm going to love him regardless.

OK. Back in my seat. Maybe I should try and get some sleep . . .

Nope. Not going to happen. Got restless legs.

Perhaps I'll go to the loo for something to do.

Just as I get there, the door folds back on itself and Sasha squeezes out, looking suspiciously damp of eye.

'It was the movie – it was really sad,' she blusters,

noticing my concern and hurrying back to her seat before I can remind her that she was watching the Bond stunt-fest *Die Another Day*.

It must be the altitude, I shrug, contorting myself into the cubicle. Time to take a long, hard look at myself in the mirror. I recoil instantly – airplane lighting, what was I thinking?

Taking a stroll along the aisle, I'm amused to see the positions people are trying to sleep in. One woman has her head on the tray table. I can't decide whether she looks like she's passed out at a dinner party or is about to be guillotined. The man ahead of her has wriggled into the gap between his seat and the window and is trying to arrange himself so his head is on the seat. It can't be worth it. The two girls along from him have got the right idea – they're yakking their way through the flight. That would be me and Zoë if we'd sat together. I eavesdrop as I pass. 'If you love him you've got to tell him!' one girl insists.

If only it were that simple. Would you risk losing your best friend over such a confession? Although I did once try that popular non-verbal form of communication with Elliot once. We were at a house party and he had to leave early and I – already drunk in *excelsus* – didn't want him to go. I followed him out into the driveway and we were suddenly alone. I don't know if it was the contrast of leaving a cigarette-fogged sweatbox to emerge into the cool jasmine-scented night but I felt compelled to reach for him – it started as a playful stay-a-while tug back but then I stumbled

37

into a herbaceous border, and as he righted me, I instinctively *carpe diem*-ed and kissed him. And he kissed me back. It seemed to last for ever and with every microsecond that passed I fell deeper, lost in wonder and swirled up with feelings of delight and realization. It *is* you! Years of daydreaming had not prepared me for the bliss that enveloped me. I swear I went to a higher place.

At one point I'm sure I heard Zoë calling Sasha: 'Come and look – she's done it!'

But then he was gone. I stood there wondering if I'd imagined the whole thing, then the biggest smile spread across my face. I knew it was real.

I staggered back and propped myself against a wall, closed my eyes and tried to prolong the sensation for as long as possible. The warmth, the smooshiness of our mouths, the lightest bristling of the goatee he had at the time. The way he reached down to my heart and welcomed my whole body to his. I didn't want to go to sleep that night in case the feeling slipped away in my dreams. Indeed, hangover gremlins did take a large chunk of memory but they left me with more than enough to treasure to this day.

He called the next morning just to make sure things weren't going to be awkward between us. Though I'd conveniently forgotten about her the night before, he actually had a girlfriend at the time and there seemed little chance of a rematch so I simply apologized for lunging, blamed the booze and then asked after his hangover. 'Oh, I wasn't drinking,' he replied. My inner cringe was the equivalent of a hundred crunches.

That was six years ago but Zoë's never let go of the 'he kissed you back' factor. I long to know if there were any tingles on his behalf, if he ever relives the moment like I do. If I had a videotape of the kiss it surely would have come un-spooled by now.

But then even the best repeats eventually become tiresome and there came a time when I thought I'd have to let go altogether – basically when we couldn't have a conversation without him mentioning Elise. It could just be something in passing – 'I've been round at Elise's all weekend . . .' – or unbeknownst to me she'd be there when I called and I'd hear a noise and he'd say, 'It's Elise – she's just slipped into an ecstasy coma because I've been stroking her back . . .' Urgh! Touching her while he's speaking to me. It just didn't seem right. So I started calling less and leaving the answerphone on more. It was such a loss, not having him in my life, but I think it was the right thing to do – I needed a break from all that unfulfilled longing and to fill the gap I submerged myself in my work. Now there's nothing I don't know about 1930s light fixtures.

As we start our descent I'm forced to accept that I've got about as much chance of winning Elliot as Zoë has of becoming the next Halle Berry. But then the captain addresses us over the Tannoy: 'Ladies and gentlemen, we will shortly be arriving in beautiful San Diego, California. The temperature is an idyllic 78 degrees and on behalf of myself and the crew, I wish you a magical stay.'

Suddenly my body surges with hope. Perhaps I'm being given one last chance? After all, this is America, land of dreams! Anything is possible! Maybe the mere fact that we're in a new environment will make him see me in a new way!

I close my eyes, cross my fingers and make a wish – *'Let him love me!'* – just as we bump down on to the runway.

3

Judging by the trepidation on the faces surrounding the luggage carousel, people have a greater fear of losing their luggage than they do of flying.

'The first round of suitcases never seem to get touched,' I muse as I watch them rotate.

Elliot returns from his trolley-corralling duties with a fine pair of fillies.

'We'll share this one.' Elise latches on to the first before shunting the other towards the rest of us.

I don't want to have to say thank you out loud in her direction so I let it rattle to a halt of its own accord.

'There's mine!' Zoë lunges for her fake Louis Vuitton, loading it on to the trolley with a WWF grunt.

'Ours! Quick!' Elise commands Elliot.

Sasha is next.

But I continue to wait.

And wait.

We haven't yet had the essential burst-in-transit case spilling embarrassing undies so I don't give up hope just yet. Maybe if I look away it'll come. I turn to find Elliot shoving the books he was reading on the flight into his suitcase to lighten his backpack, prompting Sasha to do the same. But as she pushes her geisha saga in one side, it forces a work of non-fiction out the other. Elise swoops on it before Sasha even realizes what has happened.

'*Repacking Your Baggage!*' she reads. 'God how anal – travelling with a book on packing?!'

Sasha blushes and tries to snatch it away from her.

'Oh no! Even worse! It's one of those self-help books,' Elise takes a closer look. ' "*How to release the dead weight of your past and carry only uplifting essentials . . .*" Talk about taking coals to Newcastle. Don't you think there's enough of this mind-cult nonsense in California?'

Elise thinks this is hysterical. Sasha looks plain mortified.

'You're not really into this are you, Sash?' Elliot looks concerned.

'Someone recommended it,' Sasha mumbles as she retrieves the book and rams it back in her case, but in the bluster a further three spill out. I quickly gather them up to protect them from prying eyes – all except my own. *Louise Hay's Self-Esteem Affirmations, One Day My Soul Just Opened Up,* by Iylana Vanzant and *Getting the Love You Want.* I wouldn't mind reading the last one but I'm as surprised as Elliot that Sasha's into DIY psychiatry. Maybe it's to do with her giving up modelling – she's got a whole new life ahead of her so she's having an emotional spring-clean before she moves forward. Well, good for her!

'Have you read Barbara Sher's *Live the Life You Love*?' I venture.

'Oh not you too!' Elise rolls her eyes.

'It's meant to be really good.' I ignore Elise. 'Plain-talking but practical.'

Sensing Sasha wants the topic dropped I turn back to the carousel.

'Come on, customized wonder-case!'

Right now I'd even settle for mine to be the one trailing thongs and tatty bras, but there's no sign of it. More worrying still, bags are no longer being spat from the shute.

We wait a further ten minutes before I face the fact that, for once, the queasy anxiety that my suitcase didn't make it is founded.

As I fill out the appropriate forms the others reassure me that it's going to be fine and I'll have my case back by tomorrow. All the same, I can't help feeling picked on by the universe.

'You're welcome to borrow anything of mine,' Sasha offers as we trundle towards Customs.

'Thanks but I'd look like a stilt-walker who forgot her stilts.'

'We're the same size!' Zoë pips.

'*Where?*' I splutter, surveying her wondrous curves – what I wouldn't give for a cleavage you didn't have to winch together. 'Around the ankles?'

'Same *height*,' Zoë grasps at straws.

I try and picture myself in a Zoë ensemble but realize I'd feel like an overly-bedazzled Eurovision Song Contest entrant.

I notice Elise isn't offering to loan me anything. Not her own clothes anyway.

'Surely Helen can sort you out?' she reasons, not knowing what an unlikely prospect this would be.

Helen, bless her, is trapped in some kind of M&S timewarp – her trademark look is peg-pleat trousers and a gold chain worn over a polo neck jumper. Not particularly offensive to the general populus but a classic case of *What Not To Wear*, as far as Zoë's concerned – if an outfit can't double up as a Christmas decoration she's just not interested.

I wonder how Helen's wardrobe has adjusted to suit the hotter weather. I have a feeling she'll be in knee-length skirts and logo'd polo shirts. So not me. Not that I'm any great style icon – my knack for accessorizing is restricted to rooms. I can hunt down the most inspiring vase to become the focal point for a whole room but when it comes to shopping for clothes I buy variations on the same theme over and over, mistaking recognition for desire. If I'm honest, being without my suitcase doesn't so much deprive me of fourteen outfits as one outfit fourteen times.

'Lara!' Elliot snaps his fingers in front of my face. 'Where'd you go?'

For a moment I stare stupidly into his eyes, unable to flick back to 'just your pal' quick enough.

'Do you want to put that on here?' Elliot tugs at the strap of my outsize shoulder bag.

I look at his khaki canvas suitcase nestling beside Elise's hard shell and shake my head. 'I'm OK,' I insist.

Even carry-on luggage can be prone to gooseberry complexes.

As we trek through the airport to Arrivals, the thing that really jumps out at me is the fresh turquoise and white signage – it seems so bright and breezy, sending the distinct message: 'You're in California now – get happy!'

I decide to give it a whirl, for Helen's sake.

'Can anyone see her?' I squint at the crowd.

'I don't even know what she looks like!' Elise shrugs.

'Light brown hair, dead straight, probably tied tight back,' Zoë starts at the top.

'Always burgundy No. 7 lipstick and little gold hoops in her ears,' I fill in the details. 'Beauty spot just below her left eye.'

'I never noticed that.' Elliot scrunches his brow. 'Like the one on your lip?'

My hand goes to my mouth. He noticed mine!

'I thought she'd be standing here with a clipboard ready to tick us all off.' Elliot pictures the scene.

'Handing out copies of the itinerary . . .' I have the same image in my head.

'Does anyone know what she's got planned for us?' Sasha queries.

'She was really vague when I asked her,' I admit, only now realizing how out of character that was. 'She just kept saying she'd tell us when we got here.'

I don't want to say this out loud but I have a suspicion that my impending birthday has got something to do with the secrecy – I turn thirty a week from today and there's no way Helen is going to let that milestone go by without a bang. I grin to myself – how fun that it's going to be as much of a surprise for the others as it will be for me. I don't mind what we do, I'm just chuffed that we'll all be doing it together.

No sooner has that thought formed in my head than Elise shoots it down.

'I suppose we'll be doing our own thing most days,' she predicts with an underlying threat. 'I mean, you can't expect six individuals to all be satisfied by the same things.'

'It's never been a problem before,' Sasha counters, instantly wise to Elise's Elliot-snatching plan.

'Yeah, we have a good time whatever we do,' Zoë and I agree, keen to let her know we won't be letting Elliot go without a fight.

'Well, I'm sure we'll meet up in the evenings,' Elise faux-soothes, retreating behind Elliot.

Sasha, Zoë and myself exchange a dubious look. She'll never make a musketeer, that Elise.

Elliot, meanwhile, is oblivious to the tug-of-war going on around him, his mind still on Helen. 'I wonder if she's going to cook for us,' he ponders. 'I've had dreams about her Sunday roasts!'

'Oooooh!' We all go ga-ga at the memory. And not just of the food. We used to have quite a routine going. While Helen set a-basting Elliot would get the papers, then – once we'd eaten ourselves silly – Sasha would offload the freebie beauty products she'd acquired that week and Zoë would apply them to us all, Elliot included, while we read the papers to her. Early evening I'd go down the video shop and choose three movies – one comedy, one indie, one classic – that everyone except me would intermittently kip through. It was then my job to fill in any gaps in the plot succinctly and evocatively. I loved it! I was the sentry who would not sleep!

'Remember how we'd swear we wouldn't eat another thing all day and then come teatime Helen would get all those homemade cakes out . . .'

'And now she's doing it as a job!'

'I can't believe she's given up a career in the board-room to make cupcakes,' Elliot laughs.

'God, I know – I'd be a complete ball if I was a pastry chef,' Zoë groans.

'Is Helen overweight?' Elise perks up.

'Just a regular size 12,' I happily rain on her parade. 'She's actually ideally suited to the job because she never eats dessert.'

'Yeah, she used to cook us these amazing chocolate mousse cakes and never so much as dip her little finger,' Elliot confirms.

'And it's not that she hasn't got a sweet tooth,' Zoë chips in, 'she's just got this amazing self-discipline.'

Elise frowns, 'I don't get it. Why would she sur-round herself with all that temptation? Are you sure she hasn't got some kind of eating disorder?'

'Definitely not,' I shake my head. 'It's only sweets she avoids.'

'And yet she cooks them on a daily basis?' Elise is still struggling with the idea.

'The thing is, she's good at it,' I explain. 'And she

47

likes to bring people pleasure – like with us, it was enough just to see the look on our faces when we'd take a bite of her latest creation.'

'That's Helen, isn't it?' Sasha sighs. 'She loves to see her friends happy. I miss her worrying for us and interfering in our lives. It's not the same over email.'

We all concur and then look hopefully for a sign saying Hel's Beau-Belles amid the Mr Esposito and Clark Family cards. Nothing.

'If she's going to be a while, I'm going to the loo.' Elliot darts off.

Elise watches him until he disappears into the Gents and then tugs at Sasha's peasant sleeve: 'Got any more pick'n'mix?'

I'm desperate for her to say: 'No, and you should know because you scoffed the last handful!' but of course Sasha's far too passive and settles for a simple, 'Sorry, all gone!'

'I don't know where you put it all!' Elise chimes in, before continuing her cadging mission with a request for chewing gum.

'There's a kiosk right there,' I say, pointing behind her.

'Oh, I can wait. I'll get some later.' She dismisses my suggestion until Elliot rejoins us. 'Unless you want something, bunny?'

'What's that?'

'You want some gum, Mickey?' she coos, pinching his chin.

'That'd be great, I can still taste that burrito from the plane,' he grimaces.

48

'Can you get me some while you're there?' Elise propels him in the direction of the kiosk.

That woman seems to have a serious aversion to buying anything herself.

'Wait! I'll come with you,' I volunteer. 'Anyone else want anything?'

'Just water, sparkling if they've got it,' says Sasha, reaching into her purse.

'That's OK!' I wave her hand away.

'Get us some water too,' Elise calls after Elliot.

Get *us* some water! What are you – two humps, one camel?

Duds. Nips. Tootsie Rolls. American candy sure has some funny names.

'Look at this – who'd buy a bar called Big Hunk?' I hoot.

'Why you – as a present for me, of course!' Elliot reasons.

I chuckle then get a stab of nerves. This is my first moment alone with Elliot since The Announcement and I feel I should really say something poignant and congratulatory. I quickly try out a few test runs in my mind but I can't seem to give any sentence that contains the words 'Elise' and 'engagement' a positive spin. There's only one thing for it – bravado!

'*You're getting married!*' I give Elliot what I mean to be a playful punch on the arm but my true feelings turbo-charge my fist.

'Ow!' he yelps, nursing his biceps. 'Yes, I am. Since when did that warrant GBH?'

I chuckle out loud but think to myself: 'When the groom needs some sense knocking into him.'

'So, what do you think?' he asks, turning to me and looking for a second as if my opinion might make a difference.

I look away, not wanting him to read my expression.

'It's disgusting!' I cry.

'What?!' Elliot gasps.

'That gum, it's wintergreen!' I point to the pack he's just picked up.

'It's all the same, isn't it?' Elliot frowns, trying to find the ingredients.

'Tastes like Germolene mixed with minicab air freshener,' I assure him, grateful for the diversion. I just couldn't give him the eye contact he was looking for.

Quickly I try and compose myself in case he asks again but before he gets the chance, Elise barges between us.

'What's taking so long?' she whinges, snatching the gum out of Elliot's hand. I watch with bemusement as she scrumples through the wrapping as if in search of Willy Wonka's golden ticket.

'Lara and I were just talking about the wedding,' he informs her.

'You haven't told her?' Elise halts before the gum reaches her mouth.

'Nooo,' Elliot shakes his head.

'Told me what?' I laugh. Can it get any worse?

'Nothing!' they chorus.

I feel uneasy. I can't begin to imagine the wedding

day Elise might have in mind. If I was the wedding planner I'd opt for a blind drunk ceremony in Vegas: that way there'd still be the chance of switching the bride at the last minute.

'Urgh!' Elise spits, mouth shrivelling to a shrewish pinch. 'What flavour is this?'

I smile to myself. I think I'm about to acquire a new taste.

'Still no sign of Helen,' Sasha says as she joins us. 'And now we've lost Zoë.'

'Uh oh!' Elliot shakes his head.

'Celeb-sighting. Got to be,' I deduce, switching my eyes to *OK!* vision.

'Lara, come and look over by Arrivals with me,' Sasha tugs at my arm. 'You two stay here.'

It's not like Sasha to take the lead, but all becomes clear as we round the corner and find Zoë flattened against a wall.

'Quick!' she beckons.

'What's going on?'

'Sasha's got something to tell us.' Zoë looks fit to burst.

In fact, so does Sasha. It's a long time since I saw her face so animated.

'Go on . . .' I urge.

'It's not her real name!' she tells us gleefully.

'*What?*' Our eyes widen.

'I saw her passport.'

I knew Elise was hiding something.

'What is it?' Zoë gasps.

'Same letters, different order,' Sasha teases us.

51

'Oh I love aneurysms!' Zoë claps.

'Anagrams,' I correct.

'I-L-E . . .' Zoë rearranges the letters.

'Just tell us!' I scream, checking that the Es are still by the kiosk.

'It's—'

'Wait! Give us a clue!' Zoë is way too playful for my liking.

'I'm guessing her mother was a big fan of *Coronation Street.*'

We take a moment and then yelp, '*Elsie!*'

Sasha shushes us as I giggle, 'Oh my God! Like Elsie Tanner?!'

'Elsie Fake Tanner more like,' Zoë hoots.

Oh how healing bitching can be! We're so slack-limbed with laughter we can barely stand up. Our attempt at a composed return to the kiosk looks worryingly like three OAPs body-popping.

'You all right?' Elliot looks concerned.

We nod vigorously in lieu of speech.

'No sign of her?'

Emphatic head-shaking and a whimpering noise like a balloon losing air from Zoë.

Elliot frowns. 'It's not like her to be late . . .'

Suddenly we're assaulted by a flap of flip-flops and flail of arms. I try to focus but all I can see is a blur of sun-streaked, sea-straggled hair whinnying with glee.

We recoil as one, causing the blonde banshee to cease pogoing. She stands panting and grinning before us, seemingly awaiting a reaction.

52

I see freckles. New ones – her skin has a brown base but strong pink accents as though some rays snuck through sunscreen this very morning and she hasn't had a chance to bronze over them. Her outfit is a tangy selection of citrus brights. She looks shiny and fresh and supernaturally happy.

Elliot is the first to speak, gingerly trying out the word: 'Helen?'

'Come here, you!' She flings her arms around Elliot, squeezing him as if she's trying to pop a beanbag.

We gawp and peer closer, hands reaching out to touch her, as if that might trigger some sensory recognition.

'Is it really you?' I locate her beauty spot amid the freckles.

'Lara!' she cheers, throwing herself at me.

Though semi-obscured by the hood of her top, I see Sasha and Zoë exchange an incredulous look, then merge squealing and bouncing into the hug.

Elise just looks confused, as if peeved that she wasn't in on the 'before' shots of the transformation.

'And you must be the future Mrs Harvey!'

Elise takes my smile and smears it over her own face. Helen knows? She knows they're engaged! She must have given her seal of approval, not that she's ever met Elise . . . I don't understand. Why would Elliot tell her before the rest of us? Before me? And how could Helen have kept such a bombshell to herself? Surely she could have warned me? I watch her take Elise's arm and think, Who is this woman?

'Don't worry, they haven't been playing a trick on

53

you!' Helen comforts Elise. 'I'm not quite the same person I was a year ago.'

'Is that a real tattoo?' I notice the wave motif on her ankle.

'How does that jewel stay on your toe?' Zoë magpies in on the twinkles.

'You look amazing!' Elliot speaks for all of us.

'Nearly as blonde as you now, Sash,' Helen smooths Sasha's silky veil.

'And nearly as tanned as me!' Zoë giggles, comparing an arm.

Helen takes a deep breath, assessing us one by one, looking fit to burst. 'So!' she grins, keen eyes sparkling. 'How was the flight?'

'Forget the flight! What's going on with you? What's happened?'

She goes to speak, then checks herself. 'I'll tell you later.'

'Tell us now!' Zoë insists, still hyped up on 'Elsie' hysteria.

'I'll tell you over tea – the top of the Jensens' wedding cake got dive-bombed by a seagull so we've got loads of free cake.'

Elise's eyes light up. As do mine – now there's something I hadn't thought of: I could ice her then prop her out on a deck to be pecked to death . . .

'Come on!' Helen chivvies me. 'The car's right outside.'

4

'Got your camera?' Helen asks as Elliot heaves the last piece of luggage into the back of Helen's silver People Mover.

'Right here.' Elliot taps his hip pouch.

'If you want sit up front, you'll get some great shots going over the bridge to Coronado.'

In one move Elliot leaps to the front seat, eagerly training his lens on the windscreen in preparation.

'Room for one more.' Helen holds open the passenger door.

'You go, Lara – you got the raw deal on the plane,' Sasha prompts.

'Well . . .' I hesitate, noticing Elise's (Elsie's!!) pointy-toe hovering over the step.

'Come on, up you go!' Zoë blunders in front of her, boosting me up alongside Elliot.

In the rearview mirror I watch Elise slide along into the seat behind the steering wheel. Then I see her eyes flash with panic – she's just realized she is no longer connected to Elliot on either the vertical or horizontal plane, and there's a whole gearbox obstructing her diagonal reach! She goes to switch places with Sasha who's just settling into the middle seat, but it's too late. Zoë is bumping them closer as she takes the other window spot, then Helen slam-clunks the door into place and seals her fate.

'We're on our way!' whoops Zoë. 'I can't believe we're all here.'

'I know,' Elliot grins. 'It's ages since we were all together. When was the last time – Helen's leaving do?'

'No, Sasha was in Cape Town on a job,' Helen reminds him. 'Before that.'

Elliot asks the panel on the back seat.

'What?' Elise snaps. 'I can't hear you from back here!'

Elliot repeats the question, oblivious to her huffiness.

As Sasha recalls the exact date, I can't help narrowing my eyes at Elise: you just sat on an eleven-hour flight with Elliot and now you're begrudging me a fifteen minute car ride? Look at her acting all left out. If she can't hear, all she has to do is lean forward, everyone else is managing. Surely she can't resent us reminiscing? We haven't seen Helen in over a year.

'What about the time we went to that Bucking Bronco bar in Watford!' Zoë chuckles. 'Maybe we could do it for real out here. This is the Wild West, isn't it?'

'You're kidding – my groin still hasn't recovered.' Elliot shifts in his seat.

'You were a natural!' Helen laughs. 'Randy the Cowboy!'

'Oh no!' I cringe. We called him that for weeks. He certainly had a knack – we reckoned it was because his legs are so long he got to tuck them under the bull whereas the rest of us just flailed around, cheerfully impaling ourselves on the horns.

Elliot inspects his left index finger – slightly misshapen since that day from gripping so hard – and sighs. 'That was a great summer.'

The best, I think to myself. All those beautiful hungover sunrises we saw in.

'I'll never forget—' begins Elliot, but before he can finish his thought, Elise has strained forward into front-seat territory. Instead of pawing at him she jabs Helen.

'The air conditioning isn't working back here,' she complains. 'I think you've got it all switched to the front.'

'It should be coming out here,' Helen reaches her hand back and runs her fingers over the vent.

'I'm OK,' Sasha shrugs, ever neutral.

'Well, I can't breathe,' Elise wheezes, slightly over-playing her bid to get attention.

'Here – I'll open the window,' Zoë offers.

Suddenly a flurrying blast of air whips up a wind tunnel effect and amid the bluster I hear a piercing scream. I wrench round to find the whole side of the People Mover missing – nothing but a seatbelt between Zoë and speeding tarmac.

'Hold on!' Helen urges.

The vehicle lurches as we veer over to the hard shoulder and screech to a stop.

'What happened?' Elliot scrambles around in his seat.

'I was just trying to open the window!' Zoë wails.

'You pulled the door handle!' Sasha gasps.

While we take a moment to let our battering hearts settle, Helen runs around to slide the door closed again, this time tapping on the window to indicate the lock to Zoë. She depresses the button with a trembling finger.

'Are you OK?' Elliot asks. He unbuckles himself so he can give Zoë's knee a comforting squeeze.

Zoë nods, still in shock.

'You'd better buckle up, we're off again!' Elise snaps as Helen starts up the ignition.

'I wondered what it was, that rushing sound.' I shudder. 'Imagine if you'd got sucked out!'

'It would have been awful – I'd have died before I got famous!' Zoë frets.

'You could've been famous for the *way* you died,' Sasha suggests.

'I think they already made a movie about that,' Elliot notes.

'Did they?' I frown. 'What?'

'*Gone With The Wind*!' Elliot hoots.

We all fall about laughing. All except Elise. It seems that nothing makes her more miserable than Elliot having fun. I'm telling you, if she gets through the week without me squashing her into a smoothie blender it'll be a miracle.

*

We continue flying down the freeway, banked on either side by soft swaying grasses that remind me of the wispy hairs on a balding man's comb-over. Lulled by the muted tones, I do a double-take at the shock of purple spilling over the concrete exit ramps – what looks at first like a giant splurge of paint is actually densely layered flowers.

'Trailing lantana,' Helen acknowledges my interest. 'It grows—'

'Check out that rollercoaster!' Elliot cuts in, unable to contain his excitement. 'Sorry, but look!'

'Wow!' I gawp, making out a bright blue loop of steel held up by vast concrete Roman numerals.

'You want to go on it?' Helen looks playful.

'Now?' I balk.

'It looks like it's on the way . . .' Elliot looks hopeful.

'Actually, it *is* the way!' Helen grins, sliding off the freeway and following the curve of the road until we're approaching the 'rollercoaster' head on.

'Oh my God!' I gasp as we mount it.

'Welcome to the Coronado Bay Bridge!' Helen introduces us.

Within seconds our altitude increases tenfold and we find ourselves suspended high above the sea, the skyscrapers of downtown San Diego behind us and a sand-fringed island ahead.

This has got to be the automobile equivalent of tightrope walking – the edge barriers don't seem nearly high enough, and my stomach feels as if it's just gone head-first over a high jump.

'Over to the left is Mexico!' Helen directs our gaze to the hazy mountain range.

As Sasha's eyes widen, Zoë starts singing, '*Tequila!* Du-duh-da-da-da-da-duh-duh!'

The rest of us would join her but our hearts have leapt into our mouths and there's no room for any vocal gymnastics. Gripping the dashboard, I dare myself to peer down at the elegant sailboats crossing the bay – little white triangles set against the blue like crisp handkerchiefs in a blazer pocket.

The relief is palpable as we begin our descent. We slow to join the line of traffic at the tollbooth then turn down a darling street lined with ice-cream-coloured clapboard houses. I wind down the window and lean out, wanting to take in every detail – the old palm trees with their shaggy dreadlocked grey bark, the ginger cat sprawling on the pavement begging for a tummy rub, the rose petals strewn on the neatly clipped grass.

'Is this where you live?' Elise asks, unable to keep the envy out of her voice.

'No, I'm about twenty minutes up the coast, at La Jolla,' Helen tells her, then locates Zoë in the rearview mirror, 'Your Spanish stretch to a translation?'

Zoë's longest relationship to date was with a Spanish barman but that was five years ago now.

Zoë frowns, 'Spelt J-O-L-L-A but pronounced HOYA?' she checks. Helen nods.

'Rings a bell but, no . . .' Zoë shakes her head. 'Tell us!'

'The Jewel,' Helen shimmers.

We sigh in unison. This is all so magical. Elise can do

60

her darndest but I know now that I won't regret coming on this trip. I'd forgotten how uplifting sunshine and a new view can be.

'Hotel Del Coronado!' I spot the sign for Helen's workplace. We all tug at our seatbelts trying to get the first glimpse of the infamous landmark – a white-washed wooden palace with dark red turrets, stretching along acres of pale blond shoreline.

'They say the Hotel Del is one third sand, one third sea and one third fairytale,' Helen smiles, winding up the driveway. 'But most people just call it the *Some Like It Hot* hotel!'

'Just think, Marilyn stayed here.' Zoë coos, utterly enraptured.

Every year since we met I've hunted down some quirky piece of Marilynabilia for Zoë's birthday so I know how much this means to her.

'Remember the bit in the film when they arrive at the hotel for the first time and there's all these ancient millionaires in wicker rocking chairs on the porch?'

'I've never liked black and white films,' Elise announces.

This is sacrilege to Zoë but she's too mesmerized by the guy in the stunted bowler hat who's stepped forward to greet us to care.

'Checking in?'

'Just visiting.' Helen leans across to him. 'Grant, these are the friends I was telling you about.'

'Heeyy! Welcome!' he cheers as we spill out of the People Mover. 'You must be Elliot –' he shakes his hand. 'And your fiancée . . .' His finger wavers like a water diviner between me and Elise. Then settles on me! My heart leaps as I redirect him to Ms Tanner. They have to break it off now – the doorman thinks we're a match!

'I'm Lara,' I tell him.

'Sasha!' The Beautiful One shakes his gloved hand. 'And this is Zoë!'

The bowler hat's eyes bulge at Zoë's cleavage then, as a luggage trolley brushes past, he stammers. 'Mind your, er, backs!' Still transfixed. I'm sure Marilyn herself had a similar welcome.

'Shall we?' Helen beckons us up the tiered redbrick steps, pushing through the glazed glass doors and leading us from dazzling sunshine into ye olde underworld of dark wood panelling, creaky balconies and antique lifts. The lobby is dominated by a Liz Taylor of chandeliers – a great bejewelled blancmange with dangling baubles flashing rainbows across the room.

We take a moment to inhale the towering floral display then disperse. Elliot gravitates to the cosy library area (for all his high-tech ways he's always had a thing for old books with frayed fabric spines. Elise thinks they're musty and unhygienic, which is why I send him bundles of them at regular intervals). While he studies gold-stamped titles like *Moon Tide* and *Midnight Plus One*, Elise seems to be having a bit of a moment with a gold velvet armchair, sinking into it with a distant look as though a misty memory is playing in her mind. Meanwhile Zoë and I are drawn as one to the exotic Martini menu – 'I fancy a Violette – Skyy vodka with a dash of cranberry and blue curaçao!' she reads.

And Sasha, where is she?

I turn back to see that she never made it further than the ante-room, having been waylaid by a suitor. Nothing new there. I feel almost sorry for him – he doesn't stand a chance. Not because he's unattractive, which coincidentally he is (unless you like your men to have the purplish complexion of the semi-strangled). It's just that if he's paid her any kind of compliment she'll have instantly switched off. With Sasha you can forget 'You had me at hello!' It's more a case of 'You lost me at "You're gorgeous!" '

However. It would seem Mr Plum has gone for something original, because he's holding her attention longer than most – perhaps she can't take her eyes off that golfball-size boil on his neck – but still she's shaking her head. He's offering her his card. She's declining. He's insisting. She's pointing over at Zoë. Strange. Zoë can find something shaggable about most men but I think this one may be a flabby earlobe too far. He pulls a face, she reluctantly accepts his card, then quickly tucks it into her tasselled handbag before hurrying over to join the rest of us.

'What did he want, apart from the obvious?'

'Who?' Sasha blushes.

'That guy,' I point back but he's gone.

Sasha shrugs and studies the floor.

Curious. Why would she try and deny the encounter? But before I can probe further, Helen sweeps us through to the Palm Court and offers us Afternoon Tea served by waitresses with buns and bustles.

Within minutes of settling around the table we're presented with the best-dressed cake stand I've ever seen – three layers, each with a distinct personality: at the top sit the dainty-girlie-frilly items, all frosted icing and sugared pastels, then comes a succulent fruit-topped selection, and at the bottom the rich browns of the chocolate, coffee and nut offerings.

'Helen, you've excelled yourself!' Elliot admires her handiwork.

I look at the anticipatory rapture on everyone's faces and think how B&Bs really talk up their break-fasts – quite logically of course – but what if our attraction was a legendary teatime? That would be a lovely bonus at check-in. You'd feel indulged the second you were through the door.

'Lara, are you going to try something?' Helen prompts me. 'I did the mini donuts specially for you.'

My life is one big quest for the perfect donut. I like them light and fluffy with a slightly crispy shell, as opposed to those solid doughy cushions that are so common.

'Perfection!' I gasp. 'Just a hint of jam and it's the quality stuff with pips and everything!'

Helen grins proudly, grabs an éclair and takes a giant bite.

I can't quite believe my eyes. In the old days, if a raisin got wedged in her teeth she'd consider that her treat for the month. I wonder if there's some new culinary equivalent of wine-tasting – take a bite, roll the food around the palette and then spit it out. But no, she swallows. *And* takes another bite.

'Mmm, and you've got to try these,' Helen raves, plucking one of the flaky pastries oozing custard. 'I know it looks messy but I tried adding a little almond paste to the filling and it's worked out really well.'

'I like these chocolate-dipped Florentines!' Sasha enthuses.

'I have two every morning for breakfast!' Helen smiles. 'Aren't they divine?'

I look at Zoë. She nods at me as if to say: You ask. So I do.

'Helen . . .' I try to sound casual, not wanting to make a big thing of it. 'Since when did you start eating your own creations?'

She laughs gaily. 'I don't know, one day I just got this *appetite*!'

'I don't get it – you're eating all these treats and you're looking slimmer than ever. What's your secret?' Zoë wants to know.

'Please don't tell me you've found true love, I'll have to kill myself,' I whimper.

'As a matter of fact I have met someone!' Helen beams.

'Traitor!' I joke but inside I'm crushed. Is there anything left of the old Helen? I mean, it's one thing to get a makeover but deliberately withholding earth-shattering gossip (I still can't believe she knew about Elliot's engagement first!) and now finding love. I feel a twist in my stomach and I'm having to work hard to keep smiling.

'His name is Reuben,' she sighs, looking elated.

'When do we get to meet him?' Elliot enquires.

'Soon,' she says, mysteriously.

'How did all this happen?'

'You really want to know?'

Yes!' we insist.

Helen takes a second to look at each of us, almost as if she's assessing whether we're really ready for her reply.

'Well . . .?' Sasha eggs her on.

She takes a breath and whispers: 'The California Club!'

'The what?' We all lean forward, eager to learn more.

'Miss Hill,' a waiter interrupts, 'the mother of the bride wants to thank you for the cake, have you got a minute?'

The second Helen is out of earshot we begin our speculation.

'It's got to be a Weight Watchers thing,' Zoë asserts. 'It's just like in the ads when people lead these fabulous zesty lives after they've dropped six stone. Look at her – she's glowing.'

'She wouldn't be allowed chocolate éclairs if it was Weight Watchers,' Sasha observes.

'Maybe it's just all the extra sugar making her hyper,' Elise opines.

'I reckon it's a surf club.' Elliot gets practical.

'There's more to it than weight loss, she's toned, she's lithe – look at her body.'

Elise raises an eyebrow.

'Not that I was,' flounders Elliot.

'Could be,' Sasha muses. 'She's got the look, she's right here on the beach, San Diego's the surf capital of California, isn't it.'

'I think it's a dating agency: "*The California Club – bringing together sun-kissed singles . . .*"' I suggest, hoping I'm not making it too obvious which aspect of her transformation is preying on my mind the most.

'Oh no.' A look of horror flashes across Elise's face. 'What if it's one of those dreadful change-your-life cults!'

'What if it's Scientology?' Sasha murmurs.

'Oh my God! I wonder if she's met John Travolta!' Zoë gasps.

'She's far too level-headed – she'd never sign up to a cult,' Elliot tuts.

'A year ago she'd never leave the house without a serum-smoothed bob, and now look at her!' Zoë points out.

As we lapse into silent contemplation I give myself a chill. 'You don't think she's got us over here to recruit us, do you?' I ask, unsure of whether that would be a good or a bad thing.

'You can rely on my bullshit detector,' Elise bristles. 'If I sense a whiff of mind control I'll scream the place down.'

'Whatever it is, she looks pretty good on it!' Elliot says.

'Yeah, I'd give it a try.' Sasha looks wistful.

'I wonder if she can get us temporary membership,' Zoë ponders.

'I don't think we should mention it again till she does,' Elise decides.

'Why not?' Zoë frowns.

'That way we'll know if she's trying to convert us.'

'Ahhh!' we nod, all going along with Elise's paranoia for some inexplicable reason.

'So it'll be like a test?' Zoë checks.

'Exactly!' Elise confirms.

'So we'll just keep—'

'Quiet!' Elise shushes Zoë. 'She's coming back!'

We all resume 'mmmmmm-delicious' poses with various pastry props and act as though our conversation got no further than eulogizing the lemon meringue pie. Helen surprises all of us by not mentioning The California Club again, although instead of this being a relief, it just fuels our curiosity. But we daren't cross Elise so soon after we vowed silence on the subject, and besides, I don't know if I'm ready for any more revelations yet.

I study Helen closely as she chats merrily. Can she really be as happy as she seems? My stomach continues to curdle. This is about her, not me, so why am I feeling so introspective, so grey sitting next to her. As Elliot brings Helen up to speed on his recent promotion (strangely unwelcome – he preferred his former job and the relative absence of responsibilities to his new power status and company car) I feel I'm slipping away, as though I am watching the others from behind a Perspex screen. Elliot and Elise's lives are about to change as they become husband and wife, Sasha has begun a new chapter, having given up her modelling, and Zoë is busily applying for new jobs but look at me – my hair's the same, my job's the same, and as for my love life, I thought it was just coasting along in nothingness but it turns out that even that just got a hell of a lot worse.

Of course there is one big change coming in my life but it's a longed-for opportunity being taken away rather than presented to me. Not even Helen knows I'm going to lose the B&B. But I've decided I'm going to hold on to that revelation a while longer. I couldn't talk about it now without being overwhelmed with self-pity. I have to tune into the good around me. Focus on the positive. Have another cake.

5

I tilt my head at the swathe of sky unravelling for miles in either direction from our vantage point on the beachfront terrace. The wisps of clouds look to me like powdery icing sugar blown across a sheet of blue silk.

'Phwoar – hello!' Zoë whistles as three bare torsos in grey shorts jog by in such strict formation they look like a six-legged Chippendale.

'There's a Navy SEALS base on the island,' Helen explains. 'They're here every day.'

'Welcome to paradise!' Zoë mutters, then sits forward and points to where the flat bands of sand meet the sea. 'What's going on there?'

We follow her gaze to five fully-dressed silhouettes dodging the lapping waves. Head to toe in black, they seem to be transplanted from another era. I remember Helen saying the hotel had a ghost and I'm about to ask whether these might be visiting spooks when we realize they are in fact an Amish family – Dad and sons sporting braces and straw boaters, the mother and daughter in matching bonnets.

'It looks like a scene from *The Piano*,' Elise gawps.

'Now I've never seen that before!' Even Helen is bemused. 'Come on, I want to show you something.'

'Is this the haunted stairwell?'

'Not yet.'

Helen leads us beyond the tennis courts to a private bungalow with its own gated entrance.

'We can't go in because it's occupied, but this is the Beach House where Marilyn Monroe stayed during filming.'

As Zoë throws herself against the railings, crying 'I want to touch it!' I find myself wondering how I might have lured a celebrity to stay the night at the B&B and then named the room after them. The Orlando Bloom Suite, in an ideal world. Doesn't that sound fetching? But then I experience a stab of regret. Why are ideas presenting themselves to me now when it's too late to implement them?

'Do you like it, Lara?' Helen asks.

'How many does it sleep?' I reply with a question.

'Well, there's one king, two queens and a sofa bed—'

'Room enough for all of us!' Elliot decides. 'How much?'

'$2,300.'

'Please tell me that's for the week.'

'A night.'

'I've got to find a millionaire,' Zoë scans the horizon.

'Have you been inside?' I ask, dying for a glimpse. The outside is a basically plain white box, albeit a box

71

topped with a red tile roof and tailed with a border of clashing pansies and snapdragons.

'Of course!' Helen nods.

'Well?' I prompt her.

'Maybe you'll get to see it for yourselves soon . . .' Helen gives a mischievous twinkle.

Zoë swings round, 'Oh Helen, you haven't! Can we . . . Are we . . .?' Zoë splutters, pawing at Helen's sleeve.

'Do you mean a tour? A night?' Elliot tries to get the specifics.

'You'll have to wait and see!'

'Not this too!' Zoë wails. 'Helen, you're killing us with all this suspense!'

Elise gives Zoë a dark look.

'Aren't I wicked?' Helen chirrups, unfazed. 'Come on, let's go back to the main hotel, I'll tell you the hotel ghost story.'

'Do we get to hear the end?' Zoë grumbles.

Helen takes her arm. 'Of course!'

I follow behind. Helen can't have wangled us a night in the Beach House, surely? $2,300 worth of accommodation! Unless . . . Maybe The California Club is some kind of local hotel mafia . . .

'What are all these metal things sticking out of the ceilings?' I ask as Helen leads us along one of the extra-wide corridors.

'Sprinklers. This building is mostly wood and one of the owners was so terrified of how quickly a fire would spread that he had gazillions installed. Now you'd have more chance of drowning than burning to death.'

'Speaking of death,' Elise finally finds a subject she feels an affinity with. 'You mentioned a ghost . . .'

Helen continues for a couple more paces then turns to face us. 'Kate Morgan was just twenty-four when she put a gun to her head and shot herself, right here in the hotel. She checked in with no luggage following an argument with her husband on a train bound for San Diego. He got off in Orange, she continued on and waited for five days for him in this corner hotel room. When he didn't show she took her own life.'

Sasha, Zoë and I sigh. What woman can't relate to the madness-inducing frustrations of the waiting game.

'Poor girl,' Sasha exhales.

'I wouldn't feel sorry for her!' Elise pouts. 'Why didn't she just go home? It's ridiculous!'

I wonder if Elise has ever cried over a man. It strikes me that I know nothing of her love life before Elliot.

Helen shrugs. 'This was 1892, maybe it wasn't that simple.'

'Do you know the exact date?' Sasha asks.

'November 24th,' Helen replies.

Elise goes white. 'That's my birthday!'

Now she's spooked. Good for Sasha! Her granny was a psychic, and I can't help but feel she may have just dropped by.

'We've had reports of extreme changes in temperature, strange sounds, fragrances, people tripping on the step where her body was found . . .'

'She doesn't realize that she's gone.' Sasha looks sad.

'She can't understand why people can't see her, why they just walk through her.'

I lean out on the balcony overlooking the pretty courtyard. 'Isn't that funny,' I muse. 'To everyone else here this place really is heaven.'

'Yeah, if it wasn't full of Americans it would be great.'

Thank you Elise. Back from the brink.

I try to exchange a look with Sasha but her eyes are averted and if I'm not mistaken her bottom lip is trembling.

'Back in a mo!' she swiftly excuses herself.

'We'll be in the terrace bar!' Helen calls after her.

As the others move away, I discreetly drop back then turn to follow Sasha, finally locating her in the Ladies, staring miserably into the sink.

Catching sight of my reflection she looks startled and blusters, 'Did you see this? They've got an automatic soap dispenser – you just wave your hand under the nozzle—'

'Are you OK?' I cut in, concerned at how disturbed she looks. I'm fairly certain it's not just the ghost story unsettling her.

She looks at me for a second and then starts feverishly frothing her hands like a pin-up version of Lady Macbeth. 'I just feel a bit queasy, I think it was the pecan pie – I'm not very good with caramelized nuts.' Sasha is a terrible liar. She knows it too, so she has another go: 'Or it could be the jet lag, you know I read it can actually cause depression in some people.'

'Is it Helen?' I gently enquire.

'No! Of course not! Why would it be?' she reels. 'I'm really happy to see her!'

'Me too, it's just . . .' I hesitate before shuffling out on to a limb. 'It's just thrown me a bit how much things have changed for her.'

I check for a smidgeon of empathy on Sasha's face, find it, and proceed.

'She's the last person I expected to have some kind of life epiphany. I mean, it's really exciting and I'm so pleased she's met someone but it was always us two who never had a boyfriend and now she's got one and—'

Sasha holds my gaze.

'I feel left behind,' I finish.

'Oh me too!' splurges Sasha. 'She looks so alive. Before, I don't know, I always felt something was missing from her life too. Like we were both going through the motions,' she sighs, adding, 'We never actually spoke about it but I'd look at her and think *something doesn't fit right*, and now she just looks so complete and content.'

I've never felt more in common with Sasha than I do right now. To look at us as a group, you'd think she would be the number one having-it-all contender but Helen has trumped the lot of us.

'Are you afraid it's never going to happen for you?' I ask, brimming with empathy.

Sasha nods.

'It should make us feel better, shouldn't it? Like she's giving us hope!' I smile.

'I know, it's weird. I am pleased for her. But I'm

75

also . . .' Sasha squints as she plays name-that-emotion.

'Jealous?' I suggest.

'Not jealous exactly . . .' Sasha frowns.

'I am,' I confess.

'Oh me too!' Sasha wails. 'I hate myself for it. She totally deserves it.'

'She does,' I confirm. Funny how it still hurts.

'It's just . . .' Sasha sighs, 'I feel like I don't know her any more.'

'She's crossed over.'

'Become one of them.'

'The Happy People,' I gurgle.

'People with lives.'

'And we're still us.' We sigh in unison.

I lean against the marble wall, wondering what we do next. I didn't even know how bleak my life was until I saw Helen looking so vibrantly in her element. I was even reasonably resigned to losing the B&B – it seemed like too much work to fight for it. Before I left I was only interested in coming on holiday and forgetting about it all. But now . . . Now I'm all at sea.

'Do you really think this California Club is the key?' Sasha queries.

'There's definitely something to it,' I decide. 'You don't get that level of transformation just from a change in the weather!'

As soon as I've said it I disagree with myself. Of course all this sunshine could be the answer. Maybe Helen's found a way to liquefy it, so now pure radiance pumps through her veins.

'Whatever she's got, let's hope it's contagious!' I joke, trying to lighten the mood.

'Maybe she'll be able to give us a few clues on how to get it.' Sasha plays along.

'Yeah – we've got an insider on our side now. This is great!'

It's taking every ounce of my strength to try and jolly us up. Ordinarily this situation would qualify for a whole evening's wallowing and soul-searching but we need to buck ourselves up in a matter of minutes so we can put on a bright face for the others.

'It's not like there's only enough happiness in the world for a few people, is it?' Sasha asks, sounding a little uncertain.

'Of course not. There's an infinite supply!' I cheer.

'Yeah!' Sasha dries off her hands in an efficient 'glad we got that sorted' way.

'You know what else – maybe we were holding each other back, thinking it was OK to stay the same because we weren't the only one,' I suggest. 'Maybe we didn't want to be the first ones to get a man or a life.'

'I guess a rut can get pretty cosy when your best friend's in it with you,' Sasha sighs.

'It's a theory,' I acknowledge. 'Now this could set us free!'

'Wow!' Sasha takes a moment to process the thought. 'Whatever has happened to Helen could be the best thing to ever happen to us.'

I know neither of us really believe it and that later our minds will weave back to our respective problems but it's good enough for now.

'Ready to face the music?' I ask.

Sasha smiles a yes. 'Thanks for—'

'That's OK. You know me – I love a bit of cubicle counselling.'

So many toilets, so little time . . .

On the way to the terrace bar we make a conscious effort to go from introspection to commenting on our surroundings and the people infiltrating them: mainly bumbag-toting tourists and what look like the local gentry – old folk with whisked up hair and heavy jewels.

'Curious mix you get here,' I comment. 'By the way, who was that guy?'

'What guy?' Sasha does it again.

'The one with the—' I tug at my earlobe.

'My God! Weren't they huge? Up close they looked like big fleshy cuts of meat!'

I wait for her to reveal his identity.

'You know, my dad convinced himself his ears were getting bigger as he got older and so I looked it up in a medical dictionary and—'

'Sasha!'

'Well, he *says* he's a movie producer.'

I gawp. Only Sasha could get a casting call within two hours of touching down. Fortunately I'm all envied-out – I just want the juice.

'He gave me this spiel about how I was "a less smooshy-faced Cameron Diaz" and perfect for his next movie,' Sasha obliges.

'Why didn't you say?'

'You know I'm not into that,' she squirms. 'Even if he was for real.'

'He could be!'

'Which is why I suggested he take a look at Zoë. But I didn't want to introduce them until I checked him out.'

'Wise move,' I acknowledge, getting an image of Zoë hyperventilating with excitement and then dragging him, boil and all, on to a casting couch. Whether he liked it or not.

'If he is legit, I thought maybe she could meet with him when we go to LA.'

'Did he say anything about her? "Halle Berry with hair extensions?" "Tyra Banks with a human-size forehead?"'

Sasha chuckles and shakes her head. 'Just that she looked more music video than actress at the moment.'

'Oh,' I say, disappointed for her.

'But we can easily sort that,' Sasha notes. (She's learned a fair few styling tips in her time.)

'Here they are!' Helen heralds our return. 'We're ordering martinis.'

'I've got a Spudtini!' Elliot looks pleased with himself. 'Pure potato vodka.'

'You're such a man,' I tease, settling into the wicker chairs they've aligned for us.

For a while we sit in contented silence watching the sun back-light the waves – as they rise up we can see clear through the glassy green water. I'm hypnotized watching them fold over, froth up and then slide in on layers of silver-grey, and I'm just about to comment on the idyllic silence when a lifeguard truck splashes through the shallow waters informing everyone within a mile radius that they are now off duty, so should you enter the ocean, you do so at your own risk.

I doubt many would venture in now. It's amazing how quickly the temperature drops early evening. I give a little shiver.

'You cold, La?' Elliot reaches over to rub my bare arm. 'Here, put this on.' He pulls off his sweater in that weird way men do, reaching back and dragging the whole thing over his head for maximum hair-rumpling potential. It's still warm as he heaps it into my lap.

'But now you'll be cold,' I half protest, slurring rather more than anticipated. (I made the mistake of thinking I could handle an XXL Supertini.)

'I'll be fine,' Elliot assures me. 'I've got this one to keep me warm,' he adds, concertina-ing Elise with his embrace.

'Careful!' she whines, wriggling free.

I can't help but snort out loud – I love how Elise makes out she's this fragile sugar-spun waif who'll snap if you hug her with any kind of sincerity. Oh to set Zoë-The-Human-Pulverizer on her.

'Shall we go down on to the beach for the sunset?' Helen suggests, noting that all the drinks are satisfactorily drained. 'If we go over to that humpbacked ledge it feels like you're sitting on the edge of the world looking out . . .'

'Won't the sand be cold now?' Elise complains, reluctant to leave her floral cushion.

'I'll get some blankets.' Helen jumps up.

'I'll come with you,' I volunteer, eager to compensate for not being 100 per cent embracing of the new Helen, just in case she's noticed.

'It's just through here . . .' Helen leads the way.

'I can't believe the changes in you,' I pipe, trying to sound as upbeat as possible.

'I can't believe I lived like I did for so long,' Helen sighs.

'How do you mean?'

Helen stops. 'Oh you know, I was putting so much energy into being the me I always saw myself becoming, not really stopping to ask whether I was happy.' She frowns, and for a second I see a flash of how she used to be and I don't want her to go back. Why should she? She's found a new way to live.

'So then what happened?' I ask quickly, afraid she'll dwell too long on the past and lose her newfound bliss.

'Reuben took me surfing and I didn't recognize myself out there!' she smiles. 'And it was a good feeling. In that moment I just let it all go.'

'How you thought things should be?' I check, wanting to be clear on how the miracle began.

She nods.

'We lay out on the beach all night and all these thoughts kept whizzing through my head and I just kept coming back to the same thing: "This is it! This is what really matters – the rest is just a distraction."'

I get a rush of vicarious adrenalin.

'Is that when you gave up your job in Arizona?' I ask. I'm still not sure of the details.

Helen nods. 'That night, when I went back to

Reuben's apartment, I sent a faxed resignation letter to work. I didn't want to risk going back on Monday and slipping into my own routine, losing my nerve.'

'That was a big step.'

'Yes it was, but I had some help.'

The California Club, I think to myself. I want to ask more but I'd feel sneaky getting information before the others.

'Here!' Helen loads my arms with an array of Mexican rugs and throws.

'Are these all yours?' I admire the streaky ridges of colour – mint to pink to burgundy to blue to brown, like a series of woven sunsets.

'Yup, I've got quite a collection going – little tip I learned from your mum: why sit on one thin layer when you could be snuggled in seven!'

Mum never believed in travelling light to the beach – there was no need. We were so close we could make five trips if we wanted. Everyone else was on damp towels with rolled-up T-shirts propping up their heads, while we looked like some sumptuous bedouin scenario with windshields and cushions and fleece blankets in jewel-bright colours. I feel swimmy with nostalgia and contemplate telling Helen about the B&B, but I don't want to ruin the mood, besides the others will be getting chilly.

'Great blankets!' Zoë covets them the second we reach the dune.

'I got them at this market in Tijuana, fiver each,' Helen brags.

'I'd love to go shopping there!' Zoë enthuses. 'I bet Lara could find some real treasures.'

'The border's only twenty minutes away,' Helen tempts her further. 'My sous-chef actually lives over there.'

'Imagine commuting to work from a different country every day!' Elliot smiles. 'That's so cool.'

As we snuggle into the blankets Helen deftly rustles up a mini beachfire and then we all bliss out as the sun puts on the most spectacular show, melting from hot gold to moody orange and then seeping across the sky, turning the clouds alternately pink and baby blue. This performance has many acts and just when we think it's going for a subtle fade-out, a blinding electric yellow streaks the vista and we gasp at the beauty and ingenuity.

'There's definitely a magic in the air here.' Helen inhales the last breath of sunshine then continues speaking, almost as if in a trance. 'I just feel so free, so happy for every little thing.'

The rest of us stare at her through the now misty darkness, as one by one she strikes at our Achilles' heels.

'I feel lighter, not just physically but in my heart. I feel loved, connected, part of the world . . . So peaceful and yet so energized. So hopeful . . .'

There's a silence while we contemplate what it would be like to feel even one of those things whole-heartedly. The want in us is palpable. It's not just me and Sasha.

'So come on, Helen!' I beg, all out of patience. 'Tell us about The California Club!'

Elise shoots me a poisonous look but everyone else gives an encouraging, 'Yeah!'

She beams back at our expectant faces. 'OK. But I'm going to ask you all to do one thing first.' Sitting up on her haunches she rummages in her rucksack, this time pulling out a little block of paper and a collection of biros.

'Are we playing some kind of game?' Elise sneers.

'No, I just need you all to write something down,' she explains, handing out a sheet of paper and a pen to each person. 'Ready?'

We nod, looking a little wary.

'I want each of you to write down what you'd most like to happen during your vacation here.'

'Vacation?' teases Elliot in his best Valley Girl voice.

'Holiday, whatever!' Helen dismisses his friendly carping.

'Do you mean like a list of activities?' I ask.

'Stick my hands in cement on Hollywood Boulevard, get discovered by a movie director, shag Josh Hartnett,' Zoë offers.

'Well, you're halfway there but I'm not after a list. This is more of a wish. What would be the one thing that would make your holiday complete?'

'Shag Josh Harnett!' Zoë affirms.

'Don't say it out loud, just write it down. No conferring and no more questions,' Helen sternly addresses our furrowed brows and open mouths.

Elise is the first to scribble, somewhat aggressively, on her page. Then Elliot, with a casual scrawl, obviously not fretting too much over his choice.

'Now what?' Elise asks impatiently.

'We just sit quietly until the others are done.' Helen takes their pieces of paper and then Zoë's, closely followed by Sasha's reluctant offering.

'I think my wish might be a bit of a lost cause,' she frets.

'It doesn't matter,' Helen reassures her. 'Just as long as it's heartfelt.'

Now everyone is waiting for me.

This is obviously just some funny little quiz to amuse Helen but I don't want to miss out on the chance of having a wish come true. Just in case. But how can I write down what I really want – for Elliot to realize that he loves me, not Elise! I already wished for it on the plane and I don't want to negate that, and besides, I have a feeling these are going to be read out loud at some juncture. What then? I look around me for inspiration. I'd love to swim in that glittering sea or cruise the coast in a convertible but that's hardly original. Aware of the others' eyes upon me, I dig my toes beneath the dusty sand to the cool damp beneath.

What do I want? Honestly? I'd be happy to stay around this fire for the next two weeks. Everything I need is here. I sneak a peek at the faces reflecting the flickering yellow light . . . It's been so long since I had the chance to catch up with everyone, I feel swollen with fondness for them all. Well, nearly all. If Elise morphed into a giant toasting marshmallow life would be just about perfect. So how can I phrase 'spending quality time with my beloved friends' without sounding a cheeseball?

I take the pen, do my darndest to focus on the page and write, 'I wish I could have some special one-to-one time with each of my friends, enough to create a memory that would last a lifetime.' I can't believe I wrote that! Is that even a sentence? I'm just about to screw up the schmaltz and start again when Helen reaches over and swipes the page from me.

'All done!'

'But—' I protest.

'It's best to go with the first thing that pops into your head!'

'But, really, Helen!' I squirm, mortified. My first thought would be the Elliot love wish. Maybe I should've . . . Oh no!

'Right!' Helen folds the pages and puts them back in her rucksack, zipping the bag closed with an air of ominous finality. 'Let's get you to the hotel.'

'Is that it?' Zoë asks, as we all continue to eye Helen's rucksack, fearing for the future of our slips of paper.

'For now,' she smiles.

'Thank God!' Elise rolls her eyes. 'I thought we were going to be led in some weird pagan ceremony.'

'Don't be silly,' Helen laughs, getting to her feet. 'That's tomorrow.'

'What?' Elise blurts.

'But Helen!' I scamper to my feet. 'You still haven't told us about The California Club – what is it?'

'Tomorrow,' she says, steadily.

Our five voices tangle in an exasperated squeal but frankly we're too tired to argue.

'Tomorrow, you promise?' I need some assurance.

Helen nods. 'Trust me, it'll be worth the wait.'

6

Sunlight slides under the curtains and creeps up to my eyes. I smile realizing I'm waking up in one of the most enviable scenarios known to man – in bed with Sasha. And there's a light guttural snoring coming from the foot of the bed, which is something of a relief as there was no sign of Zoë when I turned out the light at midnight.

'I'm just going to grab a hot totty at the bar!' were her last words to us.

Sasha and I mused over whether she meant a 'hot toddy' but decided it was actually more likely that she'd spotted an appealing barman while we were checking in.

It was after dark when we presented our seasalt-frosted faces to the reception staff at La Valencia – a baby-pink mission-style hacienda overlooking La Jolla cove – and then left a trail of sandy footprints to our rooms, or better yet, villas. Elliot was particularly tickled that he and Elise were assigned 'Ocean Villa Eleven' – going some way to fulfilling his hankering to be a part of the Rat Pack. Zoë, Sasha and I were in

Ocean Villa Five. And in Fifteen, Goldie Hawn. I kid you not. At first we didn't believe Zoë when she came screeching in from the balcony to inform us of our celebrity neighbour, but this time she was right.

Turns out La Valencia has been a Hollywood hideaway since the 1930s. In those days Zoë might have been yelping that she'd just seen Greta Garbo or Charlie Chaplin reclining on their sunloungers. (Not that I can picture either of them getting busy with the coconut tanning oil.) Anyway, since then it's become such a beloved local institution that most of the antiques in the public rooms have been donated by former patrons. I think it's lovely that they wanted to be a part of their favourite hotel.

I wish that one day I could've inspired that kind of devotion with the B&B – how wonderful to know that every chaise or vase had a personal history rather than an Ikea price tag. Despite not having the same taste as my mum I have to acknowledge that she had chosen every item with love. So many of the other B&Bs in our square stopped at the bare minimum – every item in the room provided a function or it wouldn't have a place. The rooms I love have treasures that are just there for pleasure. Those are the things that give a room a personality. Some people want bland, they don't want to engage with their environment and that's fine, but I like to walk in and get a sense of character. That way, even if you're alone, you feel like you're in great company.

As I lean over to take a sip of water a thought strikes me – it's almost as if Helen knows that I'm on the verge of giving up the B&B and she's trying to tempt me into keeping it by showing me all these sumptuous hotels: *look at all the fabulous possibilities* . . . But she can't know. I haven't discussed it with anyone except Mum. I thought it would be best to make the decision first and tell them when it was a fait accompli. That way it wouldn't seem such a big deal – just a case of 'it's done, accept it'. And yet it seems wrong to make a decision without consulting them. Especially Zoë because it really was her home for seven years.

But maybe I'm overestimating how upset they'll be. The B&B hasn't been part of their lives for a while now. Sasha was the last person who came to stay and that was six months ago. They've moved on. Maybe it's time I did too. Maybe they'll think it's a good idea. Maybe it is! Yes, I've felt a flutter of five-star inspiration since arriving in America, but I'm assuming that we will be staying six of us to a motel room the rest of the week – two nights at La Valencia is totally skewing our accommodation budget. (When we quizzed her on the extravagance, Helen assured us that there's a reason why we should make the most of luxury now. Not that she'd tell us what that reason was. I just hope it doesn't involve camping.)

Anyway, I'm not going to think about it any more. I came here for a break. I stare up at the white fir-beamed ceiling and wiggle my toes beneath the 10 billion thread count sheets. If it wasn't for the chronic jet lag I'm sure I would have had one of the best night's sleep of my life.

As I pull myself up to a sitting position, eager to see

this place in daylight, Sasha responds by snuggling deeper down. I'm relieved to find her looking so serene in repose. She seemed troubled and distant during the evening, but fell asleep as soon as her golden head hit the goosedown pillow. In the absence of Zoë, I watched TV for a while and then sat out on the balcony in the dark, listening to the rustle of the palm trees and deep breathing of the sea, wondering what the next fourteen days holds for us all.

It was so unexpected, being given a wish. I mean, I always thought if a genie wisped out of a lamp I'd ask for a million pounds, true love and an end to period pain but this wish was different. *What would we most like to happen during our time here?* If I had to guess, I'd say Zoë's would involve sex and a celebrity – her two favourite things; Sasha, either surgery to make her look like Kathy Burke or maybe a surprise Prozac prescription; Elliot's dream would definitely be Disneyland with no queues; Elise . . . probably something simple like, 'Make Elliot's friends go away.'

I'd love to be a fly on the wall and see how she is with him when we're not around. Maybe she saves all her bristling for us and is sweetness and light when they're alone. I wonder what they're doing now? Lying in each other's arms, feeding each other chocolate-dipped strawberries, no doubt.

'Are you indecent?'

There's a rat-a-tat on the door and Elliot strides in, hair still wet. Dimples dimpling.

I do a quick check that my pyjamas aren't offering

an impromptu peep show as he darts for the window.

'Get ready for some California sunshine!' he cheers, unhooking the white plantation shutters.

He laughs at my blinded-by-the-light pose and then does a double-take at the body on the put-me-up bed.

'Oh my God! Check out Zoë's maracas!'

'Elliot!' I exclaim. It's not like him to be so crude. I make a move to redress Zoë's modesty but the tightly tucked counterpane has me bound to the bed.

'I mean literally!' He reaches down and picks up two hand-painted maracas, giving the rattling beads a rhythmical swish. 'Where'd she get these?'

'Mmmmfff,' Zoë stirs.

'Zoë?' Elliot leans over her.

She squirms away. 'Don't make me eat the worm again!'

Elliot's eyebrows raise.

I make a silent prayer that it's a tequila worm she's referring to and suddenly feel a bit guilty for letting her out of my sight.

'Wow. She's out of it! What time did you lot get to bed?'

'Sasha was about ten,' I begin.

She raises a slender arm and flickers her fingers in acknowledgement.

'I watched TV till midnight.'

'Does your telly rise up out of this box here?'

I nod.

'How cool is that?' Elliot grins.

'As for Worm Woman,' I continue with our alibis: 'no idea.'

Elliot looks back down at Zoë and frowns. 'What's that black line between her eyebrows.

Freeing myself from the bed, I scuttle over and gasp. 'It's the Frida Kahlo monobrow!'

'The what?' Elliot laughs, stepping back and stumbling over a giant paper-wrapped roll. 'Where'd all these Mexican blankets come from? Did Helen—'

Suddenly Sasha sits bolt upright in bed as if she's been yanked up in traction. 'She couldn't have!'

I immediately get Sasha's drift and spin around. 'Where's her bag?'

Sasha locates it in one leap. 'Passport!'

We all crowd round, scrabbling through the pages and discover the word MEXICO, freshly stamped.

'She must have gone shopping in Tijuana!' Sasha reels.

'I can't believe she left the country while we were sleeping,' I gasp.

'Zoë?' Elliot gently shakes her.

She opens one blurry eye. 'Si?'

We chuckle at our somnolent signorita.

'I think we should let her sleep,' Elliot decides, tucking her maracas in beside her like a teddy bear. 'You two coming to breakfast?'

'Can you wait five minutes while I have a shower?' I ask.

'No problem,' he obliges. 'Sasha, you OK? You look a bit queasy.'

'Yeah, I'm not hungry, I think I'll get some air down by the sea and then meet you back here.'

I experience a flicker of concern but decide not to hassle her.

'Five minutes . . .' I repeat but as soon as I step into the marble vastness of the bathroom I realize I've been a little optimistic with my timing – it takes five minutes just to reach the shower and when I pull the glass door shut behind me I discover it seals to create a steam room and it seems criminal to waste such an exotic function. So I don't.

I appear fifteen minutes later with highly flushed cheeks and a rumbly tummy.

Breakfast is served al fresco on the Tropical Patio, a charming tiled courtyard interspersed with tumbling flowers and manicured men in salmon pink cashmere V-necks.

'Look at the pretty tablecloths,' I coo as the waiter guides us to our designated table.

'Gorgeous!' Elliot grins.

'Elise!' I startle myself saying her name. For one blissful moment I'd actually forgotten she was on holiday with us.

'Morning, sleepyhead,' she smirks.

I smirk back. Had to get in an 'I was up with the larks' dig, didn't she?

'Where's the rest of your cronies?' she asks.

I take a don't-hit-her breath then launch into an overly cheerful, 'Well, Crony One – Sasha – is at the beach. And Crony Two, Zoë . . .'

I catch Elliot's amused eye and find myself sniggering.

'What's so funny?' Elise snaps.

'You wouldn't believe us if we told you,' Elliot shakes his head and does a little maraca motion with his hands.

I titter uncontrollably, then hold my knife along my eyebrows, setting Elliot off again.

'What?' Elise is getting impatient now, miffed that she's not in on the joke.

I feel simultaneously mean and triumphant. Last night on the way back from the beach she was laying on all the couple schmaltz: 'Remember when we were in bed, programming our mobile phone rings?' or 'You were talking in your sleep again the other night, Mickey Mouse.' Urgh! Sickening! Well this is payback.

I hide behind my menu trying to decide whether I'm brave enough order a spirulina juice or whether celery and fennel would be a wiser option when Elliot caves and fills her in on Zoë's exploits.

'I suppose we should be grateful she didn't bring back a whole Mariachi band,' he concludes.

Elise's response? Laughter? Incredulity? Disapproval? None of the above. She simply clicks her fingers and summons the waiter as if Elliot had just related the weather report for the day. She can't stand him to have fun if it doesn't revolve around her. I stick a fork prong into my palm to stop myself screaming.

'What would you like?' The waiter has his pen poised.

Elise jumps straight in: 'I'll have a chocolate mocha, he'll have a latte. Shall we split the crab and avocado omelette with chive *crème fraiche* and get a stack of cranberry cassis pancakes?'

'Why don't you just get what you want and I'll get what I want?' Elliot dares to question her food order.

The look on her face very clearly announces: Sulk brewing.

Elliot looks back at the menu. 'Actually the pancakes sound good, let's do it.'

I guess I'm not invited to their plate-swapping picnic. I order the ginger pancakes with homemade apple butter and defy them not to want a forkful.

As the parade of food begins I wonder out loud if Helen might be joining us.

'She won't be here till noon,' Elise announces. 'Says we're to meet her in the lobby at exactly twelve.'

'When did she call?' Elliot queries.

'Just after you left to knock up the girls.' Elise frowns at her choice of phrasing then continues: 'Apparently she's got a surprise for us – maybe she's going to reveal where we'll be staying after tonight.' Elise grizzles. 'I'm not sure I like all this "Wait and see!" stuff. If I wanted suspense I'd have gone on a Murder Mystery Weekend.'

If only. Though it's not too late to arrange a little strychnine in her mocha chocolata ya-ya.

'I think it's fun,' Elliot rallies. 'Anything could happen!'

'I just hope there's not going to be loads of packing and unpacking. I hate that.'

'Count yourself lucky you've got a suitcase to unpack,' I mutter.

'Still no sign of it?' Elliot sighs.

'Express is just across the street, it's similar to Next,' Elise informs me. 'We could come with you and pick something out, if you like?'

I see this supposed kindness for what it is: a ploy to get Elliot to buy something for her.

'Thanks but I think I'll wait till Helen gets here to see what occasion I'm dressing for,' I tell her.

'Suit yourself.'

We fall into an awkward silence. I feel so self-conscious in front of Elise, almost as if I'm acting. I can't be my normal self because that would mean gabbling away to Elliot and she gets all huffy if the conversation doesn't revolve around her so all that's left is innocuous nonsense.

'Did you know Pearl Jam once stayed here?' I make a conversational bid. 'And Barbra Streisand. Imagine them doing a duet!'

Nothing.

'You know where I'd like to stay?' I try a new tack. 'The Madonna Inn!'

'Oh God!' Elise rolls her eyes.

'It's nothing to do with Madonna herself,' I hasten to explain. 'It's actually the surname of the owner – Mr Alex Madonna. He built it himself.'

'I think I remember you mentioning this before.' Elliot furrows his brow. 'Didn't his wife decorate the rooms with all these crazy themes?'

I nod delightedly. 'Cowboys and cupids and cavemen!'

'You've got to be kidding, it sounds so tacky,' Elise sneers.

'I think the word you're searching for is kitsch,' I try a little banter.

'Kitsch, retro, camp – they're all just euphemisms for bad taste. You of all people should know better. I thought you were supposed to have an eye for style.'

Could she sound any more patronizing? As it happens, you can't get too kitsch for my tastes. It's MFI and pastels that push me over the edge. I guess it's in my blood, but my environment really affects me. As do the people in it, I think, eyes narrowing at Elise.

'I think I'll take a few bits to Sasha,' I say, scraping the fruit salad garnish on to a side plate along with a rogue muffin. 'See if she's hungry.'

'See you at high noon,' Elliot says as he waves me off.

Elise doesn't even bother to look up. Urgh – manners!

Walking away from her gives me an instant sense of relief. I find her presence so tainting, especially when the others aren't around to dilute it. But I'm not going to let her spoil this holiday. I take a moment to inhale the fresh sea air and shake her off, then skip down to the beach. It's such a beautiful day, how could anyone be anything other than elated?

Then I spy Sasha draped limply over a bench. The sleeping angel has long gone, leaving a miserable mortal in her place. I suppose it was too much to hope that eight hours' kip could cure her woes. Woes which

I'm starting to take seriously. The self-help books seemed harmless enough and the episode in the Hotel Del loos was entirely understandable, but then last night as I sloughed off my crystallized make-up in the bathroom I caught her glaring at her reflection as if she was in a staring contest with her darkest enemy. Seeing as I'd be clambering up on to the marble sink top to kiss the mirror if I was her, I couldn't understand the dirty look.

I was about to dismiss it as a mis-squirted skin freshener incident when it got more bizarre – she slathered thick cream over her face then dragged her fingertips down, creating streaks of white so that for a strange moment it looked like she was staring out from behind prison bars. I thought about trying to peel off her face and swapping it for mine to see if that would cheer her up, or at least make her appreciate what she'd got, but instead I simply said, 'You all right?'

She took a second to rejoin the world, sluiced her face with icy water, then said: 'The thing we wrote at the beach – the wish?'

'Yes?' I encouraged her, handing her a towel.

'I went back to the looks thing again. You know, people not seeing the real me, just what I look like?'

I nodded as she dabbed her flawless skin dry. Always hard to sympathize when I'm standing beside her in front of a mirror to full compare & contrast effect.

'I don't even know if that's the real issue any more,' she fretted. 'I'm just so afraid that they're right. What if I *am* just a pretty face?'

I'd never seen Sasha look so scared. I set down my toothbrush to give her my full attention.

'I say I want people to get to know the real me, but who is that? I don't know. I don't even know if she's worth getting to know.'

'Oh Sasha, don't be crazy!' I rallied her.

'I know I piss you off, going on about this—'

'No, you don't,' I assured her. 'I just get frustrated that you can't see all your other qualities. All the reasons we love you.'

'I just feel like I don't fit in anywhere,' she quavered.

'You just haven't found your groove, that's all.'

'What if I haven't got one?'

'Everybody's got one. Everybody's got something that they were born to do.'

Not everyone gets to find it of course, but I don't want to labour that point. Instead I said, 'Some people find theirs later in life.'

And straight away I thought: Other people take theirs for granted. Look at me – years of practising my home styling skills in anticipation of transforming the B&B and now the groove I thought I was gradually growing into is gone. Was I wrong? Is there something else for me out there? I was so sure.

'Maybe I should have just stuck with modelling.' Sasha sounded defeated as she pulled on her stripy pyjama bottoms.

'You hated it,' I reminded her.

'I know, but at least I was good at it.'

'If you hated it, it wasn't your groove,' I confirmed.

'It was just a red herring – something you needed to get out of your system.'

Sasha shrugged then suddenly changed the subject. 'Have you seen the shutters above the bath? They open out on to—'

I knew she wasn't really done but I didn't want to push it. It wasn't a conversation that could lead to an easy resolution and at that point I thought a good night's sleep would probably serve her better than a pep talk from me. I guess now it's time for Plan B.

As I get closer to her beachside bench I see a tear trickle from her eye, so I slow down and then casually slide on to the seat beside her and stare deliberately out to sea, trying to give the sun a chance to dry the streak so I don't have to comment on it and thus put her on the spot. But when I finally turn to offer her a slice of breakfast pineapple, her face is flooded.

'Sasha, what is it?' I'm shocked and put my arms around her, ready to catch her if she falls.

'I'm lost, Lara,' she wails. 'I wonder if I should just go home.'

'What?' I gasp. 'We haven't even been here twenty-four hours!'

'I just don't think I can do it.'

'Do what?' What on earth is going on in her head?

'Have fun. Jape around. I mean, where does Zoë get the energy to go to Mexico of an evening?'

'I don't know,' I marvel. I'm still fighting visions of her dancing on a table, a small Mexican man between her teeth.

Sasha sniffs. 'When I was at home thinking about

this trip I imagined myself laughing in the sunshine, but now I'm here I feel just as bad as I did then. Worse even, because I look at you all having fun and I feel such a killjoy and I hate myself for not being able to loosen up and join in.'

I'd hardly say I've been a barrel of laughs since we arrived but it never crossed my mind to turn around and go back home.

'It's early days, Sasha, you said yourself jet lag can be a downer for some people.'

'I know but—'

I'm not done. 'If you went home, how would that make you feel?' I turn her to face me.

Her eyes remain downcast.

'Miserable . . . defeated . . . a failure . . .' She sinks lower. 'But that's OK – you're supposed to be miserable living in London. Everyone is. I can blame the tubes and strikes and the weather, but here – it's blue skies and golden sands and swaying palms and I can't stand it!' Sasha covers her face with her hands. 'I mean, if I can't be happy here there's no hope for me. I might as well—' she halts herself with a choking sob.

I blink, stunned. She's even worse than I thought. As I try and think what to say next, Sasha uncovers her eyes and takes in the look on my face.

'You see? This is exactly why I have to go. I'm just going to ruin it for everyone else.'

'You wouldn't . . . you couldn't . . .' I begin.

'I just . . .' Her eyes flick around searching for the words, something to make sense. Then in a small voice, she says, 'I don't like being me any more. I don't know if I ever did.'

'I'll swap!' I suggest with a faint smile.

'Do you want to feel like this?' Sasha looks me in the eye.

I shake my head. Because I already have. 'Maybe this is the worst bit,' I suggest. 'If you've been really depressed then you're not going to get happy overnight, there'll be some resistance. Your body is probably addicted to all these negative pheromones or whatever they are, and at first it's going to reject any happy beans, but soon you'll be addicted to them instead.' I'm sure there must have been a better way to phrase that.

'But I don't even want to try. How lame is that?'

My heart goes out to her. That's just how I felt when I first heard about the B&B. It scared me too much to care so I opted for apathy. But that only provides a temporary numbing, as I am beginning to find out.

I take Sasha's hand and try and be tactful. 'It's not like we're expecting you to be the life and soul of the party.'

'Why would you? I never have been, have I? What exactly *do* I bring to the party?'

'You bring Sasha!' I cry, exasperated.

Before I can list her lovely calming qualities she says, 'Admit it. It would be easier if I wasn't here.'

'I don't know why you'd say that,' I frown, peeling back the strands of hair that have become stuck to her face with tears. 'You haven't done anything to bring us down. Of course we all want you along.'

'Not like this.'

'Whatever state you come in, we want you here,' I insist. 'If you want to slump in the back of the car while we're driving round, or build sandcastles on the beach and fill the moat with your own tears, that's fine. If you want to go to bed early, or not get up at all, that's fine. If you want to wander off and have some alone time – fine – you don't have to be what you think we want you to be. You don't have to be fake cheerful. You're entitled to your feelings. We'll be more than happy to have a laugh with you when you feel like joining in, and if you don't that's OK too. If this is your hour of need, do you think we're going to turn away?' My eyes well up with emotion. I mustn't cry. If we both lose the plot, who'll save us? I have to be strong.

I take a breath and wait for the tightening in my throat to subside. I watch the furrows in Sasha's brow soften and for a moment she seems to take comfort, but then she slips again.

'But it'll be such a downer for everyone.' I sense she's about to scrunch up.

Oh no you don't! 'It would only be a strain if we spent all our time trying to cheer you up. If you say it's OK that we just let you be, it'll work out fine.' I try and sound matter-of-fact, as if there's simply no way I'm letting her go. I'm holding tight. I can do this.

'Anyway, we don't even know where we're going to be tomorrow, let alone how we're going to feel,' I remind her. 'Aren't you at least curious to find out what Helen has planned?'

'I suppose,' Sasha concedes.

'Oh come on, it must be good or she wouldn't keep us in suspense all this time. She's on to something, you can tell by looking at her. Do you really want to miss out on a chance of experiencing the kind of joy she's brimming with?'

Sasha shakes her head.

'I know I don't!' I answer my own question. 'I want to know her secret.'

I think it's working. Sasha's juddering breaths are beginning to even out.

'Is that papaya?' She eyes the mini fruit platter.

I smile. She's back in the game. 'It's all yours,' I tell her. Then I look at my watch. 'And you've got exactly sixty seconds to eat it.'

'Is she here?' Sasha looks up, mid-mouthful, eyes wide.

My heart pounds as I nod a yes. I reach for her hand – 'Come on, let's go!' – and together we race up to the lobby. Two dented spirits in search of some hope.

7

'Your party awaits you in La Sala . . .' The receptionist seems to know exactly who we are and why we're here. 'Please come through.'

She guides us down a tier of terracotta tiles into a lounge swathed in jewel-bright tapestries seemingly stitched with threads of topaz, sapphire and emerald. A trio of black wrought-iron candelabra bear down on us from above and straight ahead, dominating the room, is a magnificent floor-to-ceiling window. The glimmering sea entirely fills the frame, with just one gangly palm tree in the foreground. It's like desert island wallpaper, but for real.

Elliot is sunk deep into a smooshy leather armchair, deeper still when Elise dumps herself on to his lap. Now from certain angles you can't see him at all. We take the gold brocade sofa, Sasha and I, sitting either side of Zoë, who grips our hands with ever firmer fervour. Meanwhile Helen inhales a nerve-quelling breath and leaves little smudgy fingerprints on the highly polished wood of the piano as she positions herself with her back to the window, eyes trained beyond us on reception.

'That's all of us!' Elliot prompts her.

'We're just waiting for . . .' Her face lights up. 'Here he is!'

We turn back and see a man advancing in a sleek navy suit, sharp white shirt and sky blue silk tie. His thirtysomething face is tanned, his hair stylishly groomed and there's a tiny diamond stud winking from his left earlobe.

Zoë's nails are now so deeply embedded in my palms I think they'll probably stay there even when she finally releases her grip.

As he passes us, he acknowledges our 'Who he?' glances with a courteous nod and takes his position beside Helen, clearly a man on a mission. Assured of our full attention, he breaks into a disarming smile and says, 'Welcome to your first meeting of The California Club!'

There's a buzz of anticipation and a speedy exchange of 'This is it!' looks.

I can't believe we're so out in the open. Surely we should have travelled blindfold in the boot of a car to some mystery location? At the very least I would have expected an underground bunker and the speaker to be lit by a flickering match. Instead he's flooded with sunlight and standing before a panoramic backdrop in a 'All of this could be yours' kinda way. Maybe that's the intention. Or maybe only official members get to go to CC HQ.

'I've got tingles!' Zoë squeaks with excitement. She's scooted so far forward with eagerness that her bottom is only making the most token contact with the sofa seat. Any second now I expect her to drop to the floor adopting the 'on your marks' position, cocking her ear for the starter pistol. She's so ready for this.

'My name is Alex Daniels and I'm the Club President. Helen has asked me here today as she would very much like you to share in the rewards she has experienced as a direct result from joining our cult, er—'

'What?' There's a gasp of horror from his audience. Even Zoë flinches.

He looks stricken at his mistake. 'Er, club!' he corrects himself then grins broadly. 'Just fooling!'

There's a wobbly sense of relief in the room.

'I realize some of you may have reservations about our organization but The California Club has no intention of turning you into identikit zombies. Quite the opposite. Our aim is to wake you up to the thrill and fulfilment of being the best possible you.' He takes a breath. 'So my first question is this: Are you ready to change your lives?'

'Yes!' hoots a lone voice.

He steps towards it. 'I'm guessing you're Zoë?'

She nods wide-eyed, as if he just told her she was the Chosen One.

He extends his hand. 'Good to meet you.'

She shakes it with ligament-dislocating vigour.

He laughs, 'I can see we're going to have some fun channelling that energy of yours!'

She has no idea what he means but looks enthralled.

'You must be Sasha.' He moves on.

She nods shyly, staring at his Italian leather shoes. He continues to hold her hand until she looks up into his dark blue eyes.

'You're going to be fine,' he assures her. 'More than fine.'

Sasha looks doubtful.

'Try to believe me. If you go with this you could be the biggest surprise of the group.'

Sasha looks ruffled and turns away, eyes glossing with tears as she attempts to control the sea-swell of emotions within.

I'm next. Surreptitiously I wipe my clammy palm in anticipation of the handshake but he switches direction and moves towards Elise. Oh no! I've been deliberately overlooked. Why?

'Elise?' He stands before her.

'However did you guess?' she sneers, giving him a challenging look.

'Why, Helen told me, of course. This isn't Amateur Psychic Hour.'

Hah! She chews her lip like a petulant teenager.

'Anyway,' he continues. 'It's always nice to have a cynic to convert, so welcome.'

Before Elise can froth a reply he addresses a denim knee, 'Is that Elliot under there?'

Elliot struggles to free his arm, quickly shaking off the pins and needles before his hand meets Alex's.

'Hi!'

'I guess you're wondering what you've got yourself into?' Alex raises a knowing eyebrow.

Presumably he's referring to The California Club

109

but I allow myself to think he's picking up on some kind of reservation Elliot may have about Elise.

'I can handle it!' Elliot struts his macho stuff.

Alex smiles and says, 'It's you who's into roller-coaster rides, right?'

'Yeah,' Elliot grins.

'Well, you're going to get one!'

'Sounds good to me!'

I wouldn't be so thrilled if Alex said that to me, it sounds vaguely threatening. But why would The California Club want to rattle our cages? We've come here for pleasure, we made that quite clear at Passport Control.

'Lara!' he turns suddenly to face me.

Oh thank God!

He leans close.

'What's it going to be with you?' He studies me, boring into my soul.

I try to project flair, confidence and success but suspect he can see through to my confusion, fears and lonely wee heart.

'I guess we'll have to wait and see.'

Oh no! I'm an unknown quantity. I want to be fine, more than fine! Not wait and see! I demand a recount! You've got to give me more than that!

Seemingly sensing my needs he adds, 'But I suspect it may be your turn.'

My turn for what? Am I supposed to know what he means? My turn to be with Elliot? My turn for love? My turn to put the rubbish out? What?!

Alex strolls back over to the window and takes a

more casual position to address us now, resting on the arm of a busily patterned chair. 'My second question is: Are you really ready to get what you really want?'

Zoë jolts a 'Yes!' out of me. The best he can hope for from Sasha and Elliot is a tentative nod. As for Elise, he doesn't know how lucky he is that she's making no response at all.

'OK. Last night each of you wrote a wish on a piece of paper. Today we're going to take the first step to making those wishes come true.'

'Oh great!' Elise rolls her eyes.

'On behalf of The California Club I'm going to make you an offer. It's entirely up to you as a group whether or not you take it—'

'We'll take it!' blurts Zoë.

Elliot urges Zoë to cool her jets until we've heard the whole proposition.

'Now this isn't a one-tap-of-the-wand thing. Ninety per cent of the work will come from you,' Alex informs us.

My heart sinks. There's always a catch, isn't there? Always the word 'work' running alongside any chance of dreams being fulfilled. I'm off the idea already. Let's just have a holiday and have done with it.

'So my third question is this: Would you be prepared to give up one week of your stay in California to make your wish come true?'

Wary silence. Even Zoë is mute, not wanting to be selfish and put her desires ahead of the group.

'What exactly do you mean by that?' I query.

111

'The California Club has arranged for each of you to spend seven days in pursuit of your wish.'

Again Zoë flutters with excitement. But she's the only one.

'Because of the variety and nature of your wishes, each of you will be sent to a separate location.'

There's a muttering of solidarity: no way – we're sticking together.

'You'd send us all to different places?' Zoë hopes she's misheard.

'Yes,' Alex confirms. 'Well, all, that is, except for Lara, but I'll come to why later.'

What? Me? What have I done now? Why do I feel like the outsider again?

'Why can't we stay together?' Zoë pouts.

'Because you all want different things.'

'Can I change my wish?' Elise asks.

Alex shakes his head. 'We go with what you wrote last night.'

'Then forget it!' she huffs.

Zoë looks pleadingly at her.

'I'm sorry but my wish is crap.'

'And yet it was your choice. Your wish.' Alex reminds her.

'Yeah but I didn't know it was going to lead to this.'

'None of us know where things will lead in life but it's an important lesson – your thoughts and words are powerful. Choose them wisely.'

Elise wrestles herself free from the chair and turns on the group. 'Are you just going to sit around and listen to this crap?'

'Let's at least hear the thing out – we're not committing to anything,' Elliot reasons.

Oooh goody – does that include each other?

Elise groans and goes to stomp off but Elliot tugs her back on to his lap, winding himself in the process.

'Why does it have to be for a whole week?' Elliot asks, trying to position Elise so she's not compressing any vital organs. 'Couldn't we just do it for one or two days? I don't know about the rest of the wishes but mine could easily come true in an afternoon.'

There's a murmur of assent.

I could certainly have quality time with every one of my friends in a day – breakfast with Sasha, lunch with Zoë, tea with Helen and dinner with Elliot. And maybe a bit of the night-time for good measure. Just through to sunrise or something. Elise is no friend of mine so she doesn't count. Sorted!

Alex shakes his head. 'Unfortunately there is a process in making these wishes come true. If you do not experience the process, the wish itself will be invalid.'

'What are you proposing?' I dare to ask.

'Yeah?' the others chorus.

'I'm afraid I am not able to disclose the details until you have committed to the seven days.'

'You want us to say yes to giving up a week of our holiday without knowing where we're going or what we're doing?' Elliot talks it back to him in his most unconvinced tone.

'There is a very special incentive at the end of all

113

this,' Helen prompts Alex, sensing we need a carrot –
and fast!

'Yesterday you all visited the Hotel Del Coronado,
yes?'

'Yes.'

'And you liked it?'

'Gorgeous/beautiful/magical!' Our adjectives over-
lap.

'Well,' he smiles, confidently. 'If you all complete
your week, you will earn yourselves five nights' complimentary stay.'

Now that's tempting.

'Helen's teas!' Sasha's eyes light up.

'I could sip mandarin martinis and watch the Navy
SEALS training,' Zoë gurgles.

'Could we hire a jet ski?' I ask.

'All those books . . .' Elliot gets misty.

'All for free?' Elise speaks.

A-ha. Alex has just discovered the way to her heart.

'That place is what, $200 a night?' she asks.

I remember the tariff in my bag and pull it out:
'$230 for a regular room. $650 for a junior suite.'

'We're going one better than that . . .' Helen can't
keep it in any longer: 'We're offering you the Marilyn
Monroe Beach House.'

Oh my God! I gasp. That's some carrot!

Meanwhile Zoë has become a human firework of
excitement and instantly starts campaigning: 'So, in a
way, we'd be earning –' she leans over my shoulder,
keen to play to Elise's weakness – 'nearly $12,000-
worth of prize for seven days work!'

'Still. Seven days,' Elliot's not convinced.

Helen steps in. 'I realize you guys are just out here for two weeks and to spend half of it on some crazy scheme seems a bit excessive but trust me, it'll be one of the best things to ever happen to you.'

We all stop flapping to listen to Helen.

'California will always be here – the beaches, the palm trees, the convertibles, the babes – but you might never get this chance again. I'm not going to force you, but I will get down on my knees and beg you to do this because I know how happy it can make each and every one of you.' Her voice quavers with genuine emotion.

We take a moment to mull over her words. Her insistence seems to be born out of real concern for our lives. Maybe we're in a bigger mess than we thought. I look at Sasha. She's definitely on the brink. If not this, what? What will save her? Zoë's so wound up, she's likely to explode any minute. Maybe this could switch her to implode, which would be considerably less messy. Elise. Well, that girl has issues. Elliot. He does look tired. A bit pallid. Maybe he needs a dose of greenery. And what about me? I came here to escape the biggest upheaval in my life, hoping to regain some feelings of security, and yet here I am being presented with more uncertainty. Maybe that's the point. Maybe I'm supposed to have a practice run here so when I get back, things won't seem so daunting. All the same . . .

'Why don't you take a moment to decide?' Alex says, as he escorts Helen through to the lobby, leaving us to debate.

*

'Come on you guys, it's the chance of a lifetime.' Zoë remains the constant positive.

'For you, maybe,' Elise spits.

'Zoë, perhaps you'd like to get us some drinks?' I suggest. Her peppiness is only making Elise more cantankerous.

Zoë obliges but Elise strops off regardless. Elliot follows, leaving Sasha and me alone.

She turns to me. 'So, what do you think?'

There's a glimmer of hope in her eyes. I can't risk extinguishing that.

'Maybe it's the chance we've been waiting for?' Do I sound convincing enough?

Sasha holds her hands up to her face, making a little teepee over her nose, then takes a breath. 'We've got to do this, haven't we?'

'What have we got to lose?' I'm still not sure.

'I think we need to want this.' Sasha gives me a serious look.

I look back at her. She's right. If we're going to go for it, we have to be wholehearted.

'Of course, if Elise doesn't agree in the first place, none of us get to try,' Sasha notes.

Suddenly I want this more than anything. If she's got the power to take it away from me, I want it all the more.

'I'm in,' I tell her.

Sasha inhales, looking both terrified and excited, a new determination forming in her eyes. 'Me too!'

I grin and hug her, closing my eyes as I press my

cheek to her bony shoulder and whisper, 'I'm so proud of you!'

'Don't – I'll cry!' Sasha laughs.

'God – imagine staying at Marilyn's Beach House!' My mind leaps ahead.

'Everyone!' The others have returned and Helen reconvenes the meeting before I can get too carried away. 'Do you have a verdict?'

All eyes are on Elise. She knows she holds the casting vote and she's milking it for all it's worth.

'Well?'

I cross my fingers, Sasha gnaws a nail, Zoë scrunches her eyes closed. Nothing. Elliot nudges Elise into making a response. She makes a big show of crumpling her brow like she's in pain then concedes, '*All right* . . .' with a look of supreme martyrdom.

We all charge across the room and pile on top of her in a noisy, boisterous hug. Not a scene I visualized happening in this lifetime.

'That's wonderful,' Alex claps his hands together. 'I just have to go back to HQ and confirm the arrangements and then we can meet again at about 4 p.m.'

'Is that when you'll tell us where we're going?' Zoë asks.

'That's right,' Alex confirms.

'Oh my God!' Zoë bounces with glee.

'Well, enjoy your afternoon. I know Helen has got something special planned.'

'Thank you so much.' Zoë gives Alex's hand another digit-mangling squeeze as he leaves.

*

'Am I OK in this?' I nudge Helen and tug at yesterday's travelling outfit. 'Only my suitcase hasn't arrived yet.'

She gives me a sympathetic smile. 'Don't worry, where we're going you won't need clothes.'

As she marches ahead towards the door, the rest of us exchange worried looks. No clothes?!! Oh God! Not only is Helen part of a cult – turns out it's a nudist cult!

Elliot leans close and whispers: 'Gives a whole new meaning to the term "Moonies", doesn't it?'

8

'You *can* go naked if you prefer,' Helen chuckles when Elliot tells her what we were expecting. 'I just meant you didn't need any of *your* clothes: we supply everything here.'

We're at La Jolla beach. About to brave the waves. In wetsuits. I feel somewhat daunted.

'Helen, are you sure about this?' I ask, handling the dense black foam.

'Yes, yes – put it on. I've worked out the sizes, they should be a good fit.'

Zoë's already in hers, zipper straining over her cleavage like she's doing a rubber fetish shoot for *Playboy*, Sasha is sleek Catwoman, Elise is refusing to join in and Elliot is pissing himself laughing – 'I look like the stick of liquorice in a Sherbet Dib-dab!'

In actual fact he looks divine. His tousled hair and lean physique suits the surfer look. He's even got the right stance. I remember him saying he used to go to Newquay as a kid, before he got pale and into computers.

Helen gives me a final hoik and I've squirmed into

mine. It feels tight and restrictive yet bendy and pliant. Strange. Part of me wants to claw it off, but as I begin to calm down from the effort of getting it on, I adjust to the sensation of having a second coarser skin and reach out to shake Elliot's hand, 'Hi, Liquorice Man? I'm Lara – the human tyre!' Elise is not amused. 'I don't know why we couldn't just stay by the hotel pool.'

'There's no better cure for jet lag than surfing,' Helen insists. 'You'll feel totally revitalized after, I promise.'

'She's right,' Elliot agrees. 'In fact I think I'm going to brave it in my shorts – I want to feel the water on my skin . . .'

'You'll freeze!' Elise warns him.

'I'll be fine,' Elliot contends. 'Bracing is good!'

I experience a flutter of lust as I watch him peel himself free of the wetsuit – it's all a bit slo-mo after-shave ad for my delicate sensibilities.

'What colour rashguard do you want?' Helen nudges me, emptying a bag of stretchy surf T-shirts on the sand. 'You're supposed to wear them under your wetsuit but if you put them on top I'll be able to keep track of you.'

Zoë nabs the pink, Sasha green, Elliot blue, Helen opts for yellow and hands me the red. Red for emergency. Red for STOP!

'Helen, I don't know if I can,' I bleat, noticing a surfer lose his footing and get whisked into a foamy froth out at sea. It's all too easy for me to imagine the pounding-drumming-glugging pressure as he claws his way up to the surface, gasping for air.

'You can stay with me,' Elise offers. 'I'm not going in.'

Suddenly I'm Yasmin Bleeth, hurdling the waves. What's a little light drowning compared to death by Elise?

'OK,' Helen commands our attention. 'Before we get in the water there's some basic stuff you should know. I could tell you myself but instead I want you to meet the woman who taught me and totally upgraded my life – Isabelle Tihanyi, she's co owner of—'

'The California Club?' Zoë jumps in.

'Actually no, she's the woman who started Surf Divas – the world's first surf school for women.'

'Um, Helen.' Elliot tugs at her elbow, laughing. 'There's something I've been meaning to tell you all these years . . .'

'That's fine,' Helen assures him. 'They make allowances – Guys on the Side, they call it. Besides, you're so pretty all we need is pop a couple of clams in your suit,' she teases, grabbing his pecs.

'Get off!' he laughs, batting her away.

'She's over in the carpark so I'm just going to help her with her gear, back in a mo.'

'Helen!' I call after her.

'What?' She turns back.

'Are we allowed to tell each other our wishes yet?'

Helen grins broadly. 'I was wondering when you'd get to that. Go ahead – you've made your commitment. *Spill!*'

*

We huddle up.

Zoë jumps straight in with her wish: '*I want to swap lives with a Hollywood actress!*'

No surprises there. Not sure how. The California Club can pull that one off without kidnapping someone, but it's a good wish with high glamour potential. Jammy cow.

Zoë tags Sasha.

'*I want to find the one place in California where looks don't count!* Oh, it makes me sound so vain!' Sasha cringes.

'No, it doesn't,' we assure her, not envying her her wish. She could easily end up in Death Valley with a load of parched skulls, or maybe trampling grapes in the Napa Valley. Hmmm, all that aromatic wine, maybe not such a bad option.

'Elliot?' I prompt.

'*Get me to a theme park!*'

Reassuringly predictable.

'I don't really know how they're going to string that out into a week-long activity,' he frowns. 'I'll just end up with massive osteopath bills and probably get done for stalking Minnie Mouse.'

I never thought I'd be so happy to hear Minnie's name used in its proper context.

'Were those your exact words?' Elise checks the small print.

'More or less. I did say something about it being the biggest theme park, because I had Disneyland in mind, but really I'd be just as happy with Magic Mountain or Universal Studios.'

'What was your wish?' Zoë asks Elise.

'I don't want to talk about it.'

'Don't be silly, you can tell us.'

'Look it's bad enough I have to do it without dwelling on it ahead of time.'

Sounds intriguing. And unpleasant. Which is good. 'Lara?'

'I can't remember my exact wording,' I lie. 'I just said I wanted to hang out with you guys.'

'Awww, you old softie!' Zoë pulls me into a hug. 'What a waste of a wish!'

'So basically, there's no mystery with what Zoë and I are going to get – she's doing the movie star bit, I'm doing rollercoasters,' Elliot summarizes. 'Sasha – who knows? But it won't be LA, that's for sure.' He turns to me. 'Lara, I don't really see how your togetherness thing is going to work if we're all whizzing in different directions.'

'That's true,' Sasha looks concerned.

'And Elise—'

'Don't!' she warns.

'You may as well—'

'Aloha!' We turn to find ourselves greeted by Helen's mentor – a voluptuous nutbrown surfer woman wearing a red sarong and straw cowboy hat that creates a lattice effect of light and shade on her smiling face. 'I'm stoked to meet you all!'

She digs her surfboard in the sand and shakes our hands.

'You ready to rip up those waves?'

'We'll give it a go,' I offer, meekly.

'We're not expecting you to become Kate Skerrit in

123

a couple of hours, we just want you to enjoy yourselves,' she encourages. 'Our motto at Surf Divas is: "The best surfer in the water is the person having the most fun!"'

'Isn't that great?' Helen twinkles, clearly dying for us to get a taste of what has become her ultimate pleasure.

I want to give it a go for her sake but at the same time I suspect that one woman's euphoria is another woman's snot-streaming nose and salt-stinging eyes.

As Isabelle takes us through the basics, I wonder if this is a deliberate ploy to distract us from dwelling on what we've just agreed to do with The California Club – there's so much more to take in than I anticipated: when entering and exiting the water do the jellyfish shuffle (shuffle the sand between your feet so you don't splodge down on one of the slippery suckers and get stung); don't pull the board by the leash; if you lose it shout, 'Loose board!' to warn other surfers but don't feel obliged to be a board caddy if you see someone separate from theirs; no tailgating; no tea parties (sitting round chatting in groups); always keep your eye on the horizon so you know what waves are coming your way . . . I even learn that waves come from storms far out at sea and that Americans pronounce Buoy 'boo-ee' rather than boy.

But it's still not time to get in the water. We have to master the vital art of 'popping up' – going from lying stomach flat on the board to jumping into your classic crook-kneed surfer pose. Not nearly as easy as it looks.

I've got the board anatomy down pat – the 'deck' is the part you stand on, the 'rails' are the sides, the 'nose' and 'tail' are self-explanatory – but I can't pop-up for the life of me. Isabelle tries telling me that as a girl I should understand that getting ready to go out is half the fun but my legs are beginning to wibble.

Despite this bit being on dry land, Elise still won't join in, preferring to tell us what we're doing wrong: 'Lara, you're too far forward/Lara, you've got something on your thigh – oh it's cellulite!' That kind of thing.

Isabelle discovers my problem is that I'm 'goofy', which isn't slanderous, merely the name for people who should have their left foot forward, as opposed to their right.

And then finally it's time to get wet.

'We want you to stay good-looking when you're fifty so lather on the sunscreen,' Isabelle says. She hands us an industrial-sized pump. 'Don't forget your hands and the tops of your feet,' she adds, slicking such a thick layer on her face she could do a passable impression of Casper the Ghost.

'Let's go!'

'What am I supposed to do?' Elise whines.

'You can set up camp and guard our clothes.' Helen refuses to pander to her sulk. Instead she dives straight in and powers out to sea, turning the board over and ducking under the waves she can't glide over.

I still can't quite get my head around her being so skilled at something I've never even see her try before. It makes me wonder what hidden talents we all might have if we were just given the chance to try something new every week.

Us girls are barely waist deep in white wash when Sasha gets hit on by her first surfer dude. We make out the words 'narly' and 'hot' but advise him to take his sharking elsewhere because we don't *speaka da lingo*. Poor Sasha – she's not even safe from suitors out at sea. As we get into deeper waters I half expect Neptune himself to rise up and ask her for a date.

For at least an hour we mess around paddling like fury, only to tumble before we've even got semi-upright. Isabelle and Helen make great cheerleaders, encouraging us to get back out there but only Elliot has any real success. I watch him catch a wave and then fall back and break its glassy arch. Seconds later he surfaces, a little disorientated, shakes his head to right his internal compass, and clambers back on his board. This time he pulls it off and looks absolutely triumphant. It's the most active I've seen him in years and it's undeniably sexy.

'He's doing a great job, isn't he?' Helen paddles over to me.

'Amazing,' I beam, unable to take my eyes off him.

'Still?' Helen says simply.

I look at Helen. 'Always.'

She takes a deep breath and flips on to her back so she's using her board as a lilo. 'I don't know why he can't see it's you.'

'Me?'

126

'You,' Helen repeats. 'I thought he was nearly there and then Elise comes along.'

'Nearly there? What do you mean?' I swish closer.

'It was just a feeling I had. Before I left, you two seemed to be closer than ever.'

'We were.' I feel a twinge of sadness. 'Then she . . .' I tail off. 'So, you were the first to know about the engagement!' I have to bring this up.

'Don't read too much into that, they had a reason for telling me, I just can't say what.'

Once again I feel frustratingly in the dark. Does everyone know something I don't?

'It feels weird, him having secrets from me,' I confess.

'Well, hopefully you'll get a chance to talk on this trip. Get back to how you were.'

'Do you think that's even possible now?'

'Anything's possible,' Helen insists.

I sit quietly for a moment.

'What do you think of her?' I venture, trying to sound casual though Helen has always been able to see straight through me.

Helen twists on to her side. 'You want me to say something bad, don't you?'

'If you could!' I joke.

'I'm not going to,' Helen sets me straight. 'I made a No Negativity pledge to The California Club.'

'Oh. OK.' I look down at my board, feeling a little bit told off.

'But if I did have to . . .'

'Yes?'

'I'd find it *really* easy!' she teases.

I grin back at her. That's all I need to know. I gingerly match Helen's belly-up position, feeling a bit like I'm lying on an extra firm water bed. Every time a wave sloshes me, I spasm like I'm about to tip up but Helen just rolls with it.

'You look so comfortable out here,' I note, shaking off the latest dousing.

'It took me a while, Reuben has been amazing. He used to be a lifeguard so I felt in safe hands.'

'A lifeguard, really? Did he teach you any tricks?'

Helen thinks for a moment. 'Well, if you do try and rescue someone you first have to acknowledge that you are seriously putting your own life at risk – most times they'll grab on to you in the panic, pushing you under so you have to pretty firm with them and get them to follow your instructions or they'll drown you both.'

'How firm?'

'Splashing water in their face or bending their thumbs back to breaking point if they continue to grab at you—'

'Oh God!' I gasp.

'It's a life and death situation,' Helen asserts. 'I think the best trick if someone has locked their arms around you is to push them upwards by the elbows and you go down deeper into the water – they're not going to follow you there, they want to get up!'

'All this just to get them to behave – then you have to rescue them too!' I shake my head.

As Helen explains the various procedures, I watch

128

the sun sneak behind the one cloud in the sky. My skin feels taut and tingly like I've braved the elements and my muscles ache from exertion. It's chilly without the direct rays but I'm reluctant to go in, wanting to prolong the anticipation of wrapping a warm towel around me as long as I can.

'Do you ever pinch yourself – you know, that this is your life now?' I ask.

'Every day,' Helen affirms.

'Really?'

'Sometimes twice a day.'

'And it's all because of The California Club?'

'Well, a lot of this was here already . . .' Helen flicks me with seawater to make her point.

'I know that!' I swipe her back. 'But it really works, this programme or whatever it is?'

'It does if you believe in it.'

I think for a moment. 'Do you think I could have chosen a better wish?'

No reply.

'Helen?' I look over and find her sights eagerly trained on a guy in khaki shorts loitering on the edge of the carpark. There's something weird stuck to his leg . . . I try to focus – oh, it's a tattoo – one of those jagged Maori tribal prints running the length of his right calf. I'm about to comment on how that design has been done to death when I notice the delight in her eyes.

'Is that Reuben?' I ask.

'I'll be back in ten!' is her reply as she slides on to her stomach and swooshes back to the shore.

'As in Hang Ten?' I call after her, feeling strangely giddy.

My wish may be a bit wishy-washy but Helen doesn't like Elise. All is well with the world.

I continue to bob on my board as a daddy surfer skims past with his three-year-old son *on his shoulders* then return my gaze to Helen and the tattoo guy – they seem deeply engrossed. He's wearing sunglasses and the hood of his sweatshirt is up so I can't get a good look at his face but he definitely looks cool. I wonder if it is her boyfriend. Let's see if they kiss.

'*Yikes!*' There's a thud-jolt as Zoë's board collides with mine.

'I think my hair is dreading,' she frets, with good cause. 'Me and Sasha are going in. You coming?'

'Where's Elliot?' I twist around, scanning the swell.

'Way over there.' Zoë points to where the current has lured him south. 'Maybe you should go and round him up?'

'OK,' I smile, enticed by a vision of the two of us floating into the sunset together. What a life we'd have: taming seahorses, diving for sunken treasure, playing Frisbee with the starfish.

I glance back at Elise, still hunched grumpily on the shore even though Helen is now by her side, her khaki-shorted friend nowhere in view. Can't have been her boyfriend then or she would have introduced him.

Flipping on to my stomach, I start propelling myself through the water towards Elliot. I'm just thinking how chilled he looks sitting there – staring out to where the dark green waters meet the streaky orange sky – when his spine straightens and he looks strangely alert. Uh-oh – I fear the mother of all tidal waves looming on the horizon but no, it remains sloppy-choppy as far as the eye can see. All the same, I get a nervous chill. I don't like coming this far out to sea.

I throw another glance back at the shore. From my long-distance squint it looks like the girls are tucking into some goodies. I want to get back to safety and snacks but the pull to be with Elliot is stronger. I'm nearly with him now, just twenty or so metres to go.

Head down I paddle on until, amid the sloshing water and my grunting efforts, I realize I can hear my name, 'Lara! Lara! LARA!' getting louder and more frantic. I scramble into a sitting position. Where's Elliot gone? His board is dragging sideways but I can't see him. My heart batters at my ribcage. All of a sudden I spot his contorted face straining out of the water, 'Get help!' he yells. His panicked eyes meet mine and then he disappears under the slapping waves, forced down by a heavy hand.

Where he sinks, an old man rises up, wild with fear. Limbs thrash and flail. For a moment I think Elliot is being attacked but as their positions reverse, I realize he is trying to save some old geezer and the old geezer is trying to use him as a float, just as Helen predicted. Helen! I swivel around and call and wave frantically towards the shore but the wind just blows my cries back into my face. Even if they did hear me, they're too far away to act fast enough. One more look at Elliot and I've plunged into the water, tears mingling with the salt. Got to get to him and do the elbow push-up shove and then break the old guy's thumbs! Is that right? Oh God! What if I cack-handedly elbow someone in the throat or concuss them with the surfboard I'm dragging behind me?

For the first time in my life I ask myself, 'What would Pamela Anderson do?' Not having a body double to hand, I enter the fray grabbing for something – anything – to pull up to the surface. What the hell is that? I gasp for air. Eurgh – old man's bottom! I splutter as I come face to face with Elliot.

'Quick, pass your board over!' he gasps.

I yank it to me by the ankle strap.

'Grab on to that!' he urges the old man, wriggling free of his desperate grasp.

The old man grips the board as if he's hanging from a window ledge, not entirely convinced he's alive.

'Reach across,' I guide him, using all my strength to push his saggy-skinned legs up to the surface so he can lie out flat.

Now I'm panting. Through stinging eyes I look for Elliot. He's nowhere to be seen. Milliseconds before cold dread sets in he appears on the other side of the board.

'Are you OK?' I gasp.

'Yeah, you?' he chirrups, jaggling his ears with a level of blasé-dom reserved for the seriously in-denial.

I decide to play along with him and shrug, 'Never better!'

'Great! Hop on!' Elliot motions for me to slide on to the back of the board.

As he holds the front steady, I take my position. 'If only we had something to paddle with, it'd be like *Hawaii Five-O*!' I declare.

'Meets *One Foot in the Grave*,' Elliot mutters before politely enquiring, 'Are you all right, sir?'

Three successive blinks apparently means the old man is fine.

'OK, your turn,' I tell Elliot, patting the board.

'I can't.'

'It's OK, I'm sure it'll take all three of us.'

'No really, I can't.'

I frown confusion.

'He pulled my trunks off in the struggle,' Elliot whispers.

As my eyebrows raise, my eyes drift downwards.

'Don't look!' he exclaims, frantically swirling up the water around his groin.

'I'm not looking!' I lie.

I can't believe I've just had a near-death experience and now I've got a silly smile on my face.

9

'Don't be surprised if there's a news report tomorrow saying half your ocean is missing.' Elliot collapses on the sand back at base, still spitting seawater.

'If the news says anything it'll be "*Jet-lagged hero saves saggy-bottomed old man*,"' cheers Helen.

'Followed by "*Raven-haired beauty saves jet-lagged hero*."' Elliot winks at me.

'Wash your mouth out with this.' Elise thrusts her lukewarm bottle of Evian at Elliot.

I smile. I know it's the compliment not the salt she wants him to swill away.

'I've got something better than that.' Helen rummages in her rucksack, producing a bottle of José Cuervo tequila, a stretchy-string bag of limes and a penknife. 'Thought we'd have a few shots to revive us.'

'Cool!' Zoë enthuses.

'Did you bring any salt?' Elise reaches over to nose in Helen's rucksack but Helen is too quick for her: 'Just lick your skin!' she grins, whipping her bag out of reach. 'Suck, swig and bite the lime – *Yeah!*' she husks, passing the bottle to Elise.

134

'But my skin's not salty, I haven't been in the water,' Elise complains.

'I know!' Zoë whoops. 'Let's do it so we lick each other!'

A collective 'Ewwww!' greets her suggestion.

'I think it works better when there's more than one guy present,' Helen notes.

'I don't mind,' jokes Elliot.

Elise finds this hysterical. In a parallel universe.

'Well, just for one round, then,' concedes Helen. 'We'll spin the bottle to see who licks who.'

'And where!' Zoë whispers under her breath.

Half an hour later I've tasted Sasha's collarbone, Helen's bellybutton and the inside of Zoë's left knee, twice. Though I'm horribly dismayed I didn't get to lick any part of Elliot, I am at least grateful that my tongue is the type that can become a spear-like point at the tip – when it came to licking Elise's toe I was keen to make only a pinhead point of contact. And even that *Urgggh!* I shudder at the memory.

'Oh buggering bollocks!'

I look up to find Zoë wrenching angrily at her hair.

'What's the problem?' I ask.

'I can't get the comb through it – it's gone all matted and weird. Feel that!' She extends a tendril to me.

'Zoë, that's a piece of seaweed,' I sigh, yanking it free.

'Oh.'

I smack her hands away and use the stretchy lime

bag as a band to tie her hair up on her head where she can't mess with it any more.

'Thanks,' she smiles, seemingly satisfied with the bunched wheatsheaf look.

A comfortable lull settles. I wonder if now might be the moment to tell everyone about the B&B? I'd rather not make the announcement in front of Elise but if we're going our separate ways tomorrow I can't really put it off much longer.

'Um,' I shuffle up on to my haunches. 'I've got something to tell you all . . .' I begin.

Helen's mobile rings.

'Hold on!' she halts me.

Saved by a *Surfin' USA* jingle.

She 'mmmm-hmmm's into the phone and then flips it closed.

'He's back,' she announces

My big news is forgotten in the dash back to the hotel. I'm secretly relieved – I'm not sure I'm ready for the outcry. I've got to look confident and assured when I tell them – they have to believe that I think it's for the best. Whether it's true or not.

Alex is already in position in La Sala when we bundle in and take our seats.

'Who shall we start with?' He shuffles through our paper wishes.

'Elise!' we chorus, curiosity getting the better of us.

'Ah yes,' he says. *'I want to gate-crash a self-help group and tell them to get a life!'*

We all burst out laughing. All except Elise. That'll teach her to be so judgmental!

'Don't tell me you're going to have me walk on to the set of *Oprah* and tell her to get a life!' she scowls.

'Actually that show is taped in Chicago but even if it was here on the West Coast we wouldn't make you do that. You'd get lynched.'

'Beaten to death by two hundred empowered housewives,' grumbles Elise. 'What a way to go.'

'We think you could benefit from getting a little inside knowledge of the self-improvement groups you are so scathing about. You might be dismissing something that could really help you.'

'I don't want to be helped!' she protests. 'I'm fine as I am. I certainly don't need to get all pally with my inner child or have my guardian angel over for tea!' Elise strops off towards the door then skulks behind a pillar, not quite bold enough to exit altogether.

Meanwhile Alex turns his attention to Zoë. *'I want to swap lives with a Hollywood actress.'*

'Are you going to send me to LA?' Zoë leaps to her feet. 'Oh please! Oh please!'

'Yes we are. You'll be right in the heart of Hollywood and we're going to make it as real an experience as possible.'

Sounds a bit cryptic.

'Do I get a choice of stylist, cos I really like Phillip Bloch—'

'You'll get a detailed brief on arrival,' Alex shushes her and turns to Sasha. 'For you, we've found the perfect place where looks don't count – the Tiger

137

Tiger animal preserve. It's where all the retired movie cats go. Believe me, they don't care whether you're Pretty Woman or the Elephant Man, so long as you treat them right and feed them on time.'

Sasha looks mortified. She never was the world's greatest animal lover. Surely Helen could have advised The California Club against such a mismatch?

'Will she have to muck out the cages?' asks Elise, from behind the pillar, obviously trying to find suffering in other people's choices to console her.

'She'll have the full animal care experience,' is all Alex is prepared to say.

I catch Sasha looking at her nails, presumably deciding that if they're going to get wrecked she may as well start chewing them now.

Me, I'd love that – getting up close to those majestic creatures. I guess that just gives me something else to be envious of Sasha for.

'Elliot!' Alex continues. '*Just get me to California's biggest theme park.*'

'Bring it on!' Elliot cheers.

'Did you know that the biggest park in the state is actually Yosemite National Park?'

Elliot pulls a face. 'I didn't realize there were rides at Yosemite, I thought it was all . . .' he spits the final word: '*nature.*'

'It is.'

'So what's the "theme", then?'

Alex shrugs. 'Trees, I guess.'

'Bit tenuous, isn't it?'

'Maybe it would do you some good,' Helen

ventures. 'All that time you spend in front of computers.'

'So this isn't really about making my wish come true, it's about me doing what you think will do me good?' Elliot challenges Helen, with a fond smile.

'You might like it,' Zoë chips in. 'Great outdoors, camping, bears.'

'Do you want to swap with me?'

'No.' Zoë shrinks back, getting protective of her assigned glitz.

'What about Lara?' Sasha asks on my behalf.

Alex takes my scrumpled sheet and reads: *I wish I could have some special one-to-one time with each of my friends, enough to create a memory that would last a lifetime.*

'Agghhh – it sounds so corny,' I wail. 'It's just I haven't seen much of you all lately.' I apologize for being schmaltzy.

'Not very comfortable with baring your heart, are you?' Alex notes. 'No wonder you couldn't write down what you really want.'

I blanch. How does he know what I really want? My eyes dart around the group to check they don't know what he's getting at. Elliot looks oblivious. My eyes flick to Helen. Of course – she must have told him.

'So what's she going to do?' Zoë wants to know.

'Well, Lara will be dividing her time between you all. In the seven-day period she will visit each of you at your locations, keeping you company and getting the quality time she craves.'

I wish he'd stop embarrassing me like this.

'She'll also act as the central contact point. She

wants to be more involved in your lives and she's going to be. Any messages or information you need or want to get to each other will go through Lara.'

'Are you saying I won't be able to talk to Elliot for a week?' Elise stomps back out from the shadows.

Alex nods, 'That's right.'

I swear I see a flicker of relief on Elliot's face. Peace. Seven squwawk-free days. I'm happy for him. And then I realize I'll be getting it all. The only person she can complain to.

Elise recognizes the look of dismay on my face and tries to recruit me. 'Lara, you don't want to be shunted from pillar to post, do you?'

Before I can answer she continues, 'You've never driven in America and you'll be all alone in the car. For hours. I mean, it's what – six hours from LA to Yosemite?'

How does she know that off the cuff? There's something shifty about the time Elise spent out here. She hasn't regaled us with any stories and it's not like her to pass up a chance to gloat. I have to find out more.

'Actually she'd be flying that leg of the trip,' Alex counters, 'but yes there will be a fair bit of driving in between.'

Much as I want Elise to be miserable I'm not sure if it's worth it if the rest of us are too. Elliot's not that keen on trees, and we could do the movie star thing in LA anyway – well a 'faking it' version at least. I'd love to see the lions and tigers but maybe Sasha would do better swinging by Elise's self-help group and getting a little therapy while she's here. I don't want to hurt

140

Helen's feelings but I'm ready to forget the whole thing.

'At this point you may well be feeling that some of you are getting better deals than others. You may even be questioning why you should put yourself through this at all,' Alex once again seems to read my mind. 'Well, if you don't try you'll never know. Life will go along the way it always has. Maybe that's fine. But maybe you want more. And if you knew how to get more, I'm guessing that you would have taken those steps already; so give us the benefit of the doubt. Maybe we know something you don't!'

He's got me. It's all too intriguing. On paper our tasks don't sound too life-changing but there he goes again with this hazy insinuation that miracles will occur.

'I would really love for each of you to enter this with an open mind and heart,' Helen urges. 'If you harbour reservations they're just going to be an extra obstacle for you to work through. And try not to make premature judgements. Where you begin is not where you will end up.'

Not for me, that's for sure. I'm going to be travelling all over the shop.

I half expect Alex to pass around a companion book on enlightenment The California Club way, but instead he concludes by telling us we need to be packed and checked out by noon tomorrow.

'Oh and for your reference, Lara, the order of your visits will be: Sasha, Elliot, Zoë and finally Elise.' He hands me a sheet with a list of names and their assigned destinations, then bids us a wonderful last night of freedom.

I watch Helen walk Alex to the door and give him an extended hip-to-hip hug. Just as well Reuben's not looking. Mind you, these groups are always big on hugs. I wonder if I should donate one to someone. By the look on her face, Sasha has the direst need.

'Yours is great!' I try and encourage her. 'Nothing to worry about!'

'Unless I end up neck-deep in tiger poo or thrown to the lions,' she quivers, gripping me tightly.

'Other than that.'

'Other than that, no!' A faint smile appears on her face. Then fades.

'But what about you?'

'Suits me. This way I don't have to watch them together.' I glance over at the Es, who are arguing.

'What about the driving?'

I shrug. 'What's the worst that could happen?'

'You get car-jacked, lose your way, the engine explodes and you plunge to your death over a cliff edge?' Sasha suggests.

'Other than that,' we chorus.

'You are going to have to spend some one-on-one time with Elise,' Sasha warns.

'It looks like she'll blow it long before I get there. I doubt I'll even have to worry about it.'

'OK, gang.' Helen returns to the group. 'I've booked a table at the Sky Room for 7.30 but I thought we could start with cocktails in the bar at seven?'

'Perfect!' We approve.

'It's pretty swanky so I'm popping home to change into something devastatingly chic,' Helen winks, adding: 'I suggest you do the same!'

The atmosphere instantly fogs with what-to-wear panic. I'm so desperate I'd consider mugging one of the other guests for an outfit but the only females to hand are a cluster of grand dames with bullet-proof hair and gobstopper-size pearls.

It is thus with supreme joy that I discover my beloved suitcase waiting for me back at the villa. There's just one catch – when I excitedly unzip it, I find it empty.

'Where's everything gone?' I look around the room as though the contents might be playing hide-and-seek.

Zoë slides back the wardrobe door. 'It's all here – the butler must have unpacked for you!'

'And it's been pressed,' Sasha notes as she inspects the drapes of fabric.

'What are you going to wear?' I ask the girls, dismayed that I no longer have an excuse for looking dodgy.

Zoë opts for strapless black with her gold cuff-bracelets and Cleopatra collar, Sasha reaches for her white trouser suit and – six changes later – I settle on my long swishy skirt and sparkly sea-green top. (Elliot once said it matched my eyes so it's been a secret favourite ever since.)

After three consecutive showers, we line up in front of the steamed-up bathroom mirror to do our make-up. Even Sasha, who rarely wears any, is joining in.

'How do you think Elliot's going to get on in Yosemite?' Sasha asks, expertly shaping her left eyebrow.

'No gadgets or computers? He'll short-circuit for sure.' Zoë dabs what looks like real gold leaf on to her eyelids.

'Not really one to languish in his own company, is he?' I note, fluffing pink on to my cheeks.

'Mind you,' Sasha nudges me, 'he will have company for a couple of days . . .'

'. . . and nights,' Zoë bumps me from the other side.

I grin. 'Oh don't! I can't believe I'm actually going to get some time alone with him!'

'Out there in the wilderness, under the stars . . .' Sasha teases.

'Hot chocolate spilt on one sleeping bag – forced to share the other!'

We giggle at Zoë's perfect plan.

'You know how people who have near-death experiences sometimes entirely change the way they live?' Sasha takes the more scientific approach. 'Well, what if he got pinned to a rock by a bear, just managed to escape, fell into your waiting arms and then realized that's where he's meant to be!'

My heart twizzles up to the ceiling. 'If only!' I sigh, giddy from the fantasy. 'I just hope he sticks it out till I get there.'

'Hey – we should have a bet on who's going to drop out first,' Zoë giggles.

'Oh well that's easy – Elise!' Sasha reaches for the eyelash curlers.

'Don't underestimate how tight she is,' I caution. 'You saw that look in her eye when she heard how much the Marilyn Monroe Beach House is worth per night. I just know she's thinking up ways to get the cash alternative.'

'Do you really think she'll last the week?' Zoë queries.

'Think of all the material she'll get from the experience – she'll be dining out on it for years.' Except she's not funny, she's just a bitch, and they're easy targets.

Sasha dabs cologne that smells of fresh linen behind her ears. 'If you had to swap with someone, who would it be?'

'Probably you,' I decide. 'I mean, LA would be amazing and I'd love to get all dollied up and go to a première or something but I think it would be even more incredible to get up close with a tiger, maybe even touch one.'

'Fed up with having fingers, are you?' Sasha flinches, setting the glass bottle back on the counter.

I chuckle and address Zoë: 'What about you?'

'Yours,' she tells me. 'You get to dip into everyone's wishes and experience all these different things – wilderness, kitties, glamour, and all that crazy spiritual stuff – I wanna get Reiki-d!'

She's right. Suddenly I feel the luckiest of all.

'I'd swap with Elise,' Sasha announces.

Zoë jolts her liquid liner with surprise.

Before she can speak I jump in with, 'Do you think they might have some answers for you at the retreat?'

and slip Zoë a cautionary look, trying to convey the words: Tread carefully if you're going to comment!

'Maybe,' Sasha sighs.

'What kind of answers?' Zoë asks, looking confused.

'Oh you know, just how to find true happiness and inner peace,' Sasha shrugs, smiling.

'Oh,' Zoë frowns.

'Wouldn't it be great if someone could just walk up and say, "Here's exactly what you need to do to be deliriously happy for the rest of your life . . ."' I muse. 'Or, when you've got a potentially life-changing decision to make, there would be someone you could call who could ensure you made the right choice.' I get wistful.

Every time I think about selling the B&B I get an uneasy feeling and I can't tell whether that's nostalgia or nerves or my instincts screaming, 'Don't do it!' If only there was some wise, neutral force I could consult, that way I wouldn't feel all the responsibility was on my shoulders. I'm so afraid that if I make the wrong decision now I might regret it for ever. If I let the B&B go, I'll never be able to get it back. But do I really even have a choice? *Enough!* Stop thinking about it. Let the universe decide!

'It's all that rooting around in your psyche that puts me off self-help stuff,' Zoë shudders, testing the heat of her tongs. 'I'm not sure I want to step into the mire.'

'I was thinking about getting some, um, professional help just before I came away.' Sasha squirms.

'What for?' Zoë still doesn't get it.

'Well, I haven't been feeling too chirpy lately and—'

'You're all right, Sash!' Zoë hugs her, inadvertently smudging caramel foundation on to Sasha's shoulder. 'Anyway, what stopped you?'

'What you just said – I was worried I might make things worse. Or that if I chose the wrong person it might mess with my head.'

'Of course it's perfectly possible it could be illuminating and a change for the better!' I try and be positive. 'Who knows, Elise could be giving this place a test run for you and then you end up going there and finding yourself.' Gotta give her hope.

'Imagine finding yourself and discovering you don't like yourself.' Zoë inadvertently puts a dampener on things.

'Well that would be a bummer,' I admit.

For a moment we all look fearful of our futures then Sasha proves the surprise saviour: 'Juicy Tubes at the ready?' she rallies the troops as only a model can.

We hold up our trio of glosses – lychee, melon and strawberry – and then ooze on the goo until our lips are inch-deep in sticky shine. 'Yum!' Zoë licks away the excess.

'Well, that's our appetizer,' Sasha does her darndest to make a joke. 'I'm ready for the main course now!'

10

'Where are the Es?' Zoë sets down her leafy Caipirinha cocktail to check her watch. 'They're half an hour late.'

'Well, Elise did say that they might stay in and get room service cos this was going to be their last night together in a while.' Helen looks disappointed.

'You're kidding?' Zoë scoffs. 'It's not like we're making them sleep apart, they could at least join us for dinner.'

'Shall we go on up to the restaurant?' Sasha suggests.

We're just shuffling off our bar stools when Elliot rushes in looking harassed.

'Sorry I'm so late. Elise wasn't feeling too bright so she's decided to have an early night. I just ordered her some soup.'

Which roughly translates as: We had a huge argument – she was insisting on dinner *à deux*, I explained that I see a lot more of her than I do my friends and it would be rude to miss the farewell meal and then she threw herself sobbing and screeching on to the bed and frankly I couldn't bear to spend another second in

148

her selfish, manipulative company so here I am. I may be slightly exaggerating the last bit but that's the gist, I'm sure.

We take the lift up to the top floor and then spill into the Sky Room with its starlit panorama of the cove. As the *maître d'* shows us to our plum velvet booth, there's a shuffle to get the seating order right – first Elliot gets nudged into place then it's like the parting of the Red Sea as the girls make sure I end up next to him. I love my friends!

As we mellow to the glow of the candlelight we realize there's a couple at every other table in the place. If you listen closely you can almost hear the proposals. Chez us, however, all breathless rapture is directed at the 'modern French' menu. It's the details in the sauces and sides that get us – yes the spicy ahi tuna tower sounds intriguing in itself but the fact that it comes with fresh mango and strawberry and is garnished with a mandarin vinaigrette makes it nigh on irresistible. But then we read about the Muscovy duck confit with braised Belgian endive and pink peppercorn brandy sauce and our tastebuds fairly swoon.

'It's like the equivalent of giving a vegetable a double-barrelled name,' Elliot decides as he scans down. 'Fire-roasted tomato just sounds so much fancier!'

Giddy from ordering rosemary jus and scarlet orange reductions we opt for a cheeky bottle of Perrier Jouet to toast The California Club and our impending adventures.

'Thanks for bringing us here, Helen,' I beam.

'Well, I thought that seeing as some of you will be spending the next week living off the fruits of the forest –' she winks at Elliot '– we should do it in style!'

As I let the champagne bubbles crackle on my tongue, I realize I have a small window of opportunity before the arrival of the bread basket to steal the floor: 'Remember earlier at the beach I said I had something to tell you?' I venture, nervously.

Nodding.

'Well, my mum's moving to Spain and—'

'Spain? Since when?'

I wanted to get it all out in one go but Helen's tripped me at the first hurdle.

'Um, since she met this fella who's got a villa complex out there. He wants her to run it for him.'

'What about the B&B?'

'She's giving it to me!'

There's a collective gasp and a sensational whoop from Zoë. 'That's fantastic!' she shines. 'You can finally do it up how you want!'

'Oh Lara! Congratulations!' Elliot cheers, pulling me into a lop-sided hug. 'Your own B&B, it's what you've always dreamed of.'

'It's going to be the most original and stylish in town,' Helen decides. 'A whole building showcasing your talents!'

'Well . . .' I try and cut in but I can't stop the barrage of excitement.

'We could all come down and help you strip wallpaper!' Sasha laughs, looking as if she's just found her purpose in life.

'Oh my God – what a brilliant idea for reality TV show!' Zoë gasps. 'The making of Brighton's newest B&B – we'd all be stars and your B&B would be famous!'

For a moment I get caught up in the sheer elation around me but then reality slaps me in the face and I blurt, 'I'm selling it!'

'What?' four voices snap.

The expressions on their faces range between stunned and uncomprehending.

'Why?' Elliot takes the next step.

I take a breath and tell them. 'The whole place needs rewiring and revamping and I just don't have the money.'

'I thought you were doing well,' Helen frowns.

'We're doing OK but the rewiring alone would cost £20,000 and that involves ripping up floorboards and drilling through walls so I'd have to redecorate after, which of course is what I'd want, but that's at least another £30,000 on top. £50,000 to do what I really want. And the whole time we're working on the place, we'd have to be closed so we won't have any income.'

Trust me, I've thought this through.

'Can't you just do a few rooms to start with?' Sasha asks, trying to hold on to the dream.

'I thought about that but it puts a limit on the money I can make. If I don't get at least an 80 per cent occupancy over the summer I can't make it through the winter months.'

'You need to find an investor, someone to go into partnership with,' Helen decides.

'I wouldn't know where to begin,' I confess. 'And I haven't got much time.'

'I'd love to help, Lara, but I'm just scraping together every last penny for a mortgage.' Elliot looks regretful.

'Are you buying a house with Elise?' Zoë still seems to be struggling with the concept of the fiancée creature as a permanent fixture. As am I.

'We're putting down a deposit when we get back,' Elliot nods.

I wonder who's paying more.

'Sure you don't want to relocate to Brighton?' Helen prompts.

'Actually I'd love to move back but obviously Elise's work—'

'No, no, don't be silly!' I trill. I'd rather squat in an amusement arcade than share my home with Elise.

'I haven't got a bean,' Zoë sighs. 'This whole trip is on credit.'

'My savings aren't going to last much longer,' Sasha reveals. 'I haven't worked in months.'

'I'm not asking for your money, any of you,' I insist. 'If anything, I'll be able to lend you guys some. The property should go for a million!'

Gloomy faces all round.

'But where would you live?' Zoë frets.

'I suppose I'd buy a flat or a small house, one with a nice big guest room.' I force a smile. 'And then invest the rest or whatever you do with spare money.'

I haven't got very far with thinking this version of my future through. Every time I imagine what I'd do with my newfound wealth, instead of feeling flush and fanciful, I just feel sick and want to cry. I can't shake the feeling that letting go of the B&B is giving up my soul and I'll just end up sitting there counting my money in an empty, echoing shell of a building. But really, what alternative do I have? I simply can't afford to keep the B&B. I have to be practical.

More pressingly, I have to convince the others that it's for the best.

'Honestly, it could be an exciting new start,' I insist. 'Who knows, maybe I'll move to Spain too!'

No one's falling for that.

The bread basket arrives. A couple of hands reach half-heartedly for a seed-speckled roll while the others wave it away.

'Did we order enough wine?' Zoë drains her glass. 'I think we need more.'

'It's a lot to let go of,' Elliot sighs. 'All those good memories.'

'I thought it would always be there.' Sasha looks particularly sorrowful.

'It felt like a real home.' Zoë's eyes well up. And she never cries.

'There's got to be a way to get round this,' Helen is determined. 'Together we can come up with a solution!'

No! I resist. I daren't feel hopeful so I try a new tack, 'Maybe I don't want to.'

Silence.

'Do you mean that?' Helen looks concerned.

'Look, with Mum gone, it'd just be me in a house full of strangers. That's no fun.'

For a second I think they're going to buy it but then Sasha gets an idea. 'Maybe I could move in, rent one of the rooms?' she says, brightening. 'I don't know why I'm still in London, there's no reason any more.'

Zoë follows her lead: 'And if I moved back we could be like Charlie's Angels, only landladies!'

'Remember when we used to imagine all of us living there together?' Elliot reminisces. 'I always thought that would be the perfect life: we could come and go as we pleased but there'd always be someone you could talk drunken gibberish to at 3 a.m., someone to challenge at backgammon or make Marmite on toast for. Someone to laugh with . . .' he sighs. 'I've never been as happy as when we all used to hang out.'

'Me neither,' Sasha agrees.

'Mmmm,' Zoë concurs.

Even Helen, who has moved on to greener pastures, seems misty-eyed.

I force down the lump in my throat with a forkful of potato *au gratin* and a large gulp of Pinot Noir. All I ever wanted was for us to stay together for ever. I'd love to believe that they'd all come back to Brighton and we could go back to the way things were but the reality is that they moved away for a reason and I can't keep hanging on to the past. I have to let go. Not my forte, but here goes:

'My mum's putting the B&B on the market while I'm away,' I inform them, feeling like an executioner.

'She said she'd call if there's a serious buyer. I gave her your number, Helen, hope that's OK.'

'That's fine but you'll have your own mobile tomorrow,' Helen reminds me.

'Oh yes! The Batphone!' I laugh, trying to jolt the conversation back to The California Club. 'Can I count on a few *cris de coeurs* from Yosemite?'

Elliot looks at me, knowing exactly what I'm trying to do, then does the decent thing and plays along. 'I might need you to arrange an emergency airlift at some point!'

'Don't you dare,' Helen warns. 'You're all going to complete your week and you'll all have the time of your lives. Even if it doesn't feel like it at first.'

'Is that what happened to you, Helen?' Sasha asks. 'You still haven't said.'

'Yeah,' wheedles Zoë, 'What did The California Club make you do?'

Good girls, move on . . .

'I can't really talk about it until you've completed your week,' she demurs.

'Give the game away, would it?' Elliot narrows his eyes.

'Exactly.'

'Hmmm,' I muse. 'Well, I'll tell you one thing, it's not going to be dull!'

'Speak for yourself.' Elliot rolls his eyes. 'I think I might purchase a Game Boy before we get dispatched.'

'I can't wait!' Zoë's sparkle returns. 'Imagine if I got to meet Josh Hartnett!'

The B&B isn't mentioned again. We chat on through desserts of hazelnut charlotte with crème praline and honey-roasted white peach with panko-fried (none the wiser for eating it) coconut crème pâtissier until we've eaten ourselves into a state of paralysis.

'I can't move!' I complain, rubbing my over-sated belly.

'Shall we get a liqueur?' Elliot summons the waiter.

For once Zoë chooses beauty sleep over boozing. 'I want to look my best for the casting agents!' she tinkles, prompting Sasha and Helen also to call it a night.

'Shall we take our drinks outside?' Elliot suggests.

Stepping out on to the terrace I feel as if I'm stepping into a dream – just me and Elliot on a balmy night under a scattering of superbright stars, serenaded by the swish of the inky black Pacific. It would feel so natural to lean into him and have him slip his arm around my waist. For me, anyway.

'Are you lonely in Brighton, Lara?' Elliot startles me with his directness. 'I never thought that you might be, until tonight.'

I look down at the aqua gel of the hotel pool and try and form a reply: 'Well, I miss you. All. Of course. But um, I've got some really nice clients, sometimes I go to Browns for cocktails with the Langhams or Daniella will get us tickets for the Theatre Royal because her mum works in the box office. It's nice.'

'But not a riot.'

'Not exactly,' I concéde. 'Not counting last night, I can't remember the last time I was drunk!'

'You know what I miss? Going into town, bumping into someone you know and saying, "Let's go for a quick one!" then ending up down the pub till 1 a.m. I suppose a lot of the university crowd have moved on now?'

'Yeah, most of them are in London. I still see Denny around.'

'How is he?'

'Same as ever.'

'Stoned?'

'Every waking moment.'

Elliot laughs and shakes his head. 'I can just see him fitting in at one of Elise's dinner parties.'

'Really?' Maybe I've pegged her wrong.

'I'm kidding! They're too formal for words. It's all her new work colleagues, and they're so competitive, even socially. Nobody dares drink more than one glass of wine for fear of showing any kind of vulnerability.'

I smile. It was always the opposite with us – the more you disgrace yourself the more you're welcomed into the bosom of our family.

'I don't know why she does it to herself,' Elliot continues, slumping over the railing. 'She seems to find the whole thing so stressful.'

'I think most people do,' I point out. 'We were just spoilt having Helen preside over our soirées.'

'You're right. She's a natural, that one.'

'So you're buying a house.' I don't know why I'm bringing this up again. 'That's a big step.'

'It's about time I grew up.'

'Is it?' I ask.

Elliot looks up at me. 'It's what you're supposed to do, isn't it?' He sounds unconvinced. 'Anyway, Elise is keen to settle down. I know she can seem cynical but she's actually quite conservative when it comes to having a house and a family.'

Family? That's one conversation I don't want to have – the mere thought of Elise pregnant makes me want to scream, 'Spawn of the devil!'

'Have you met her folks?' I ask.

'Just briefly.'

'Did you go to their house?'

'No, they visited us. Why do you ask?'

'No reason,' I chirp. I'm still trying to put together the Elise dossier but information is hard to come by. Now I'm wondering how much Elliot himself knows about the woman he's planning to marry.

'Did you get on with them?'

'They're OK. Super-keen on me – not that I want to sound big-headed!'

I smile. Elliot could never do that. Even saying 'Mosquitoes love me!' feels immodest to him.

'They can't wait for us to get married,' he continues. 'I suppose most parents are like that – they think they'll be able to relax if they know someone is taking care of their baby.'

I've never got that feeling from my mum – *hurry up and get married so I don't have to be the primary worrier any more*. Mind you, she did once say that she knew I'd be safe as long as Elliot was around. As if he was my guardian angel as well as my best friend. I wonder how she's going to react when I tell her he's engaged. I'm not sure I want to, it just makes it all the more real if she knows.

'Oh well – as long as you're having fun!' I shrug, eager to change the subject.

A dubious look passes over Elliot's face then he giggles like a child.

'Remember after that all-nighter on the beach we had to prop Zoë under a tree while we were trying to get a cab?'

'And no one would take her so we ended up carrying her all the way home . . .'

'. . . and the next morning she woke up and she had a dead beetle in her knickers!'

We splutter with mirth.

'And then I got you a taxi and you opened the door into an oncoming car and it ripped it straight off!'

'I'll never forget the look on that cab driver's face,' I cringe.

'What about when Helen's dad rang up and asked you out on a date and you said yes!'

'Don't!' I blush. It was April Fool's Day but I didn't twig until too late. I thought he was being genuine – I knew he hadn't been out with anyone since he split up with Helen's mum and I didn't want to be the first person to reject him.

'That was just mean!' I pout.

'He loved it!' Elliot laughs. 'He'd have gone through with it, given half a chance. I don't know what it is with you and older men, my dad always had a thing for you too. Said you were a keeper.'

'I loved your dad,' I softly say.

Elliot has a quiet moment and then says: 'We'll always be friends, won't we, Lara? I can't imagine my life without you in it.'

He holds my gaze a little longer than I can stand.

'I'm always here for you,' I whisper.

He takes my hand and gently kisses it, as a distant clock strikes midnight. 'We should probably get to bed.'

I close my eyes and sigh. *If only . . .*

11

Elliot is the first to leave the next morning. Then Elise, also flying to her destination, somewhere up the coast near Big Sur. Sasha and I drop Zoë at the train station in San Diego and then begin our car journey inland.

I think for all of us, the look of pride and hope on Helen's face is what keeps us going. When it came to saying goodbye even Zoë was wishing we could all just stay by the beach. What gave me the final push was remembering that this was my last chance for two whole nights alone with Elliot – it has to be worth it for that.

'What do you think they're going to make me do, exactly?' Sasha frets just twenty miles down the road from La Jolla. 'Surely you need training for this kind of thing?'

'I have no idea. All it says here is that the place is run by Carrie Shandrew, there's one other full-time guy – Ty – and a volunteer called Nina. Oh and they've got fifty-four big cats. Wow.'

The car engine revs wildly in response. I was

expecting to drive but Sasha asked if she could, to take her mind off things. It's obviously working a treat.

'Are we on the 15 freeway for a while?' she asks, itching to get into the fast lane. Anyone would think she was in a hurry to get there.

'Yup. We just need to keep an eye out for Temecula, that's when we switch to the 215.'

'Then what?' she hustles.

'Cruise to Riverside, then jiggle around a bit.'

Sasha darts a look at me.

'Don't worry, we'll be fine. Have a Jelly Belly.'

I rattle the box over Sasha's palm. 'Oh look! You got red, white and blue – how patriotic – for America *and* the UK!'

What can I say? It's the little things that make me happy.

'What flavours are they?' Sasha looks suspicious.

'You tell me!' I challenge, deciding this will be a good car game.

Sasha pops the white. 'Coconut.'

'Correct.'

'I'm going to guess blueberry for the blue without even tasting it,' she decides.

'How bold! Also correct!'

'Eurgh, that's revolting!' she swiftly follows it with the red. 'Cherry.'

'Almost,' I grant her.

'It's definitely cherry.'

'Very Cherry is what they have on the box.'

Sasha rolls her eyes. 'Now you!'

The jelly bean game lifts our spirits and takes us as

far as Temecula. By which time, unsurprisingly, we're feeling rather sick.

'I can't believe you've eaten all the Juicy Pears,' Sasha groans.

(It was such a taste sensation, I emptied the whole box into my lap and picked them out one by one.)

'I can't believe you thought Pink Grapefruit and Top Banana would taste good together,' I counter.

Sasha grimaces at the memory. 'Can you put them away? Just knowing they're there is making me nauseous.'

I oblige. 'Gummi Bear?'

'Oh go on then!' Sasha rustles into the bag. 'So, how do you think the others will get on?'

'Well Zoë's going to love it, no matter what. That girl is out to have a good time in this life and woe betide anyone who gets in her way.'

'I wish I was more like her,' Sasha sighs. 'She's so gung-ho, party-hearty, make-the-most-of-every-situation. Where does she get her energy?'

'No idea.' I shake my head. I still haven't got over the maracas.

'Do you think LA will be what she thinks it's going to be?'

'Even if isn't, she can handle it.'

'I just hope she doesn't get disillusioned, she's been dreaming about going there for so long.'

Uh-oh. Sasha's starting to worry about other people when she's already got her plate full worrying about herself.

'Fret ye not,' I advise. 'Zoë would have just as good a time at a Dyspraxia benefit as the Oscars.'

'It's a gift.'

'A blessing,' I agree. 'In fact, if I ever have kids that's the one thing I'd wish for them – not the fingers of a concert pianist or an IQ of 200 but a sunny disposition.' I reach for my bag. 'Let's give her a call – christen the Batphone!'

'Aaaghhhhhhhhhh!'

I hold the phone away from my ear. 'Zoë, are you OK?'

'Oh La, this is brilliant! I'm just passing one of those big water viaducts like Danny and Crater Face raced along in *Grease*! It's all graffittied and there's these little rows of flowerpots by one of the spillage pipes, I think someone lives there. Oh God – there's a naked man bathing! No way!'

The phone cuts out.

I look at Sasha. 'Do you think it was wise to let her loose unescorted?'

'Probably not,' she concedes.

I try Zoë's phone again but no reply – she must be in a tunnel, I'll try again in a minute.

'How are we doing?' Sasha nods at the map.

'Let me see . . . we're nearly at Moreno. Not far till our next freeway change.'

'Would you say I've got a melancholy disposition?' Sasha asks, trying to sound casual about her *non sequitur*.

'Did someone tell you that?' I ask, treading carefully. She nods. 'The make-up artist on the Will Young

164

video shoot. It's one of the most depressing things I've ever heard. It makes me think I'm going to feel like this for ever.'

'You could look at it another way – if you accepted that melancholy is your natural state rather than trying to reinvent yourself, then any good times would be a bonus.'

'Is that supposed to make me feel better?'

'Yes, but I can see why it wouldn't,' I admit, then try again. 'I remember watching this interview with Carrie Fisher and she was saying she's given up trying to fight her depressions when they hit, she's even given her miserable alter ego a different name so if someone rings up for her she says, "Mildred's in town" or whoever, so people know which state she's in.'

'Sounds scary!'

'I think it's quite a good way of dealing with it. At least she knows Mildred is just visiting.'

I can't quite believe it but I seem to be experiencing a craving for a tangerine jelly bean. I try to sneak the box on to my lap without alerting Sasha.

'I think I'd find it too exhausting being Zoë,' Sasha decides. 'In my next life I'm coming back as one of those naturally contented people. You know those folk who seem comfortable in their own skin.'

'Like Elliot,' we say in unison. He really is the most relaxed individual I know. Or at least he was.

'91 freeway, exit here,' I direct Sasha before asking, 'Do you think he seems different?'

She pulls a contemplative face.

165

'I don't mean in a Helen dramatic-new-identity way, just not quite himself.'

'Like when Aaron Spelling brought back a different actor to play Blake's son in *Dynasty*?' Sasha deadpans.

I chuckle. 'No. He's obviously the same guy, it's just . . . his little twinkle's gone.'

'I didn't know he had a little twinkle,' Sasha teases.

'I think the E numbers in the Gummi Bears are getting to you,' I tut, then smile to myself: that's two out-of-character jokes in a row. The fact that Sasha's nearly at her mission destination seems to be giving her a boost. Or maybe it's just the hysteria setting in.

'I haven't noticed, to be honest.' Sasha tries to give my question about Elliot its due. 'He was a laugh at the beach.'

'Yeah. I just got the feeling that he was holding himself in check. Like he'd mess around and then pull back, as if Elise might disapprove or something.'

I'm so transparently trying to kick-start some Elise-bashing. I swore I wasn't going to bitch about her any more but I can't help it.

'You know, I wouldn't have thought Elliot was her type,' Sasha muses.

Excuse me? Elliot's everyone's type, surely?

'Not saying that he's not fantastic, but I probably would have put her with someone a bit more . . . a bit less . . .' Sasha can't seem to find the words.

'What?' I laugh, dying to know.

'Maybe someone older or richer or more catalogue model good-looking.'

I smile to myself. I love that Elliot's appeal is quirky.

To me he is the most beauteous thing I've ever laid eyes on but at the same time I have to acknowledge that he has one of those 'All my own work!' faces. And I don't mean in surgery terms. His face seems to reflect his personality as opposed to being a mask of inherited beauty. Of course, Sasha is quite the opposite. She's all about genes and expensive moisturizers. I can't help wondering, if she gets her other wish and discovers her inner identity, will we be able to see a change in how she looks on the outside? I guess we'll just have to watch this face.

The scenery seems to be flattening out and getting progressively more nondescript the closer we get to Rialto so I go back to sorting through the CDs, stacking them on the dashboard in a bid to find a track that will quash the soul-searching and bring an air of frivolity to the proceedings. Best give REM a miss then. Ah! Found it. I slide out Sugababes and skip on to track six of a compilation album.

'*The Lion Sleeps Tonight*!' Sasha instantly recognizes the opening. 'Very funny!'

We're *awimmawaying* to our hearts' content when the phone rings. It's Zoë.

'It cut out before, I don't know why.'

The background noise has changed. 'Where are you now?'

'In a cab. I just left Union Station.'

'Seen any movie stars yet?'

'Actually this area is kinda weird and run-down.'

Zoë sounds fascinated rather than freaked out but I

want to know more. 'Describe it to us,' I say, putting her on speakerphone.

'Everything's dirty and low-rise, there's a woman in a purple balaclava walking along with a baby, she's just gone into the 98 cent store . . . It's like a mish-mash of nationalities, all the restaurants . . . there's Armenian, Mexican, Creole, Salvadorean, Tantra . . .'

'Tantra? Isn't that a type of sex?'

'I'm just reading the signs . . . Cambodian Buddhist Temple, Far East Auto Services, Casablanca Futons . . .'

'Are you serious?'

'Five T-shirts for $10.99, drinking water 20 cents, 99 cent store . . .'

'Hey, you're moving up!'

Zoë chuckles. 'I just saw a road called Avenue of the Athletes!'

I imagine a pole-vaulter being forced to fly over a pyramid of baseball players just to get to his front door. 'What happened to Avenue of the Stars?' I demand.

'That's what I want to know! It's all pawn shops, lino warehouses and dentists round here.'

I wonder if The California Club has done this deliberately to shake up Zoë's idea of LA being glamour central. I hope they know what they're doing. If they even partly extinguish her spirit they'll have me to answer to.

'Dollar World!' Zoë screeches, delighted.

Bless her, she'll get to Beverly Hills even if it's one cent at a time.

'Now it's getting all trendy-edgy, everything's

vintage and surplus – hey, La! You'd love this – I just saw this shop called the Den of Antiquity!'

'What road are you on?' I want to see if I can find her on the insert on my map.

'I can't see a sign. Oh wow! There's a bus just like the one in *Speed*!'

'Riverside Avenue, isn't that the one we want?' Sasha points ahead.

It's all happening at once.

'And a cop car!' Zoë whoops. 'How exciting! They're handcuffing two boys. They have the sexiest uniforms ever!'

Sasha and I exchange a concerned look.

'Zoë, we have to go, are you going to be OK?'

'Of course! And you two are together so that's cool, I don't care about Elise. It's just poor Elliot – the sooner you get to him the better.'

Amen to that.

'Call me if there are any problems,' I insist.

'Will do!'

I wish I could hang on until she's safely arrived at her destination but I have to return to my role as navigator.

'We're nearly there,' I tell Sasha. 'Just take the second turning on the left and—'

Sasha suddenly swerves down the first side road.

'Not this one!' I yelp, bracing myself against the dashboard.

'I know,' she cries, ramming on the brakes and lurching into a dusty gravel lay-by.

I struggle to control the clattering landslide of CDs.

'I just needed a minute,' she explains, looking shocked by her own actions, breath juddering in and out as she continues to clutch the steering wheel as if she's fighting a magnetic force.

'All right,' I say softly, not wanting to disturb her any further. I clutch the CDs to my lap and stare steadily ahead. Just keep calm and still. Any sudden moves could set her off. I stop chewing my tangerine jellybean, press the zesty gelatine to the roof of my mouth and mould it with secret swishes of my tongue.

A battered red pick-up truck passes us. Sasha's gaze tailgates it until it disappears from view, then slowly she releases her grip, leans back in her seat and closes her eyes. Even now there is little sense of relief. Her lips may be motionless but I know she's delivering a feverish pep talk on the inside.

Not wanting to interrupt the conversation she's having with herself, I wait. And wait. My eyes flick to the dashboard clock. It's now 5 p.m. so I take a chance on speaking.

'Do you want to get out and have a walk around?'

She shakes her head.

I return to the staring contest I'm having with the yellow line dividing the road. Oh no. I've got an itch brewing on my left shin. Just ignore it, it'll die down of its own accord, I tell myself. I must remain composed. Aaaghhh – my leg spasms and shoots out as if someone thwacked my knee with a reflex hammer, causing a handful of jelly beans to jump playfully in the air.

'Sorry!' I mutter, unsure why I'm apologizing.

Sasha blinks at me then quickly rouses herself, reaching for the ignition. 'We're going to be late!'

'Are you all right? Do you want me to drive?'

'I'm fine!' she says, briskly perpetrating a tyre-scuffing U-turn.

As we pull back on to Riverside Avenue I open my mouth to emit a platitude, something like, 'Don't worry, Sasha, I know you're scared but I'll be your real-life guardian angel.'

Instead I find myself saying, 'Did you know that one in four people experience some form of mental illness in their life?'

'What did you say?' Sasha winds up her window to silence the rushing wind. 'One in four people what?'

I can't believe I said that out loud. 'Are allergic to cats,' I lie.

'I wonder if there are any statistics about the number of cats that are allergic to people?' Sasha muses, with a certain poignancy to her voice.

I laugh 'I wonder.'

'I mean, it's possible, isn't it? Maybe that's all it was. Just an allergy.'

'All what was?'

Sasha's face clouds over again. I'm losing her.

'Sasha?'

'It's . . . I . . .' she flounders and fails to find the words to express her angst.

I can't finish her sentence for her. I have no idea what she is trying to say. But I'm sure she'll feel better once we get there. Actually, I'm not sure of that at all, but I can hope. Reluctantly I go back to focusing on moving my finger a fraction of a millimetre along the map with every tyre rotation. 'Agua Mansa!' Finally our road. 'This is it!'

Sasha takes the turn but immediately has reservations: 'This can't be right . . .'

'Why not?'

'There's just a lot of ducks!'

'What?' I follow her nod to the right and see endless pens of pure white quackers and not a pond in sight. 'How bizarre!'

'And over there – ostriches.'

We roll by the gawky creatures, which for some reason look to me like black-feathered bagpipes. I wind down my window for a better look.

'They're living dangerously – imagine if the tigers got out!'

'What a wonderfully reassuring thing to say just before I move in with them.'

'Sorry!' I grimace. *'Here!'* We're suddenly upon the sign: TIGER TIGER. A NON-PROFIT RETREAT FOR RETIRED ANIMAL ACTORS – hey we're going to see celebrities before Zoë, how weird is that?' I try and make a joke.

Sasha slams on the brakes so hard my seatbelt locks and gives me a diagonal garrotting. I've had smoother rides in a bumper car.

'They won't like me,' she blurts, experiencing a resurgence of nerves.

Before I can assure her that everyone warms to her once they get over wanting to believe that she's a vain 'n' vacuous ice queen, she adds, 'animals don't like me.'

I want to laugh but decide against it.

'What makes you say that?' I ask.

'It's true. They can tell—' she halts herself.

'Tell what?'

Sasha looks as if she's about to retreat into her catatonic state. No pun intended. I have to do something.

'Gosh look at that!' I say, praying for something to leap into my sight line so I can follow through.

'What?'

'I think I just saw a . . .' I scrabble out of the car as if I'm tracking something in the foliage.

'Oh my God, yes!' Sasha joins me. 'He's looking right at us!' She shrinks behind me.

I can't believe she can actually see my imaginary distraction. Where is it? Suddenly I lock sights with a pair of golden eyes. Benevolent rather than predatory, they seem to be saying, Oh, it's you!

'That's Ryan,' a voice behind us says. 'Our VIP guest. He's a liger – that's half lion, half tiger.'

Now his expression seems to be saying, I know, I don't get it either.

We turn to find a cosy-looking brunette. 'I'm Carrie,' she smiles, warmly shaking our hands.

I can see the relief on Sasha's face: thank God there's going to be someone nurturing around.

'It's actually pretty good timing you being here this week,' Carrie continues. 'I have to go to San Francisco to try and raise some funds—'

'When do you leave?' Sasha panics before Carrie even finishes her sentence.

'Day after tomorrow. I'll be gone a coupla days so Ty will welcome an extra pair of hands.'

Sasha's fretful look returns.

'How about I give you a little tour of the place before it gets too dark?'

I nod on Sasha's behalf.

'We'll start with Freddie. He's the devil himself, it'll be all downhill after that.'

Here kitty, kitty, kitty . . .

12

'We're not too picturesque yet,' Carrie warns us as she raises the horseshoe clip on the gate and grinds it open. 'This is actually a disused water plant. The city of Colton donated it to us when they heard we were being moved on from our last home.'

'Why did you have to leave?' I ask.

'The local council decided they didn't want us there any more, said they'd kill the cats if we stayed.'

'Are you serious?' I'm shocked.

She nods a grave yes, motioning us through the wire fencing. Suddenly I'm gawping at a writhing mass of leopard spots. It's like an animal print Magic Eye. I blink, trying to correct my vision.

'I've never seen so many cats in one place!' Sasha tries to take it all in.

'We've got sixteen leopards, a mix of Northern Chinese and Asian, the Asian are the smaller ones . . .' Carrie points over to a pair hanging back from the group. 'Those two were in a Brooke Shields movie called *Born Wild*.'

'Oh wow!' I haven't seen it but I'm sure it's an impressive thing to have on your CV.

'They're all entertainment cats, born and bred in captivity.'

'Is that a panther?' Sasha enquires.

'Black leopard,' Carrie corrects her. 'You can see his markings better if the sun shines directly on him.'

We squint at his self-patterned fur, just about making out the dark chocolate spots.

'Is he going grey?' Sasha notes the tufts of silver over his nose.

'Yeah a couple of them are getting old now and osteoporosis is setting in.'

It's then that we notice the stiff arched spines like a humpbacked bridge and wince in sympathy.

'This one looks in his prime, though,' I say, pointing to the sleek individual who's keeping a keen eye on us.

'That's Freddie.'

'Freddie as in Kruger?' Sasha gulps spotting his flick-knife claws.

'He went out on the road with Janet Jackson for her Rhythm Nation Tour.'

'Really?' Zoë would love this! I wonder if the cats have evening get-togethers and swap celeb stories under the stars.

'Freddie runs this camp.' Carrie sounds suitably respectful. 'He's top cat.'

'The indisputable leader of the gang' plays in my head.

'Why is that one separate?' Sasha nods over to a black leopard with a mangled ear who's restlessly prowling and hissing, clearly peeved at being barred from the party.

'With leopards there can be only one leader,' Carrie explains. 'Freddie and Malachi like to tango – if we'd left them in together one of them would have died.'

As if to prove her point, Malachi flares up and hurls himself at the caging. My heart goes out to him, it just doesn't seem fair. 'Can't you divide up the rest of the leopards so they get a gang each?' I suggest.

Carrie smiles and shakes her head. Malachi skulks into his shabby wooden hut and then sticks his head up through a tear in the roof.

'We build them nice boxes but they just tear them apart.' Carrie shrugs, moving on.

'Here's Ryan again.' Carrie bows to the liger. He gives us a regal nod which seems to say: Charmed, but please don't put on any airs and graces on my behalf.

I love him! Even at this early stage in the tour I know that he's going to be my favourite.

'How come he's a liger not a tion?' I ask hoping it's not too stupid a question.

'Actually it's tigon – that's when you've got a tiger father, lion mother. Ryan is the other way round, hence liger.'

'I seeeee!' I nod. 'He's a big guy, isn't he?'

'Eight hundred pounds.'

'What? That's nearly sixty stone!' I reel.

'Just as well he's not a lap cat, huh?' Carrie laughs, leading us to the next cage. 'This is Tyson.'

I gulp at the sight of the stocky, power-packed tiger. 'You wouldn't want to mess with him!'

'No you wouldn't,' Carrie confirms. 'He used to belong to Mike Tyson!'

He's not the only bruiser in the pack. Several of the tigers appear pumped-up and ready for aggro, while others are slender and demure. I'm intrigued by how much their coats vary in colour – from soft golden syrup tones to burnt orange sunsets and, most dramatic of all, pure white with liquorice stripes.

'That's Syntar, our white Bengal tiger.' Carrie sounds suitably proud.

He's stunning. I'd defy anyone not to get tingles looking into those sapphire blue eyes.

'He's been used a lot for calendars and photoshoots but only facially – the back end of his body has a yellowy tinge that's no good for full body shots. Not in Hollywood, anyway.'

Sasha takes a step forward. She knows what it's like to be admired only for your looks, to be scrutinized and then dismissed for the slightest flaw. They'll get along great. Beauty and the Beauty.

We continue down the open-air corridor – passing large cages either side with just the odd paddling pool, tree stump or potted plant breaking up the yards of sandy earth and wire meshing. I'm just wondering how many of these cats would trade what essentially is a spacious squat for a penthouse at the zoo when Carrie opens another gate and we step out into a dusty wasteland backed by distant mountains. Other than a row of clapped-out VWs, a tractor and a random scattering of rusty tools, it's just flat, dry earth as far as the eye can see.

'We've got two acres up at the back here. The idea is to build a free-roaming area with trees and waterfalls where the cats can take it in turns to run and play.'

'Like a day out at the park?' Sasha suggests.

'Paradise Park!' I suggest a name for it.

'Why not!' Carrie smiles. 'We're trying to raise the funds to get it landscaped . . .'

'You should charge more for your tours – is it really just $5?'

'Yeah, but until it's prettied up there's not much to see,' she admits, tugging up a tangle of weeds. 'Listen, you girls must be tired, I'll introduce you to the rest of the cats tomorrow.'

Carrie turns to lead us back to the house.

'What's through here?' I point to a gate with a NO ENTRY sign. 'If you don't mind me asking.'

Carrie hesitates then reaches for the padlock. 'These are a few of our special friends,' she says, voice softening. 'The ones that have been rescued. They're not so used to being around people so we keep them in a quieter area.'

'Oh we don't have to—' I feel bad for being so nosy.

'It's fine, just don't make any sudden moves and if they turn their ass towards you and lift their tail, make sure you jump to the side – it's like skunk spray and it goes back a good few metres so there's no point in running backwards!'

Carrie pushes open the door. Nervously we step through.

A slim-hipped tiger scrambles to her feet, checking out the intruders.

'Desiree was rescued from a restaurant in Texas. We don't declaw any of our animals but she came to us already done so we have to keep her in her own cage because she can no longer defend herself.'

I feel a pang for her: she must feel so vulnerable.

'And this is Oliver. He was found abandoned in a garage in Wyoming. He'd been left on his own in the middle of winter with no food or water and was frostbitten all over.'

Sasha's eyes well up and gently she moves closer but the instant Oliver sets eyes on her he starts freaking out.

Carrie bundles her out of the way.

'I'm sorry, I forgot – can you tie back your hair?'

Sasha looks confused as she swiftly winds her hair into a knot. Oliver gradually calms down.

'We think he might have been abused by someone with long hair, it always seems to set him off.'

I grip Sasha's hand and find her shaking.

'Ty's been spending a lot of time with him lately. We think he's making progress but after what these animals have been through it's tough . . .' Carrie shakes her head.

It seems unfathomable that anyone could be deliberately cruel but Carrie points out that there's a shocking amount of ignorance in the world, citing the man who thought that if he stopped feeding his tiger cub it would stay the same size, as a disturbing example.

'Come on, I'll show you the house,' Carrie jollies us out of our slump.

*

180

It's a pretty basic wooden bungalow with very little in the way of furniture and trimmings but the large kichen/dining area overlooking the preserve is warm and homely and smells of baked ham and cornbread (our upcoming dinner, it transpires). There's a long corridor with three bedrooms and a bathroom off it and a half-painted porch with a hammock at the end. I'm rather taken with the idea of sleeping al fresco but we've been assigned sleeping bags on an old mattress two doors down. Bit of a contrast to La Valencia.

'I'm just going to have our personal butler run a Jacuzzi for us,' I joke to Sasha as we wheel our suitcases in from the car.

It's pretty spooky in the darkness with the curious walrus-like barking of the cats. I wouldn't like to be staying here by myself and I wouldn't blame Sasha if she suddenly bleated, 'I can't do this!' But instead she seems oddly resigned to her fate, as if she somehow feels she deserves this punishment.

We're just inside the front door when the lights cut out.

'You girls OK?' Carrie finds us in the darkness.

'Fine!' we say gripping on to each other.

'Looks like we got a power cut,' she says matter-of-factly. 'Ty's moved the torches again so we're gonna be blacked out till he gets here. Why don't you come on through to the kitchen – it's nice and toasty by the stove.'

'Wood-burning?' I check.

'That's right.'

Sasha continues trembling but I heave a sigh of relief – dinner is still on, thank God!

'You two sit tight,' Carrie instructs as we fumble towards the table. 'How about I fix us some drinks?'

We nod and then realize actions alone are just not going to cut it. 'Yes, please!' we say out loud.

'Now one of these bottles . . .' Carrie appears to be sniffing a selection. 'Here it is. I guess we should be having wine with the meal but since I don't have any and this is a special occasion . . .'

Lord knows what she hands us but judging from the searing sensation in my throat and the way my eyes water from the fumes I'm guessing at moonshine. We're tiddly in seconds and chat amiably for the next half hour: it feels a bit like we're having an illicit 'lights out' conversation. We're just getting on to Carrie's divorce and how she came to be heading up Tiger Tiger when the distinctive purr and pop of a motorbike whirrs to a halt outside.

'Here he is! Maybe now I'll be able to see to carve the ham!'

The door creaks open and a figure clomps into the kitchen. 'What's going on here?' a male voice rumbles. 'You girls playing hide-and-seek?'

'Where'd you put the torches?' Carrie cuts to the chase.

'I haven't touched them – they should be right here . . .' There's a shuffling and the squeak of a hinge. 'You know what? Nina was going to get new batteries.'

'You're right,' Carrie confirms. 'Oh well, we'll manage.'

'Are you going to introduce me?' Ty prompts.

'Oh yes!' We hear Carrie chink a tooth on her glass as she curtails her slurp. 'This is Lara and Sasha. Not that you can see them, let alone tell them apart!'

'For the record, I'm the really good-looking one!' I pipe up, my squiffiness having gone straight to my tongue.

'And I'm the one who looks like she's been smacked in the face with a shovel!' Sasha giggles, apparently suffering similar symptoms.

'Carrie, I'm guessing you've cracked open that bottle of Sambucca you've been saving.'

Is that what it is? I love it. My new favourite drink.

'Yes I did!' Carrie cheers.

'Good job! I'll get a glass.'

'You got your bike back then,' Carrie calls after him.

'Yeah, she's running like a dream.'

'Sounds like an old Triumph Tiger,' Sasha observes.

'It is,' Ty's voice comes back in our direction: '1964 classic. How'd you know?' he asks with obvious delight.

'I had one. Well actually it was my brother's but he gave it to me when he moved away. Best way to get around London.'

'Well I wouldn't know about that but she sure is nippy! You ever take her on any long runs?'

'Mostly just down to Brighton – that's only an hour or two but sometimes I'd continue down the coast.'

'Man, that's the best, isn't it?'

The pair of them rap away about ccs and shock absorbers and the bliss of having sea air mingling with the exhaust fumes. Meanwhile Carrie does a pretty good job hacking at the ham and I hoik the cornbread out of the baking tray and on to the plates (sneakily snaffling Sasha's ham portion while I'm at it. She doesn't seem keen to ruin the mood by telling them she's a vegetarian just yet).

'I'm sorry we didn't bring any wine,' I apologize. 'Maybe I could go to a local store tomorrow?'

'Don't you worry about that,' Carrie shushes me. ''Nother Sambuca?'

'Oh go on then!'

This is great! I'm going to have all my dinner parties in pitch blackness from now on – it makes the whole thing so much fun. I gave up trying to co-ordinate my knife and fork after the first failed bite and am now picking at the food with my fingers and no one even knows!

'You want a napkin, sweetie?' Carrie offers, foiling me with her night-vision.

'Oh! Er, thank you!' I fluster.

'So, what's your ultimate dream for Tiger Tiger?' Sasha addresses Carrie and Ty.

Interesting. It's not like her to initiate a conversation, and she always used to wince at the mention of dreams – after all, she'd lived the dream of so many girls and look where that got her. I put it down to this lack of scrutiny – in the dark she doesn't have to be her normal self, or the person people expect her to be. As she responds to Ty talking about his trips to Africa and the ideas he's got for the preserve, her voice sounds warm, intimate even. Everything he says seems to strike a chord with her. At first I wonder how she can flirt with someone she's never seen but then I remember all the men I've fancied purely on a phone-call basis – antique dealers, new clients, wrong numbers . . . – and it hits me – BAM! She's having a blind date! She said she wanted to go somewhere where looks don't count and suddenly she's in a place where no one can even see her! I can't help wondering if The California Club didn't orchestrate the power cut themselves.

We stay up till midnight, Carrie and I yappering over peppermint stick ice-cream at one end of the table, Ty and Sasha sipping coffee and sighing at the other, then retreat to our respective bedrooms.

'Am I detecting a slight fluttering of the heart?' I whisper as I close the wonky door behind us.

'Slight?' she reels, hoarse with lust. 'I've been having palpitations for the last two hours!'

'Sasha!' I gasp.

'What?'

'I've never seen you like this! Not that I can see you now.' I laugh as she spins me around the room. 'I wonder what he looks like?'

'Oh I don't care!' she sings.

'You don't?'

'Well, I'm curious of course but if I could just keep listening to his voice,' she sighs. 'His deep, gritty voice . . . I'd be happy.'

'Even if he was some spindly little worm with one leg?' I tease.

'Oh Lara!'

'Well, he could be – if he's spent years around wild cats he could easily be missing a few limbs.'

Sasha grabs me and tells me again, 'I don't care!'

'I'll bet he's lying in bed now wondering what you look like.'

'D'you think so? What if he doesn't like what he sees?' Sasha frets.

I groan. 'Coming from anyone else on the planet that might be a reasonable concern, but you? Sasha, get real! The guy is going to freak when he sees you – he won't believe his luck!'

'Oh, I hope so!'

We wriggle into our sleeping bags.

'I'm thinking Indiana Jones crossed with Fabio,' I mutter.

'Stop it!' Sasha chortles.

'Or a lean Russell Crowe, maybe with an eyepatch?'

'Night!' Sasha tries to shut me up.

'Night!' I concede.

We lie still for two whole minutes before Sasha fidgets excitedly: 'I can't wait for morning!'

I think of the contrast to her earlier mood – crying on the beachside bench, on the verge of taking the next flight home – and experience a gratifying sense of satisfaction. We've only been gone a matter of hours and The California Club is already working.

13

'I can't look!'

Sasha and I are outside the kitchen, about to see Ty for the first time in hyper-bright daylight.

'Can't you go in then come back and tell me what he's like?' Sasha urges, backing away.

'Wait! I know!' I reach in my bag and pull out my compact, angling the mirror so I can see around the corner.

'Oh God, it's worse than we thought!'

'What? What?' Sasha claws at me.

'I thought you said it didn't matter what he looked like?' I give her a withering look.

'It doesn't. Just tell me!'

'Picture a young Danny De Vito.'

'Is he short?'

'Not so much short as wide. Khaki combats and a turtle neck.'

'In this heat?'

'Not the jumper, one of those necks with droopy excess skin.' I tug at my own.

'You're lying!' Sasha tries to peek in the mirror but I snap it closed.

'To be honest I could only see the table leg,' I confess. 'Shall we go in?'

'You first!'

I've never seen Sasha so jittery over a man so I do the decent thing and lead the way.

In the millisecond before he senses our presence we take in his unkempt mane, his tanned, scarred hands and lived-life face. It's too soon for me to say whether he's ruggedly sexy or just needs a good wash and brush up; either way he's the kind of man who could withstand anything the elements might throw at him. And I'll bet you anything he has powerful thighs. Whatever that means.

Sasha emits a sound that other women will immediately recognize as code for gorgeous. I can't wait to hear what noise he makes when he sees her!

'Sasha?' he looks up at me expectantly, onyx-green eyes sparkling.

'No, I'm Lara, this is Sasha.' I give my beautiful friend a flourish. For the first time in my life I see a man's face fall at the sight of her. 'You're . . .' he tails off, then shakes his head and throws his cup into the sink. 'I'll be outside when you're ready to start working.'

Turning on a mud-caked heel, he stomps out the door.

'I guess he's not a morning person,' I gawp after him.

'Did you see the way he looked at me?' Sasha is crushed. 'It was like he despised me!'

She's right but why on earth would that be true?

'Nooo!' I say opening the fridge. 'He probably didn't want to make it too obvious that he fancied you so he, um . . .'

'Ran away?'

'Exactly.' I put the milk and butter on the table. 'Toast?'

Sasha's over by the kitchen window watching Ty crash around the yard. 'He looks in a foul temper.'

'Maybe he's just hungover. Or worried that you're out of his league. You've had that before.'

'Does he strike you as the kind of person who would think like that?'

I open my mouth then close it. No would be the answer.

'Look, don't worry about it. I'm sure there's a perfectly reasonable explanation – maybe he's like Oliver and freaks at the sight of long hair,' I suggest.

Sasha swiftly winds her skein of gold into a twist at the base of her neck.

'There we go – sorted!' I throw Sasha an orange.

As she goes to catch it, her hair comes tumbling back down.

Judging by Ty's mood, he won't be the type to tolerate slacking or phone-call breaks so I quickly dial Elliot while we're munching our way through our slices of sourdough.

He answers straight away but sounds groggy.

'Are you all right?' I ask, instantly fretting.

189

'I don't feel too bright. I think it's the fresh air. Everything smells like those pine air-fresheners. It reminds me of my dad's car and how carsick I used to get.'

I can't help but grin. There's no one quite like Elliot. It's so good to hear his voice.

'So, what's it like, Yo-semite?' I ask giving it the homeboy inflection.

'I'm sleeping in a tent. I have to keep my food in this padlocked metal dumpster so the bears can't get to it and last night I did a strange dance with a racoon.'

'You danced with a racoon?'

'Well it wasn't exactly the *Pulp Fiction* two fingers across the eyes move . . .'

I laugh, imagining it all the same. 'What happened?'

'I'd got up in the night to get a can of Coke from the vending machine outside the convenience store; it was pretty dark and I was wishing I'd brought my torch when I sensed movement at the top of the stairs.'

'Da-da-daaa!'

'I looked up and there was this racoon stood up on his hind legs! He looked at me, I looked at him. I wasn't quite sure of the road rules – who was supposed to back up? – so I decided it should be me and I took a step backwards. He moved his little foot forwards. I took another step, so did he. And then when we were both back on the tarmac we moved slowly round in a circle, never taking our eyes off each other!'

'That's amazing! Are you two friends now?'

'No, he just ran off into the night, haven't seen him

since – he doesn't call, he doesn't write . . .' Elliot gives his most pitiful sigh. 'It's just me, alone in the wilderness.'

'Is it beautiful there?'

'The trees are green. The rocks are big. What else is there to say?' Elliot mutters, clearly bored.

'What have they got planned for you?'

'They want me to do a bear walk.'

'You didn't get naked enough at La Jolla?' I tease.

'Not barc! B-E-A – oh forget it.'

'No go on, tell me!' I prompt.

'It's just this thing for the visitors, a guide takes a group of about twenty on this walk through the meadow and gives them a little chat about the local bears and their habits.'

Before I can comment, Elliot asks, 'When do you get here?'

'My flight's not till early evening tomorrow. I was thinking of stopping off to surprise Zoë before I go to the airport—'

'Can't you come here earlier?' Elliot whines.

'I'm sorry, it's all pre-ordained.' I sound stoical but inside I'm thinking: 'Is there a way to bring it forward? Maybe I could—'

My phone bleeps.

'Hold on a second, there's another call coming through.'

'Lara?'

'Zoë!'

I experience a pang of guilt at my willingness to leapfrog my visit to her.

'Hold on a mo!' I flick back to my previous call. 'Elliot? I've got to go, another of my subjects needs me!'

'Have you spoken to Elise yet?'

My heart sinks. 'No.'

'Well, send her my love.'

'OK!'

'And—'

'Gotta go!' I cut him short. I can't deal with the mush. I'd rather challenge Malachi to a scrap.

'But I haven't heard about how you're getting on!' he protests.

'I'll call you later.'

'You'd better.'

'I will.'

I click back to my other call.

'Zoë! You're up early. How's our glamour girl?'

'Great!' she whoops. 'I love limo land!'

'Seen any stars yet?'

'Queen Latifah came in yesterday.'

'In where?'

'In? I mean on – on the set!'

'You're on a movie set?' That's too exciting. I'm sure even if they're filming a story about pygmies Zoë can wangle herself a walk-on part. 'What movie?'

'What?'

'What's the movie called?'

'It's a secret!'

'Oh.'

'Lara, when are you getting here?'

I don't want to spoil my surprise visit tomorrow so I

give her the official schedule spiel – 'Three days' time.'

'Three days or three nights?'

'Well, it's Tuesday today, I'll be with you Friday.'

'Oh.' She sounds disappointed.

'You're having fun aren't you?'

'Oh yeah, it's the best, I just want you here to share it with. I gotta go – I think I just saw Kate Hudson!'

'What's she up to?' Sasha is eager for an update.

'No idea,' I admit. 'No mischief yet or I'm sure she would have said.'

'You sound concerned.'

'No, she just didn't seem herself. Anyway, I'll see for myself tomorrow. Shall we?'

Sasha and I set out into the baking heat, ready for whatever Taskmaster Ty throws at us. As it happens he's nowhere to be seen but we do find Carrie chatting to a pair of tigers.

'Hey!' she greets us. 'How'd you girls sleep?'

'Fine!' we chorus. Amazingly this is true. We may be in the middle of nowhere but we certainly weren't worrying about intruders in the night – forget Beware of the Dog, we had fifty-four cats watching over us.

'Did you meet Cosmo and Caesar yesterday?' Carrie asks.

When we shake our heads she continues: 'Siberian tiger brothers. They don't like anybody else and that's fine, we just keep the two of them together.'

'They're massive!' I gawp.

'Nine-and-a-half-feet long and about three feet from their shoulder to the ground. You'll notice with the Siberian tigers they've got big fat heads . . .'

I want to rush and cover their ears – there must be a nicer way to put it.

'. . . and their stripes separate as they get older, see?'

She's right – it's like Gisele pulling on a catsuit meant for Kylie.

'With the Bengals, the stripes remain close.'

'It's Stephanie about the cubs,' Ty cuts in, appearing out of nowhere to hand Carrie a mobile phone. Carrie excuses herself, leaving Ty to glare at us. Seeing as he doesn't seemed inclined to resume the tour, I decide to be bold and ask a question.

'I meant to ask yesterday, what are all those ducks doing up the road?'

'They're nothing to do with us,' Ty grunts. 'They're being bred for Peking duck – 3,500 about to be slaughtered any day now.'

Sasha shudders. We won't be having Chinese take-away for a while.

'And the ostriches?'

'Ostrich burgers are big in LA,' he shrugs. 'Lean meat, less fat.'

In a bid to avoid eye contact with us, Ty whips out a pair of pliers and sets to bending some spiky prongs of fencing round to a safer position.

'So what kind of things will Sasha be doing while she's here?' I ask, starting to feel a little indignant at his attitude.

'Oh we're going to have her manicuring claws, getting the panther coats to shine like a Pantene ad,' he deadpans. 'Maybe improve their catwalk skills . . .'

194

That would be a good pun if it wasn't delivered with such spite.

'I guess we really should begin by finding one that matches her outfit,' he continues. 'How about you, Carlito?'

A fuzzy-furred snow leopard rears up and throws himself against meshing. Sasha stumbles back, terrified.

'No? Well, maybe she'd do better with the ladies.' Ty lets himself into a cage of seven or eight slinky-hipped tigers. 'Hey girls,' he greets them as they swish around his legs like house cats. 'I guess they just look like walking handbags to you, huh?' he stares pointedly at Sasha through the fencing.

Sasha looks as if she's been slapped. I'm too stunned by his aggression to speak. Could this just be his strange sense of humour?

'So you're a model?' He comes out and says what is obviously gnawing at his guts.

'Ex,' Sasha clarifies.

'D'you know Kate Moss?'

'I worked with her once but I wouldn't say we were friends.'

'She's no friend of ours either.' Ty rumples the fur on one of the adoring tigers at his side. 'She claims she cares about animal welfare then goes out in a vintage coat with a fur collar and when someone asks her if it's real she's all, "I dunno!"' he snorts. 'If she cared, she'd know.'

'Not all models are that fickle,' I tell him, hoping it's true.

'What about Naomi Campbell?' he challenges.

I knew she was coming next. 'You mean that hypocrite who claimed she'd rather go naked than wear fur, then paraded down a catwalk in dead animal skins?' I rally, hoping to beat him at his own game. Before he can speak I add, 'Look, there are plenty of beautiful women in this world who genuinely care about animal rights.'

'Yeah, but funny how they always choose the beautiful animals to protect, isn't it? Ones they consider worthy of their looks. Go save a hippo or an alligator, that'll impress me. All we need is another damn supermodel who thinks this is some kind of photo opportunity!'

'This wasn't my choice!' Sasha protests, finally speaking up. 'I was placed here.'

'What is this – community service?'

Sasha looks despairing. This is going to be a tough week.

'Sorry about that,' Carrie returns. Not a moment too soon. 'We've got cubs arriving tomorrow, I just needed to arrange an early pick-up.'

'Cubs?' I brighten, falling straight into Ty's 'aren't they cute?' trap.

'We don't breed here, that's not what we're about,' Carrie explains, 'but that'll be the second batch of cubs we've had this year. These ones over here are about five months old.'

Carrie leads us forward to a trailer with two inquisitive, roly-poly, chewy-tustly cubs frolicking inside.

'Cassidy and Kid.'

'As in Butch and Sundance?' Sasha enquires.

'No, David Cassidy and Kid Rock,' Ty sneers before skulking back over to the yard.

'He's teasing, take no notice,' Carrie breezes.

I can see Sasha getting even more paranoid – it's not just animals that don't like her but animal people.

'The cubs help promote us. We take them out on the road to local fairs to get people interested in visiting us here and hopefully adopting a cat or making a donation.'

The two cats get into a lively scrap, squealing as they chomp on each other.

'They're getting to the age where they're trouble now. They're even more rambunctious in the cooler weather.'

'Can you still handle them?' I ask.

'Well, they're starting to want to bite – they think it's fun to use your leg like a chew-toy!'

Ouch!

Out of the corner of my eye I see Ty letting himself into the padlocked area, presumably to do some more counselling with Oliver.

'Did Ty grow up around big cats?' I'm curious.

'Not really, he didn't start as an animal trainer until he was twenty-eight. Before that he was an actor.'

'Ty was an actor?' My eyes widen in disbelief. I can't imagine him being too obedient on set.

'But he doesn't really like to talk about that time in his life.'

Well, that's good to know. I load the ammunition, getting ready in case he decides to attack Sasha again.

We spend the afternoon clearing stray debris and weeds from the wasteland and testing each other on the cat names.

'I wonder how big Cassidy and Kid will be by the time this is built?' Sasha ponders, straightening her back. 'Wouldn't it be great if we could just magic it up by the end of the week!'

'That would be one in the eye for Ty.'

'Wouldn't it?' Sasha gets a rarely seen glint of determination in her eyes. 'There must be something we can do.'

'I don't know what. We don't know anyone here. Maybe we should find out how far along they are over dinner?'

'Good idea!' Sasha nods. 'Then we can come up with a plan!'

Though Carrie is happy to chat away about Paradise Park – or rather her hopes for it – it turns out they don't even have enough money to purchase a single bamboo shoot at present. Ty utters barely a word throughout the meal and excuses himself directly after a helping of peach cobbler, gruffly announcing, 'I'm going to spend the night with Stella.'

Later as Sasha and I lie side by side in our sleeping bags, Sasha asks, 'There wasn't a cat called Stella was there?'

'I don't remember,' I mumble, trying to mould my pillow to better accommodate my head.

'Do you think that's his girlfriend?'

I stop pummelling. 'You don't still fancy him, do you?'

'No,' she pouts.

It's too dark to tell if she's blushing so I reach out and touch her skin. *Hot!*

'Sasha – you do!'

She squirms, then reasons, 'It's just . . . there's something about him. The way he is with the cats.'

'But he's such a grouch! And he's been so mean to you.'

Sasha doesn't reply, just muffles into her pillow giving a resigned huff of: 'Of course he's got a girlfriend.'

Oh yeah, he's a real charmer, I think to myself. The last thing I want is for her to get even more hurt than she already is. Of course her emotions are out of my hands but unless Ty starts being a bit more civil, I'm going to have to have a word with him – warn him off before I leave. He might be scary but he doesn't know how fierce I can be when it comes to protecting my friends.

I hunker down into my sleeping bag. Hmmm. This has been a good lead up to camping, it won't be so much of a shock to the system now. As a matter of fact I think I might enjoy it – Elliot and I in a little nylon triangle making shadow puppets and telling racoon stories, how cosy!

I try and picture the others tucked up – Zoë in some

satin-swathed mirrored boudoir, Elise strapped to a metal hospital bed, or similar. Then a lion roars. Wow, this is a trip! I'd actually feel pretty content at this moment in time if it wasn't for the sound of Sasha softly crying.

14

'Lara, quick!' Sasha shakes me. 'You've got to come and see Ty!'

I open one reluctant eye. 'What's he doing now? Mounting Naomi Campbell's head on a plaque for the lounge?'

'Just get up!'

I yawn, creaking my body into a sitting position. 7 a.m. Not good. 'I think I just had a dream where he dared one of the lions to put *their* head in *his* mouth,' I shudder.

'Quick!' Sasha urges, unzipping the sleeping bag to spare me having to wriggle out. The second I'm on my feet, she's yanking me down the corridor on tiptoe.

As we approach Ty's room, she guides me to the best vantage point, just outside his doorway. At first all I see is a sun-shrouded silhouette but gradually, as my eyes adjust, the detail reveals Ty sitting nursing a tiger cub eagerly sucking on a baby bottle, white-tipped ears flipping forward rhythmically with every glug. I look back at Sasha and smile. Even with an ogre in the frame, it couldn't be a cuter picture.

'Isn't it amazing?' she whispers.

As Sasha's no animal lover I can't help wondering if, in her eyes, the cubs have been upstaged by the sex appeal of the man holding them. Until now I'd been so put off by Ty's hostility, his hottie licence had automatically been revoked. But, this current situation easily affords him a second chance. I turn back and peer a little closer. It's only now I notice that his shirt is entirely unbuttoned and that his smooth leather-brown skin forms a couple of neat creases just above his belt buckle.

Still focusing on the cubs, Ty says, 'Do you wanna come and say hello?'

I freeze. Has he seen me? Perhaps he's talking to someone else.

'Lara?' He looks directly at me.

'Um. I'm not really dressed . . .' I tug at the collar of my pyjamas.

'They won't mind,' he shrugs, adding, 'This is no catwalk' as he notices Sasha.

Oh, he just had to go and spoil it, didn't he? Sasha turns to leave but I grab her hand and pull her in alongside me.

'Wanna hold one?' Ty extends an arm with a dangling furball on the end.

'Are you sure?'

'Just make sure you put a hand under their butt so they feel secure.'

The cub looks so much like a toy I'm surprised to find him warm-bodied and wet of tongue. I shuffle him round so I can rumple the fur on his head. It's soft but not as sleek and silky as I was expecting. In fact, bar his downy pink tummy, his stripy beige ensemble looks and feels like teddy-bear fur that's worn and tufty from excessive cuddling.

'That's Max.'

'Hey boy,' I coo, besotted.

'Short for Maxine. It's a girl,' Ty corrects me.

'Oh.'

I go to pass her to Sasha but she immediately backs off.

'No, it's OK.'

Ty looks up, surprised.

'You can take her,' he says gruffly.

'I'm all right, I'd rather watch.'

'They haven't got fleas, if that's what you're worried about.'

'No, I'm not really good with animals, she'll probably start crying.'

Ty hesitates a moment and then says, 'Take Theo. He won't cry if he's got a bottle in his mouth.'

Lordy Miss Claudie! Are we having a breakthrough? I watch Sasha awkwardly take hold of the cub, trying not to break the contact between his busy mouth and the bottle. 'It's easier if you sit,' Ty suggests, offering his seat.

I watch him watching Sasha and for a moment I see his sneer merge into something that could be mistaken for longing but then he looks towards the ceiling and gives an almost imperceptible shake of his head. I would love to know what's going on inside his mind. Maybe one of the gurus at Elise's retreat could give me an insight?

'Mwwaacch!' Uh-oh. There's a weird bleating-squawking sound coming from Maxine.

'What should I do?' I panic.

'Just set her down on the floor,' Ty tells me.

She looks relieved but also slightly bewildered to be back on all fours. After taking a couple of uncertain steps she plonks herself down and starts chewing on one of Ty's shoes.

'Do you just let them roam around?'

'Not outside. We'll keep them in the house for a few more months.'

'In a cage?'

'In a kids' playpen actually.' He nods over to the corner where there's a wooden-barred one all set up. 'When they're a bit older we'll take them out like Cassidy and Kid for publicity – it helps us raise funds for this place.'

I sigh. 'I can't believe Hollywood is only an hour away. All those mega-buck movie stars . . . What about Julia Roberts? She doesn't seem to lead a particularly extravagant lifestyle – didn't she have a really cheap wedding? She must have a spare million she could donate.'

'I know she likes horses!' Sasha chips in.

'We feed them horses.'

'What?' I gasp.

'If they've been put down from an injury or something.'

Silence.

'Breakfast?' says Ty, scooping up the tiger cubs, one in each hand.

Sasha and I exchange a queasy look.

For the first time I see Ty grin. 'I'll get the coffee on.'

By the time we get to the kitchen Ty is long gone, having just left us a scribbled note, 'Finish what you started yesterday.' Hardly poetry but I notice Sasha stash the piece of paper in her pocket as if it were a personal love letter. It concerns me that she still seems to be craving him but I decide to say nothing, for now.

After fortifying ourselves with toast and apricot jam we resume our clearing of what will one day be Paradise Park. I'd swear we'd only been working for an hour when Ty calls, 'Lunchtime!'

'Thank God!' I cheer. 'I'm starving again!'

Sasha leans her garden rake against the wall and I switch off the hose I've been using to fill Ryan's playpool and together we hurry towards the house.

Ty stands waiting beside a marble tabletop just outside the kitchen. As we approach he throws down a slab of bloodied meat.

'Are we having a barbecue?' I ask.

'It's Tahira's dinner, not yours. I need it cut into cubes,' he instructs, handing Sasha a knife.

'I'm vegetarian,' she says, shrinking back.

'Just as well I'm not asking you to eat it then, huh?' Again he thrusts the knife at her.

'I can't.'

'Is it horse?' I ask ghoulishly.

'No,' Ty rolls his eyes.

Sasha contemplates the moist flesh. 'It feels like murder.'

'D'you wanna try and be a bit more dramatic?' he scoffs.

'How can you call yourself an animal lover and do this?' Sasha gulps.

'It's not nice but it's a fact of life. These cats can't hunt for themselves, I've got to do what it takes to feed them.'

Sasha raises the knife, blanching as she goes to make the first incision, then stumbles back, shuddering.

I reach out to her. 'Are you OK? You don't have to do this.'

'No, you don't,' Ty confirms.

We look up at him, surprised by his compassion.

'Just go along and tell Tahira she's going to go hungry today. She's the one in the back cage. I'm sure she'll understand.'

And with that he turns his back, heaving a wheelbarrow full of quartered chickens towards the cages.

My phone goes. It's Elise. The last person I want to speak to but I remember my promise to Helen to give her equal airtime and seeing as Sasha has ducked out to the loo, I listen patiently to an exhaustive rant about what a waste of time the morning's 'Facing your Fury' class was. When she's done I tell her that I know at least one person who could benefit from a little anger management, i.e. Ty. Elise is not convinced so I proceed to gross her out with the chopping-raw-meat story.

'I mean, why is he bullying Sasha like that?' I wail,

forgetting for a moment that I don't value Elise's opinion enough to hear what she has to say.

'It's obvious,' Elise clips. 'He fancies her.'

'Bit of an Ozzy Osbourne-style courtship, don't you think? No, it's not that.'

'Are you sure?'

'Trust me, you wouldn't think so if you saw how he looks at her.' Other than the fleeting moment with the cubs, it's been pure visual vitriol.

'Ah, but that's a reaction to how she's making him feel about himself, not what he really feels about *her*.'

Blimey! Two days at Guru Camp and she's already fluent in psycho-speak.

'Wait there – let me get Martha, she's brilliant at this kind of thing.'

'Elise!'

'What?'

'I thought you said it was all hokey crap!'

'Well, it's no use to me because I don't have temper tantrums but for some of the frothing-at-the-mouth crazies here I'd say it's been quite beneficial.'

What a wonderfully supportive environment she must be supplying for the rest of the group.

Martha comes on the line, fully briefed.

'I need you to tell me exactly what he's said and then we'll work out a way to get him to roll over,' she promises.

It's got to be worth a shot so I relate every sentence Ty has spat at Sasha. When I'm done Martha says she could do with some more background information and reminds me that this isn't my battle to fight, but I don't agree – Sasha is wounded and even if she wasn't I'd feel protective. Besides, it's actually easier fighting other people's battles, don't you think? At least that way you know it's worth the fight.

The rather more pressing factor is that I've only got a matter of hours to sort this thing out. I can't just drive off and leave her, I'd feel I was throwing her to the lions. Now I've got a few starter insights from Martha (and Sasha's occupied in the loo) I decide I'm going to confront him. Even if he does have some pretty lethal friends on his side.

As I open the gate the leopards start freaking out – hissing and screeching, scrapping with flick-knife claws flailing. A couple go at each other on their hind legs while another opts for curious intimidation tactics – crouching low and twisting its fully fanged head up at another. The noise of the fracas is incredible.

What on earth is going on? Do they know that I'm out to get their master? Has Freddie's arch-rival Malachi instigated some crazy mutiny? Then I see Ty trundling up with a fresh wheelbarrow of chickens. They know it's feeding time and they obviously have very strong feelings about whether they want a leg or a wing.

Ty tips the wheelbarrow upright at the fencing, pressing the meat into waiting jaws. I expect them to savage their quarry, gulping it down in one but instead they find their own private space to dine, away from the dusty-earthy floor – either on the top of the den box or on the concrete border of the cage, presumably to prevent the 'sand in your sandwiches' factor. I watch Freddie lick the skin until it stretches away from the pink flesh and slithers up into his mouth. Taking a moment to debate which bit to eat next, he decides to break it down, splintering the bones with a satisfying crunch.

'They eat the bones,' Carrie tells me, having snuck up while I was engrossed in leopard table manners. 'It's a great source of calcium for them – good for their teeth and bones.'

'They were so ferocious just now,' I marvel.

Carrie nods. 'You've got to remember these animals are essentially wild.'

Same goes double for Ty, I think to myself as I watch him press a handful of raw McNuggets through the cage for a less pushy member of the pack. The leopard chomps them down then licks Ty's palm to make sure she hasn't missed any delicious gristle.

'I'm just going to get some supplies from the vet, I'll be back in an hour or two.' Carrie pats me on the back.

'OK,' I nod, instantly drawn back to the leopards. Having enjoyed their starter they return to the barrow buffet for seconds and thirds. I wonder if they ever tire of chicken. Maybe, just maybe, one of them is craving a little braised tofu.

'Where's your friend?' Ty shouts over.

'She's just thrown up,' I say, as pointedly as possible. No reaction.

'Doesn't that bother you?' I narrow my eyes at him.

'She's a model isn't she? I'm sure she's had plenty of practice.'

I want to scream, What the hell is your problem? but he's coming straight at me with the wheelbarrow. I leap back to avoid a clash. He glowers at me as he passes. I take an indignant breath. What's that smell? It's not the raw chicken or animal droppings. Something more fumey. Not petrol. Turps? I do have a painting chore this afternoon. Then I twig. Whiskey. It's fading now but it was coming from Ty's mouth.

Is he Mr Angry because he's an alcoholic? Perhaps I should take Martha's advice and gather a bit more information before I confront him. As I wander through the pens I stop beside an unfamiliar furry face.

'What's your name?' I ask, searching for a plaque.

He makes a sound akin to a weight-lifter's grunt but I can't translate.

'Here it is!' I pick up the wooden sign and hook it back on to the fencing. 'Troy.'

Something clicks in my head – 'Troy! Of course, Helen! She'll know what to do.'

I dial her number, praying I'm not disturbing a crucial spurt of icing.

'Hello?'

'Helen! It's Lara. I think we may have a problem.'

I bring her swiftly up to speed on Ty's unacceptable behaviour but Helen is dismissive.

'Sasha'll be fine, she's dealt with enough designer histrionics in her time.'

'But this is different,' I contend.

'How so?'

'Well apart from the fact they were shrimpy queens and he's a big macho lug, she fancies him.'

'And you're worried it's some kind of manifestation of her self-loathing, the fact that she's attracting abuse to her?'

'Does everyone start talking like that when they move to California?'

Helen laughs.

I restate my case, Cali-style: 'I'm just concerned that, seeing how fragile she is at the moment, maybe this isn't the best environment for her.'

'Please don't worry, Lara. It's going to be fine. This place has been carefully selected by The California Club. Besides, it's just five more nights. If she has any major problems she can always call you.'

'But what if I'm in Yosemite? That's hundreds of miles from here.'

'Zoë's just an hour away in LA. If she can't terrorize him into submission, no one can.'

She's got a point.

'Everything is going to turn out for the best, trust me.'

'If you're sure . . .'

'I am. Listen, I've got to go, my soufflé is about to collapse.'

The line goes dead.

I turn to Troy. He looks at me as if to say, If Helen says it's OK . . . then shakes his mane. I sigh and return to the house to get my next assignment.

For the next few hours I busy myself painting fence posts, while Sasha gets her first lesson in animal environment hygiene. No prizes for guessing who assigned the tasks. Still, I reckon Ty is going soft in his old age because he's given her cages without tigers in to clean.

It's now 1 p.m. I'm running out of time – just half an hour before I'm due to leave. I look over at Sasha. Whereas I'm already on my fifth fence post, she's made almost no progress clearing out the first cage. She keeps stopping, leaning heavily on the shovel and visibly fighting back the tears. If it wasn't for Ty's watchful and ever more belligerent eye on us I'd go over and comfort her. But I know that would only bring on another tirade.

'How are you getting on?' Carrie appears by my side.

'Fine, just two more to go. Did you get what you needed from the vet?'

'Yup, just going to administer it now.' She looks over at Sasha. 'I guess she's not used to getting her hands dirty,' she says.

'Really, she's not like that,' I insist.

'Does *she* know that?'

Good question.

'To be honest, this is all quite new to her – she's only recently stopped modelling so the new non-model her, the real her, is still a work in progress,' I explain.

'She's trying to find out who she is on the inside?' Carrie enquires.

I nod.

'Does she still think all she's got is her looks?'

'I'm afraid so.'

'No wonder she's not ready to let go.'

I look at poor Sasha. Warring with herself. I know part of her wants to throw down that shovel, climb head-first into her sleeping bag and weep until next Tuesday. I wonder if I should tell Carrie how depressed she is, perhaps ask her to ask Ty to lay down his arms. And legs and torso, for that matter. If he didn't speak he could really be quite attractive.

'You know she's doing it the wrong way round, don't you?'

'How d'you mean?' Is there some special technique to shovelling poo that I don't know about?

'She can't find herself and then let go of her looks, she's got to take a leap of faith and let go of her looks first.'

Easier said than done. Of course this would be as good a place as any to get hideously disfigured, which would be a start.

'I don't think she's naturally vain,' Carrie muses. 'It's just been very deeply ingrained in her.'

Sasha hoiks up the wheelbarrow to deposit the stuff she's cleared but hits a rock two paces along, the barrow flips on to its side and everything she's just cleared comes tumbling out.

'Oh no!' I cry.

'Maybe you should show her how it's done,' Carrie suggests.

'Me?'

Carrie raises an 'I dare you!' eyebrow.

I grin back. 'OK! Why not!'

I set down my paintbrush and run over to Sasha.

'You seem to be having way too much fun, mind if I join you?' I say.

'Oh Lara!'

I hold up a hand, as if somehow this will freeze-frame her before she starts blubbing. Oddly it seems to work. 'Now I don't know what kind of warped individual you are, but according to The California Club this is your dream come true so I think it's about time you started embracing the poo!'

Sasha blinks in disbelief. 'Embracing the poo?'

'Come on now, you are in gorgeous sunny California ankle deep in tiger excrement, what more could you want? Think of all your poor model friends getting bunions in their Manolos, shaking from the diet pills—'

'Going barefoot at Pink Sands in Barbados, sipping champagne in Paris,' Sasha cuts in.

'Right!' I waver.

For a moment I think Sasha's going to have a 360-degree revelation and decide she wants to go back to modelling till she's advertising anti-wrinkle creams and Zimmer frames, but then her expression changes.

'If they could see me now!' she hoots.

'What would they say?' I grin, egging her on.

She looks down at her muck-encrusted feet and then around at the ramshackle set-up and the hazy mountains beyond and a big smile erupts on her face. 'They'd say I was mad!'

'Well, that's one piece of the puzzle in place!' I cheer.

'Am I mad?'

'Walking away from a life of privilege and luxury? Of course!'

'Maybe I want more from life.'

'Well, what would that say about you?' I probe.

'That those things don't matter to me? That I tried them and they were nice for a while but they didn't float my yacht.'

'So what would you call someone who followed their heart and threw it all away even though they didn't know what was coming next? Someone who was willing to take a chance on a new life, even though they didn't know what it was?'

Sasha takes a deep breath then purses her lips.

I wait.

Then she says it.

'Brave?'

I nod.

'I'm brave!' She tests out the sentence and likes how it fits. 'I'm brave!' she says, bolder now. 'Look at me!' she laughs, wielding the spade. 'Owwww!' She doubles up in pain.

'What?' I run to her side.

'Splinter!'

'Let me see.' I take her hand in mine.

Suddenly the sound of sarcasm fills the air.

'Aw, did you break a nail? Let me go call the 24-hour manicurist – we have one on standby for just these kind of emergencies . . .' Ty camps it up as he passes.

This time Sasha doesn't crumble. She just picks up a clod of dry poo and throws it at him.

215

Unfortunately (or maybe extremely fortunately) she's a terrible shot, misses him by a mile and he walks on oblivious, though I very much doubt he could miss our hysterical laughter.

'Well it makes a change,' I sigh, wiping my eyes.

'What does?'

'Having a man hate you for your looks instead of a girl.'

I decide to take my leave while Sasha is riding high. After a quick farewell tour of the cats (it's a particular wrench to walk away from Ryan – something about the way he looks at me, so knowing . . .) I move on to the humans, and hug Carrie. No sign of Ty. Shame.

As Sasha walks me to the car, it occurs to me that Carrie will be gone in a matter of hours (off to raise funds in San Fran), leaving Sasha alone with Ty at night.

'Are you going to be OK?'

She nods.

'Just keep in mind that it's his problem,' I advise her. 'He's obviously got some massive chip on his shoulder.'

'I can handle him!' Sasha tells me, still thriving on her newly discovered bravery. 'You just concentrate on making the most of your time with Elliot. And give Zoë my love – let me know how she's getting on.'

'Will do,' I smile.

I give Sasha one final squeeze and then hit the accelerator – City of Angels here I come!

15

I stand before the grand art deco building at the crossing of Hollywood and Highland. Wow! Zoë really is living the life. The granite has been sculpted to look like drapes of material slung between the tall pink columns and even the cement flashes and sparkles with embedded glitter. It looks more like a giant dressing table constructed with Carole Lombard in mind than an apartment block, and any minute now I expect Zoë to emerge in marabou-trimmed chiffon flicking ash from an elongated cigarette holder into some poor minion's bare hands.

It's what she's always wanted – a life of unreal glitz to finally obliterate her grim and grimy past. Although I actually think she was already doing a pretty good job herself, creating a new life. She thought so too until she started buying into the media idea that your life isn't complete unless you have your own camera crew following you twenty-four hours a day. Before that she had a good balance of doing something worthwhile by day (her job at the Dyspraxia Foundation) and partying like a maniac at night. And she was happy.

But lately that undue sense of entitlement that people have today has been rubbing off on her. She's come so far but it's still not far enough. She wants the dream – the Malibu beach-house, the Valentino dress, the convertible Mercedes – everything but the *Vanity Fair* cover husband. (She'd rather have a series of coverboy lovers.) I wonder whether she's managed to secure a date with Josh Hartnett yet – presumably she's been given a little black book featuring every eligible movie star in town. Maybe she's with him right now.

Stepping closer, I peer in the darkened windows. Hmmm. Unless she's squatting in the old Max Factor museum I've been given the wrong address. Hold on, this is 1660. I want 1650 . . . I check out the building next door and read the squiggle of pink neon in the window – *Mel's 50s Style Diner*.

This can't be right. I step inside and ask the girl on the till if there are apartments above the diner. She tells me it's all offices so I try calling Helen on her mobile but it goes straight to voicemail. Oh well, I may as well suck up a quick root beer float while I await her call.

The diner is huge with endless chrome-trimmed booths, giant blow-ups of black-and-white photos on the walls and ridged aluminium pipes snaking around the ceiling, lending a somewhat out-of-keeping warehouse-conversion feel to the place. Each table is set with regulation sugar-shaker, pourable mustard and a dainty china vase containing a spray that looks exactly like a wedding buttonhole – one pink carnation and a smattering of gypsophila. Perhaps I'm missing something and it's really a prom corsage.

Mentally I slip on a pair of bobby socks and start flicking through the tunes on the mini-jukebox: *Mr Sandman, Chantilly Lace, Candy Girl* . . .

'Welcome to Mel's!' The waitress sets down a glass of iced water on my table. 'What can I get you?'

'Actually I haven't had a chance to—' Hold on. There's something familiar in that voice. My eyes slant sideways . . . 'Zoë!' I screech, practically jumping out of my booth.

'Lara!' she screams, sending a cluster of paper-covered straws flying in a fluster of mortification. 'What are you doing here?'

'Looking for you!' I splutter, incredulous at the little white pointy napkin in her hair. She's even got a name badge, for God's sake.

'But–but . . .' Zoë flusters, looking so guilty you'd think she'd just been caught trying to run out the door with a stash of hamburger patties in her pockets.

'I don't know why *you're* acting so surprised,' I cut in. 'You're the one wearing a pinny!'

Zoë cringes and covers her face. There I was expecting those hands to have been manicured to doll-like perfection when the reality is she's even managed to gnaw through her acrylic nails.

'Why didn't you tell me you were working here?' I reel as my visions of her sprawling in the back of a limo with Colin Farrell et al. fizzle and fade.

'I didn't want you to know!' she wails, looking sheepish.

'But why?'

'I made such a big deal of the Hollywood high life I was headed for and this isn't exactly what I had in mind.'

I can see that.

'Why didn't you ring up to bitch and moan? I would have done!'

'I didn't want to bring you down – you know, set you worrying that I was having a bad time.'

'And are you?' I ask softly.

'Smell my hair . . .'

'Cheeseburger with extra onions?' I hazard a guess.

'Tuna Melt and twisty fries,' she corrects.

'Oh Zoë!' I sympathize. She didn't deserve this. She only wanted to have some fun.

'Is this going to last all week?' I ask.

Zoë nods, visibly crumpling at the prospect. 'Apparently waitressing is the most common profession for a Hollywood wannabe so here I am.' Her shoulders slump further. 'And we thought Elise would be the first to bail out!'

'You wouldn't!'

Zoë shakes her head. 'No, of course not. No matter what.'

I didn't think so. She's a trouper, is Zoë, she'll find a way to turn this around, I'm sure.

'Maybe they've got some auditions lined up and international superstardom is just a day or two away?' I suggest, groping for some hope.

'Maybe.' Zoë's not convinced.

I look down at the table. I don't know how to make this better. Hold on – I wonder if Sasha kept the number for that fleshy-lobed director guy from the Hotel Del. Maybe he could do something.

'Everything OK?' A chipper waiter with a face crying out to be plastered across a billboard stops by.

'Yes, sireee!' Zoë zaps herself back into perky waitress mode. 'This is my friend Lara.'

'Heyyy! I'm Todd.' He extends the hand not holding a chocolate malt shake. 'You coming out with us tonight? We're going to the Beauty Bar – $10 for a cocktail and a manicure!'

'I wish I could but I've got a flight at 7 p.m.'

'Oh no – I don't finish till ten,' Zoë sighs. 'We can't even have a proper chat.'

'Don't worry, I just wanted to say Hi!' I try and calm her. I'm beginning to regret dropping by – I only seem to be making things worse for her. 'Tell you what – I'll just spend the next two hours eating my way through the menu so you can keep coming back to my table,' I tell her, swiftly scanning the options. 'The '57 Ford Omelette sounds good.'

'The Elvis Scramble is better,' Todd recommends, bowing out to deliver his shake.

'I can't even show you round my hood,' Zoë pouts.

'I'll be back in two days,' I say and give her hand a surreptitious squeeze.

'Hey!' Todd reappears still carrying the shake. 'I just thought – if you want I can cover your shift till seven?'

'What?' Zoë blinks.

'That way you can hang out and see your friend off at the airport.'

'Really?' Zoë's face lights up like a spotlight has picked her out.

'Sure, I could use the extra cash, I'm saving up to get new headshots.'

'He's an actor,' Zoë says proudly.

'Do you think it's allowed?' I lower my voice. 'You know, California Club regulations.'

I don't want to see her relegated to washing dishes.

'They'll never know!' Zoë starts untying her apron. 'Todd, you're an angel.'

'Don't I know it!' he winks. 'You girls have fun!'

We exit Mel's with linked arms and a spring in our step.

'At least it's sunny!' I rally.

'Yes it is,' Zoë smiles up at the palm-tipped skyline with newfound glee. 'Really, it's not so bad. Todd keeps my pecker up.'

'And vice versa?'

'No, he's gay,' she laughs, guiding me across the road. 'You know there are some crossing signs that actually count you down across the street now – 20 seconds, 19, 18 . . . the numbers flash up on a display like in the movies when the bomb is just about to explode!'

'Really?'

Zoë nods, looking tickled, then suddenly gets serious. 'I guess I just got my hopes up too high,' she confesses. 'I wanted the whole thing handed to me on a plate and here I am handing out plates myself! How ironic.'

I love how Zoë's mind works.

'Has it made you think any differently about the whole fame game?' I wonder out loud, hoping some good has come of this.

'Well, not so much the waitressing itself but the stories the other girls tell me.' She shakes her head. 'I mean, some of them have got their heads screwed on but they can't get a break, others are totally delusional and I reckon they're still going to be sloshing lemonade when they're sixty. You think I've got it bad, you want to hear some of them talk – they really believe that someone's going to run in one day and say, "Our leading lady has singed off the left side of her face with a pair of straightening irons and we need you on set *now*!"'

I'm fairly certain that scenario has played in Zoë's head a few times. Personally my favoured daydream involves being a stand-in for a tardy actress during a kissing scene – the director wants a run-through for lighting and camera angles and subsequently the leading man decides he prefers kissing me, the other actress is fired and my movie début is secured. Actually, that particular fantasy has always been more about me getting to kiss my favourite movie stars than becoming one myself but I can see how easy it would be to start wishing your life away.

'So how does all this make you feel?' I ask Zoë, curious as to whether The California Club has succeeded in bringing her down to earth with a bump, if that was indeed the plan.

'Sad, I guess,' Zoë replies. 'It does happen for some but I'm fairly certain it's not going to happen for any of the girls I'm working with. At first I listened to them and thought, "Yes but I'm different, it could happen to me!" but then I realized (a) they're all thinking that and (b) I've never even taken an acting lesson – what makes me think I can just swan into this town and be discovered? What is there to discover, anyway?'

It occurs to me that Zoë is already discovering a fair few things about herself, but for all her super-positivity she hates it when people get all deep and analytical on her so I say nothing.

'Anyway, enough about me!' Zoë changes tack. 'What's going on with you?'

'Well, as you know I'm just off to see Elliot in Yosemite—'

'I mean about the B&B. Talk about dropping a bomb!'

I find myself inadvertenly coming to a halt. Apparently I can't walk and lie at the same time.

'I really think it's for the best—' I begin.

'No you don't.'

I sigh. I can't fool Zoë, she knows me too well, knows my heart inside out.

'It's OK, I understand,' she says, not wanting to make me squirm further. 'I was just thinking the other day – imagine if the first time I walked through the door there, someone had said to us, "You two girls are

224

going to be walking arm in arm down Hollywood Boulevard in ten years' time!"'

'We would never have believed them!' I finish her thought.

'How could we? How could we have seen this future for ourselves? Just like we can't see what's coming next. I mean, just cos it's looking a bit bleak now doesn't mean it's not going to get better, does it?'

'No,' I say simply.

'My life got so much better the day I met you,' Zoë says, hitting me straight in the heart.

'Oh Zoë!' I give her a big sisterly hug, eyes spilling over in an instant. 'We're going to be fine!'

'Of course we are,' she sniffs, never one to wallow in excessive sentiment. 'So, d'you want to see some stars?' she twinkles, blinking back her tears, more than ready for some escapism.

'Of course!' I enthuse, squishing my puffed-up heart back down to normal size. 'Show me!'

Twenty minutes later we've trodden on some of the greatest names in movie history – Al Pacino, Marlon Brando, Meryl Streep – and some big surprises.

'Can you believe that David Hasselhoff has a star on Hollywood Boulevard?' Zoë gapes at the gold-trimmed pink granite.

'And look – Tony Danza! Remember him?'

'Excuse me, ma'am!' A tousled blond sidesteps Zoë.

'Oh my God! Was that Brad Pitt?' she yelps. 'It was! Freaking Nora! And look – Drew Barrymore!'

Before I have time to tell her to get a grip I find myself exclaiming,

'George Clooney!'

We clutch each other, getting whiplash as suddenly the tourists and hookers on Hollywood Boulevard find themselves outnumbered by celebrity A-listers.

'Where've they all come from?' I cry, dodging a petite Reece Witherspoon and bear-like John Travolta.

'Well, it is the Oscars in a few days,' Zoë manages to reason through her hyperventilation. 'Maybe they're having some kind of rehearsal dinner?'

She could have a point: the Kodak Theater where the awards are held is just across the street. All the same, I can't believe they're just milling around un-entouraged.

'Isn't that Audrey Hepburn?' I gasp, coveting her little black dress.

'Yes!' Zoë whoops.

'Hold on, she's dead!' I frown.

Calista Flockhart walks past. There's something not quite right about her . . . there's flesh on them there bones!

'They all seem to be heading for the Hollywood Roosevelt Hotel,' Zoë observes.

'Let's follow them!' I suggest, advancing hot on the heels of Samuel L Jackson.

The entire lobby is abuzz with celebs all doing what Sandra Bullock refers to as the cocktail laugh – throwing your head back and cackling open-mouthed.

'Julia Roberts!' Zoë and I cry in unison. We're pointing in different directions. We're both right.

It's at that point we're handed a brochure: *'The Reel Movie Awards. Hollywood's Premier Celebrity Lookalike Ceremony,'* I read. 'Aha! that could explain why there are seven Marilyn Monroes over at the bar.'

'Some of them are really good but look at that Tom Cruise, he's got to be six foot, dead giveaway that it's not the real deal.'

'I think Hugh Grant's making a move on Meg Ryan,' I nudge Zoë. 'Actually they'd make a cute couple, wonder why they've never got together in real life?'

'Oooh, I want to play dress-up!' Zoë yearns. 'That's the best thing about being an actress – trying out all those looks.' Suddenly she jolts herself. 'La! I just remembered! Betty at work was telling me about this amazing fancy dress place near Vine, they make you over into a movie star and then they film you doing a five-minute scene from your favourite movie! Do you wanna go?'

'Do I have a choice?' I grin.

'I was saving it until you got here and now—'

'I'm here!' I hoot.

'Come on!' Zoë bundles me back out to the street sending an unconvincing Keanu Reeves flying. 'He needs to work on his *Matrix* moves,' she mutters as we scurry back to the car.

Cruising down Hollywood Boulevard, I try to imagine it in its heyday with men in tweed knickerbockers and loud-hailers and women in satin gowns and clasp purses. Now it's all touristy shops selling tacky T-shirts and over-the-knee stiletto boots in glittering Perspex for that essential Prostitute Barbie look.

'There are some real nutters round here,' Zoë confides. 'The further away you get from Mann's Chinese Theater the seedier it gets.'

'Sounds scary,' I worry.

'They're more the type to jump out at you and talk gibberish than do you any real harm,' Zoë assures me.

'I hope you don't go walking round here at night.'

'This is it!' Zoë points to the right. 'There's a carpark round the back.'

Once inside we're greeted with row upon row of bewigged Styrofoam heads from rainbow Afro to Marie Antoinette. There's a sign telling us to wait for an assistant before trying anything on but no one is around so I cover my own short black hair with a sleek waist-length wig. Imagine taking ten seconds to get ready in the morning, I muse as I smooth it in place – no bad hair days, just good Cher days.

'This tiara looks like a cathedral!' Zoë is dazzled by the heaps of fake ice in the jewellery case, then moves on to a parade of ornate Venetian masks and then – hello? – a case full of boobs and bums available in shiny plastic or squishy foam. I'm amused to note the price tag on the boobs – $12.99 *a pair*. Like you're just gonna buy a single breast.

Sensing movement above me I look up to see a rail of stroke-me feather boas – just out of reach, all swirling in the air conditioning. When I look back, Zoë is gone.

'Where are you?' I call.

'Over here by the decorative barbed wire!' she replies from the depths of the all-year-round Hallowe'en aisle.

'Oh that's nice,' I shudder, picking up a sword that bubbles with blood.

'I wish The California Club had placed me here,' Zoë sighs. 'Imagine getting to dress up as a different person every day.'

'This coconut bikini would be ideal for Tuesdays,' I tease, finding another nook of goodies: 'Real coconut shells, available in small, medium or large.'

'Look at this!' Zoë is distracted by a giant furry kangaroo costume with a pouch designed to accommodate a life-size baby. 'I am so getting that for when I'm a mum.'

For a moment I just stare at Zoë. There is no one like her on earth. Then I spot the booth where the filming takes place. Zoë can't see it because she's trying on a pair of 'Chop Suey Specs'. How PC.

As I catch sight of my reflection in the Mirror, Mirror on the Wall I'm forced to acknowledge that it's going to take a fair bit of work to turn me into a Hollywood starlet. 'How long have we got, Zo?' I worry.

'Let's see,' she says, setting down a genie lamp so she can study her watch. 'It's just after 3 p.m. now, flight leaves at 7 p.m. We could have an hour here, an hour for an early dinner in case Elliot is planning on feeding you barbecued squirrel, an hour to get to the airport and one hour to check in. Plenty of time!'

'Hoorah!' I cheer, heading back to the wigs.

'Holy Mary!' Zoë hisses, stopping me in my tracks.

That's her nickname for pierced people, on account of all their holes/perforations. I discreetly turn and find a face peppered with metallic acne glowering at me from behind the counter. Even the girl's ears are tattooed and she has what looks like a corkscrew skewered through her bottom lip.

'Bet she's handy to have at parties!' Zoë notes.

'Wouldn't be any good at blowing up balloons, though,' I wince.

Heaving herself out of her deadbeat slump, Holy Mary introduces herself: 'I'm Vixen and I'll be your transformer today.'

Her delivery is pure morgue menace. She obviously wants to get the ordeal of transforming us over and done with as quick as possible and wastes no time assigning us a celebrity lookalike each: 'You I could do as Lara Flynn Boyle in *Men In Black 2*,' she addresses me. 'And you' – she squints at Zoë – 'Beyonce in *Goldmember*.'

We exchange a dubious glance. I suppose we should be grateful she doesn't want to make us into Elvira and Morticia, or the scariest of them all – Christina Aguilera – but it's not what we had in mind.

'Um . . .' we falter.

Vixen tries again. 'Catherine Zeta-Jones and Jennifer Lopez?'

She's still not looking beyond our natural colouring. Hasn't she seen the wig changes in *Charlie's Angels*? Surely in Hollywood anything is possible.

'I want to be Marilyn!' Zoë asserts.

Vixen rotates her tongue stud and gives me a look as if to say: If you tell me you want to be Whoopi Goldberg I'm going to resign.

I try the diplomatic approach. 'Your suggestions are great but we were thinking more of classic Hollywood stars.'

'That's kinda old,' she sneers. 'But if that's what you want.' She thuds a hefty Book of Looks on to the counter and pushes it towards Zoë.

'What about Carmen Miranda?'

'Would you want a bowl of fruit on your head?' Zoë counters, not enjoying this girl's attitude.

'I take these two beauties!' A heavy Russian accent announces. It belongs to a sixtysomething man with a lush sweep of white hair and expertly shaped eyebrows. Sending Vixen to prepare the Harry Potter costumes for the dry cleaners, he introduces himself as the shop owner, Boris, and apologizes for his niece.

'She's very skilled at the make-up but lacks charm,' he admits. 'Now! Let me see.' He studies our faces carefully. Something about his manner and the low rumble of his voice has us entranced. 'You want heyday movie stars, yes?'

We nod, hypnotized by his violet-lensed eyes.

'You would make wonderful Liz Taylor, *Cat on a Hot Tin Roof*,' he strokes my jaw.

I purr appreciatively, 'Oooh yes, that would be lovely.'

'And you have Marilyn's curves, that is for sure.' He gives Zoë an appreciative once-over. 'You leave rest to me!'

231

Zoë claps her hands together with delight as he flips the Book of Looks around to face her. 'OK honey, which Marilyn you want to be?'

First up is the iconic white flare-up dress from *Seven Year Itch*.

'Too obvious?' Zoë voices her concern.

'Little,' Boris acknowledges.

Next, pink satin and diamonds.

'Too Madonna, *Material Girl*,' Zoë frowns.

'What about an outfit from *Some Like It Hot*?' I suggest, remembering the Hotel Del.

'The nude beaded dress?' Boris's eyes light up. 'I think it will stretch.'

'Oooh yes!' Zoë enthuses, envisioning herself sheathed and shimmering.

'Maybe you want to do mini-movie scene together? I could make you good Tony Curtis,' he tells me, 'you have his clear eyes, black hair, we could do a little dimple here . . .'

I bat his hand away as he goes to smudge brown eyeshadow on my chin.

'I want to be a girl!' I protest.

'Oh go on, La!' Zoë begs, taken with the idea. 'We could show Helen – how funny would that be? She could put a picture of us up at work!'

'Can't you come back and do that with Todd?' I frown as Boris tries to set a captain's cap on my head.

'No?' he frowns, looking plaintive.

'No!' I pout. 'Isn't there something we could do together as two females?'

232

'Marilyn starred in *There's No Business Like Show Business* with Ethel Merman,' Zoë recalls.

'Thanks a bunch. I think Tony Curtis is prettier.'

'I've got it!' Boris swishes down the rails and in one flourish produces two floor-length red sequined gowns: '*Gentlemen Prefer Blondes*!'

'Of course!' Zoë whoops, grabbing my arm. 'You get to be Jane Russell!'

'Gentlemen also love the ladies with the black hair,' Boris winks at me.

'Sold!' I cheer.

'We wouldn't even need a wig for you,' he says, sweeping my hair over to the side and flouncing it up, 'We set you just so.'

'This is so exciting!' Zoë squeaks. 'What do we do first?'

'Take off your clothes!' Boris announces.

I knew there'd be a catch.

'Or at least your tops.'

I can't believe he's trying to negotiate a strip. Then he hands us robes and explains that he doesn't want to get any make-up on our nice outfits. Fair enough.

'You want I play you the movie while we do the make-up?'

'Oh yes! Can we sing, *'We're Just Two Little Girls from Little Rock!'* Zoë requests.

'Why not?!' Boris complies.

*

As Boris pastes on a mask of foundation he tells us stories of Hollywood's first make-up artist – George Westmore – and how his six sons all followed his

233

brushstrokes to create a dynasty of creative geniuses heading up make-up departments at Paramount, Warner Brothers, 20th Century Fox et al.

'They were responsible for taking Rita Hayworth's natural black hair and make it strawberry blonde!' he begins in his stilted accent, continuing with revelations that Shirley Temple's ringlets were supplemented by hair bought from a local whorehouse and how Errol Flynn turned up drunk to every make-up seating for the swashbuckling flick *Captain Blood* and even resorted to injecting oranges with vodka when Perc Westmore confiscated his bottles of whiskey disguised as hair tonic preparations!

As Boris highlights our browbones he tells of how Marlene Dietrich taught Ern Westmore a nifty alternative to heavy black greasepaint – she held a lit match under the base of a china saucer until a smudge of pure carbon collected, then mixed in a little baby oil and used it as shadow around her eye!

'I love all this stuff – tell me more!' Zoë begs as Boris applies what look like the wings of a blackbird to her lids.

'Well, George Westmore was first to invent false lashes – he had hand-laced a wig for young starlet named Billie Burke and talked her into letting him do her make-up. To help define her eyes he clipped tiny pieces of hair from the wig and pasted them on to her lashes one strand at a time! That was 1917!'

'This is so relaxing,' I sigh, eyes closed, as Boris tends to my lashes.

'You know Mont Westmore once went to Gloria

234

Swanson's home to do make-up before filming and found her still in her bed,' Boris yarns. 'He was too afraid to wake her – she had such a dark temper – so he did the whole thing while she slept!'

'So movie stars really do wake up with a full face of make-up!' I laugh.

'Still, please!' Boris carefully lines my lips. 'Another time he went to do the same for Mae West but she greeted him stark naked and refused to cover herself up so he left!'

'Morals are a terrible hindrance,' Zoë sighs. 'Wow, Lara you look stunning!'

'No peeking please till I finish,' Boris scolds.

Zoë leans back in her chair, waiting her turn.

'Even today Ms Russell is most striking woman,' Boris informs us. 'Strong, passionate, smart.'

'It's amazing to think she's still around,' I muse.

'She's not only legend who lives. Lena Horn is still good-looking woman and you see Debbie Reynolds – now she is Mrs Adler in hit sitcom *Will & Grace*!'

'That's Lara's favourite!'

'I love Jack!' I just manage to squeeze out the words before Boris applies layer upon layer of lipstick so red and thick and luscious I suspect he's using strawberry jam.

Boris finishes Zoë's face and our respective hairdos with precision flair then announces: 'Now the dresses . . .'

'Wow! They weigh a ton!' I gasp, confusing the plunging V-neckline with the high side-split on the leg.

'They say Ginger Rogers's gowns were so heavily

235

beaded that they made her feet bleed when she danced.'

'Ouch!'

'Sequins is OK, just a little rash!' he smiles, handing us our jewellery – two diamond bracelets on one arm, three for the other. 'Turn around, I put on necklace.'

Again diamonds, surrounded by rubies. We pat the jewels flat.

'Earrings . . .' he continues.

I feel my lobes squish to the size of bottle tops from the metal clasp.

'You'll get used to it,' Boris consoles, sensing my pain. Then he takes Zoë's hand and slides a ruby ring into place, looking for all the world like he's her adoring groom.

'One final touch . . .'

He hands us each a red sequined cap sprouting white feathers, securing them on our crowns with a pin.

His eyes shine with pride. 'Ready for your close-up?'

Zoë takes my hand and squeezes it tight before nodding.

'First close your eyes!' he instructs as he guides us to the full-length mirror. 'Now open!'

I have a bit of difficulty as my false lashes have intertwined, lacing my lids closed but I can hear Zoë practically choking with delight. Boris rushes to my aid and carefully prises open my eyes. I get a rush of hysteria at the sight of the glittering vamp before me and twist around to admire the sumptuous alien form that has invaded my body.

'We look like real women!' Zoë giggles, hands traversing her ever more exaggerated curves.

'Sirens!' Boris corrects. 'What man could resist you now?'

He's got a point – the dresses seem to have a powerful sexual presence of their own, demanding a certain sassiness from the wearer. I find myself arching my back, jutting a knee forward and placing a come-and-get-it-boys hand on my hip. How I wish Elliot could see me like this. The double-take alone could jolt the block in his brain that's preventing him from falling in love with me.

'Look at you blonde!' I exclaim, finally tearing my eyes away from my alter ego to gawp at a barely recognizable Zoë.

'Look at you bouffant!' Zoë reels at my big hair.

'I love it!' gently I touch my rollered set. Amazingly it still feels like hair despite all the spray. 'We look so glamorous!'

'I wish we could stay like this for ever!' Zoë breathes, taking a closer look at her beauty spot.

'This may be my finest work,' Boris sighs contentedly. 'Although I did a fabulous Liz Hurley last week.'

'Gosh, I didn't think women liked her enough to want to dress up as her,' I ponder.

'Oh no, honey, it was a man. The men make the best Liz Hurley, also Celine Dion.'

'You're a genius!' Zoë plants a perfect red cupid's bow lip-print on his cheek.

He looks dotingly back at her. 'You are something

special, lady.'

'I know it says no photographs with your own camera but can we just take a quick one with you?' I plead.

'How can I deny you anything?' Boris gives a little bow.

I scrabble through my bag, emptying the contents – map, scrumpled tissues, make-up, receipts, plane ticket, earring I've been missing for years, half-eaten Tootsie Roll and a spatula from an Immac kit (why?!) – on to the counter.

'It's in here somewhere . . . Ah!' I hold up my trusty disposable.

We lean in and grin as Boris instructs us to: '*Say sleaze!*'

As I shove the mess back into my bag, Zoë remains lost in wonder at her reflection.

'This is what I wanted, Lara. To feel like a movie star, just once.'

I stop what I'm doing to look at her, feeling my heart swell again and affection radiate from my eyes – there is something so rewarding about seeing your friends blissfully happy.

'Camcorder ready!' Boris informs us.

And now we're going to immortalize this wonderful moment on film!

16

'Excuse me, Miss Russell,' Boris raises a finger as we take our positions in front of the blue screen.

I give him the full diva arched-brow.

'This is your airline ticket?'

'Oh God!' I whistle relief as I shuffle over and grab the slip of paper. I could so easily have left without it. Checking the details I read out loud: 'MISS LARA RICHARDS. LAX to FRESNO-YOSEMITE INTERNATIONAL AIRPORT. Yup, that's me. Going to see my beloved. Just the two of us and the wild wilder—'

Suddenly I freeze. My eyes are on the departure time.

'Oh no.' I fill with cold dread.

'What?' Zoë yelps.

'What time is it now?' I ask, trying to remain calm despite the feeling that I'm being sucked into quicksand.

'Just past 4 p.m.'

'Oh no, oh no.' Underneath the pancake foundation I've turned a wispy Cate Blanchett white.

'Lara what is it?'

'My flight leaves in an hour.'

'No, you said 7 p.m. . . .' Zoë cranes over my shoulder. I watch as realization followed by angst contort Zoë's face. 'Oh shit.'

'I just saw the 7 in the 17.00. I thought—' I shake my head, foiled again by the 24-hour clock. I take a breath as my brain races trying to think of a way round this. I know Helen said it was the last flight of the day but maybe I could find another airline? Or would that break The California Club code? If I hired a car and drove, maybe no one need know? But it's a six-hour slog. Oh God, oh misery, oh Elliot! – slipping ever more out of reach.

'You are packed?' Boris cuts into my downward-spiralling thoughts.

'Suitcase is in the car,' I sigh. For what it's worth.

'You can still make it.'

'What?' I'm not convinced, Helen said I should allow an hour to get to the airport and then check in an hour before the flight so unless Boris has got a fully working replica of Chitty Chitty Bang-Bang out back we don't stand a chance.

'Do you really think we can?' Zoë takes the role of the believer.

'Freeway is no good now but you can take Western Avenue most all the way.'

'But we don't even know where Western Avenue is!' I panic.

'Is simple. I show on map.' Using the glitterstick he traces the path to the airport.

Zoë and I stare at the shimmering snail-slick,

paralysed by the prospect of negotiating unfamiliar roads at high speed.

'But maybe this flight is not so important?' he shrugs.

Suddenly we're animated. 'Oh yes it is!' we insist.

'Well, then!' He makes a grand shooing motion with his arms.

'Oh my God!' we cry, lunging for the door only to find our stride severely restricted by the dresses. 'The costumes!'

'Quick, turn around!' I twizzle Zoë and fiddle frenetically with the sequence of hooks and eyes at her collar. 'Keep still!' I squeak as she kicks off her shoes, dropping three inches and causing me to catch the top hook in her wig.

'Aaaghh!' Zoë screeches as her head wrenches back. 'Undo the zip!' She panics, reaching around behind her, wriggling as if she's been doused in itching powder.

'*Stop!*' Boris bellows.

We look up from our grappling, startled by his vocal amplification.

'Much as I would love to watch you two ladies undress one another . . .' he smiles, savouring the moment for a millisecond longer than our schedule can allow. 'I trust you, so GO! You bring back tomorrow, OK?' He squeezes Zoë's elbow as he herds us to the door.

She reaches back and smothers him with a feather-up-the-nostril hug. 'I'll be here before breakfast, I promise – thank you so much!'

For a moment his face fills with transcendental bliss as his hugging hands discover her zip has descended as far as her G-stringed bum. But before Zoë even realizes what's going on, he zips her back to decency.

'Tomorrow,' he concludes, eyes misting with delicious anticipation.

'I'll drive!' Zoë snatches the keys from my trembling hands as we do our hobbling version of a Benny Hill dash to the carpark.

'You sure?' I frown. This surely isn't the best time for experimentation.

'You'll be too stressed. Just read the map,' Zoë insists.

'But—' I'm thrown. I've never seen Zoë take control before. And she's not messing – the engine is already revving.

'Get in!' she commands.

I leap into the passenger seat, twisting around to check the street name. 'Er, this is Vine so left out of the carpark and down two blocks to Sunset.'

We screech into the street, only taking the wrong side of the road for a hair-raising thirty seconds.

'Shit!' Zoë laughs, yanking us back over to the right.

I try to laugh too but only manage a petrified wheeze.

As we power down Western Avenue I steal a glance at Zoë. Were it not for the fact that she looks like some freakshow granny driver (hugging the wheel with her shoulders up to her ears, wig yanked back to her collar and a bank-robber stocking showing at the front of her head) I'd be impressed – she's driving like a rally driver.

'Wow! Look at this v-v-v-vehicle!' I gawp as we slow at the lights, drawing level with a hot pink corvette.

'It's Angelyne!' Zoë gasps, glimpsing the face beneath a peroxide flounce of hair.

Even in a town overrun with surgically enhanced blondes there's no mistaking the kewpie-doll looks of Hollywood's most infamous and aging wannabe.

'Can you believe that? She's looking at us like *we're* the weirdos!' Zoë tuts, inching forward, eager to get just that little bit closer to the airport.

The second light turns green. She's off.

'Blimey! Girl racer!' I brace myself on the dashboard as we surge ahead of the traffic.

Zoë smiles. 'Dad sent me on a defensive driving course last summer. He said I was such a bad driver I'd probably need to make a speedy getaway from an irate motorist at some point. Whoah!' She swerves to avoid an outrageously handsome man exiting a gas station in a silver convertible. I wait for Zoë's lecherous comment but it doesn't come. Her eyes are trained on the road ahead.

'How come you've never driven when we've been places before?' I'm suddenly curious.

'I don't know – it was always like you and Elliot were Mum and Dad and me and Sasha were the kids in the back,' she shrugs. 'I didn't think there was any point messing with the equilibrium.'

I smile. 'You're a good driver.'

Zoë floors it.

243

'A little bit fast . . .' I gulp as we gobble up the miles. 'Oh God!' I close my eyes as we swoop across three lanes in one go.

'Our exit!'

'Is it?' I look down at the map, desperately trying to locate us.

'It had a big airport sign, don't worry, we're going to do this.'

I look at the clock on the dashboard. 11 p.m. Helpful. If I make this flight I'll take it as a sign that I have to tell Elliot how I really feel. Pact!

'What airline is it?' Zoë asks, already approaching the first terminal.

'Um. Skywest.' I check my ticket.

'OK, when we get there, I'll pull up right outside and you just run in.'

'What about the car? I'm supposed to drop it back at Enterprise.'

'I'll do it.'

'But how will you get back into town?'

'I'm sure one of these nice gentlemen will give me a ride,' she says eyeing a fleet of prowling black limos.

'Skywest! Pull in!' I blurt, suddenly spotting the overhead sign.

Zoë skims the kerb and pops the boot. The second my suitcase hits the pavement she hollers, *'Run!'*

I obey but instead of an athlete's springing gait all I manage is a tic-tac shuffle.

'The dress!' I turn back in panic.

'I'll sort it with Boris!' she assures me.

'Aren't you running low on sexual favours by now?' I fret, suddenly loath to leave her.

'Never!' she grins, waving me through the automatic door.

'Vegas?' the check-in girl enquires without looking up, seemingly unfazed to find her peripheral vision filled with sequins.

'Fresno,' I correct. 'I'm really late. Can I still get on?'

'Let's see what we can do.' Her fingernails do a frantic tap dance across the keyboard. My heart leaps as she nods for me to heave my suitcase on to the metal plate. There's hope!

'You can make it if you run but I can't guarantee your luggage will get on board.'

I roll my eyes. Surely it wouldn't happen twice?

'That's OK. I'll take my chances.'

She hands me my boarding pass like it's a relay race baton and says, 'Gate 17. You're gonna have to Flo-Jo it!'

There's only one thing for it, I hitch up my skirt, exposing my pink skin-socks for all the frequent flyers to see, and then *charge*.

Heckles are surprisingly few. Far more common is: 'Hey look, Mom, they must be shooting a movie!' followed by slack-jawed gawping around the concourse for camera crews.

The departure lounge is deserted bar the ticket-taker cheering me on to the finishing line. I'm ready to cry with relief as I stumble jelly-legged down the prefab corridor and on to the plane but it's not quite

245

over – as the last person on a full flight I have to play hide-and-seek with the one remaining seat. All eyes are on me as I slink my sequins down the aisle. You'd think someone would raise an arm and say, 'Coo-eee! There's a free one here!' but no – apparently my fellow passengers want me to suffer for delaying take-off. It's working: my already sweaty pink face now takes on the radioactive glow of embarrassment.

Naturally the one remaining space is a middle seat: a man with extra-long legs extending into the aisle has to unbuckle himself and step out in order to let the freak in the fancy dress in. Sliding past him with a salvo of *Sorry!*s I get entwined in his headphones. It's an excruciating palaver and yet all of a sudden I don't care – frankly I'd sit on his lap and sing *Diamonds Are a Girl's Best Friend* if I had to – all I can think is: *I made it!* I'm on a flight that is taking me to Elliot and for the first time in years I'm going to be truly alone with him.

After this farrago, telling him that I love him is going to be easy.

17

My luggage decided not to join me on my journey to Yosemite. No surprises there. What has thrown me, however, is the dramatic change in the weather. I left LA in streaky pink sunshine and now I'm convinced that our one-hour hop up the coast involved a diversion to Lapland.

It began with a noticeable drop in temperature when I stepped on to the airport concourse, but there was no real hint that a whirling snowstorm lay ahead. (I'm sure Enterprise wouldn't have given me a white rental car if they'd known I was about to become invisible on the roads.)

Initially I drove quite happily, watching plastic chains like Days Inn and Dairy Queen give way to officially quaint establishments like Elk Lodge and The Ol' Kettle café, where the big news on the menu was that 'Wild Hare is Back'. I also passed several outdoor outfitters but they were all closed. Who'd have thought I could look so covetously at a puffa gilet? And what I wouldn't do for a pair of cashmere gloves! I can only endure occasional eyeball-drying blasts from the car heater – any longer and it gets too 'can't breathe' claustrophobic. As a result my frozen fingers are hooked around the steering wheel like eagle claws. An eagle with highly manicured nails, I muse, admiring my glossy red talons.

The snow began just as I passed through Coarsegold – one racetrack curve in the road and the landscape made a startling switch from spring greens to winter wonderland. It was like entering another dimension. Did I miss the segue scene? I guess I should have given more credence to the promise of Sleigh Rides ten miles back. As the snow began to lightly tickle the windscreen I couldn't help but smile – it just didn't seem real – every frisky pine tree branch was heaped with two inches of sparkling sugar, the surrounding hills became mounds of desiccated coconut and the compacted ice on the roads offered the perfect surface for serving vodka. Even though I'm alone I find myself sighing 'It's all so beautiful!' out loud, and wondering if this is what life would be like inside a snow-globe.

My pessimistic alter ego has a rather different take on the situation: 'We're going to die!' she howls. She's got a point – the roads are becoming more randomly squiggly, the drops more sheer and the snowfall is now so vigorous and enlarged, it feels like the car is being pelted with flour bombs. I've been aware of a pick-up truck bearing down on me for some time and decide I'm going to have to pull over and let him pass. Again the shrill voice has other ideas: 'Are you crazy? We need to keep them behind us so when we skid into

248

oblivion they'll see us go and be able to call for help!'

'Jesus!' I gasp as the truck passes me, swerving perilously close to the cliff edge. I wonder if the driver's loss of concentration had anything to do with the sight of my very un-wilderness-friendly ensemble? I must look like a lost drag queen in a Christmas special. Perhaps I should put on my hazard warning lights just to prepare people. Not that there's another car for miles . . . I shiver again. I'm freezing! I suppose I should be grateful I didn't end up in the skimpy slip from *Cat on a Hot Tin Roof*, although I wouldn't mind a Liz Taylor wig right now – that mat of synthetic fibres would at least keep my head warm.

Wondering exactly when I should become hysterical with fear, I crawl onwards, blinking at the white eternity. I have no idea how much further it is to go and I daren't take my eyes off the road for a second to check the map. I'm going to have to stop. And I should probably call Elliot. I pass a sign (hoorah!) for Wawona and roll into the next available lay-by. OK. Let's see if I can find where I am. Moccasin, Bootjack, Cedar Crest – ah, here we are . . . Wawona. Nearly, anyway. The windows are all misting up so I switch off the engine. I'd say there's at least another 30 miles to go to the camp. At minus 2 m.p.h. that should take . . . oh lawks, it doesn't bear thinking about. I reach for my phone and notice with alarm that the battery has died. Naturally the charger is in my suitcase. Aaaaghhh! I'm just going to have to keep going. The sooner the better.

I turn on the ignition. Nothing. I try again. No response. My heart starts to pound. This is serious.

'No. No. Noooooooooooooo!' I wail, trying to push away thoughts of Elliot discovering my frozen corpse days from now – I can just see him trying to remove my rigid body from the car only to have my arm snap right off in his hand. Not a good look. Have to live.

My only hope is a passing Samaritan but it's not likely anyone is even going to notice me: the car is blending too well with the scenery. If only it was red.

Hang on. *I'm red*. Red and sparkly. A human flare. I'm going to have to try and flag someone – anyone – down. I fling open the car door and then slam it shut immediately. It's perishing out there! OK. Plan. I'll wait until a car comes in view and then leap out at it. But then I'll probably kill them as well as me. Oh God!

I try the ignition again. Dead.

OK. Mind over matter. I am lying on a tropical beach, glossy from the humidity. That's maybe pushing it. Let's try the Sunset Strip – Zoë and I are sucking on a smoothie. Agghh – brainfreeze! No. Try again. I'm eating soup. Spicy Thai Tom Ka soup. In a woolly jumper. Boiling! In one swift move I leap from the car and slam the door behind me, trying to let as little icy air sneak into the car as possible. Now what?

I pace. Not quite as fast as I would like as my train drags in the snow, holding me back. I decide I'll just have to jog on the spot – not easy in stilettos . . . So I flap my arms around. And then I break into the '*We're Just Two Little Girls from Little Rock*' routine. Twice. For a moment I'm not scared. This is fun. Surreal. Cold. But

fun. I'm mid-way through the Jane Russell gym solo –
'*Is There Anyone Here For Love?*' – when a black Cherokee
jeep swings into the lay-by behind my car. Saviour in the
house! I scuttle over to the tinted window, which duly
lowers to reveal a broad-shouldered thirtysomething
male behind the wheel. I can't really see his face
beneath the peak of his baseball cap but I think I may
have found a Tony Curtis chin for Zoë.

'Everything OK?' he enquires.

I don't know what I expected him to say but surely,
considering the circumstances, he could have done
better than that?

'Miss?' he pursues.

The altitude must be affecting my attitude because I
find myself cooing: 'Yeah everything's fine, I've just
been booked by Park Services to entertain the
motorists along this particularly monotonous stretch
of road.'

After a millisecond's hesitation he shows me his
Matt Damon dentistry courtesy of a dirty great grin.
'D'you do requests?'

'No but I have a few!' I shiver, partly from the cold,
partly from the sexy curve of his mouth.

'I take it you need a ride?'

'A ride. A floor-length *faux*-fur coat. A pair of yeti
boots and something hot and delicious to eat,' I
suggest.

'Grab your stuff and get in,' he manfully instructs
me.

I don't need telling twice. As I go to dart off he calls
after me: 'Do you need a hand with anything?'

'No, I'm going to leave the dead body in the trunk for now!' I holler back and then quickly check to make sure I haven't started an avalanche. Nope. All is well. I grab my handbag and the car keys and then hop up into the passenger seat of his jeep, trying in vain to keep the thigh-high split sealed at least to knee level.

'I'm Joel,' he says, offering me a warm hand.

'Lara,' I tell him, enjoying the thawing sensation I experience from his touch.

His car is toasty-warm without being an eyeball-roaster and better still he reaches back behind the passenger seat and hands me an XL grey fleece.

'Here, you can put this on if you like,' he says taking the first corner a little swifter than I would have liked, especially with only one hand on the wheel.

'Do you have anything in red?' I query. *Eyes on the road!* I screech as his withering look lingers too long on me. 'I was kidding, sheesh!'

I pull on the fleece, zipping it up to my nose and pulling the cuffs down over my mottled purple claws. Something about this stranger makes me feel curiously playful but I don't want to scare him – he has potentially saved my life, after all – so after I've explained where I'm going, I sit quietly.

'I know I'm not going to get a straight answer but where've you come from?' he asks, understandably dying of curiosity.

'LA,' I reply, keeping it simple.

'Figures. Is this what you starlet types are wearing to go hiking this season?'

'Yeah, these heels make great crampons,' I tell him.

He chuckles delightedly.

'Also implements of death,' I threaten, removing one so I can mock-skewer his head.

'OK, I won't ask any more. You just sit there and be a nice little hitch-hiking, breakdown psycho or whatever you are.'

I smile contentedly – the plummet-to-your-death scenery looks a lot less threatening now I have a travelling companion.

'So what's your story?' I turn to face Joel

He shrugs. 'Nothing nearly so intriguing as yours. I'm just coming in for a friend's wedding. Thought I'd make the most of the trip, stay an extra night and get a bit of climbing in before kick-off.'

'Are you a mountaineer?' I gasp.

'Well I couldn't make a career of it but yeah, I like to climb. You know, the bride's the real El Cap freak—'

'El what?' I interrupt.

'El Capitan, you must have heard of it – world's largest granite monolith?'

I look blank.

'Ninety-six per cent sheer rockface . . . You've seen all those Ansel Adams photographs, right?'

I make a noncommittal grunt and, in a bid to distract him from my ignorance, ask if he's climbed it.

'Sure! Jen and I used to race each other up at least once a month!'

'Is she an ex of yours?' I say, getting on to the more important details.

'Yeah. We were together a year – that's pretty major for me!'

'So what are the odds of you yelling, *"Don't marry him, marry me!"* in church?'

'That's not going to happen,' he smiles. 'We ran our course.'

Hmmm. Must be nice to feel something is done, that you've had your fill, I think to myself. I'm always leaving the table wanting more.

'You know, she originally wanted to get married halfway up, hanging from a ledge,' Joel continues.

'Can you do that?'

'Oh yeah! But her ninety-year-old grandmother wasn't keen.'

'Funny that,' I frown. 'So where are they having the ceremony now?'

'At the Awahnee Hotel. Do you know it?'

I shake my head.

'It's this great old mountain lodge built in the Twenties. The décor is all Native American – a tribute to the local Miwok and Paiute tribes.'

'Sounds cool.'

'Some people think it's cheating – you know, coming out to the wilderness and then staying in a luxury hotel – but come the end of the day, I like my creature comforts without the creatures!'

'Oh me too! I'm supposed to be staying in a tent tonight but the thought of it in this weather . . .' I shudder.

'Are you visiting someone?'

'Yes,' I nod, swallowing back my tale of unrequited love. I'm not quite sure if I'm keeping shtum to protect him from a girltalk minefield or because I want to seem available because I fancy him. *Interesting* . . .

Joel waits a few seconds and then says, 'Is that all you're prepared to say on the subject?'

'Not necessarily,' I squirm, trying to focus on the Merced river, racing to our left. For a moment I'm transfixed by the icy-green froth thrown up as it bounces over the rocks in its path, but I don't know how much longer I can hold out.

'How about we play twenty questions?' he suggests.

'You can have five,' I allow.

'OK but you have to tell the truth,' he insists.

'Go ahead,' I say, feeling a little wary.

'Is it a guy you're staying with?'

'Yes.'

'Thought so. Boyfriend?'

'No.'

'But you want him to be your boyfriend?'

I hesitate. Am I ruining my chances – however microscopic – if I say yes?

'Yes or no?' he pressures.

'Yes,' I blurt.

'But there's an obstacle of some kind?'

'Yes,' I confirm.

'A big one?'

'About ten stone, I reckon.'

'A-ha! Ten of your British stones would be 140 of our pounds so we're talking a person here. Most likely a woman.'

'Do you want a yes or no to that?' I check.

'No – wait up, I have to use my last question wisely. Is she here in Yosemite, too?'

'No.'

'Are you interested in making him jealous?'

'That's six.'

'Actually that's a different kind of question alto-gether. I'm offering you my services . . .' He gives me a sly look.

I study him a little closer. If you were looking for a guy to make another man jealous he would do nicely – strong physical presence, confident manner, cool clothes, big car. He's perfect.

'It wouldn't work.' I shake my head.

'Hey, I can make a pretty attentive suitor-stroke-love rival, you know.' Joel looks put out.

'He just doesn't see me that way. Whatever you did, it wouldn't change his mind.'

'But that's what you're here for, right?' he ventures.

I can't deny it.

'Is this –' he waves a hand towards my spangles '– get-up an attempt to change his image of you? Or is this how you normally dress?'

I can't help but laugh. Joel is being so sweet and patient with me. If he hadn't mentioned his ex I'd presume he was gay.

'If I had something else to change into I would,' I tell him. 'But my suitcase is still at LA airport.'

'Well, I can easily lend you something but person-ally I think you should rock up and give him the works – you never know.' Joel winks.

Up until now I had only thought of the embarrass-ment factor of what I'm wearing, not the vamp potential. But I'm not convinced. 'He'll just laugh,' I protest.

'Don't be so sure – you look hot! Do you think I would have stopped for you if you'd just been in jeans?'

I give him a playful punch.

'Seriously, I think any man would find you pretty hard to resist right now.'

My heart does a little flip. And I can still feel the sensation of his super-toned biceps on my knuckles. All my quippy sarcasm deserts me in favour of a good old-fashioned 'Take me now!' sensation.

'Great! It's still open!' Joel's attention shifts to a tin-roofed trading post on the roadside. 'This is my favourite store. I just need to get a few provisions. You coming in?'

I look down at my bottom half and then back at him.

'OK, you stay put. I'll be back in five.'

'With snacks?' I ask, hopefully.

'As much beef jerky as you can stomach!' he teases.

'And herbal teabags – I've got a craving!'

'If they've got them, they're yours!'

Making sure he's safely in the shop, I unzip the fleece and peer down inside. Could this outfit really do the trick? *If only.* At least it's had some kind of effect on Joel. I wonder what kind of girls he usually goes for? I hope Jen isn't typical – she sounds all too Pepsi Max for my liking. What kind of woman wants to get married hanging from a rope? I'm just about to start rifling through his CDs when I get a mischief spasm and find myself jumping out of the car and scurrying around the back to hide without even really knowing why.

Five minutes later he emerges from the shop. I hear him open his car door and then stop.

'Lara?' He turns around to search for me and DUMPF! Direct hit! Right in the mouth. I rub my chilled hands together as he spits out the snow.

'Oh-ho-ho, you'll be sorry,' he says, dumping his brown grocery bag on the car seat and tearing after me.

Before he can fill his hands with snow I hit him again, this time in the chest – left pec, ten points. I've already prepped an arsenal and have a serious advantage but it doesn't stop me screeching like a banshee when he lobs one at me.

'Gotcha!' he cackles, delighted that he's ruined half my movie-star hair with his first shot.

The second of Joel's missiles knocks me off my feet. I watch as the offending snowball falls to the ground, still intact and streaked red with my lip gloss. Stunned, I wipe the remainder from my face.

'That's not blood, is it?' Joel blanches, rushing to my side.

I nod, looking like I'm about to cry.

'Let me look,' he frets, tilting my face towards his. As he inspects my mouth I reach up and shove a handful of snow down the back of his shirt.

'You evil little witch!' he howls as I wriggle free.

Now it's gone beyond snowballs – we're just scooping up great armfuls of powdery snow, more akin to a water fight. Staggering backwards to duck a dousing I trip on my train and splat into the snow, pulling him on top of me. Unintentionally, honest. I try and writhe free, knowing he's going to wreak an icy revenge any second.

'Now I've got you!' He looms over me.

I start frantically kicking and screaming, 'Get off! *Help!*' I struggle and strain. 'Aaaaaaaaghhh!' I squeal as he gives me a crushed ice collar.

'*Stop!*'

Suddenly his weight is lifted off me and I see him yanked back by the scruff of his neck as a familiar voice cries: 'What the hell is going on?'

Panting, I sit up and push my soppy, straggled hair from my eyes.

'Elliot!' I wheeze.

'Lara?' He reels.

Joel looks more intrigued than ever as he shrugs himself free from Elliot's rough grasp.

'I was just coming to meet you!' I blurt. 'What are you doing here?'

'We got a report of an abandoned car near Wawona, I was worried it might be you.'

'It was. Were you coming to rescue me?' I ask, feeling either dreamy or mildly concussed, I'm not sure which.

His look softens. 'Thought I might return the favour,' he smiles. I flash back to the surf drama and Elliot's absence of trunks and feel quite dizzy with lust. For a millisecond I could swear he's feeling the same way but then the state of me distracts him. 'Lara, what happened to you?' he frowns, shooting a dirty look at my burly assailant.

'Oh, this is Joel.'

'Do you two know each other?'

'Know each other? Haven't you heard? We're engaged!' Joel lunges at me and waves the ruby clunker on my wedding finger under his nose.

Elliot looks utterly bewildered.

'Not really!' I say, reaching out to Elliot but his look doesn't change. Before I can explain further, a real-deal park ranger appears by Elliot's side.

'Everything OK, son?'

'Yes, Mr Gediman – this is Lara.'

I shake his hand, apologizing: 'I don't normally look like this.'

'It's her car,' Elliot continues. 'The abandoned vehicle.'

'Are you all right, miss?'

'I'm fine. Joel rescued me.'

Elliot looks a little put out.

'Great, well, I'll go ahead and get the car off the road. Elliot, why don't you get a ride back to camp with your friends?'

'Um, well . . .'

'That's OK,' Joel assures him. 'Plenty of room in the Jeep.'

Still he's reluctant: 'I don't want to put you out – where are you headed?'

'I'm staying at the Awahnee,' Joel announces, as he slots behind the wheel.

'Of course you are,' I hear Elliot mutter as he finds himself in a rather unfamiliar position – taking the back seat.

18

'Welcome to the Ahwahnee,' the uniformed valet parker greets us as we pull up in front of the hotel entrance. 'Please ensure that all food items are removed from the vehicle before you leave,' he continues, slinging Joel's luggage on to a trolley.

'We didn't have any in the first place,' I lament. And then I remember the convenience shack stop.

'Joel! Where're the snacks?'

'In the seat-well,' he remembers. 'Good call.'

'Is this yours?' The valet rattles a box of Celestial Seasonings at me.

'It's just a few herbal teabags,' I explain. He's looking at me as though he just found a kilo of cocaine.

'The bears will tear the car apart if they smell them,' he growls. 'You have to take them with you.'

'OK,' I bleat. No refreshing cup of Orange Zinger for the bears tonight, then.

'He's exaggerating, surely?' I hiss at Elliot as we follow Joel down a wooden-log walkway lined with gold lanterns and hanging baskets.

'Actually, no. They get about four hundred bear break-ins here each summer.'

'You're kidding!' I have visions of teams of bears in balaclavas moving around the carpark after dark, methodically inspecting every vehicle with a flashlight.

'They go for anything, even a scented lip balm!'

'They eat lip balm?' I'm incredulous.

Elliot rolls his eyes. 'They think it's fruit or sweets from the smell.'

'And it's not as if they replace your car door when they realize they've got it wrong,' he warns.

'You seem to be getting into the swing of things,' I smile.

'Don't be fooled. I'm still hoping you've arranged to get us air-lifted out of here!'

The cranberry carpet of the walkway leads us to the cold stone floor of the lobby. There are geometric tribal patterns stencilled beneath my feet and lamp-shades of taut animal hide in the lounge area. I appreciate these authentic details and note with bemusement that there's what looks like a confession box next to reception. Maybe Elliot and I can sneak back later for a game of priest and sinner – 'I know you are promised to another but I must have you!'

'Do you guys want to go ahead to the bar while I check in?' Joel suggests.

'We'll just stay for one,' I reassure Elliot as we wander through. 'I've got to at least buy him a beer for saving me.'

Elliot still seems a little prickly on the subject and laments: 'Bet you wish you were staying here.'

I go to protest but nothing comes out.

'I know I do,' Elliot mumbles.

'Nevermind, we'll have fun at Camp Elton,' I assure him, reminding him that we decided every time we referred to his camp we would re-name it in honour of a fabulous homosexual.

'I was going to do us a barbie but I'm not sure I can get the fire started in this weather.'

My stomach yawps in anguish.

'OK, you two, I've made a dinner reservation for 8 p.m., my treat!' Joel appears behind us. 'That's if you'd care to join me?'

Elliot and I exchange a 'should we?' look. I daren't be the first to say yes – I don't want to spoil Elliot's plans – but part of me is thinking: Thank you sweet Jesus – rescued for the second time in one day!

'Come on, why suffer unless you absolutely have to?' Joel reasons.

When Elliot acquiesces with a simple, 'Oh go on, then!' I feel a thrill of anticipation. Dinner with two gorgeous men – what could be better?

'Can I get you a drink?' Elliot offers Joel.

I smile, feeling proud as he does the next-best-thing on the manly list.

'Sure, just give me five minutes to zip up to the room and dump my stuff,' Joel nods, then turns to me: 'Lara, do you wanna grab a hot shower?'

My eyes widen – I can't believe he's being so forward!

'W-w—?' I stammer.

He nods over to the mirror above the bar. Robert Smith from the Cure stares back at me. Quickly I try to wipe away the smeary lipstick from my face but only succeed in staining my hand red. I'm a mess.

'And maybe we could find you something more suitable to wear?' he adds.

Until now I didn't care that I was half-fleece, half-sequins but people are beginning to stare.

'I think it might be a good idea,' I concede.

'Although I kinda like seeing you in my clothes!' Joel reaches for the fleece zipper and pulls me towards him. 'Shall we?'

Could he be any more flirtatious? I don't know what to do with myself.

'I'll wait here.' Elliot turns away and stares intently at the cocktail menu.

As soon as we're out of his earshot Joel whoops, 'It's gonna be a cinch!'

'What is?'

'Having him fall in love with you,' Joel taunts.

'Don't say that!' I flinch, punching him in the deltoids.

'He's halfway there already.'

'I know he loves me as a friend but—'

'Trust me. We can do this,' Joel asserts.

'OK,' I blink.

Right now I'd believe anything he says – I feel utterly in his power and if that hot shower happens to come complete with him as a human loofah I won't be complaining.

'After you.' Joel motions me into the crowded lift then, just as the doors squeeze closed, he booms, 'Can I have my fleece back now please?' over-enunciating to be certain everyone hears his request.

I look at him. Surely he can't mean *now* now.

He manoeuvres his hand free and makes a 'gimme' motion with his fingers.

If he thinks he can humiliate me by making me reveal my glittering torso in a lift populated by conservatively dressed sixtysomethings, he's right. But I do it anyway. I feel he's earned a thrill at my expense.

'That was priceless!' Joel whoops, wiping a tear from his eye as we career down the corridor to his room.

I'm laughing too but more from nerves than the image of the neck-cricking double-takes I prompted – it's been a long time since I was alone with a man of such blatant sexuality. It doesn't help that he's humming *The Stripper* as he unlocks the room door. I wonder what he has in mind in terms of a change of clothes. He can only have hiking gear and a dress suit for the wedding. Please don't say he's going to make me go to dinner in a customized pillowcase.

The room is chintzy-grand with two heavy king beds, a pair of winged armchairs and a cherrywood table set with a bottle of Merlot and a fancy cheese and fruit platter.

'Help yourself!' Joel says, knowing I'm so hungry I could eat one of the scatter cushions.

'You've got a balcony!' I say, sending splinters of water biscuit into the carpet.

I step out, only to recoil instantly from the cold. I'd forgotten we were experiencing the Ice Age.

'You must be frozen to the core.' Joel captures me and vigorously rubs my arms. 'Don't worry, we have ways of making you warm!'

My eyes stray to the nearest bed. What is it about this man that has me wanting to get wanton? One slight innuendo and I'm wondering what the possibilities might have been if Elliot wasn't waiting downstairs. Elliot. I feel a shimmy of disloyalty but then remind myself that I'm a free agent. He's never exhibited any carnal interest in me, like Joel.

'Ready for that shower?'

I nod.

He leads me to the bathroom and pushes open the door. I step inside then turn to face him: my hand is on the handle but I'm reluctant to close the door in his face. He holds my gaze, looking intrigued rather than wolfish, then smiles, 'Well, much as I'd love to stay and watch . . .' and retreats into the room.

As I turn the lock I struggle to suppress a whimper of lust, settling instead for a flamenco clatter of heels on the tiled floor. He's so sexy! I try and shake the feeling from my limbs for fear of becoming possessed and concentrate instead on the way the tiny hexagon tiles on the walls create a lovely whitewashed honey-comb effect. Better yet, the glass shelf above the sink is crammed with 'we-can-rebuild-you' mini beauty products.

I grab the bottles of juniper shampoo and matching body lotion and stick my head around the door. 'Is it OK if I use these?'

Joel looks up from unsheathing a black evening suit and grins: 'Knock yourself out!'

I dip back into the bathroom and set the shower running. This is such a bonus. If I had gone with Elliot I'd probably be cowering behind a canvas sheet having the contents of a watering-can emptied over me. I reach around to undo my dress but even backed up into the mirror I can't judge hooks and eyes. Frustration! I twist and arch and even try pulling the skirt part up over my head but then realize the potential horror of getting it stuck above my waist like a giant version of those neck cones people put on dogs to stop them biting themselves, and quickly tug it back down. There's only one thing for it – call in the experts.

'Um, Joel?'

He looks bemused to still find me dressed.

'Sorry to bother you but could you just help me get this off?' I fluster.

'My pleasure,' he says, striding over and deftly addressing the various zips and poppers. This is not a man who ever struggles with a bra strap, I'm sure.

He catches me looking at him in the bathroom mirror and I blush as I feel the steamy air meet my bare back.

'OK, that's great. Thanks. I'll be really quick.'

'No rush,' he smiles, waiting for me to resume eye contact with him.

I manage it for just a second before busying myself

with the vital task of moving the towels from the rack to the loo seat and setting them in a symmetrical stack.

'You have fun!' He exits, closing the door behind him.

It's been a while since a man undressed me so I take a moment to lean against the cool glass of the door as I once again turn the lock. I feel all swimmy and succumbable, if there is such a word . . . Suddenly I leap back as a loud rap jolts my ear.

'Lara?'

I gulp. It's him again. This is more than I can stand. I think it's best if we just get this *frisson* over and done with before I explode. I prise the door open and give him my most seductive look.

'I found this in the wardrobe.' He hands me a white floor-length bathrobe.

'Oh! Fantastic! Thank you!' I exclaim, somewhat over-enthusiastically. He doesn't want me naked after all. I bury my face in the robe to mask my disappointment.

'OK.' He smiles into my peeping eyes. 'See you in a while.'

Finally I step into the shower, hoping to wash away the jumpy never-been-kissed imbecile that's taken over my body and liberate Lara the Femme Fatale.

I emerge fifteen minutes later a good deal calmer, buried under acres of robe and wafting juniper from every pore.

'It's a shame this isn't a health spa hotel,' I muse, perching on the end of the bed securing my matching towel turban.

'Feel in need of a little pampering, do you?' Joel ladles on the 'poor baby' mockery.

'No, I was just thinking they let you wear towelling robes to dinner in places like that, don't they?'

Joel contemplates me for a moment then says, 'Well, there is one way you could get away with it.'

I look down at my bulky fluffiness. 'Dress it up with diamanté?' I suggest, unconvinced.

'No you fool – room service!'

My eyes widen with glee. Right now I can't think of anything more fun.

'What about Elliot?' I ask.

'He can eat downstairs with me, like a grown-up.'

'Oh.' My face falls.

'Don't be silly, there's plenty of room at the table, we'll just get them to bring an extra chair. And if we wrap up we can have aperitifs on the balcony.'

'Can we get wine and everything?'

'Sure. I won't tell your parents if you don't,' he teases.

I flump back on the bed, losing my turban in the process.

'Your hair looks good wet,' he says, rescuing the towel then reaching over to tousle my damp locks.

I look at him, wondering what it must be like to have the confidence to touch another person so easily, knowing that they'll love the sensation. So much of my pre-foreplay just goes on in my head.

'Shall I call down to the bar and have them send up Elliot?'

I nod, forced to rein in my imagination yet again. It's just dinner he's offering.

Joel makes the call then hands me the room service menu. I study it for some time. 'What are you having?' I sigh finally, unable to make a decision.

'I'm torn between the crispy-skinned salmon and the citrus-roasted chicken.'

'We could get both and have half each,' I venture, playing the Elise couple-order game.

'I like your style!' he cheers, just as there's a knock at the door.

'Just a minute!' Joel calls out. 'Put your heels back on,' he whispers to me.

'What?' I laugh. 'With this?' I'm still in the robe.

'Trust me. It'll just punch up the fact that you're not wearing anything under there.'

My breathing seems to have become exaggerated. Maybe he's on to something. I slip my feet into the shoes and go from snuggly to sexy. Potentially. But then I go and spoil it all by opening the door with a big grin on my face. I'm too happy to be sexy. If Zoë could see me now!

'Greetings!' Elliot slurs, pretty happy himself, propped on the doorframe trying to not to spill three margaritas.

'Welcome to our humble home,' I say, relieving him of two glasses and leading him into the bedroom.

'What's with the shoes?' he frowns.

'Oh!' I quaver, losing my nerve. 'My feet were cold!'

Joel rolls his eyes at me as he hands Elliot the menu. 'We need to make a swift decision before this one passes out with hunger,' he urges.

Elliot scans the menu. 'How about the pork T-bone

270

with tobacco-fried onions?'

I spare a thought for Zoë's hair as Joel says, 'Great. Why don't you two brave the balcony while I place the order and jump in the shower.'

Elliot and I obey, trying not to mist up the view with our breathing. It's still far too cold to be out here but who am I to question my new lord and master.

'This is weird,' Elliot notes as we gaze out over endless elongated Christmas trees. 'I'm used to being at ground level with all the grass and deer droppings and now I'm up here with the sky and the treetops!' He reaches out his hand and allows a series of slo-mo snowflakes to melt on to his pale caramel skin.

'Beautiful, isn't it?' he sighs.

'Mmmm,' I acquiesce. I always thought Elliot had the most elegant hands I'd seen on a man. I'd watch them flitter across a keyboard and imagine them pattering on my skin. My eyes glide up to his face. Even the distraction of Joel can't lessen the impact. Every time I look at Elliot I want to stroke his tawny hair and softly lean my cheek against his and breathe the same breath.

Feeling my eyes upon him, Elliot lets the collected dribble of water slide from his palm into my drink.

'There you are – bet you never had a real snowflake in a cocktail before!'

I smile. How can I not love this man?

'The wilderness *is* growing on you!' I marvel.

'Are you crazy?' he scoffs. 'Do you know how hard it was for me not to strap myself to Joel's TV when I walked past?'

'Are you really hating it that much?'

'It's not so bad now you're here,' Elliot concedes. 'At least I thought . . .' he halts mid-sentence.

'Yes?' I query.

'Nothing.'

I wait for him to continue but his mouth is clamped shut.

I shrug and raise my glass. 'Anyway, cheers!'

'Cheers,' he chinks. 'To . . .' He pauses, eyes prying deep into mine. 'What shall we drink to?'

The question seems particularly loaded. I look at him, wondering if I'm ever going to have the nerve to tell him how I feel. Of course, now isn't the time and 'To us!' isn't going to cut it. Perhaps we should toast Mother Nature for the wonder of Yosemite. Or Helen, for bringing us here. Or Joel for rescuing us from trying to start a campfire with damp twigs.

'To getting drunk!' I suggest uncouthly, knocking back my glass.

'To getting drunk and the swift return of your suitcase!' he adds, downing his. 'Your feet must be killing you in those.'

I grimace and make a mental note to ask Joel if I can borrow some socks when he gets out of the shower.

'They look sexy though,' he adds, looking a little embarrassed.

'Really?' I brighten, clicking my heels together like Dorothy.

'You know, if he offers for you to stay the night here, you should go for it!' Before I can splutter a response Elliot continues. 'I'm not being funny but you'll be a lot

272

more comfortable here and you know, it's cool . . .' He nods back at the room, conveying the words, *If you two want to get it on*, without actually saying them.

I'm stunned. Having Elliot presume that a little hanky-panky is in the offing makes me feel strangely fluttery inside. Could it be true? Could I really pull a stud like Joel?

'I don't think that's what he has in mind,' I say, reminding myself that Joel is actually more interested in seeing me get together with Elliot.

'I do. Why wouldn't he?'

The more pertinent question is, Why wouldn't *you*, Elliot? but I don't ask it.

'Urgh!' I shudder. 'I'm perishing, shall we go back inside?'

Elliot grabs my towelling lapels together. 'All I'm saying is: please don't feel you have to hang out with me just because . . .' he falters. 'Just because that's what you came here to do. Maybe this is what The California Club had planned for you all along.'

'Are you trying to get rid of me?' I narrow my eyes.

'NO! *God*, if you knew how much I've been looking forward to your visit!' He looks pained. 'I just don't want you to, you know . . . miss out.'

'Miss out on what?' I raise an eyebrow. I can't believe he's trying to get me a sex life.

Elliot sighs heavily. 'If you've met someone, I . . . oh I don't know! I wasn't expecting to have this conversation.' He shakes his head. 'I just feel like there's this vibe between you two, which is fine, of course – why wouldn't it be?'

The last question seems to be directed to himself. I've never seen Elliot get in such a tangle. He's usually so articulate. Just how many tequilas has he downed?

He huffs a breath. 'So.'

'So?' I smile, wishing I could read his mind.

'You just seem . . .' he begins again.

'Yes?' Oh please tell me! I feel different too but I don't know what it is.

His eyes search my face as if he's trying to identify a familiar feature in a stranger's face.

'Animal, vegetable or mineral?' I prompt.

He rolls his eyes.

'Just get inside!' he groans, pushing me back in to the warmth.

As the boys make macho smalltalk, I try to make sense of the jumble of feelings I'm experiencing. How could I *not* want to lie beneath the stars with Elliot? It's what I've been dreaming of since our roles were assigned. And yet, now that I'm here, all cosied up in this room, I can't imagine leaving Joel and his happy band of hormones. I look at him, seen for the first time without his baseball hat. His hair is as black as mine but shorn like an Army-enlisted Elvis, his eyes are so dark you can't distinguish the iris from the pupil and yet they shine beguilingly like glossy ebony. Next to his robust geometric form, Elliot looks so much softer and sweeter – he definitely has the more gentle spirit and that's what has always drawn me to him. But tonight, I seem to be hankering for something stronger.

'Do you want red or white with your dinner, Lara?'

Joel asks, wrapping me the dark velvet cloak of his stare

How can I make that decision? Joel is of course the red: bold and sultry, I'm drawn to his power and naughtiness but my heart just melts at my pet Pinot Grigio Elliot – aromatic, golden and true.

'You choose!' I slur, passing the buck.

All I know is that right now the notion of *not* concluding the evening kissing someone seems *utterly utterly* unthinkable.

19

'So what happened?' I'm on the phone to Zoë, the following morning.

'Well, when it came to it, Joel invited us both to stay over: "There's plenty of room – two big beds. You wouldn't mind sharing with each other, would you? Old buddies?"'

Zoë gasps at his daring. 'What did you say?'

'"Fine by me!" I was quite piddled by that point.'

'And Elliot?'

I sigh. 'He was all, "I've got to get back to Camp Norton but Lara, you should stay!"'

'Oh no!'

'He even said: "Make the most of the facilities!"'

'Nooooo!'

'I know! They're both trying to hook me up with the other man!'

Like I would have had the energy either way – I'd been slipping in and out of consciousness for the previous half-hour so by that point all I wanted to do was crawl into a pit. It became a case of 'If the nearest one happens to be the cleanest, softest, comfiest one, so be it.' As the boys went off on a tangent discussing driving conditions in Yosemite, I stumbled over to the nearest bed, threw back the covers, and pulled the sheet over my head. I seem to remember Joel offering to call for a camp bed for Elliot and then suggesting he meet us for breakfast but that's it.

'The last word I said to Elliot was "Waffles!"' I tell Zoë.

'So did you get any?'

'I haven't been down to breakfast yet.'

'No!' Zoë screeches. 'Did you get any action with Joel?'

'Unless he's got a very light touch and I've suddenly become a heavy sleeper, no.'

'Oh Lara!'

'Oh don't!'

'What a wasted opportunity – two guys and nothing,' Zoë tuts.

I don't want to dwell on my failures so I swiftly change the subject: 'By the way, Joel put Boris's dress in to be dry-cleaned late last night so as soon as I get it back I'll FedEx it to him.'

'You may as well just bring it with you when you come to me – there's only a few hours in it.'

'If you're sure?'

'Oh yes, Boris was an absolute darling when I went in. As a matter of fact he now thinks he owes me a favour – we got talking and he was telling me all about his grandson and the various problems he's been having at school and when I asked him to be more specific I started thinking he might have dyspraxia. His family thought he was hyperactive cos he could never sit still and he was always shrieking but they never wanted to take him to a doctor because they were afraid of what they might say. Boris got straight on the phone to his daughter and I got my office to fax over some information and now they're really excited that they may have found out what his trouble is.'

'Wow! Nurse Harriott, that's amazing – what gave the game away?'

'Just little things like it's still not obvious whether he's left- or right-handed, he doesn't like wearing new clothes, gets defensive of being touched, frequently spills drinks – a lot of the key symptoms,' Zoë breezes. 'And when I told them it's statistically likely that one child in every class of thirty is prone to this, they didn't feel so alone.'

'Well done you!'

'It felt pretty good to be able to help, I must confess. At the diner I'm still getting used to the fact that people only interact with me cos I can get them stuff from the kitchen!'

'How's it going there?'

'Oh not so bad, Todd's a treasure but the closer we get to Oscar night, the more bitter the wannabe girls become!'

'Sounds like they make excellent cautionary tales,' I suggest.

'Yes they do. Anyway, I just wanted to let you know I'm on an early tomorrow so I should be done around 1 p.m.'

'Why don't I meet you back at your apartment, just in case there's any delay getting back from here?'

'Oh. Well. If you want . . .' Zoë sounds unsure.

'It makes more sense.'

'Right. Um. I'll give you the address.'

I jot it down.

'Where is that exactly?'

'Oh it's this hip new area, you'll see.'

'So what are your plans for today?' I ask.

'Working and then taking a Stars' Homes tour around Beverly Hills to see how the other half live. You?'

'Well, first on the list is shopping for a new outfit – my suitcase has gone AWOL again.'

'Oh no! What are you wearing now?'

'Joel's lent me a T-shirt and the pair of trackie bottoms he normally wears to go jogging.'

'Is that where he is now?'

'I think so. I woke up and he was gone.'

'Shoes?'

'I'm wearing the hotel slippers as flip-flops till we get to the shop.'

'Ingenious!'

'I know,' I beam as I wiggle my toes with pride. My only concern now is my face – I feel there's this unwritten rule that you can't wear make-up in the wilderness so I've tried to go easy on the eyeshadow and lippie but still feel like I'm going to be ambushed and scrubbed down with coal tar soap.

'Is it still snowing?'

'I haven't dared to look yet.'

'What exactly are you supposed to do in a national park anyway?'

'I don't know. I think Elliot's giving his first bear talk. Other than that, I'll leave it up to the boys.'

'Hark at you with your love triangle!' Zoë laughs, then gets serious. 'Listen, don't mess up this opportunity – you've only got tonight to do the right thing.'

'Which is?'

'I can't decide,' Zoë muses. 'I mean, Elliot is your true love but Joel sounds a hottie and you might never get another chance with him.'

'I might never get another night alone with Elliot – I still can't believe he's getting married.'

'Well you know what I'd do.'

'I can't sleep with both of them!'

'Lara!' Zoë sounds outraged.

'What?'

'What kind of girl do you take me for?'

'Sorry.'

'But you've got a point there.'

'Have I?'

'I think you need a bit of compare and contrast. You should at least kiss both of them.'

'Zoë. I've spent the last ten years trying to kiss Elliot and I only succeeded once.'

'Well, I think it's about time you got an update, just to be sure he can still make you feel all woozy.'

'But how? What makes you think that tonight is going to be different to any other?'

'*Because it has to be,*' Zoë says simply.

Her words hit home. This is it. This is for real.

After I bid Zoë farewell I sit up in bed and stare across the room. I said I'd do it – take the chance to be alone with Elliot to tell him how deeply I feel. If not now, when? But how will I begin? And considering how much alcohol it'll take to get my nerve up, how will I be able to get the words out without slurring? I might have to get a bit more guidance from Joel. He seems to have a bit of know-how on this subject.

In the meantime, I make my second phone call of the day, this time to Sasha. She sounds bright but I suspect she's putting on a breezy voice so as not to worry me.

'How's the ogre?' I ask.

'Just the same,' she sighs. 'I don't understand it. He's so cool with everyone but me. And you saw him with those cubs.' Her voice mellows.

'Surely you can't still fancy him?' I gasp.

'I still fancy the guy I met on the first night. I keep waiting for him to reappear.'

'Have you tried cutting off the electricity?'

'I've thought about it!' Sasha laughs.

'So what are you doing in the evening? It must be weird now it's just the two of you.'

'Well, last night I cooked then he read a book while we ate and as soon as he was done he went to bed.'

'What about you?'

'I was knackered but I couldn't sleep. Since you've gone I've spent most of my time trying to work out how I could raise some cash for Paradise Park. I'm sure if I could find a way to contribute he'd show me a bit more respect.'

'You reckon?'

'Well, maybe not but I'd at least feel I'd proved something to myself. I want to be able to leave here knowing I made a difference, however small.'

'What did you have in mind?'

'Well, that's the problem. I desperately need to talk to Zoë, she's got far more experience of the organizational side of these things. The charity events I've done were no different to any other catwalk show, we just didn't get paid so I'm really none the wiser.'

'When were you thinking of doing this?'

'I thought the day after The California Club week is up.'

'That's just four days from now!'

'I know. I was hoping Zoë could show me some short-cuts.'

'I guess the main thing is that you've got to think of a good enough hook to get them along in the first place.' I decide. 'Once they see the cats they'll start writing cheques.'

'Mmm, I've had a few thoughts but I don't know how practical they are. I know The California Club said all communication had to go through you but I was wondering . . .'

'Oooh you little rebel!' I tease. 'Are you after Zoë's phone number?'

'Would it hurt? I mean, in the grand scheme of things, which is more important – helping those tigers or obeying a pointless rule?'

'We don't know that it's pointless,' I point out.

'I wouldn't abuse it,' Sasha insists. 'Maybe if you

primed her and then the next day I gave her a call? Or she could even pass any information through you? There's got to be a way round it.'

'I guess one phone call won't do any harm,' I concede. It's so great to hear Sasha fired up about something, the last thing I want to do is put a dampener on proceedings. 'I'll call her now.'

Sasha whoops with gratitude. 'Thanks, Lara! Ryan will thank you for this!'

I make sure Sasha knows I'll do anything I can to help then dial Zoë. Following her success with Boris's grandson she's raring to take on another project and promises to devote all her time in between serving blue plate specials to the cause!

I smile to myself, happy to be in on it to some degree. But my pleasure is short-lived. I have to phone Elise.

'Oh Lara, I was hoping you'd call.'

I must have caught her mid psychic channelling class. Instead of her usual impatient bluster, she sounds pensive and unsure. 'Would you say you're Elliot's closest friend out of the group?'

'Er . . .' I falter.

'I know he's close with Helen but the way he talks about you, that's the impression I get.'

'Oh?' I can't help but smile.

'It actually used to irritate me,' Elise chuckles dismissively. '*Lara this, Lara that, she's so fun, so creative blah-blah* but then I realized two things . . .'

I don't like the sound of this.

283

'One is that he sees you as a mate rather than a woman.'

Oh cheers, thanks a lot.

'The other is that he may have a past with you but his future is with me.'

Amazing. Go on, stick that knife in further, you only skewered three of my vital organs – why not go for the full shish-kebab?

She does.

'I mean, it's all very well having your buddies to play with but when it comes to being a grown-up, it's all about one-to-one commitment, wouldn't you agree?'

'I wouldn't know Elise, I'm not thirty for another two days. Maybe then I'll morph into a fully fledged adult and agree with what you're saying.'

'Two days, is it?' she coos. 'You know, Elliot wanted to make a big fuss but I told him no woman wants to be reminded she's getting older!'

You utter cow! You will be punished! I wonder what he had in mind – must have been good or she wouldn't have scuppered it.

'What did you do on your 30th?' I ask, still seething but not wanting to pass up the chance to gather a little more info on Madam X.

'Me?' Elise asks.

You heard. 'Or can't you remember – I realize some time has passed.'

'No, I remember,' she sounds distant. 'I was out here, as a matter of fact.'

'Doing what?' And with who?

Silence.

'Elise?'

'Look, I've got to go,' she blusters. 'But I need to ask you something about Elliot – you know how private he is, always playing his cards so close to his chest . . .'

Not the Elliot I knew. My Elliot was always an open book, an open heart. What has she done to him?

'The thing is . . .' she sounds shifty.

'Yes?'

'Honey, I'm home!' Joel bursts in, looking gleeful. 'Ready for breakfast?'

'Who's that?' Elise snaps.

'Joel, say hello to Elise . . .' I don't know what I'm thinking but I hand over the phone.

'Hey! How's it going? You discovered the meaning of life yet?'

A pause while Elise talks.

'So no hot tutors to give you a bit of hands-on healing?'

I hear a faint squeak of outrage down the phone.

'Oh yeah, that's right. I met him last night, he seems a cool guy.'

Back to muffled vocals. I lean closer – something about not realizing that Lara had any long-lost friends in California.

'She doesn't. We just met yesterday. It was the red sequins that did it for me!'

Again a pause.

'What can I say? She's a true one-off. A very attractive one-off . . .' He eyes me lasciviously.

'Is it OK if we talk tomorrow?' I ask Elise, grabbing the phone back.

'OK, just tell Elliot he's the most wonderful, kind . . .'

I hold the receiver away from my ear. Tell me something I don't know. For a moment there I thought she was having doubts. She probably just wants advice on what to get him for a wedding present. I sigh heavily and replace the receiver. Why can't she just vanish? Forget all these gurus and psychics, what I need is a good old-fashioned witch.

20

'Where'd the snow go?' I gasp as Joel swoops back the curtains to reveal a happy sunshiny day – nothing but perky green scenery for miles.

'You like?' Joel grins, sensing my surge of joy and anticipation at being granted the perfect spring day.

'Oh yes!' I say, skipping out on to the balcony. 'You know, if I didn't have such a disgusting hangover, I'd be feeling all revitalized and zingy about now.'

'Fresh air! It'll get you every time!' Joel notes, reaching for my hand. 'Come on, let's get stage two of the Woo Elliot campaign under way.'

'Oh you can forget that!' I grumble, following him across the room. 'Last night he gave me his blessing to get off with *you*!'

'Really? Nah, that's just his defence mechanism kicking in,' Joel shrugs, ushering me out the door. 'But still, it's good to know.'

I turn back to see if he means what I think he means and he greets me with an exaggerated wink.

'What was that?' I hoot. *'Carry On up El Capitan?'*

'Well, there's no reason why the bride and groom

should be the only people having great sex tonight!'

'Joel!' I reel.

'Sorry, weddings always make me horny,' he apologizes, jabbing the lift button.

Blimey. Maybe tonight is the night after all.

The Ahwahnee hotel breakfast easily makes it into my Top 10 Alternatives to Weetabix: eggs foresta with spicy vegetable hash and a sneaky side of raisin brioche washed down with a keg of cranberry juice, all served in a trestle-beamed banquet hall creaking with wrought iron chandeliers. Most dramatic. Yet even this can't pip my all-time number one breakfast – the five of us Beau-Belles hung-way-over at The Grand Hotel in Brighton gorging on bacon and eggs and a fifteen-storey stack of toast. The night before we'd been to a summer ball that coincided with Zoë's birthday so we'd decided to go all-out with full *Buccaneers*-style ballgowns and beauty spots and treat ourselves to a suite – three in the bed (me, Sasha, Helen), Elliot on the sofa and Zoë in the bath. Her choice. The next morning over two hours and at least ten cups of tea we dissected who snogged who, who vomited, who flashed, who cried, who hid the band's cymbals, etc. (And wondered what on earth people who behave themselves of an evening have to talk about the next day.)

Not that any of the middle-aged Americans at the tables around us seem to be having a problem with producing lively banter. Maybe it's because the break-fast hours at the Ahwahnee are so civilized – no 9 a.m. cut-off here. I'd definitely have extended the breakfast hours at the B&B if I was in charge. Who wants to get up early on holiday, especially in a clubber's paradise like Brighton? I'd serve the full monty till noon. And happily deliver fry-ups to the bedroom instead of a paltry croissant in a basket.

'Where's your mind at?' Joel tickles my chin.

'Breakfast in bed,' I tell him.

'You only had to ask!'

I smile and roll my eyes. 'Are you done?'

Joel takes a last slurp of his café latte then helps me and my bumper belly to my feet.

'That was so good,' I sigh, then lean close. 'Did you get the stash, man?'

Joel gives his rucksack a pat.

Despite warnings about keeping all food in sealed canisters, we set off from the dining room wafting chocolate chip muffins from beneath the leather-trimmed canvas. (As much as I initially admonished him, I too am secretly hoping to attract a bear.)

'Now. Elliot's imagination will have been running riot overnight,' Joel begins as we head towards the lobby. 'You'll want to play on that when you see him.'

'Do you think he'll presume that we, you know?' I furrow my brow.

'Well, it would have been slightly more convincing if you hadn't passed out before he left but nevertheless, alone with a man of my dastardly charms . . .'

'. . . I didn't stand a chance!'

'Exactly. So when you see him – Oop! Here he is now.' Joel raises his arm to greet my dishevelled friend. 'Elliot! Good morning!'

'Morning,' he mumbles, shuffling over like one of the living dead.

'Sleep well?' Joel chirrups.

'Not really,' Elliot croaks. 'I woke up looking like Benicio Del Toro!' He tries to joke away the bags under his eyes. 'You?'

I look at Joel to see how he's going to answer. Joel looks at me. A wicked smile spreads across his face.

'Not that it's any of my business!' Elliot back-pedals, looking mortified.

I bite my lip and stare at the floor, knowing I can't be trusted to maintain the mystique if I speak.

'Er, Lara, I don't know what your plans are for today . . .' Elliot's talking to me like he doesn't know me, this is so bizarre '. . . but I'm doing a bear talk in an hour and I wondered if you wanted to come along?' Judging by his anxious tone of voice, he needs the moral support.

'Of course! I'd love to!' I possibly over-enthuse. 'That's if . . .' I look to Joel for approval. Am I allowed out by myself?

'You go ahead. I've got a climb planned. Either way, I think our first stop had better be a clothing store,' Joel decides as I trip up yet again on his trackie bottom legs trailing over my feet.

'There's a good one just up here at Yosemite Village.'

Elliot guides us, walking a few paces ahead, thrashing at the undergrowth with a stick. Joel gives me a knowing look but I'm not convinced – is this the behaviour of a jealous man or a friend merely peeved that they're not getting the attention they're used to? Of course, it's also possible Elliot is just grouchy from lack of sleep. He was in a tent, after all. I look up at the sunlight glinting through the leaves and decide I'm not going to let second-guessing games ruin my mood: even though I'm picking my way along the dirt track in slippers I have a spring to my step that I haven't experienced in a while. Being engulfed in greenery feels so new and exciting. I wasn't expecting to experience such a lift. Could there be a Grizzly Richards in me, trying to get out? If I stayed here long enough would I grow a beard? There is that concern.

Once inside the clothes shop the boys turn into a male version of Trinny and Susannah (but with a disappointing lack of boob-grabbing), assessing my physique and colouring and trying to decide what will suit me best.

'How do you feel about forgoing traditional hiking colours?' Joel queries.

'Sorry?'

'Only I think you'd look good in this heather T-shirt,' he suggests, holding the soft purple up to my face.

Elliot nods his approval and then thrusts a pair of trousers at me. 'Look, these are great – you can unzip them at the knee and make shorts!'

'How fabulously versatile!' I coo. 'Maybe I'll be really daring and just wear the knee-to-ankle bit!'

Neither of them laugh – they're concentrating far too hard on completing the outfit.

'What about getting some proper hiking boots?' Joel suggests.

Elliot's not convinced. 'I think that's maybe going too far.'

'There's not much else here – she should at least try a pair.'

'She'll never wear them again.'

'Hello?' I remind the chaps that I am over four and able to make up my own mind.

'Can I git yer somethin'?' the gruff lady shop assistant doesn't seem to like the way I'm handling her Timberlands.

'Do you have these in a UK size 5½? I think that's about 7½ US.'

As she rifles through the boxes I sit on the bench and roll up the trackie bottoms, unsheathing my sparkling scarlet toenails. She finds my size but there's a moment of hesitation before she hands them to me – she obviously has doubts about whether the boots are going to an appropriate home. 'Hope you don't mind me saying,' she grunts, 'but yer real feminine!'

Elliot snickers into the rack of hats. I don't blame him. I've never been called that before. Especially not as an insult.

The boots are even heavier than they look. 'They'd snap my ankle in a second, wouldn't they?' I try to win her over by seeking her advice.

'Why dontcha try these,' she says offering me some strappy-Velcro open-toe numbers. 'They got sturdy soles and y'can always wear socks if yer git cold.'

'Sold!' I say, eager to be on my way.

On our way out we find ourselves in the camping accessories department. Elliot and I are admiring a mosquito net-cum-hat that gives you that essential beekeeper look, and an ingenious solar-heated camp shower, when Joel sneaks up behind me and presses something into my hand: 'Here – present for you.'

I rustle open the brown paper bag and pull out a shiny silver package with a Mountain House logo.

'Is it coffee? Oh no – freeze-dried blueberry cheese-cake!' I hoot as I read the label.

'Just in case you get stuck in the snow again with no food!'

'That's brilliant, thanks!' I give Joel a kiss on the cheek, then continue my inspection. 'Is it powder or something?' I ask squeezing the foil between my fingers.

'Why don't you try it?'

'Oh no! I'm going to save it for a real emergency.'

'I wasn't sure which flavour you'd like – they also do seafood chowder and scrambled egg with real bacon!'

'No way!'

'Wait there!' Joel darts off again.

Elliot looks wistful. 'I should have done that. The old me would have done that.'

'What do you mean?' I ask, concerned by his tone.

'Remember the time I bought you that *King & I* plate?'

I smile. 'Of course!'

It was part of a set commemorating Rodgers & Hammerstein's 'contribution to musical theatre'. Elliot paid £7 at a flea market but it was the fact that he'd remembered my favourite duet that really made it invaluable. *We Kiss In A Shadow* was the title.

The fretful look remains on Elliot's face. 'Lara, do you think I've changed?'

'How do you mean?' I need specifics before I blunder in and let him know that I think Elise is sucking the fun out of him.

'I don't know what it is. I feel like I used to have more energy, more zip!'

'Zip?' I grin.

'Oh, you know,' Elliot smiles shyly. 'Or am I imagining it?'

'No, you had plenty of zip. You were always up for a laugh – in fact, you instigated most of our capers. Remember that trip to Butlins to see Bucks Fizz?'

'Please don't hold that up as a prime example!' Elliot despairs.

'It was great!' I laugh. 'Everything we did was great, however silly.'

'Maybe that's it,' Elliot looks like he's hit upon something. 'I don't think I've done silly in a while.'

'I'm sorry to hear that,' I say, gravely.

'Do you think it's gone, or can I get it back?'

'Stick with me, buddy,' I grin. 'You'll get more silly than you can stomach.'

'Really?' Elliot looks hopeful.

'We'll do something fun this afternoon. Something you've never done before.'

'Can we do a runner from here?' Elliot suggests.

I shake my head but before I can answer Joel reappears with another gift, this time for Elliot.

'Didn't want you to feel left out, dude!'

'Th-thanks,' Elliot stammers, accepting a T-shirt

bragging I MADE IT TO THE TOP! 'Did they have any that said, I STOOD AT THE BOTTOM AND LOOKED UP?' He gives a wobbly smile.

Joel laughs and slaps him on the back. 'You should give it a go – I'd be happy to take you up, if you fancy it?'

'Oh no!' I cry. 'Not that I don't think you'd be a natural,' I tell Elliot. 'But I just couldn't bear to watch.'

'You're not coming up then, Lara?'

'Are you insane?'

'Partially,' he admits.

'I'll be happy on that little trolley thing that tinkers around the valley floor, thanks very much,' I tell him.

'OK, just promise me you'll wave as you go past.'

'As long as you promise not to wave back,' I shudder.

It's nearly time for Elliot's bear talk. Joel joins us for the initial stroll through the meadow then breaks away from the pack.

'Look out for me on Half Dome,' he tells us. 'Otherwise I'll see you back at the hotel about 6 p.m.'

I turn to Elliot. 'Is there some plan I don't know about?'

'His friend rang while you were in the changing room – Jen? – she says we're welcome at the wedding reception tonight.'

'Really? Do you want to go?'

'I thought you probably would.'

'I'm not sure – it does throw up another clothing dilemma.'

'Your suitcase should definitely be back with you by this afternoon but if not one of the bridesmaids will have something you can borrow – apparently they've come with a full-size trunk just for one night.'

'OK, I'll think about it,' I concede.

'That's my group.' Elliot nervously points out a small gathering of hikers.

'Go David Attenborough!' I cheer as Elliot takes his position.

'From the chaparral-covered foothills to the high Sierra crest there are 4–600 black bears roaming Yosemite,' Elliot gets off to a poetic start. 'We often get asked whether you can outrun a bear. Well, the fastest human can run 23 m.p.h. A bear can run between 25 and 30 m.p.h. You might think you're in with a chance but let me tell you this – a bear can keep up that pace for ten hours!'

We all 'oooo', impressed.

'Now, you'll hear me talking about black bears but did you know that only 5 per cent of them are actually black? The majority are in fact brown or even cinnamon and vanilla.'

He's doing great! I give him a discreet thumbs-up. He responds by offering another fact, seemingly for my benefit. 'You've probably all been warned about bear break-ins. This is a serious problem – the bears are smart. Now, if they see a bear trap they've learned they don't slam hard so they leave a foot out then back out once they've nabbed the food. And when it comes to sniffing round cars, they do it at night while we're asleep.'

A six-year-old in a pink anorak sticks up her hand. 'If they're so clever why don't they break into the grocery store at night?'

His first heckler. Elliot opens his mouth then closes it, saved from having to come up with a response as all eyes are drawn to a frazzle-haired woman strolling by with three dogs and one cat on a leash.

'So!' he says, regaining our attention. 'Now we're going to play a little game and see if we can learn a bit about the noises a bear makes.'

He hands out a series of cards each with a different instruction on it. 'Clicking teeth' goes first.

'Very good,' he praises the little boy giving his milk teeth a hearty gnashing. 'That's a signal a mother gives her cub to climb a tree.' He points to the next child, who obviously got 'Grunt.' That means 'Come here now!'

An elderly gentleman hums. 'This is what bears do when they are content!' he tells us.

'We need a couple for this final one . . .' Elliot looks around. No volunteers. 'Lara – may I?'

Whatever it is, he may. I step forward and allow him to nuzzle at my face.

'Any idea?'

'Kissing!' squeals the pink anorak in delight.

'Correct!' Elliot cheers.

Don't stop! I yell internally.

I remain in a state of bliss until, for his grand finale, Elliot pulls what used to be a black bear out of his rucksack. It's skinned. Dead. Rolled-to-fit. Horrible. As he unravels it and passes it around the group one man shoves his hand up its head like a puppet.

'Where are its eyes?' pink anorak asks, on the verge of tears.

The bear is passed from one reluctant pair of hands to the next. When my turn comes I shrink back from its bristly touch.

'Whose idea was this?' I hiss at Elliot.

'Apparently it's standard – I think it's supposed to be educational,' he shrugs.

That's as may be, but it's not an image you want lingering. As Elliot concludes his talk I notice his group has gone from twenty fascinated faces to forty revulsed palms desperate for a bit of soap and water.

'If you drop the bearskin bit I reckon your show could run and run!' I congratulate Elliot as we head back to base to hitch a ride on the Valley Floor trolley.

As we step on board Elliot sneaks a packet of huckleberry jelly beans into my hand. 'I know how you hate cheesecake.'

My eyes well up and I clutch the jelly beans to my heart as if he'd kissed each one and then resealed the packet. Could it be that the old Elliot, the authentic Elliot, is making a comeback?

'All aboard!'

Our driver is Sam, a man of yeti-like height with a Bill Murray delivery. Gawping up at El Capitan we ask if he's a climber.

He shakes his head, 'I don't like heights. I don't even like being this tall.'

Apparently the average scaling of El Cap takes three to four days. Those who attempt it kip in sleeping bags pinned to the rockface and poop in containers they then have to carry with them to the top.

'Why would you?' Elliot shakes his head. 'Why, why, why?'

On to stunning Bridal Veil waterfall. That's the most common name for a waterfall, don't you know? Sam tells us how pure the tap water is in Yosemite and ridicules the fools (that'll be us) who pay for imported mineral water while in the park.

'Do you know Evian is naïve spelt backwards?' he notes before dazzling us with infinite geological facts.

'He's nearly as good as you,' I nudge Elliot.

I love this. I feel like we're on a date. Not one either of us would have chosen in our wildest dreams but a date nevertheless.

'Ew! Squished rabbit!' I point to a splattered furball on the road.

'Roadkill café, open 24 hours . . .' Sam deadpans.

Which reminds us – lunch!

After a platter of nachos with melted cheese and salsa we mooch around the Ansel Adams art gallery and then watch the 23-minute documentary on Yosemite – the closest we could get to going to the movies.

'I miss civilization,' Elliot sighs.

Funny, he hasn't said he misses Elise.

We conclude our out-of-character behaviour with a

299

two-hour horse ride. It seemed a 'silly' thing to do as Elliot has always actively avoided horses and has never even sat astride a seaside donkey but amazingly he relishes every clod-hopping, nostril-flaring second. Me, I like horses and I like the idea of cowgirling it through the countryside but in reality I find it staggeringly uncomfortable and always end up feeling bad for the blatantly bored horse. However, the sight of Elliot in his crash helmet makes the whole trip worthwhile.

'You look like you're about to be shot out of a cannon,' I tell him, then collapse with giggles yet again, inadvertently letting the reins go all slack.

'At least I can control my steed!' Elliot taunts as my Amber chomps down a tree.

I wrestle her head back to an upright position then chuck Elliot a curve ball: 'You know last night you said meeting Joel might be what The California Club had in mind for me?'

'Well, I don't know, I was just saying . . .' he panics, seemingly regretting his prediction.

'I was just going to ask what you think it had in mind for you?'

Elliot expels the longest sigh. His horse – Auburn – does the same.

'I've asked myself the same question. Over and over since I've been here. From what you've told me, I can see Sasha ending up with a new self-image, Zoë seeing the dark side of movie star glamour and Elise – well, as much as she's freaking I think it could be doing her some good. Maybe I was supposed to find inner peace.

But with all this space and time to think, I'm just questioning *everything*!'

It occurs to me that that's exactly what he needs to be doing but I decide I should let that thought pop into his head of its own accord.

'When you say everything . . .?'

'My job, the house we're about to buy, Elise's plans for the wedding, my future.'

Elise's plans for the wedding, not *our* plans for the wedding. Interesting.

'Have you come up with any answers?' I enquire, trying to stay neutral.

'Nothing conclusive,' he admits.

'Well, it's early days,' I shrug.

'Don't remind me!' Elliot groans, then snaps out of his fug. 'So. Joel. Are you two . . .?'

'What?' I give Elliot my blankest look.

'Oh come on, you shared a room last night, you'd both had a fair bit to drink . . .'

'I don't know to what you are alluding!' I tease. I could never lie to Elliot so the next best thing is to leave the matter open to interpretation.

'You used to tell me everything,' Elliot complains.

'Is he the kind of man you'd see me with?' I turn the tables, wanting to move on yet keep Joel in the conversation.

Elliot pulls a face. 'That's a tricky one.'

'Just out of curiosity, who would you see me with?' It's been ages since our last heart-to-heart.

Auburn clops on several paces before Elliot replies. 'I really don't know. Someone charming to wine and dine you and be all masterful and knowledgeable about life?'

'That's not at all what I want,' I counter, ducking under a low branch.

'What then?'

'Someone sweet and funny who really gets me,' I blurt. 'Someone who doesn't show off or lie or get competitive or put me down,' I flash through my previous relationships. 'A best friend,' I gulp. 'Anyway, lists don't mean anything. I've met people who seemed perfect on paper and they didn't do anything for me, or I didn't do anything for them.'

'You've got to have that desire, haven't you?' Elliot acknowledges.

'But it's so much more than lust, isn't it? I think there are people your heart just feels drawn to. People who get to you in a way unlike anyone else.'

'It wasn't really like that with Elise,' Elliot reveals. 'There was something there, other than her being such a rock when my parents died, and so we decided to make a go of it. It felt really grown-up.' Elliot frowns. 'Grown-up love? Doesn't sound very alluring, does it?'

No, but I know where he got the term from.

'How does it feel?' I ask.

'Safe. Different. More structured. Not really how I thought it would feel with the woman I was going to marry but there are always doubts, aren't there?'

'I suppose.'

'Don't you think?'

'Maybe it's healthier that way. When there are no

302

doubts there's no reason to hold back and then your heart just bungees and goes spinning out of control.'

'Sounds fantastic. Am I missing something?'

I smile, enigmatically I hope.

'So what are your reservations with Joel?'

'I don't know. Maybe I should go for it.' I dare myself to go one step further. 'I mean, do you know anyone who can make me a better offer?'

Elliot looks as if he's wrestling with an alligator internally.

Keen to leave that thought marinating a little longer I nudge Amber into a trot and call, 'Race you to Camp Clary!'

21

Outside the snow is falling like never-ending confetti. Inside Elliot and I lie by the fire, barely distinguishable from the cushions that have moulded to our bodies. His leg is slung over mine and occasionally his hand drops down from the back of the sofa to let his fingers absently entwine with my hair. Over and over I hear myself say, 'I'm so happy, I'm so happy!' and my heart shrugs off its pashmina to bask in the flame-danced light.

Knowing this is our last night together I go to speak but contentment gets the better of me. I don't want to hear my voice pretending to be carefree or seductive, I just want to revel in this perfect combination of physical comfort and emotional levitation.

Though it is now past midnight, the wedding party is still flurrying around us. Joel's dance card continues to be dominated by the over-seventies, who seem to see him as their last chance to grapple with some firm flesh. Elliot, on the other hand, attracted the under-sevens (now mercifully relegated to bed) on account of his 'funny accent' and funnier haircut. In order to satisfy the kiddies' need for constant conversation he toured them round the Ahwahneechee artefacts displayed on the walls – the bows and arrows and gold-panning pans and baby papooses, scrambling any historical knowledge they may have once had.

My big kick came when a little girl called Maddie told me I was like the 'pretty dark-haired lady' from *The Mummy*, so I plummed-up my accent and told her I'd just got back from the Pyramids that very day and the reason I was drinking so much wine was because it was actually a secret elixir keeping me alive.

'Are you married to Elliot?' she asked me as we queued up for the buffet.

In my tipsy state I replied that I wished I was but that Elliot was about to marry another lady.

'Why would he do that?' she wanted to know.

I said it was a very good question, especially since I suspected that Elise may have been a scarab beetle in a previous life. Then I remembered that children have a habit of repeating everything you say so I turned to take it all back. But Maddie was already at Elliot's side. I hurried over just in time to hear her ask, 'Why are you marrying another woman?'

Oh Gawd.

Elliot looked as stunned as if the shrimp on his plate had asked the question. 'Pardon?' he asked.

'Do you love her?' Maddie demanded, ever more indignant.

'Of course!'

'River deep, mountain high?' Maddie's eyes

narrowed as she referenced the Tina Turner song the bride and groom had chosen for their first dance.

'I guess.'

'I guess isn't good enough! I guess is only as deep as a puddle or as high as an anthill!' she trounced him.

I had the feeling she was going to grow up to be a lawyer.

'What was that all about?' Elliot asked, visibly shaken, as Maddie was removed to sit with her family.

'Oh you know, kids of that age get crushes so easily,' I covered. 'I'm sure she'll get over it in a year or two.'

We then meandered over to the edge of the dance floor where the bride and groom were still smooching.

'Look how close they are . . .' Elliot noted.

'Dancing cheek to cheek all the way down,' I sighed.

Elliot gave me a quizzical look.

'It's something June Whitfield said in an old comedy sketch.'

'There's no one quite like you, Lara.' Elliot shook his head.

Back at our hearthside haven Elliot stretches, arching his back and then slumps into a new position. I dare myself to relocate a little closer to him and lay a casual hand on his forearm. His incredibly toned, muscular forearm. Since when was the bit between the elbow and the wrist so erotic? Maybe it's all his precision drumstick control. All I know is that from my toes to my fingertips I'm screaming: This one! This is a match! Let's do it!

'Oh my God, listen!' Elliot grabs me. 'They're playing our song!'

When he says 'our song' it was never remotely lyric-specific to our situation, it was just one of those tunes that got under our skin – *Would I Lie To You* by Charles & Eddie. At the time I had black hair down to my waist, which meant I was Eddie, leaving Charles for Elliot. We always argued over who got the 'Woo!' bits and 'Would I lie to you?' became our most overused phrase of that year.

Elliot laughs, seemingly untroubled for the first time today. As for me, I'm suspended in joy and yet fully aware of how far I have to fall. As much as I wish this was my life, it's not. This is a sidestep into a parallel universe showing me how things might have been if Elliot had loved me.

Suddenly the pang of longing that lives inside me swells and overwhelms me. This is all I want – this feeling with Elliot – and I want it to last and I want it to be mine, not a mirage. I can't bear how precarious this transcendental state is. I'm even dreading one of the charcoaled logs shifting for fear that the crumbling ash will prompt a shift in mood.

'Five minutes, Elliot?' Mr Gediman leans over the back of the sofa and gives Elliot a shake.

That'll do it.

I quickly blink back the tears that have lined up and sniff briskly as he tells us, 'All good things must come to an end!'

Elliot shifts forward and rubs his face.

'OK, I'll be with you in a second!'

It's too soon. I don't want him to go. If you ask me, I'll come with you, I speak to him in my head. *But you have to ask me . . .*

He doesn't.

'Maybe I could come back with you,' I suggest.

'Are you insane? And leave all this?' He shakes his head.

'But I haven't had the full park experience!' I reason.

Elliot pulls me into a hug and I feel my heart collapse.

'Come here!'

Normally I can hold it together because I'm prepared, but an hour of lying together 'as if' has played tricks on me. I can't distance myself enough. Fortunately he continues to hold me, talking into my hair: 'You know that you are more than welcome in my musty sleeping bag but I'd rather think of you here in a warm bed.' He pulls back to look at me and the usual fondness in his eyes takes on a new poignancy. I feel his hands leave my arms and move up to my face, tucking my hair behind my ears and then tracing the line of my cheekbone with the deftest touch. Then he looks at my mouth as if he's seeing it for the first time. 'You're so lovely,' he breathes.

One part of me swoons as the other screams: Don't! Don't take another step closer unless you mean it! I feel completely at his mercy. Can he tell?

'Lara,' he says simply as he leans forward and lays the sweetest kiss on my lips. I can feel it everywhere. It's more than I even hoped to feel.

'Elliot?' Mr Gediman interrupts. 'Oh sorry!'

'OK! Let's go!' Elliot jumps to his feet, tousling my hair and pushing me back to friend status. 'I'll swing by tomorrow for breakfast.'

How can he leave? How can he do that and then leave? I can't speak. I feel stunned. Every part of me is crying out for him. And he's gone.

Calling upon one of the larger tapestry cushions to fill the gap that he's left I relive the kiss. I've fantasized about a sequel to the house-party kiss for so many years and now that it has happened I'm feeling something I wasn't expecting to feel. I can't quite define it. I set aside the lust and desire and dreaminess and realize that there are traces of anger. Indignation. Some part of me is actually annoyed – as far as he's concerned I'm getting it on with Joel so why now should he make a move? Is he simply trying to regain supremacy in my heart? Can his ego not take a rival – even though he's not offering me anything he still wants 100 per cent of my devotion. But of course he's not like that.

I try and squish my heart back into its feeling-proof container but it keeps pinging out again like a jack-in-the-box.

'I'm not done! You just got me all stirred up and now you want me to lie down and play sleeping lions? I can't do it!'

'You have to!' I tell it. 'There's nowhere for the love to go. He's walked away. You have to get a grip. You have to hold it back. You have to pretend it didn't happen, just to stop yourself going insane.'

A brief swish of calm descends.

But then my heart has another tantrum. 'I don't want to feel calm!' it screams. 'That's not what I'm here for. I'm here to feel everything, to experience love. *Please . . .*'

All I can say is, 'I'm sorry. Not yet. Soon, I promise. (I hope.) Let me get you a drink.'

I'm just knocking back a medicinal brandy when the bride lunges at the bar.

'Vodka orange,' she requests. 'And make it a triple – I intend to start married life with the mother of all hangovers!'

As I do a quick double-take, she catches my eye and puts a lacy arm around me.

'What kinda night are you having?'

'Oh, great, yes – thank you so much for letting us come!'

She shrugs as she takes a swig. 'Well, I always like to see Joel happy.'

'Oh no, it's not like that!' I jump in, just in case even on her wedding day she's feeling proprietorial over her ex.

'I saw you with that other guy.' She nods over to the fireplace.

'Elliot,' I mutter, with downcast eyes.

'But he's gone.'

'Yes,' I confirm.

She cocks her head to one side. 'Don't you find it tiring feeling heartbroken all the time?'

My jaw drops at her insight into my condition. 'Is there an alternative?' I ask.

'There is tonight.'

I raise an eyebrow.

'His name is Joel. Trust me, you won't regret it.'

'Regret what?' A male voice joins us.

It's Joel. It would be.

'I'm just recommending one of the activities available at the hotel.'

'At this time of night?' Joel looks bemused.

'Oh this one goes right through till the morning.' She winks before giving him a peck on the cheek and Tina Turner-ing her way back to her husband.

'What was that all about?' Joel laughs. Before I can fudge an answer he bumps me playfully and says, 'So – was that a kiss I spied earlier?'

I attempt a triumphant twinkle: 'That was not *a* kiss. That was *the* kiss!'

'I knew if I gave you guys some room something would happen,' Joel grins then prompts, 'And yet?' noticing the smudge of sadness on my face.

Immediately I'm crestfallen. 'It's not enough.'

'Tell me what you want,' he urges.

'Everything,' I quaver. 'Everything, or what's the point?'

Joel takes my hands and wraps them around his waist. 'A kiss is a good start.'

'Yes,' I concede, leaning against his shoulder, glad of the comfort. 'And, you know, if I was here for a few more days I'd feel pretty optimistic but I'm leaving for LA tomorrow and—'

'By the way, I'll drive you,' he cuts in.

I pull back and gawp at him. 'Don't be silly, that's 300 miles!'

'I've got a meeting at the Bel Air Hotel in the afternoon so I have to go anyway, it's really you who'd be doing me the favour, keeping me company on that tedious journey.'

'Are you sure?' I succumb to a half-smile. I'd be a fool to fight his offer.

'There is one catch – we'd have to leave about 7 a.m.'

I don't need to look at my watch. Even if was 6 a.m. now I'd still go – he's taken a lonely trip and turned it into the chance to have another adventure. Suddenly I don't know what I'd do without him.

'I love you Joel,' I say, looking directly into his midnight eyes. The brandy has made me daring.

'I love you too, Lara,' he responds just as steadily.

We hold each other's gaze. It's just for a few seconds but long enough to cross over into new territory. I can feel my heart saying, What about him? He seems willing. I've got so much to give right now, please let me love someone.

'So now you're thinking, "Could we? Should we? *Will we?*"' Joel teases, leaning closer with each question.

I laugh, trying to cover my embarrassment and inner palpitations as I squeak, 'Could we?'

'We could indeed.'

'Should we?' My voice involuntarily takes on a more serious tone.

'It would definitely be fun.'

'Will we?' By now I am practically hoarse.

'That's up to you,' he says simply.

Suddenly it's right there, so close I could reach out and grab it – literally! He's talking sex, not a relationship, I know that. But what an offer. The best I've had in a long time.

I emit a tremulous sigh. 'No, I don't want to mess things up, I like things just the way they are between us.' I reach for the bar snacks but he stops me.

'Just like you're happy with the way things are between you and Elliot?'

I look confused.

'You're scared of messing up that friendship, aren't you?'

'Of course I am!' I puff. 'If I make some big love confession I could ruin everything. I'm not sure it's worth the risk.'

'It's the thing you want most in the world and you're not prepared to take a risk for it?' Joel confronts me.

'I don't want to make him feel uncomfortable,' I mumble, feeling feeble.

'It's only the truth,' Joel shrugs. 'All you would be doing is putting your truth out there. How he reacts is up to him.'

This man certainly has a way of making things sound so simple. I push a scattering of pistachio shells into a neat little circle. Maybe I am a bigger part of Elliot and I not getting together than I realize.

'I have moments when I think it's the only thing to do – to tell him how I feel – and other times I think I've just got to let go,' I explain.

'You know you're coming very close to now or never,' Joel warns. 'I reckon he can handle it, either way. The question is, can you?'

313

I take a moment to think and then squirm. 'I don't know.'

'Maybe we should give you some practice, then.'

'What do you mean?' I ask, feeling unsettled.

Joel takes my hand, which is absently pinching my pistachio shell circle into a straight line, and rumbles, 'Practise on me!'

I knew the man had killer sex appeal but I had yet to experience its full force directed at me. My stomach and loins flurry excitedly.

'I've only known you thirty or so hours but I'd say we're friends, wouldn't you?'

I nod vigorously, unable to speak.

'OK. Well, I tell you what – we're going to cross that line. Together.'

Before I can voice any concerns he leans forward and kisses me. I take a moment to register the sensation. Not bad, but it's not Elliot.

He contemplates my expression and kisses me again. More tenderly, languorously. Hmmmm. Not Elliot. *Joel.*

This time he seems pleased with my reaction. Me too.

'Again,' I request, pulling him towards me.

There's something so appealing about a man who really wants to kiss you. Someone volunteering to be with you, no conditions, no complications, no restraints.

He's right, I haven't known him long but sometimes it's better kissing a man you don't know too well because then you can kiss them with all your heart because – who knows – they could be the one. And it's not that you necessarily think they are, it's just that you don't know enough about them to be sure that they're not.

'Hey man – you up for a game of pool?' A beefy bloke slaps his arm around Joel's shoulders.

Joel turns to me as if to say, What do you want to do?

I give an exaggerated yawn. 'I don't know about you, but I'm ready for bed.'

22

'*No!*'

I've been watching Joel sleep for the past twenty minutes and it freaks me out that this is how he chooses to greet the morning-after-the-night-before.

'*No! No!*' he continues his emphatic remonstration.

His eyes are still tightly closed. Is he sleep-talking? Dreaming? *Remembering?*

'Joel?' I whisper, paranoia gnawing at me.

He groans and flips on to his side, announcing: 'NO, I don't regret it. NO, it's not going to be awkward between us. And NO, I'm not gonna try and wriggle out of driving you to Los Angeles.'

He opens one eye. 'OK?'

'OK!' I grin, totally busted.

He looks past me to the alarm clock: 5.45 a.m. 'Five more minutes?' he entreats.

I snuggle back into the warmth of his furry chest – the kind that looks like it's been blown-dry and feels like a nest made of softly spun silk.

Now Joel's said his piece I feel secure in the knowledge that he's not going to squirm away from me or pretend it didn't happen. Or pretend it was anything more than it was. I like how he's honest with me and doesn't invent stuff that he thinks I want to hear. He's the same person he was at the wedding reception last night. Only with fewer clothes. And that's the way it should be.

I don't understand why so many men shut down directly after an intimate encounter. In theory it should bring you closer together but that's rarely been my experience. Is it panic at being confronted with real emotions that throws them through a loop? Embarrassment at having shown some vulnerability? Or is it that, in trying to second guess what the girl is thinking, they mistakenly presume you always want more from them? They daren't be nice or civil in case they encourage you.

Generally the best thing to do is to get the hell out of Dodge ASAP. But not today. Today I'm going to enjoy the chest then I'm going to have breakfast with it and then take a six-hour drive with it. And it's going to be fine. More than fine. I know that because I haven't woken up feeling as if I lost something in the night. There are no regrets. Even when I think about Elliot. Yes, that fireside kiss was pure bliss, but I'm still a little miffed that he made his move on Joel's time, rather than the endless free years he could have chosen. It makes me question his motivation. All the same, I was concerned that being with Joel would feel like a betrayal. But it didn't. It felt like an entirely separate part of my life, and, if anything, I feel more balanced about Elliot today because I'm no longer quite so far behind in the *amour* stakes. Now I've had a bit of action I don't have to be resentful of my feelings for him, because this time they haven't stopped me having fun.

A big smile spreads across my face. Apparently it *is* possible to get it on with a friend and still be buddies the next day. I'd even go one step further: sometimes it doesn't ruin everything, it makes it *better*!

One of Joel's hands slips over the side of the bed and reappears with a bottle of Evian in its grasp.

'Slurp of Naïve, darling?'

I eagerly rehydrate then ask, 'Are you the perfect boyfriend?'

'As a matter of fact I'm the world's *worst* boyfriend,' he states, frankly. 'But I do a nice line in do-gooder shagging.'

'You should rent yourself out.'

'I've thought about it, but if I did it on a regular basis all my clients would fall in love with me and then where would I be?'

'Loved?' I suggest.

For a moment he looks thrown. And a little bit lost. I try to un-trigger the emotion by joking, 'I have the same problem. Once a man has been with me, no other woman can compare. I mean, you're utterly smitten now, aren't you?'

'Besotted. Being with you is like a drug. You're like those cane toads they lick in South America to trip on.'

'I'm like a *toad*?!'

He responds to my outrage by licking me from shoulder to ear in one slurp.

'Eurghhh! Get off!' I shudder, writhing beneath him. He continues the licking so I start tickling him. Bad idea – now he's licking and tickling me. I can't bear it and squeal in a state of squirmy delirium.

'Wait!' I say, holding him away from me for a second. 'Was that the door?'

'Dunno!' He grabs me again, pulling me on top of him.

'I'd better check,' I say, wriggling out of his grasp. I pull the sheet off the bed to swathe it around myself but he pulls it back. As we indulge in a farcical tug-of-war there's another knock at the door.

'Joel!' I despair. He still won't relinquish the sheet so instead I have to make do with two of the extra-large pillows – one in front, one behind – so I now look like a cuddly version of a sandwich-board street walker.

'Nice look!' Joel calls after me.

When I get to the door, I have to press the back pillow against the wall in order to free up a hand to open the latch.

'Oh! Sorry!' Elliot looks absolutely mortified at the sight of me – the muss of my hair and flush of my cheeks leaving him in no doubt that naked frolicking has been prematurely curtailed. 'Bad time?'

'Actually your timing is perfect,' I tell him. 'You've rescued me from death by tickling – come in.'

'No, no, I'm fine. I was up early and I just wondered if you fancied getting some breakfast before you left.'

'Of course! Just give us half an hour.'

'Oh.' By the look on his face he wasn't planning on hearing the 'us' word, but he quickly composes himself. 'OK. Well, no rush. You just . . .' He waves an arm back towards the bedroom.

I close the door and take a moment to assess what I'm feeling. Half of me wants to run after him and say, 'It's not what you think! Well, actually it is but given the choice I would have rather shagged you but you didn't offer and Joel did . . .' And the other half is saying, 'Now you get to see how I feel every time I see you with another woman.'

'Share a moment, share life!' Joel sings along to the jingle for a Kodak ad as he flicks through the TV channel. Meanwhile I sidestep my way across the room so as not to flash too much flesh.

Joel looks over and smiles. 'All right there, crab-lady!'

'Yes, thank, you.'

He leans on his elbow so he can get a better look at the gap between the pillows. 'Do you get that TV show *Scrubs* in the UK?'

'Yes, most amusing,' I tell him. 'Why do you ask?'

'Remember that scene where Turk's girlfriend is all miffed at him for bragging to his mates about their sex life before they've even done it?'

I look blank.

Joel adopts a feisty Latino accent and says, 'Is that how you see this relationship? As some mad dash to the finishing line? Because I'll take you into the bedroom right now and I promise you, you will be walking sideways for the rest of your life because I will have used up all your up and down!'

I chuckle, recalling last night's up and downs – they certainly went beyond acceptable quotas. I wonder what the average number of ups and downs per shag would be? Must remember to count next time. Oooh, hark at the new optimistic me presuming that there will be a next time! Instead of fearing an intimacy-free life, all of a sudden I can't wait to see who it'll be with!

'What are you looking so pleased about?' Joel laughs.

'Nothing!' I pipe. 'I'm just going to jump in the shower.'

23

'Dear God, could this be any more orgasmic?' I ask, sinking my teeth into an apple crêpe oozing raspberry purée.

'Well . . .' Joel gives me a naughty look.

Elliot goes cross-eyed staring into the bottom of his coffee cup.

Bless him, I don't suppose he's ever witnessed Lara the Sex Object before. I feel a little uneasy at the level of schmaltz Joel is peddling but I know his excessive flirtation is partly just a last desperate bid to prompt a jealous outburst from Elliot. I'm hoping for something along the lines of 'Step away from the damsel! She can never be yours for she loves only me! This very morning I awoke to find my love for her soars high above the mariposa trees!' That would please Maddie.

Instead he says: 'Do you have any tomato ketchup?' and he's not even talking to me.

As the gaps allotted for Elliot to speak go unused, Joel decides to fill them.

'Do you think you'd ever do it again, angelica – you know, embrace the Great Outdoors?'

I think for a moment. Not having camped out or endured a ten-mile trek I feel a bit like I've done the drive-by Disney version of wilderness – I've been on all the rides but spent more time foraging in the gift shop than actually experiencing the snap of a twig underfoot.

'I think if I did do it again, I'd almost need to come for longer,' I decide. 'You know – give myself a chance to get past the boredom and surrender to the serenity.'

'Is that a yes?' he asks.

'Well, I don't want to make a habit of this fresh air lark but it certainly has novelty appeal!' I try and get a smile out of Elliot. No dice.

Joel leans closer. 'I was just thinking, I'd love to take you to Lake Tahoe – we could get a cosy little log cabin by the water's edge, go skinny-dipping in the moon-light . . .'

The dreamy look on my face is for real. This man is like the promise of another world. I try to imagine what it would be like dating someone like him but somehow even the fantasy seems out of reach. He's so fully present right now but I get the feeling he could vanish at any time, without any warning.

'Whadda y'say, babycakes?' Joel slides his hand along my thigh.

'If it's got a patchwork quilt and room service, I'm in,' I announce. There's a chink of cutlery on china as Elliot savages his eggs Florentine.

'Everything all right?'

'Fine!' he trills.

'Looks good.' I prod my fork at his spinach-heaped muffin.

'Actually, Elise does a better hollandaise sauce.' He sticks his nose in the air.

For once I smile at his mention of the devil woman. If I didn't know better I'd swear we were finally getting to him!

After arranging a bag of muffins for the road (and a small care package for Elliot) we head down the exterior walkway to the car. By the third hanging basket I realize Elliot is deliberately skulking behind us. By the fourth I've hung back and linked my arm in his, knowing these are the last few steps we'll take together. By the fifth, Joel has me in a fireman's lift and is charging for the valet parking desk.

'It's the black Cherokee,' he says, pointing over to nearby carpark where his jeep is in view.

'We have a bit of a backlog, sir. If you could just bear with us.'

'I'll get it myself, no problem,' he tells the valet, exchanging a $5 bill for his keys and setting me down. 'Stay put, I'll bring it round.'

Elliot watches Joel jog off and mutters, 'I'll just run a quick marathon while I'm at it . . .' then ushers me away from the other guests awaiting their vehicles. 'Lara, I need to talk to you.'

Could the taunt about Lake Tahoe have done the trick after all? He did seem to prickle.

'It's about Elise.'

I grimace. Don't rain on my parade, mister!

'If you've got a message for her, why don't you jot it down?' I suggest, cheerfully picturing her drowning in a vat of hollandaise sauce. I'm not reciting love lines to her.

'It's just . . . I was wondering if you could let me know how she's getting on—'

'You can ask her yourself in two days,' I cut in. 'I've got the magic cellphone, remember? I'll put you on to her as soon as I get there.'

'No! I mean . . . I'd rather you had the chance to sense her mood first. See how she's feeling about us – the wedding and everything.'

'Are you worried that she might be having second thoughts?'

Elliot looks shifty.

'What is it?' I frown.

He falters, apparently struggling to find the words. When his eyes lock with mine he changes tack: 'You seem to be getting on better than ever with Joel.'

'I am,' I beam.

'Seeing you with him . . .'

My smile fades. 'Yes?'

'It's made me realize . . .' Elliot pauses, eyes searching mine. 'I'm looking at you and . . .'

I raise my eyebrows to encourage him to go on. Words are failing me but inside I'm chanting: Say you're jealous. Say you're jealous.

'I'm jealous,' he confesses.

Oh my God! I gasp. Here we go!

'I want what you've got,' he says simply.

Hmmm. I want what you've got. Not I want *you*. We're getting there *but* . . .

'You want what I've got?' I repeat, angling for clarification.

'The two of you look like you're having a blast.' I don't want to overplay the projection of Joel and myself as a Brad & Jen match-made-in-heaven so I say, 'Well, it's always like that at the beginning, isn't it? I'm sure you and Elise—'

'It was never like that with us. It was great in other ways—'

'Well, then!' I jump in, nerves getting the better of me.

A horn that has been tooting for the last few seconds now comes with a vocal accompaniment: 'Lara! Over here!'

It's Joel, beckoning to me. He mimes that he can't come back round to the entrance because of the car congestion.

'One second.' I give Elliot the 'hold that thought' finger and run over to Joel.

'Bloody hell!' I pant, leaning in the driver window. 'He's just confessed that he's jealous!'

Joel's face lights up. 'Did he say he wants you?'

'No,' I admit. 'But he wants what I have. With you.'

'He wants me?'

'No!' I scoff. 'He wants the fun stuff.'

'He wants to have fun. But not with you.' Joel talks it back to me with the cold-light-of-day glare.

'Well, he hasn't specifically said with me but—'

'Then you get your ass in this vehicle now,' Joel commands.

'But!' I protest.

'Look, he's obviously having some kind of epiphany about his relationship with Elise. Maybe it's seeing us together, maybe it's having time apart from her, maybe it's the prunes he had for breakfast. Whatever it is, great! About time! But if you stay with him now and talk him through what he's feeling, that's you finished – you'll just be counsellor girl, listening ear, damp shoulder, good ole trusty Lara, you get me?'

I turn and look back at Elliot. He looks fretful in the extreme, as if he's trying to unravel internal knots using mind control alone.

'Are you sure? I feel like I should be there in his hour of need,' I worry.

'I thought you had an appointment with Zoë,' Joel reminds me.

'I do, but—'

Joel takes my chin in his hand so he can bore into my eyes. 'You stay with him now, you're going to have to listen to him sift through every stage of their relationship. It's going to be all about her, nothing about you.'

I don't want that to happen but Joel could have a point.

'Does that sound like fun to you?' Joel enquires.

'No,' I concede, fiddling with the door lock. The shape of it reminds me of the pegs that come with a set of travel Mastermind.

'Lara.' Joel clicks his fingers like a hypnotist trying to wake up his patient. 'Your heart has been aching for him for ten years, it won't do him any harm to have a few days' misery.'

I sigh. 'OK. Just give me a moment to say goodbye.'

'Good girl. Quick pep talk and a peck and let's be on our way.'

I stride back to Elliot telling myself that discipline and restraint is the order of the day. Stay away from the light. No blubbing, no clinging, no releasing ten years of pent-up love and affection.

'Elliot. I feel awful leaving you at a time like this,' I begin.

'I know you've got to go. I don't mean to worry you, I've just been thinking about things all night and we haven't really had the chance to talk.'

I try to dodge a pang of guilt but it gets the better of me. 'I'm sorry Joel's been around the whole time.'

'That's fine. You deserve some, er, romance. I just,' he sighs, 'miss you!' He shrugs, looking sorrowful.

I tilt my head and give him a quizzical look.

'You've always been my number one girl and all of a sudden I feel I'm losing you,' he whispers, scuffing the ground.

My heart strains towards him and I confess: 'I've been missing you a lot too, ever since you've been with Elise.'

He looks me in the eye and nods, understanding. 'I was thinking about that last night. I didn't realize until now how that might have felt for you.'

Oh why are we having this conversation now, with just seconds to go? As if sensing a moment of weakness Joel leans heavily on the horn.

'I have to go,' I say, forcing myself to get practical when all I want to do is hug and reassure him and wallow in our revitalized empathy. 'So. With Elise. You just want me to see how she is?'

He nods. 'We haven't really had any time apart since we met. I just want to know . . .' He shrugs. 'I don't know.'

Poor Elliot, he looks a terrible mix of confused and despondent.

'Look, I'm sure it doesn't feel like this now and yes I am partly saying this to make myself feel better about leaving you, but having a few more nights out here to sit quietly and fill your lungs with this amazing air could help you clear your mind so you can figure out what you really want.'

He nods.

'And don't just think about relationships!' I add. 'Think about what makes you happy.'

That'll be me.

'OK.'

'And if all that thinking means you end up a total basket case I'm sure Elise will be able to recommend a great therapist!' I tease, hoping to provoke a reaction.

He gives me a playful swipe. He's coming back. 'I'll be fine,' he forces a smile.

'Really?'

'Would I lie to you?'

I grin, suddenly filled up with longing to kiss his cares away.

'One day I'll get it right,' he says.

'I know you will,' I say, hugging him goodbye, trying not to squeeze too tight.

As I turn to leave he asks, 'What about you and Joel?'

If I was being honest I'd tell him, 'I have a feeling that, after today, I'm never going to see him again!' but I'm learning to keep shtum more often so instead I say: 'I guess we'll hang out until one of us gets a better offer.'

Elliot laughs. 'Well. Good luck.'

'You too.'

This is crazy. I'll be seeing him again in three days. Why is this such a wrench?

Then, blocking myself so Joel can't see my face, I lean in and give Elliot the softest, most loving kiss on the lips.

He looks almost surprised.

'Thanks,' he sighs.

I feel a melting sensation as his eyes warm me. I can't speak. I daren't. Instead I give a muffled 'mmmff' sound and turn and run to the car.

Joel is right. I need to let Elliot work out which way is up. For once I'm going to leave things to breathe, to find their natural level. I'm not going to look back at him. I'm not, I'm not, I'm not.

24

'Eyes forward!' Joel barks, tiring of my transfixion with the wing-mirror.

'Oh, it's agony!' I wail, slumping back into my seat.

We haven't even left the park boundary and despite our strict schedule I've already tried to side-track Joel twice – once to see the Grizzly Giant (a 2,700-year-old sequoia tree), the other for a ride on the Sugar Pine Railroad – anything in the vain hope we'll loop back to Elliot.

'You're making me feel like I've kidnapped some poor little forest-dweller!' he complains, defiantly flooring. 'Off we go to the big bad city so I can corrupt you!'

'Sorry Joel!' I cringe with shame. 'You are a total star to drive me, I'd be a wreck without you.' Giving his gearstick hand a squeeze, I stare determinedly ahead, curbing my craving as we bullet past Erna's Elderberry House – could it have a cuter name?

All too soon we're back in the flat modern world – a.k.a. Fresno – with its concrete strip malls and pretzel emporiums.

It's strange to think I flew in just two days ago with one man on my mind and now I'm leaving with another.

'What?' Joel asks.

My face must be doing something giveaway.

'I was just thinking how bleak it looks round here,' I fib.

'You think?' Joel queries.

'Don't you?'

'I know something you don't.' Joel jiggles his eyebrows.

'Oh really?' I glint.

'Have we got time for a half-hour diversion?'

Oh, I see – *now* he's prepared to linger a while. Not that I'm complaining.

'Let's do it!' I enthuse.

Joel insists I close my eyes until we get there and so for ten or so swervy-curvy minutes, images of $5 Shoe World and Hot-Dog-on-a-Stick vendors parade through my mind.

Finally we bump to a halt.

'Now?' I ask.

'Not yet!' Joel cautions.

I hear him thunk his car door closed and then un-click mine.

'Keep them closed,' he instructs as he guides me across the uneven ground.

'What's that amazing smell?' I breathe in a delicate yet overwhelming perfume sent to me on a warm breeze.

'OK . . . now!' Joel whispers.

At first I can't make sense of what I'm seeing –
I seem to be entirely immersed in a fluffy pink
heaven.

'Where are we?' I gasp.

'Blossom Trail.' Joel smiles at my enchantment.
'The orchards run for miles round here. Almond,
peach, apricot . . .' As Joel continues his list – 'apple,
orange' – he reaches out and shakes the tree I am
standing beneath, showering me in soft pink kisses. I
laugh as the paper-thin silk flutters between my
fingers. For as far as the eye can see, the twisty little
trees and surrounding earth are covered in pink and
white petals. I feel like I'm in a dream scene from one
of those MGM extravaganzas – any minute now
dozens of beribboned dancers will waft by in sugary
chiffon, swirling up the confetti carpet.

'What are you trying to do to me?' I sob as Joel pulls
me into a warm all-encompassing hug.

'Nothing,' he smiles into my hair. 'Except maybe
raise your game!'

I twist around so I can see his face.

'It's all out there if you really look,' he asserts.

'Were you born like this?' I laugh, marvelling as
much at Joel as at our soft-focus surroundings.

'Like what?' Joel worries.

'With so much energy for . . . I don't know – seeking
out life's wonders?'

'I could ask you the same question.'

'I wouldn't have much of an answer.'

'Come on, you go rummaging around your antique
stores, don't you? Looking for hidden treasures.'

'This is on a slightly grander scale.'

'So open your eyes a little wider,' he shrugs. 'Like I say, it's all there, waiting to be seen.'

I look around. My heart swells just a little bit more. And then a thought crosses my mind.

'Are you trying to show me there is more to life than Elliot?'

'I'd hope you'd already know that.'

'I do, it's just . . . I do.'

'How do you feel right now?' Joel asks me.

'About him?' I think for a moment. The pang isn't quite so wrenchy-sickly as it was in the car, it's more a profound wish that he could be here with me, sharing this beauty.

'Better,' I'm surprised to hear myself say. 'Calmer.'

'Well, if it seems to be getting too much again or you're ever just feeling empty inside, here's my tip for you – try and fill yourself up with something else. You can't always get what you want romantically but the world is more than willing to offer you up some amazing alternatives.'

I get a sudden flash of Joel as a bereaved heart, someone who couldn't have his one true love and, seeing as no one else can compare, has been seeking out other and more extreme passions ever since. 'Is that what you're doing – trying to fill up your heart in other ways?' I gently probe. But he ignores my question.

'You're a visual person,' he continues. 'You should seek out the beauty in art, landscapes—'

'Your face!' I offer.

He breaks into a grin. 'If I had any sense I'd challenge Elliot to a duel and win you for myself.' Then he adds sadly, 'But I haven't.'

'It's OK,' I tell him, feeling I understand even though I'm only guessing at why he's like he is. 'We're just making the most of the here and now. And I'm loving every second.'

It's funny how some people come into your life so intensely and yet so briefly. Of course I don't want this to be all, I don't want to say goodbye today and then for us never to see each other again, but there's something finite about Joel. Something that says, Don't get too close. Make the most of me now because I can't make any promises. And that's fine. At least it's fine right now because I'm with him. I'm not sure how I'll feel when the time comes for him to leave.

'I tell you one thing,' I say, as we make our way back to the car. 'You've changed my mind for ever about Fresno!'

Two hours later we're in Cholame, pausing beside the memorial marking the spot where James Dean crashed his Porsche Spyder in 1955. I'm just musing over the fact that tomorrow I'll be the same age as him – thirty – when Joel reminds me I promised to speak to Elise today.

'Do I have to?' I whine.

'You never know, she could be bequeathing Elliot to you,' Joel suggests. 'You said she sounded a bit wobbly.'

'I think it was just wishful thinking. Hey! Maybe you

could seduce her and leave Elliot free for me?' I give Joel a '*Oh go on!*' look.

'I don't do charity cases,' he retorts.

'You did me!'

'You were an honour and a privilege.'

'Really?' I beam.

'Call her.'

I dial her number and humph a 'Hello?' into the receiver.

'Oh Lara! Can we speak later? Only the Ho'opono-pono class is about to start!'

I frown. She's either turned piss-taking to an art form or is expressing genuine interest in self-improvement. That can't be right.

'Come again?'

'Ho'oponopono,' she repeats as if I'm being deliberately dim. 'It's the ancient Hawaiian art of problem-solving. Apparently you can heal hurtful memories without having to replay them.'

I wonder why she's in such a hurry to get there. I see Elise as the kind of person who inflicts hurt on other people rather than receives it. What memory is she hoping to zap?

'It starts in five minutes,' she whines. 'I don't want to miss neutralizing the negative energies.'

'Of course not – off you go!'

I'm incredulous. And a little bit afraid. I want to hate Elise. I need to hate Elise. But it's very hard to despise people who are trying to better themselves. Oh no! What if she's developing into this angelic being and just when Elliot is having doubts she's going to reveal her new glowy-pure side and he'll fall in love with her all over again? I can't bear it!

I switch off the phone so she can't call back, and mantra 'Blossom, blossom, blossom' to myself, trying to recapture my former sense of hope and wonder but with Elise presiding over my thoughts the silken petals wither to a brown pulp.

Finally we arrive in LA.

'I think we'll take the surface streets so you can see a bit of city,' Joel decides, coming off the freeway early. 'Everyone says there's no centre to Los Angeles but I'd say this is the closest thing – you've got Farmer's Market and The Grove right here, and the Beverly Centre mall is just down there,' he points to our left and then turns down a quiet residential street.

'The houses are so pretty!' I gasp. 'And so different,' I note as we progress – Spanish-style haciendas next to mock French château with pointy turrets, Walton-style shacks with sunny porches facing twee balconies with Hansel & Gretal cookie-cut woodwork, one place a-blaze of Moroccan blue paintwork. Others are just grey motel-like blocks though some have authentic Fifties lettering and star motifs that put me in mind of *Bewitched*. As well as the obligatory palm trees, there are neatly trimmed privets, sprawling ivy, proud and pointy birds of paradise and paper-thin bougainvillaea spilling over whitewashed walls.

'They're really into fairy lights here, aren't they?' I'm tickled to note how many gardens have sets twisting around their foliage.

'Give me Zoë's address again?' Joel frowns, distracted.

I read the slip of paper to him. The doorlocks click simultaneously.

'It said Hollywood that way,' I point back to the sign we just passed.

'She's not in Hollywood.'

'But—'

'She works there, I know, but she lives in Korea Town.'

'Is that bad?'

'Decide for yourself.'

All too soon the pretty houses are replaced by dodgy-looking apartments and the chipper souls walking their dogs become bandana'd youths.

'Are we in gangland?' I shiver.

'Gangland adjacent, I think would be the estate agent's term,' Joel grimaces.

I tell myself it's bohemian. 'I bet a lot of arty types live here.'

'It's certainly cheaper to rent round here,' Joel looks on the bright side. 'What number are we looking for?'

'722,' I tell him.

'Should be 911,' he mutters.

'This is it!' I peer up at the kind of brick building I'd expect to find in New York. No glittery cement here.

'I'll come with you.' Joel escorts me to the door and scans the streets for potential sources of trouble as I jab the doorbell. I ring and ring but no reply.

'Try her at work,' Joel suggests.

'Lara!' Zoë answers out of breath. 'I tried to call you but I couldn't get through!'

That'll be Elise's fault, I forgot to switch the phone back on.

'They've changed my shift – I have to work till 6 p.m., there's no getting out of it,' Zoë humphs.

'Don't worry – well, it's a bummer for you, but I can easily amuse myself.'

'Where are you now?'

'At your apartment.'

Silence.

'Zoë?'

'Isn't it cool?' she blusters. 'It's a really up-and-coming neighbourhood!'

'Don't you get scared here?' I grimace at the sound of someone's phlegm-tastic cough and a car backfiring. I hope.

'Oh no! It's all about keeping it real. There's loads of celebs in the area.'

A man in a hairnet and fiendish moustache eyes us suspiciously as he exits the building. I can't even imagine who Zoë might mistake him for.

'I think I'll come back over Hollywood way,' I stammer, daunted by the prospect of having to stay here with her tonight. This is not the LA we had envisioned. I want to hang out by a hotel pool, not struggle to get a solitary drip out of a rusty shower-head. Maybe we could just check into the Viceroy for the next two nights, I hear it's intimidatingly fashionable – that's the level of discomfort I'm prepared to experience, not this!

'You *have* to go to Fredericks of Hollywood Lingerie Museum,' Zoë busily plans my afternoon's itinerary. 'Boris told me about it – they've got those fluffy Fembot négligés from *Austin Powers* and Ava Gardner's gorgeous nightie from *Showboat* and Tom Hanks' boxers from *Forrest Gump*!'

'OK!' I intervene.

'The best bit is the undie catalogues from the Fifties – they had blow up bras called Belle Air and there's one called Tidal Wave that you could wear under swimwear—'

'Yup, I'll definitely—' I try to cut her short. I don't think Joel's enjoying the scenery.

'Ooh! And they've even got Tony Curtis's female body shaper from *Some Like It Hot* and it's so funny cos the bra straps are fixed with those clips you get on braces instead of hooks – you know how useless men are at undoing—'

'Zoë!' I yell.

'What?'

'I've got to go. I'll just get Joel to drop me—'

'Joel!' Zoë cuts in. 'He's with you?'

'Yes!'

'Well, then I guess you don't need any tips on how to entertain yourself!'

'Actually he's got to go to a meeting,' I blush. 'But he can take me to a car rental place and then I'll whiz over.'

'Did you two . . .?'

I know exactly what Zoë is getting at but Joel is within listening distance.

'Yes, that's right,' I try and sound like I'm talking about something else.

'And?'

'Spectacular!' I cheer.

Zoë cackles with glee. 'You can tell me everything later!'

'I'll pick you up at the diner at 6 p.m.,' I conclude.

I flip the phone closed and turn to Joel. His face is still filled with disdain for Zoë's accommodation.

'Do you girls have plans for tonight?' he asks as we return to his car, which amazingly still has all four wheels.

'I don't think so,' I shrug. 'Why?'

'Oh, I just thought of something you might enjoy. I'll have to make a couple of calls but if you like I could meet you at the diner later?'

'Sounds perfect!' I'm so relieved this isn't goodbye just yet. I was starting to get pangs of resistance at the idea of being parted from him.

'OK. Let's get you hooked up with a car.'

Somehow Joel manages to talk the Enterprise clerk into upgrading me to a convertible. I can't believe my luck. It seems a waste to just go a few blocks to Hollywood. I want to fly down a freeway! I take out the map and study it. I've got four hours. I shouldn't really go further than an hour away . . . Santa Monica is meant to be nice, or what about Hermosa Beach? Palm Springs is that little bit too far. Hold on – what if I went and surprised Sasha? I get a sudden rush of high spirits. Why not? She could do with a boost, I'm

341

sure. Zoë and I have got two whole days to see the sights in LA. And if Ty would let her take a break I could help her with the Project Paradise fundraiser. I'm sure something must need decorating.

I put my foot down and floor it. After watching Joel drive I'm getting the hang of sailing through yellow lights and turning right on red, and when I get on the freeway I speed-weave willy-nilly as good as the rest of them. Admittedly in my enthusiasm I overshoot my exit and find myself in San Bernadino but at least there's still time for me to backtrack and enjoy a nice cup of tea with Sasha. I can't wait to see the look on her face when I stroll in!

However. Things don't go quite according to plan. When I arrive at Tiger Tiger the place is deserted. The cats are unattended and there's no one in the kitchen. I try Sasha's bedroom door. Locked.

I give it a knock.

A terrified voice calls, 'Go away!'

'Sasha!' I lean closer. 'Is that you?'

Suddenly there's a scrambling to the door and she drags me inside, swiftly locking the door behind me.

'What's going on? Did Freddie get out? Why are you crying?'

I take in her sob-stained face and juddering breaths.

'It's Ty,' she hiccups. 'He's totally trashed, I don't know what to do.'

I guide her to a seat, trying to calm her.

'Nina's gone to the vets and I'm the only one here.'

In the background I hear the sound of glass smashing and some male swearing.

342

'What was that?' I panic.

'He must be in the kitchen now.' Her eyes widen.

There's another crash – it sounds like the cutlery drawer being yanked asunder.

I have one thought – he's going for a knife.

25

My first instinct is to call the police.

'You can't!' Sasha stops me. 'He'd get in so much trouble with Carrie.'

'But—'

'And what if word got out? The fundraiser is in three days. Who'd come to a place where there's a madman on the loose?'

'This is America,' I remind Sasha. 'Anyone who's ever been in the studio audience for Jerry Springer would be here like a shot!' I pause for a moment. 'Maybe that's the hook you've been looking for – we could put Ty in one of the cages.'

'He's just drunk,' Sasha defends him. 'It'll pass.'

'So you're just going to stay locked in a room until he sobers up?'

Sasha nods.

'What if I called Helen?'

'What can she do?'

'I'm sure The California Club must have some SWAT team that deal with emergencies like this.'

'Let's just wait,' Sasha pleads. 'Nina – you know, the

volunteer girl? – she should be back later, I'm sure she can reason with him.'

'I haven't got that long, and besides I need a wee. I'm going to have to go out there.'

'Don't!' Sasha pulls me back.

Outside we hear shuffling-staggering down the corridor.

I sigh. There is one person I wouldn't mind speaking to but it would mean asking Elise for help. I really do need the loo so I dial her. She gets Martha straight away. I give her a whispered update on Ty-gate (with Sasha's sleeping bag over my head for extra soundproofing) and in return she tells me what she thinks the best plan of action would be. Starting with persuading him to drink a large mug of coffee.

Checking that the coast is clear, we make a dash for the kitchen, clinging on to each other for dear life. Frankly I'd rather let Freddie chew on my femur than face Ty in this state but it has to be done. I fill a mug with steaming coffee and try and calm my hammering heart.

'I'll come with you.' Sasha moves to join me but I block her. Martha has convinced me that Sasha is the reason for Ty's drinking so it would only aggravate things.

'You stay here. Unless you hear him coming, in which case go back to the bedroom.'

'But what should I do?' Sasha looks forlorn.

'Make another pot of coffee,' I instruct her.

As I creak down the corridor towards Ty's room I dip my finger in the coffee to assess it's scald-potential, just in case it's thrown back in my face. (Second degree burns, I predict.) He's not in his hammock so I proceed to the back porch. There he sits, scrunched and rocking. I fear he could lash out at any time so I keep a safe distance as I announce my presence: 'Ty?'

He flicks around, ready to attack.

'What are you doing here?'

I've definitely got the element of surprise on my side.

'I brought you some coffee.' I try to sound casual, as if I've just returned from a two-day outing to Starbucks.

'I don't need it, I got this,' he wavers a bottle of Jack Daniels in my direction. 'Want some?'

'OK!' I say, deciding it's better off in my hands than glugging down his throat. I sit down beside him but not too close, unscrew the bottle top and drag out the simple process of taking a sip. I want to say, 'Are you OK?' but clearly he's not, so instead, heart pounding, I try what Martha told me and dive in with:

'Why are you so angry at yourself for fancying her?'

His head jerks round and his eyes bore through me like a drill. Though I'm trembling inside I hold his gaze.

'If I did, which I don't, it would just make me as superficial as everyone else, which I'm not.'

I think for a moment. I am Dr Phil, I can do this. 'This dread of appearing superficial—'

'A pretty healthy trait, don't you think?' he says, defensively.

'Yes but I'm wondering if you're taking it a bit far,' I venture.

'What?' he snaps.

I gulp. 'Well, isn't it possible that you could be responding to something else in Sasha, other than her looks?'

'I'm a man, aren't I?' he sneers, adding sourly. 'Besides, what else is there?'

'You seemed to be getting on pretty well with her on the first night we were here,' I remind him.

'That was before I saw her,' he grumbles.

'What a ridiculous thing to say!' In my annoyance I forget my nerves. 'Why do you let how she looks wipe out all the good stuff you were responding to – that's just so short-sighted!'

'Listen,' he slurs. 'I was in the movie business for twelve years, you think I don't know about these skinny-perfect-pouty girls, what they can do to you?'

There's anguish in his last words. I try and soften my voice.

'I think you may have had one bad experience too many—'

'Damn right!'

'But it's not Sasha's fault that you feel this way. What has she ever done to you?'

Ty rubs his furrowed brow. All at once I see someone terrified of getting hurt again, punishing himself for having feelings for 'the enemy'.

'I'm not going to let her—' He stops himself.

'Let her what? Mess you up? Reject you? Is that why you're rejecting her first?'

'You don't know!' His voice cracks.

'No, I don't. Do you want to tell me?'

'No.'

'OK.' I take a moment for us both to simmer down. Ty takes a sip of coffee, I take a sip of JD.

'I'll tell you something: I'm not leaving here unless you guarantee you can be at least civil to her. If you can't, then I'm taking her with me.'

Suddenly all the fight seems to have gone out of Ty. 'I just wish she didn't look the way she does.'

'You and her both,' I mutter.

'Oh come on!' he snorts.

'Really, she thinks her looks are a curse – so you've already got something in common.'

'And she likes motorbikes,' he mumbles.

I smile. That is so sweet. He noticed. Underneath the hostile exterior there's a pussycat waiting to get out. Unfortunately, now the anger has subsided the self-pity is setting in.

'I just hate being like every other dumb schmuck who takes one look at her and falls at her feet. I don't want to be a cliché. I don't want a beautiful girlfriend.'

I raise an eyebrow. 'In case people think you're superficial? Are we back on that again?'

'I want to be with someone real.'

'She is real!' I cry, exasperated. 'Tell you what, why don't you wait fifty years until she's lost her looks and then make a play for her. That seems sensible. I mean, what's wasting fifty years of your life because you're worried about what other people will think.'

Ty scuffs his shoe on the boulder at his feet. 'It's not just that. I'm worried about what I'll think about myself. If I got with her—'

'And we're not saying you want to or that you will . . .' I tease.

'Right!' he agrees. 'But I'd always wonder if I'm just with her for her looks.'

'Well then, your problem isn't with Sasha, it's with yourself,' I conclude. 'So I suggest you stop taking your inverted looksism' – I frown, hoping that's a real word – 'out on her!'

He looks gloomily at the earth. I could have sworn we were getting somewhere, and now this defeated slump.

'Have another sip of coffee.'

He obliges.

'It's funny isn't it?' I muse. 'For some people it's having the glamorous trophy wife and the right sports car and fancy address, and with you it's about having the correct set of political beliefs, hating the right group of people, wearing the dirtiest trousers, all to prove you don't care.'

No reaction.

'I mean, did you have to study the history of grunge to get your hair just right?'

'I don't care about that shit,' he grumbles.

'*I don't care about this, I don't care about that!* If it's so wrong to care then what on earth are you doing here?'

He looks straight at me. 'These cats need me. Look at Oliver. What happened to him is wrong!'

Finally some passion.

'Is that how you see yourself? As some avenging angel?'

Ty shrugs.

'You're here because you care. Be man enough to admit it.'

Gawd, I hope I haven't overstepped the mark. Martha said I'd have to tussle with him but—

'I wish that were true,' he sighs.

'What then? Are you trying to assuage guilt for your over-privileged background? You think you got it too easy so you want to help poor dumb animals. Animals who can't tell you what a twat you're being?'

He takes the insult on the chin and simply says, 'I can do something for them. I can make a difference.'

'It's not either/or, Ty. You can help humans too.'

His angry eyes suddenly seem searching and vulnerable.

'You could help Sasha. You're so good at seeing the pain in these animals. Can't you see hers?' Now my voice is wobbling. 'Just think about it,' I say, swallowing my tears.

He crumbles and his head falls forward into his hands.

'She must hate me,' he says.

I shake my head. 'She should hate you. If she had any sense she would. But it's not hate, it's hurt. Your vanity is hurting her. Which is ironic, considering she's the babe and you're the dog!'

Ty snuffles a laugh. 'Where the hell did you come from?' He looks at me with something approaching affection.

'I wish I knew. If I did I'd go back there and get a

350

second one of me made up just so I could sit on your shoulder and make sure you don't mess up the rest of this week.'

'Have you got a boyfriend?' he asks, somewhat unexpectedly.

I flash to Joel but then decide he doesn't fit in that category.

'Don't be absurd,' I say. 'You know all the best relationship advice comes from people with totally crappy love lives. It makes things so much clearer.'

'Well, I hope you get the one you deserve.'

'Is that a threat?'

He laughs. 'No, you deserve someone wonderful. Someone with as big a heart as you. But preferably not such a big mouth.'

I give him a playful punch and he pulls me into a hug.

I can feel all the love he has to give and I pray that Sasha is going to get the benefit.

'Are you staying over?' he asks.

'No, I literally just came by for an hour. I've got to get back to LA by 6 p.m.'

'LA?' He grimaces. 'What are you doing there?'

'Hanging with movie stars, stylists, manicurists – your kinda people. I'll send them your love.'

He smiles and looks down into his empty coffee cup.

'I'll get you another.'

'Thanks.'

As I get up he clasps my hand, keeping hold until our arms are fully extended and I have to let go.

*

I walk back to the kitchen in a daze, not quite believing that I've got away with confronting Ty without getting lacerated. I've got to meet this Martha woman. She certainly knows her onions.

'Are you OK?' Sasha scrambles over to me as I set the coffee cup down on the side.

'Yeah, I'm fine. He's fine,' I smile at Sasha, wondering how I'm going to sum up the conversation for her.

'What did you talk about? Did you find out—'

'Basically he fancies you.' I cut to the chase.

'What? I don't think so!' Sasha flusters but her eyes flash pleasure and hope and excitement. 'Did he actually say that?'

I smile knowingly. 'You're going to have to be gentle with him, he's got some *issues*.'

'Big bad issues?' Sasha asks, looking nervous.

'I think they're get-over-able. He hasn't told me the full story. Just take it slow and let him see the real you.'

'Whoever that is,' Sasha worries.

'Well, we've got mad and brave for starters, right?'

She smiles shyly.

I take her hands. 'This is your chance, Sasha. He's as interested in discovering your personality as you are.'

'I could use an extra pair of eyes!'

I laugh, 'You'll do it!' My eyes flick to the clock. Nearly 5 p.m. 'I'm so late, I've got to go.'

Sasha squeezes me tightly. 'Oh Lara!'

'I want daily updates. Promise?'

Her eyes are misty as she pulls back: 'I couldn't have

done any of this without you. I felt like a leper being such a misery but you weren't afraid to get close.'

'I'm just sorry I didn't know how you were feeling before we came out here. I wish I could have done something sooner,' I sigh.

'It doesn't matter now,' Sasha says, bravely. 'I'm just so relieved to be feeling vaguely human again.'

'I guess that's what happens when you surround yourself with animals,' I grin. 'Anyway, it's Helen we should be thanking.'

'I want to thank you both,' Sasha asserts. 'It's not an either/or thing.'

I smile to myself. 'No, it's not. There's enough love for everyone.'

I pour a fresh cup of coffee and hand it to her. 'He needs a top-up.'

'Are you sure? What will I say?'

'Just talk motorbikes to him!'

'What?' She cocks her head, then turns coy. 'Do you really think . . .?'

'If you two haven't got it on by the end of the week I'll eat Ryan's rumpsteak. Raw. With extra flies!'

She laughs. It's music to my ears. As Sasha walks me to the car I reach out and flip her hair into a middle parting to make her a modicum less attractive, then scramble the dust as I skid on to the main road.

26

As I drive back to LA, I dial Helen and go hands-free. (On the phone that is, not the steering wheel.) She's overdue for an update and the latest developments make for headline news.

'Oh my God! Poor Sasha! Is she OK?' Helen gasps, losing her usual 'it's all part of the plan' cool.

I tell her I'm convinced everything will be peachy-keen but that The California Club should be on alert, just in case.

'Gotcha,' Helen says, still sounding shaken. 'Thank goodness you were there.'

'It's fine. I'm going to pick up Zoë from work now but if there's any more problems we'll be back at Tiger Tiger like a shot.'

'Don't you worry about that, I'll check on her. You girls just concentrate on enjoying yourselves,' Helen resumes control.

'Oh yeah, we'll be living the high life,' I mutter. 'That was a pretty harsh trick to play on Zoë – have you seen where she's staying?'

'Harsh trick or a reminder of how far she's come –

you decide.'

Helen stands strong in her defence of The California Club. 'So what are you chaps doing tonight?' she asks, on a lighter note.

'Well, actually Joel is arranging some kind of treat. I think he feels Zoë needs a little glamour to balance out the grease.'

'That's sweet. So he wasn't just a Yosemite fling?'

'I guess not.' I'm reluctant to say too much about Joel for fear of jinxing the strangely satisfying relationship we have.

'Do you think he might be a contender?' Helen queries. She always likes to know the minutiae of our love lives.

'I really don't know,' I confess, deftly changing lanes and sliding on to the exit ramp that will take me to Hollywood.

'Has he made you feel differently about Elliot?'

'Not exactly – I'll never not love Elliot, it's more that he's made me feel differently about me.'

'How so?'

'Well.' I think for a moment. 'Ever since our little rendezvous, I've been feeling more confident, more independent – more my own woman!' I laugh.

'That's quite a gift.'

'Isn't it?' I feel a swell of appreciation for Joel. 'He's been a real tonic.'

'And Elliot. How's our little woodchuck?'

'Troubled,' I confess. 'He's been doing some major soul-searching out there in the wild, wild wilderness but he's yet to have a moment of dazzling enlightenment.'

'He will.'

'How can you be so sure?' I want to believe it but I'm concerned that he could just end up depressed.

'He's no fool. Given enough time alone he'll open his eyes and see—'

Helen stops short.

'See what?'

'Just see. Ever since his parents died he's had his head down. He needs to lift it up and look around him. Things have changed. Maybe too much.'

'He thinks *he's* changed, lost his zip.'

'He hasn't lost it. He just hasn't had any use for it in a while. It'll come back.'

'Helen, you have such faith in us all!'

She laughs. 'You're my family! I'll see you right. Anyway, there's someone we've forgotten – what's going on with Elise?'

'I've barely spoken to her – she's always haring off to some class, it's like she's cramming for some spiritual enlightenment exam.'

Helen chuckles. 'I knew she'd crack in the end! I just hope it's doing her some good.'

My hope involves her getting stuck on a higher plane and not being able to come down again, but I keep that to myself.

'What do you think The California Club make of how we're doing?' I ask, curious about how closely we're being monitored.

'They feel like I do,' Helen replies: 'proud of you all.'

'So everything is as it should be?' I check.

'Yes,' Helen assures me.

I sigh contentedly. I had been wondering what on earth we were putting ourselves through but speaking to Helen makes me feel as if it's all happening for a reason.

'OK, I'm just pulling into the diner carpark now.'

'Give Zoë a big hug for me – tell her she's always a star in my eyes.'

'I will. Love you, Helen!'

I do love her. Sometimes I want to blame her for things because she's always the one in charge but deep down I know she has our best interests at heart. I can't wait for our big reunion. Just three more nights. And in the meantime, I've got a night on the tiles with Zoë and the gorgeous, masterful, sexy Joel.

'He's not coming.'

'What?'

'He came by about half an hour ago to apologize – unfortunately he can't join us,' Zoë shrugs. 'Bummer, eh?'

I quickly wipe the look off devastation off my face. I don't want Zoë to think she's not enough on her own.

'So, what do you fancy doing tonight?' I ask her.

'How about a movie?'

A movie? Zoë's the last person I'd ever think would forego a night out in favour of chomping popcorn in the dark. Poor lamb, she must be exhausted.

'What did you have in mind?'

'Just the latest Owen Wilson buddy flick . . .' she suggests with a mischievous twinkle.

Bless her, she's doing that for me.

'OK, if that's what you want,' I agree.

'I thought you'd be ecstatic,' she complains.

'Ecstatic?' I query. I mean, I love the guy but—

Zoë opens the envelope she's clutching and wafts two slips of paper in front of me. 'Tickets to the première! We've got half an hour to get ready!'

Suddenly I'm hyper-animated and spinning her round. 'Where? How?'

'Just thank Joel,' she grins.

I wish I could, in person – a Hollywood première starring my favourite actor? The California Club could learn a trick or two from him!

We dolly ourselves into oblivion and then hurtle to the movie theatre in a state of giddy anticipation but all the red carpet frenzy has subsided by the time we've found a parking spot – just the odd photographer loading his camera back into his bag and a few moping members of the foreign press dangling limp microphones complaining that they got elbowed out of the way at the crucial moment.

Having only just made it to our seats for the opening credits I spend the first ten minutes of the movie trying to regulate my breathing and bring my body temperature back down to an acceptable simmer. Even when that is achieved I can barely concentrate on the screen for wondering where in the auditorium Owen might be sitting. My eyes strain in the dark trying to make out his one-of-a-kind nose in the line of profiles in our row. No match. I settle down and try to focus on the film. Oooo-eee! That sleepy nasal drawl gets me every time. I can't believe we're going to meet him at the party afterwards!

At least we might have stood a chance if we'd got there within two hours of kick-off. I wonder if they decided to hold the party in a carpark to deliberately trick us. Three times we went past the marquee and didn't twig, presuming we were missing the entrance to some fancy hotel ballroom. When we do finally stagger up to a pair of bouncers, manfully resisting the urge to play skipping games with the red rope, an Amazonian blonde blocks our path.

'Oh no, now they're not letting any more people in – it must be rammed in there,' I wail.

'Lara?' she asks.

I nod, stunned by just how long and blonde she is.

'Joel said to look out for you. I'm Sunset. Welcome.'

Bit risky for her to be hanging so close to the Sunset Strip if you ask me, but then again she looks like that could well be her forte.

'Nice to meet you,' I smile.

I can only presume she's one of Joel's conquests but instead of feeling jealous and inferior I feel quite proud that I've played in her league.

'Is Owen still here?' I dare to ask.

'He just left,' she apologizes.

'Did he take half the party with him?' Zoë looks round the makeshift room lined with themed buffet and bar set-ups but lacking clientele.

'This is when they really need to employ some extras – to fill out the première parties after 11 p.m.!' Sunset concedes.

'If this was Brighton everyone would be sucking up

every last drop of alcohol. What's wrong with this town?!' Zoë gasps.

'Hey! Isn't that Eddie *"Rock Me"* Powers?' I point across to an electric blue seating area.

It is indeed the former MOR legend and he's still working his trademark look of rock star leather trousers teamed with a working man's plaid shirt.

'He hasn't aged at all.' Zoë is impressed. 'Still *Sexy 24/7!*' Zoë recalls one of his bigger hits.

It's then I remember her brief but all too hardcore crush on him. I tried reasoning with her at the time – he was such a doofus – but she merely pointed out that I was in love with Howard from Take That and thus didn't have a leg to stand on.

'Zoë, *no,*' I tell her, but she's already looking at him that way. Not like an idol exactly, more like prey.

'He's got a song on the soundtrack,' Sunset explains.

'A new one?'

'Yeah, he's trying to make a comeback – he's dishing out promo T-shirts if you're interested . . .' She nods over to a young girl who seems to be having a problem shifting the goods.

'Might do better if they didn't have his face on them,' I observe.

'I want one!' Zoë enthuses.

'Why?' I frown.

'I don't know, it's free isn't it?'

'All right, Elise?' I tease.

'Don't say that!' Zoë shudders. 'I just think it'd be a fun memento, for old times' sake – shall we get one?'

I can never resist that mischievous look.

'As long as you promise me you'll never wear it. Not even in bed.'

'Promise.'

'Have fun, ladies,' Sunset waves us off. 'Just remember – if you're going to get in trouble he might as well be rich!'

'Blackberry vodka?' Zoë makes a quick pit-stop at the bar.

'Why not?' I accept a freshly pulped glass to drink to the absent Owen then attempt to grab Zoë out of the way as I spot a fast-moving entourage advancing. Too late. She gets roughly elbowed by a burly bodyguard and loses her footing.

'Who was it?' She peers after them, hopping on her good foot, hoping for a sighting.

'I didn't see but I'm assuming there was a short celebrity buried in there somewhere. Oh Zoë!'

'What?' She looks down at her white top – it's covered in inky blackberry-flavoured gloop.

'Oh no,' I mutter.

'It's my favourite top!' she gasps.

'Oh no!' I say again. My mind is already leaping to the next step. 'Do you want to go home?' I suggest quickly.

'Are you crazy? We've got to at least say hi to Eddie and there's probably still a few real celebs here – surely one of them must be an alcoholic, hanging on till the bitter end.'

'I'm sure that was the last one leaving and you can't walk around with a big purple stain on your top!'

'I could always—' Zoë looks over at T-shirt girl.

'No!' I yelp. This is exactly what I was trying to avoid.

'But—'

'You promised,' I remind her.

'It's not *that* bad,' Zoë wheedles.

'No way.'

Five minutes later Zoë emerges from the Ladies with Eddie stretched across her ample bosom.

'You've given him some kind of fabric facelift,' I say, trying to tug him back to normality.

'Let's get another drink – this time we'll get ones that match our outfits!'

The girl behind the bar seems distracted as we make our order. Halfway through blending the pineapple she looks beyond us and calls, 'Goodnight, Mr Powers!' with underlying 'Take me with you!' pleading.

Zoë turns round for a final gawp, causing Eddie to do a major double-take as he passes.

'Hi! Wow, is that me?' He studies her chest. 'It's like looking in a funfair mirror!'

Zoë giggles.

'You know what I have to say next?'

'What?'

He leans in close. 'Your chest looks great with my face on it, wanna try it for real?'

Zoë laughs. For real.

He takes another look at his super-sized smile. 'Shoot, I look like the Cheshire Cat!'

'She has that effect on men,' I mistakenly say out loud.

He looks her up and down. 'I can believe that.'

The girl behind the bar 'accidentally' spills Zoë's drink but this time she's too quick and jumps out of the way – into Eddie's waiting arms. He's just about to resume flirtation when a timid assistant approaches.

'Mr Powers, your car is right outside.'

He nods acknowledgement then turns back to us. 'You girls wanna come for a nightcap? They've put me up at the Beverly Hills Hotel.'

'Oh my God! That's where the Osbournes have been filming!' Zoë squeaks. 'I heard Kelly Osbourne checked in there for two weeks when she had flu so her mother wouldn't catch it.'

Zoë gives me a pleading look. Who am I to stand in the way of a C-list shag in a five star hotel?

'All right!' we agree, ready to follow him to the car, but he stops us at the exit.

'I think we'd better arrive separately, there's sometimes press loitering in the foyer – that's how Nicole Kidman got caught,' he name-drops, deluding himself that he's in the same league. 'We don't want to end up splashed across tomorrow's tabloids, do we?'

Actually that's always been one of Zoë's fantasies but I guess it's not going to be realized tonight.

'I'm in the Sunset Suite. Just come straight up when you get there,' he smarms. 'I'll be waiting.'

27

'I'm not sleeping with him!' Zoë blurts as we cab down Sunset Boulevard.

'No one's asking you to,' I reassure her, adding 'yet . . .' under my breath.

'I mean it. I know I used to want to when I was fifteen but now I just want to be able to say that we had a drink at the Beverly Hills Hotel with someone famous. Is that wrong?'

I tell her it's perfectly acceptable – *'When in LA . . .'*

'All the same, there's something about him, isn't there? Remember that poster I had of him standing shirtless in the rain? I used to kiss his bellybutton every night before I went to sleep . . .'

I sneak a look at Zoë. Maybe this is what she needs – to get skin on skin with a celebrity to see there really is no line dividing them and us.

'The Pink Palace!' the cab driver alerts us as we pull off the road and disappear into the lush greenery disguising the hotel driveway.

I get tingles looking up at the pink bell towers with their caps of oxidized copper and jaunty flag accessories.

'This place is *so* famous!' trills Zoë. 'I can't believe we're here.'

There's a Bentley ahead of us and a limo behind as we pull up under a concrete canopy striped ivy and white. I quickly pay the driver and together we emerge on to a red carpet. Zoë's normally thrusting chest caves after just one step.

'I can't go in wearing this T-shirt!' she exclaims.

Remarkably, I'd forgotten all about it.

She looks around, as if there might just be a spare Gucci top in the foliage.

'I haven't got a pashmina or anything I can lend you,' I apologize.

Despairing, Zoë pulls Ed's face by the nose and winches it round so his whole face twists into an unidentifiable blur.

'How does that look?'

'Like you've got a third nipple,' I have to confess, tweaking the pointy end of the knot.

'What if I put it on backwards?' Zoë suggests.

We're obviously equally drunk because this actually seems like a good idea to me – as if a woman trying to wriggle around beneath a tiny top is going to draw less attention than a T-shirt with some old has-been on it.

'Everything all right, ma'm?' the doorman tries not to look perturbed.

'Fine, if I could just get . . .' Zoë does one more thrust, flashing him in the process. 'There!' she triumphs. 'OK?' She looks at me for approval.

'It's fine,' I tell her. 'A lot of the surfers at La Jolla had their tops tied at the back like that.'

This doesn't seem to be what Zoë wants to hear so I add: 'Just think, if there are casting agents here scouting for the long-awaited sequel to *Point Break*, you'll be first in line!'

'You're right!' Zoë nods, taking my arm as we stride into the lobby.

First thing we notice is the trademark banana-leaf wallpaper, second is the jutting three-tiered chandelier, its gold leaf surround adding a luxuriant glow to the room. It feels like Lana Turner could walk by at any moment.

'Imagine if the press did find out!' Zoë scours the potted palms for a prying paparazzo lens. 'I might end up in *heat* as one of the "On or Off!" couples.'

'They'd have to do a "Where are they now?" feature first,' I mutter as we try to locate the lifts.

'Well, he's obviously doing all right if he's staying here.'

'He's not paying, the movie company is,' I remind her.

'All the same . . .' Zoë shrugs, reaching for the lift call button. Her finger stops an inch short, halted by the sound of expensive laughter and chinking glasses.

I follow her gaze to the Polo Lounge. There seems to be some kind of private party within, still going strong.

'Shall we take a peek, just for a second?'

From the letters remaining on the giant pink cake we deduce that some kind of anniversary is being celebrated.

'Whose anniversary?' Zoë nobbles a waiter clearing crumby plates.

He nods to an outsized TV playing a movie on loop. 'Twenty-five years since they made *California Suite* in this hotel.'

I scurry over to the screen. 'Zoë! Remember we watched this one Sunday! It's a classic.'

'Remind me . . .' she narrows her eyes.

'Neil Simon, four stories all going on at this hotel on Oscar night?'

'Maggie Smith!' Zoë pipes as she swirls on screen in a voluminous chiffon gown.

'This is the best bit,' I chortle predicting her line about the dress giving her a definite hump.

'It cost £500 and I look like Richard the Third!' she complains.

'I know the feeling.' Zoë catches the sight of her reflection in a glass door.

We decide to have one more drink before we go up to Eddie and as we swan around jangling ice-cubes we spot two of the film's stars, Alan Alda and Bill Cosby on the patio.

'Oooh look!' Zoë points. 'What should we do? They're more famous than Eddie.'

I think for a moment then hypothesize, 'A celeb in his suite is worth two on the patio.'

'You're right. We should go for the sure thing. Not that I'm sleeping with him!'

'No.' I shake my head so vigorously I feel nauseous. 'Shall we?' I suggest.

'Let's!'

Sunset Suite: a pair of black mesh boxers greets us at the door. They look extremely pleased to see us. We follow them into the plush lounge area, elbows sparring for a rib nudge as we take in the mirrored bar, team of velvety sofas and grand piano. (One of the ones it's compulsory to lie across in a slinky satin dress.) I try to direct Zoë's attention to the twelve-seater mahogany dining table groaning under a pyramid of exotic fruit, but she's still hypnotized by the array of booze on offer. Possibly sensing that vomiting is but a Stoli shot away, Eddie dispenses with any 'Can I get you ladies a drink?' pleasantries and heads straight for the bedroom.

Zoë and I hesitate, wondering what our next move should be.

'Come on through!' he calls.

Wading through the carpet, we bob our heads round the door frame to find him scrambling into bed with a gleeful 'let's get started!' grin.

We shuffle awkwardly over to the side of the bed, dazed by his presumption. I have to admit he's in pretty good shape for his age – his biceps have that boulder-beneath-the-skin bulge and his torso is tanned and toned with a silky-smooth sheen to it. I wonder if it's his own.

'What do you think?' Zoë turns to me, acting as if she's put him on pause and he can't hear us.

I feel like an inept medical student trying to make a diagnosis. 'Oh I don't know, what do *you* think?' I bat the question back to her, swaying slightly as I do.

'I did love that *Kissing in the Rain* song of his,' she whispers. 'Remember I bought two copies in case I wore one out?'

'Er, ladies . . .?' Eddie gives us a quizzical look, clearly uncomfortable with being resistible for even a second.

'Why don't I give you two some time alone,' I suggest. Best I rid him of any thoughts of a threesome scenario right now.

'Do you play the piano at all?' Zoë tries to make polite conversation as I grope for the exit but for him the talking is done – his arm encircles her like a lasso, pulling her on top of him. I hesitate to see if she needs rescuing but already she's responding willingly to his liquor-lubricated lips. The madam in me sighs, 'My work here is done!'

My intention was to return to the lounge, perhaps to serenade them with *Chopsticks* or do a little fruit-carving to while away the time but apparently I've taken the wrong turning as I now find myself in the sumptuous en-suite bathroom. Endless toiletries are set out along the metre of pink marble. I'd say he's got a definite aftershave fetish – there's at least ten different bottles. As I squirt Davidoff Cool Water into the air I feel like I've snuck into the Gents at a posh nightclub – there's everything here but the fanned-out chewing gum sticks and the saucer for tipping the attendant.

In amongst his wares I find the hotel goodies. They sure don't scrimp on shampoo here. Normally the complimentary samples come in individual follicle portions but these are at least half the size of your average shop-bought bottle with the cool signature palm print on the label. I'd love to come up with a really covetable kit for the B&B. If I was keeping it on. Which I'm not. But just in case . . . Without thinking, I unclasp my bag and sweep the entire stash – including his aftershaves – into my bag. I've never stolen anything in my life but it seems the right thing to do. I'm just delighting in a darling little hairspray the size of a Gold Spot breath freshener when Eddie yells, 'Hey, honey, could you bring me the body lotion?'

I balk, eyes wide with guilt. Frantically I rummage through the booty in my bag. Talc, no. Sewing kit, no. Mouthwash – boy that would sting. Ha! Hand & body lotion. I throw one of the hand towels over my arm and take a casual un-thief-like stroll back into the bedroom, presenting the lotion to him like a vintage Bordeaux.

'Why thank you!' he gives me a courteous smile.

Considering the circumstances it's all very civilized, but then he has to go and whip off the tablecloth.

'Oh my God, it's *huge*!' I gasp, slamming my hand across my mouth.

'I love it when people say that.' He gives a blissful smile before trying to engage me in slathering the scented gunk over his nether regions. I pull away on the pretext of getting extra lotion – 100ml will never be enough.

Despite her fabulous sluttina persona, I know Zoë hates to be lit by anything brighter than a glow-worm so as he resumes his slippery seduction I quickly close the bathroom door and dim the bedside lamps before dutifully gathering up her discarded garments. Once in the lounge, I instinctively begin pairing Zoë's socks and laying out her clothes on the sofa, like a mum getting her kid's uniform ready for the first day of school. Finding Eddie's sheer boxers in the collection, I deem it only right that I should wedge them in my bag alongside the toiletries as a keepsake.

I sit a while, reading the room service menu and wondering if I've got time for a French onion soup, then move on to the directory of services. I fear the vodka slush puppies may be taking their toll when I discover details of the hotel's Canine Connoisseur Program – upon arrival dogs are escorted to their rooms where they will find personalized doggie cookies awaiting them! Better yet, they are greeted by name at each appearance!

I so want to run in and tell Zoë but she sounds pretty busy right now. Hmmm. I wonder if I could dedicate one room at the B&B as pet-friendly? It would mean an extra cleaning cost but if we specially customized the space it could be quite an attraction. Imagine doggy bunk beds and cat hammocks! And we could give the pets their own mini bathroom with lots of sea air pumping through to keep it fragrant. And we'd devise a special gourmet menu and arrange in-hotel visits from a local groomer . . .

I feel abuzz with inspiration, I flick onwards, eager to see what other ideas I could customize. Here's the section on the hotel's collection of on-site bungalows – apparently when they say no one walks in LA this includes stairs. I can't believe Elizabeth Taylor spent six out of her eight honeymoons in a bungalow! How gloriously unimaginative! It's like returning over and over again to the scene of the crime, determined to make it right this time.

Wouldn't it be great to do up a honeymoon suite with pictures of the world's most-married celebrities: how funny would that be – Zsa Zsa Gabor, Joan Collins, Jennifer Lopez . . . Maybe it could double up as the divorcee suite! I'd give a special rate to women who could show me their divorce papers and then tell them where they could go to pick up a Brighton hunk to celebrate their newfound freedom. I chuckle to myself and then go cold. The B&B isn't mine to have dreams for. Any day now it will become someone else's prerogative and pleasure.

My former euphoria short-circuits. I feel a wail of internal panic – I can't let it go. I get to my feet with a sudden sense of purpose – I must do something! I turn to look for a phone and find a naked and glistening Eddie looming before me.

My first thought is: 'Uh-oh – my turn!' I must look absolutely terrified because he's quick to assure me: 'Don't worry, I just need some water . . .'

Entirely unconcerned with his nudity, he strolls to the fridge and avails himself of two bottles of Evian – still doing a convincing impression of Jake the Peg, diddle-liddle-liddle-lid . . .

A few minutes later Zoë stumbles from the bedroom wrapped in a towel. She looks shell-shocked with the kind of backcombed, fright-night hair only found on

372

couture catwalks, but seems relieved to be reunited with her clothes.

'What have I done?' she mutters as she wriggles into her trousers.

'I think it's more a question of "*who* have you done?"' I snigger, rather unhelpfully.

'I'd better go and say goodbye.'

'Are you going to see him again?'

'We have no immediate plans,' she admits.

'Well, in that case I'd rather we just leave,' I urge, revealing the booty in my bag.

'Lara!' Zoë gasps.

'Sshhh! No names! We don't want to leave any clues – I've already dusted the place for fingerprints.'

'Not where my hands have been, you haven't!' Zoë winces.

'Come on!'

We belt down the corridor, aftershaves clinking, and throw ourselves into the lift. My heart is pounding and my adrenalin zinging. Please don't let me get a taste for this, I pray. I don't want to get deported before the week is up.

When the lift door opens again it's on an unfamiliar scene.

'This isn't the lobby,' I frown.

'Look! There's a sign for the pool – shall we just have the quickest peek?'

I look uncertain.

'He's out for the count, don't worry.'

Stripy sunloungers, cool cabanas and canvas

umbrellas line the 75-foot-long pool. And we've got the whole thing to ourselves: 6 a.m. and we're the only fools awake.

'This is where Raquel Welch was discovered,' I inform Zoë.

'How do you—'

'Towels, ladies?' a pool attendant interrupts, raring to do his thing.

I go to decline but Zoë reaches across me. 'Yes, thank you.'

'What are you doing?' I hiss as he prepares two loungers for us.

'Look, I've got to be at work in two hours. If I have a swim it might wake me up a bit and then I can shower here and go straight to the diner.'

'How are you going to manage on no sleep?' I fret.

'I'll be fine, the memory of all this will keep me going.'

I'm not convinced.

'La, it's fine. I wouldn't miss this for the world, I can get all the sleep I need when I'm back home.'

'What are you going to swim in?'

'Bra and knicks, there's no one else around.'

'I think I might join you,' I say, tempted by the aqua waters.

'Ten laps!' Zoë enthuses, whipping off her top. Yet again.

Although the water is a pleasant temperature there's no sun shining on it so I have to stay swimming to keep warm. Thoughts of the B&B continue to race through my head but my initial freak-out has subsided. It's out of my hands. Really, what can I do from here? I feel spacey and entirely unconnected with reality. I wonder if modern-day miracles like this are exclusive to LA?

Zoë seems to read my mind. 'Things like this just don't happen in Hertfordshire,' she muses as she floats out on her back.

I sigh, feeling a strange sense of serenity wash over me. Some people never get to have experiences like this. I feel as if we've found a little portal into the dream. We can't stay but we can enjoy a brief taster.

'I wonder what the others are doing today?' Zoë asks.

I'm just about to say they're probably not up yet, but Sasha will already be starting her chores, I know Elise had a sunrise yoga session scheduled today and Elliot certainly wasn't getting any lie-ins in his new role as a park ranger. All the same, I think I'll wait a couple of hours before I call them.

'Shall we move to the Jacuzzi?' Zoë suggests.

It's almost too hot at first but soon becomes heavenly.

'Can you believe we've got the whole place to ourselves?' Zoë coos. 'What could be better than this?'

'Well there was this one Oscar winner . . .' I gossip. 'To celebrate she asked for her bath to be filled with the finest champagne and then went for a dip!'

'I think that's what they call a *bubbly* bath!' Zoë quips.

I giggle. '$30,000 worth of bubbly – can you imagine?'

'No!' Zoë gawps. 'How do you know all this stuff?'

'I was reading while you were . . .' I tail off.

Zoë cringes at the memory.

'Was it really that bad?' I ask.

Zoë bites her lip. 'Actually I just wanted to keep laughing!' she giggles as she presses her foot against one of the water jets. 'I couldn't believe it was *him*!' She wipes the steam from her face, spreading her smile even further. 'All the times I've swooned over him and there he was getting all worked up over me!'

'That's trippy!' I acknowledge.

'I'm glad it happened. I've done it now. Maybe that's all you need with Elliot – a one-night stand to get him out of your system?'

'I'd be willing to give it a try,' I concede.

'And if it didn't work the first time you could just try, try again!' Zoë laughs.

'Exactly.'

'It's a funny thing getting what you want,' Zoë sighs. 'It's not that it doesn't live up to expectations exactly but almost immediately you want something else.'

'So what do you want most of all now?'

'Other than breakfast?'

I nod.

'I haven't decided yet. I feel like I've got all the pieces of my life laid out on a big table and I'm not sure which bits I want to keep and which bits I want to change.'

'Aren't we lucky that we have those choices?' I marvel. 'Some people feel so trapped in their lives.'

'Like my mum,' Zoë whispers. 'She can't see a way

out. But the door is always there, she just can't walk through it.' Zoë shudders, dredging herself out of the human hotpot. 'It's far too early to be getting this deep, Lara. We're supposed to be on holiday!'

While I continue to bubble and steam, Zoë does the full works in the changing rooms, emerging fifteen minutes later looking as if she's had a ten-hour sleep in an oxygenated pod. I'm starting to feel woozy groggy from lack of sleep and early hangover symptoms and can barely manage to comb my wet hair off my face. But I do smell lovely – Eternity for Men, courtesy of the Eddie Powers Collection.

We stumble back into the hotel and find our nostrils flaring excitedly the minute we're in the door.

'Food!' Zoë rapturizes.

We follow our noses along the corridor to the cute Fifties-style Fountain Coffee Shop.

'We've got time,' Zoë insists, hopping up on to a pink bar stool just long enough to tell waitress Nora her order, before disappearing to the loo.

I feel slightly nervous sitting by myself. What would I do if Eddie lurched in looking for sustenance?

A stunning employee comes in for a bagel. Her hair is flicked to perfection and her eyes are like exquisite jewels. Suddenly I feel self-conscious with my wet hair and last night's clothes.

'She's so pretty,' I sigh as she leaves.

'She's the one who gets sent up to a guest if they've got a complaint,' Nora confides. 'Nobody can stay mad when they're looking at her.'

Good strategy!

Next in is a languorously glamorous blonde with the longest, slimmest legs I've ever seen.

'How's our employee of the month?' she beams as Nora presents her with a latte.

'Who was that?' I gawp after her trouser-suited chicness.

'That's our PR lady, Wendy. She's a star.'

'She looks like Veronica Lake.'

'One of our "special guests" adores her,' Nora whispers. 'He calls her Wendacious!'

'She is!' I confirm. 'Is she going to run off with him?'

'She's already married, husband works for Rolls-Royce.'

What a team!

When Zoë returns to her stool, she raises her orange juice and cheers, 'Happy Birthday, Lara!'

'Oh my God! I'd forgotten!'

Then she hands me a paper bag. Inside is a pink rubber duck complete with Beverly Hills Hotel logo.

'The gift shop was just opening – do you like it?'

'I love it! Oh Zoë!' I give her a hug. When we separate there are two of the most luscious stacks of pancakes before us. And my stack has a little birthday candle!

'Pretty good start to the day, wouldn't you say?' Zoë grins, tucking in.

I nod, too busy drizzling hot cherry sauce to speak.

'So what are your plans for while I'm at work?'

I look at Zoë. If the roles were reversed and she had the free time she'd probably do Rodeo Drive then have a mooch down Melrose and conclude with a trip to Universal Studios.

But I'm not Zoë.

'Sleep!' I groan.

I need to get horizontal and soon. Preferably in an empty bed.

28

I'm just slipping into a coma-like sleep when the Batphone rings.

'Hello?' I can barely open my mouth, let alone my eyes.

'I've got an audition!' Zoë toots. 'Sasha's director guy with the fleshy earlobes, he wants to see me!'

'Wow, when?' I croak, still coming to.

'Tonight! I know it's your birthday but—'

'Don't be silly, you've got to go.'

'I want you to come with me. It's actually a few hours up the coast from here so I thought if we got the train we could sleep *en route* and—'

'When are we leaving?' I'm feeling caught unawares.

'In an hour!'

'Oh my God!' I ping upright.

'I need you to pack a bag for me, the shiny-pink tube dress and my J-Lo trackie to travel in and all my overnight bits.'

'Overnight?'

'Well, you never know what it'll take to get the part!'

'Zoë!'

'Kidding! Just hurry up and get here, they're letting me off work early.'

'Does The California Club know?'

'Yeah, the boss checked with them and they said provided I made up my hours later in the week, it's cool.'

'Where exactly are we going?'

'He's faxing over the details, we just get the first train bound for San Francisco.'

On the way to Union Station I try to call my posse but there's no reply from Sasha, Elliot is mid-bear talk and Elise is embroiled in homework from her Shamanic Healing seminar. Just as well, I'm too tired to have coherent conversations.

'Over here!' Zoë pogos along Platform 10 trying to get my attention.

As I approach her I'm daunted by the size of the angular silver contraption we're about to board.

'I've never been on a double-decker train before,' I marvel as we take the stairs to the upper level. 'It's so spacious and spanky-clean. Are we in business class?'

'Nope, just "coach" as they call it,' Zoë notes, taking her seat without any of the usual armrest-up-your-bottom contortions.

Suddenly I'm revived by the novelty factor of my surroundings and attempt to fold down my tray table – no mean feat considering the seat in front is so far ahead of me: it's like an elaborate Meccano project of slotting joints and extending limbs to get the table all the way over to my lap.

'I'm setting the alarm for 5.45 p.m.,' Zoë tells me as she simultaneously programmes her mobile phone and reclines her seat.

'What stop do we need?' I ask.

'I've got it all written down but it's at the bottom of my bag . . .' Zoë waves vaguely at her feet. 'Just make sure you give me a shout before 6 p.m.'

As we leave LA behind I watch the vegetation change from jutting dark green poplars – so precision pointy they look like the superglued spikes on a punk's mohican – to hanks of long grasses sprouting from the sandy earth like a crop of Limahl wigs. All of a sudden, strange yellow stacked-rock formations crowd around the train.

'Isn't this surreal?' I turn to Zoë. She's out for the count. I thought she was uncharacteristically mute.

The train conductor, however, has something very interesting to say: 'Late lunch is being served in the diner car.'

More interesting still, it appears to be being served in another era. Some time in the late Sixties, I'd say. The décor is authentically retro with squishy brown leather seating and rough-textured orange curtains. I so wish I was wearing a polyester dress and a back-combed hairpiece. But then I'd look a fool sitting with the people I'm deposited with. Opposite me is a goateed bruiser with WWF-style bejewelled knuckles, next to him his blowzy wife and opposite her, her Anne Bancroft lookalike mother, all tucking into chicken pot pie.

As I follow suit I get a sudden urge to call Joel and tell

him about the crazy birthday I'm having, then realize I can't. Ever. I don't have his number. I don't know where he works or even where he lives. In the rush to get to Sasha I forwent any of the traditional number exchanging and promises to meet again real soon. Besides, I was expecting to see him again that evening. I wonder if I could trace him through the movie première people – yeah, next time I'm back at the Arclight cinema I'll ask the usher if he's got Joel's number.

I roll my eyes, trying to keep a rising feeling of hysteria at bay. I suppose he could always contact me through Zoë at the diner. She's there for another two whole days. Oh no! How did I let this happen? Unless – maybe he passed on his number to Zoë when he came back with the tickets and she just forgot to tell me. I quickly pay for my pot pie, bid farewell to my oddball dining companions and hurry back to my seat, only to find Zoë even more comatose, now lying across my seat as well as hers.

I take a breath and resign myself to handing the Joel situation over to fate. Maybe it's for the best. What will be, will be. And what won't, won't.

In searching the carriages for a free place to sit I happen upon the viewing car. After the dining car, this looks positively space age. The chairs are groovy moulded plastic and face windows that curve up to the ceiling. I settle into one and get a full-frontal of glistening blue ocean. So this is why they call this train the Coastliner. The light glinting on the waves dazzles as if all the fish have been given little mirrors to angle at the sun. Who needs diamonds – here's the real bling-bling in this world.

I close my eyes to daydream, loving the feeling of the sun on my face. Almost immediately my thoughts turn to Elliot and our parting conversation at the Ahwahnee. What with zooming around with Joel, confronting Ty and partying with Zoë I haven't had much time to process my feelings for him. I realize now that his revelation about missing me and saying he felt he was losing me has made me feel all the more close to him. It's as if we've shared an honest moment amid all the mixed messages. Initially he was huffy about Joel, seeming peeved that he'd been ousted from being my number one guy, and in turn I was in danger of closing off a part of me to him, running with the Joel situation for all it's worth to somehow punish him for not loving me the way I want. But ever since he showed himself to be a little vulnerable, I feel we're subconsciously working together on finding a new way to be with each other, adjusting to the new circumstances in our life.

Even if he's never mine exclusively, I know now how important I am to him. It seems foolish considering all we've been through but I had been having doubts – ever since Elise came on the scene I'd felt replaced. Now I don't feel threatened by her, or anyone who might come after her. I feel like he's made me a guarantee that he'll always have a place for me in his heart, and that makes me feel less needy, more loved. It's not that I need him, to feel validated but he is so important to me it makes a huge difference to know he feels the same way. To a degree anyway!

I open my eyes again and find the sea has been replaced by dusty earth with rows of mystery plants creating lines of fuzz in the soil like the strips on the bottom of a Hoover. I wonder where we are? I look at my watch – just half an hour to go. I'd better go and wake Zoë.

This time I find her splat against the window so I'm free to slot back into my seat. As I do, she stirs and blearily asks the time.

'5.30 p.m.,' I tell her.

'OK! Let the beautification begin!' Suddenly she's wide awake. 'You might want to think about sprucing yourself up too.'

'Do I have to pretend to be your agent or anything?'

'We'll just play it by ear. Back in a mo!'

As Zoë dips to the loo, I pull out my make-up bag and contemplate my face. Why are my nostrils always the first place foundation disappears from? I dob beige over the pink and then sparkle up my eyelids, melon gloss my lips and further clog my lashes to please Zoë. Now what? I return to gazing out the window.

'Hey, look at those rusty old oil drills!' Zoë rejoins me. 'They look like they're nodding at the ground.'

'Do you think there might be an oil theme to the movie?' I ask.

'It's all top secret,' Zoë shrugs. 'I haven't been told anything. All will be revealed when we get there.'

'I'm sure it will,' I agree, amazed by how Zoë can arrange her cleavage in such a way that it gives the illusion of teetering over the edge of a precipice.

'San Luis Obispo! This is us!' she jiggles to her feet.

While Zoë summons a cab I look around the old mission-style station. It doesn't look like the kind of place geared up to accommodate Hollywood divas and coke-snorting movie execs. A teenager in beige shorts and a white T-shirt scutters by on a skateboard, no doubt on his way to appear in a Gap ad. Suddenly I feel like giving birth to 2.4 children and bagging myself one of the quaint clapboard houses painted a soothing mint green across the street.

'Cab!' Zoë calls me over.

She's starting to look excited, I guess the adrenalin is kicking in. It'll help to have a little morphine to hand if there's a casting couch scenario when we get there.

'Nervous?' I ask her.

'A bit!' She grins, looking anything but.

As we drive along, I notice she hasn't taken her eyes off me.

'What?' I demand.

'Nothing!' she trills.

'We're just about to . . .' the driver connects with Zoë in his rearview mirror.

'Close your eyes!' Zoë reaches across and puts her hand over my eyes.

'What are you doing?' I fluster.

'Sshh!'

I sense the car slowing to take a turn.

'OK, now!' I hear the driver's voice.

Zoë removes her hand.

'What's going— Oh my God!' I gasp at the lurid pink billboard before me: 'THE MADONNA INN!'

Zoë gives a gleeful gurgle at my reaction.

My mouth continues to gape like I'm in mid-dental procedure: 'I can't believe I'm here! This is my fantasy!'

'Happy Birthday!' Zoë cheers.

'Oh Zoë,' I blub. Turns out my eyes are going to spill over before her cleavage.

She pulls me into a hug.

'What about your audition?' I muffle into her shoulder.

'There isn't one!' she pips.

'You little minx!' I pull back to look at her. 'The whole thing—'

'Made up to trick you – see what a good actress I am!'

I beam at her, overwhelmed. 'This is the best surprise I've ever had.'

'It's about to get better,' she winks. 'Wait there!'

As she darts into the registration nook, I step from the cab and gawp over at the jumble of elliptical boulders – some sand-blasted smooth, others retaining their oyster-shell ridges – set around a selection of rock pools and gently bubbling fountains. The building they front peaks to a witch's hat turret and is painted the exact pink used to ice finger-buns. An enormous grin spreads across my face – it's a cross between Bedrock and a fairy grotto, with a bit of Quality Street detailing (ye olde lamps, horse-drawn carriage motif) thrown in for good measure.

I'm dying to peer inside but already Zoë's back with a key and a room map.

'I've just got to fill out the registration card but you can go on up, room 139.'

'Are you sure?'

'Yes go, your present is waiting for you in your room.'

I get a present too? This is unbelievable.

I bound up a hillside driveway that would normally have me wheezing after one stride – funny how happiness gives you so much energy. But the building at the top does take my breath away – all painted white with its three-tiered verandas and carved wooden balustrades it puts me in mind of a Mississippi show-boat. With a couple of dovecots tacked on either end. I study my map. Room 139 is on the ground floor in the middle. I burrow down a corridor and then spy the door plaque that goes with my number – Jungle Rock. Oh my God! This room is legendary!

I fidget the key in the lock and burst into a vast carpeted cave dominated by two king-size beds hiding beneath zebra print counterpanes. Though the layout is open plan the beds appear to have their own rooms. I sprawl like an animal skin on the one nearest the door and then hurtle into the bathroom. There it is – the shower that cascades down the rough-hewn rock like a waterfall! I step inside and run my hands along the patchwork of lacquered granite – blood reds, charcoal greys, mould greens and muddy aubergines, all bonded together with concrete. I take a sniff of the Madonna Inn shower gel and then dance back into the main room. Which bed shall I claim? The one I've mussed up or the one over here by the— I jump back, freaked out. There's a body in the other bed.

My first thought is that I've got the wrong room and

I dart towards the door in a panic. But then I reason that the key worked and it's unlikely someone would be calling it a night at 6 p.m. Recalling Zoë's words, I decide to check to see if the mound is in fact gift-wrapped.

Au contraire. It's naked.

And there's something familiar about the duckling-blond hair and freckly shoulders.

My heart swoons. It's Elliot.

'My present . . .' I sigh, in disbelief.

I tiptoe closer. Can this be for real? Maybe Joel was right – he just needed a prompt and then time alone to think. I kneel beside the bed and cherish being so close I can ruffle his hair with my breath. I take in every detail of his face, his dark blond eyelashes, the tawny stubble underlining his cheekbones, the soft, dented oblong of his lower lip. I inhale his smell – outdoorsy mingling with roasted vanilla. I can feel the warmth coming from his body. Am I really going to be able to touch that honeyed skin on his back? Twist my fingers in his hair, feel his body pressed up against mine? Oh Elliot, I've wanted you so much, for so long. Is this the beginning? Is my life about to get this much better? All my fantasies colliding on one day. One perfect day.

I lean closer, so I can awake him with a kiss . . .

29

'SURPRISE!'

Sensing a stampede behind me, I swivel round to find Helen, Sasha and – urgh! – Elise colliding as they rush towards me.

'I gave you the wrong key!' Zoë apologizes, bringing up the rear.

'We were all waiting in the other room!' Sasha pants as she slides beside me on the floor to give me a birthday squeeze.

'Elise, why didn't you wake me?' Elliot stirs, rubbing his eyes with the heel of his hand.

'You looked so peaceful!' she chimes.

'I wanted to be in on the surprise,' he complains.

Trust me, you were the surprise! I think to myself.

'Well, Happy Birthday, Lara!' He reaches out an arm and coaxes my head towards him. My lips meet his – soft, warm, sleepy – a two-second taster of what might have been/almost was. I cringe, imagining the scene if the girls had burst in even a minute later – me caught kissing a sleeping Elliot. Elise would have freaked, so would Elliot for that matter. It was all in my head. As if he'd offer himself to me like that. What was I thinking?

As Helen and Zoë pile on the bed, Elise smothers herself over Elliot. I can hardly bear to watch. The only good news is that she's inadvertently snagged the sheet away from him and it's gaping all the way down to his fuzzy tummy.

'So whose fabulous idea was this?' I brazen, trying to summon up my former enthusiasm.

All heads turn to Elliot.

'I just remembered the name of the place. Helen made all the arrangements.' He shrugs.

'The lying and deceit was all Zoë,' Helen adds.

Zoë chortles. 'I was so good!'

'Well, thank you all – I can't believe we're all here together!'

Elise nuzzles deeper into Elliot. I have to get away.

'So when do I get to see my room?'

'Now!' Zoë leaps to her feet. 'Come on, everyone!'

'You'll have to excuse us,' Elise leers. 'We've got some catching up to do.'

Elliot looks far too exhausted for what she has in mind. He yawns: 'What time are we eating?'

Zoë gives me a look as if to say: See, he's more interested in his stomach than shagging her.

'I've booked a table in the Gold Rush Dining Room for eight,' Helen informs him. 'Shall we see you down there?'

'Definitely!' Elliot nods. 'Both of us this time.'

I think I preferred the La Valencia arrangement.

As I close the door on Jungle Rock it occurs to me

that Sasha should really be the one waving us off with a spear.

'What's your room like, Sash?'

'Don't ask!' she grimaces. 'I'm sharing with Zoë – it was her choice.'

'Why do I get the feeling you've gone for the porn theme?' I nudge Zoë.

'You're not far wrong,' Sasha sighs.

'What?' Since when did kitsch get X-rated?

'Do you want to see it? It's right here,' Sasha offers, dangling the key.

'Oh yes! I've only seen the pictures on the Internet, let's do it!' Zoë can't wait.

'The Tack Room?' I read the plaque on the door. 'As in tacky?' I ask.

'As in ponies?' Helen suggests.

'Well, riding crops maybe,' Sasha mutters as she swings open the door to reveal a blaze of red walls, red doors, red carpet, red sofa and red leather bed-spreads. Bright pillarbox red. I kid you not.

'You don't get these at Laura Ashley,' I coo, stroking the scarlet hide.

'Welcome to the Perve Palace!' Sasha runs her fingers along the brass studs that trim the walls like a belly-chain.

'There's twisted rope on the front of the wardrobe – isn't it all a bit bondage?' Helen worries.

'I'm going to tie Sasha to the bed tonight with her own hair!' Zoë cackles, reaching to whip off Sasha's baseball hat.

Sasha leaps back as if she's just been electrocuted.

'Are you all right?' I ask, slowly moving towards her like she's a startled deer.

'I didn't want to make a big deal. This is your day, Lara.' She takes another step back.

'A big deal about what? Am I missing something?'

'No, but I am!' Sasha heaves a sigh and then removes her droopy cotton sunhat. No hair comes tumbling down.

Along with Helen and Zoë, I suck up all the air in the room with a sudden intake of breath.

'Your hair!'

'Where's it gone?'

'Did you have an accident?'

Sasha shakes her head. Gone is the swishing sound. All that remain are soft wisps of silk curling around her ears. 'What do you think?'

Helen reaches forward and rumples her flattened hair to life. 'Very Charlize Theron.'

'You didn't do it for Ty, did you?' I wonder out loud. 'To try and make yourself less attractive?'

Zoë looks confused.

'No, honestly,' Sasha assures me. 'I actually did it for Oliver. And for me.'

'Who's Oliver?' Zoë perks up. 'Is he a hottie?'

'Oliver is a mountain lion.'

'Is this going to start making sense some time soon?' Zoë frowns.

'I know it's only been a few days but I think I'm in love!' Sasha swoons.

'With the lion?' Zoë checks.

Sasha nods.

'What about Ty?' I ask.

'Don't tell me – Ty's a tiger!' Zoë tries to join in.

'No, he's the guy who's been horrible to Sasha,' Helen reminds her.

'That bastard, just wait till I get my hands on him!' Zoë growls.

'I may just beat you to it!' Sasha shares a knowing look with me.

'Have you kissed him yet?' I so want the answer to be yes.

'Has she kissed the guy she hates? What is going on?' Zoë is indignant.

Sasha goes back to the beginning, first explaining how Oliver would get freaked out at the slightest glimpse of her long hair (hence the haircut) and how the once-hostile Ty is now her suitor. And she, in turn, his suitoress. Then she answers my question: no, she hasn't kissed him yet. They're still just learning to trust each other – she needs to know that he won't get aggressive and snipey again and he needs to get over his fears that she's a diva in disguise.

'But I'd say it bodes well,' she smiles shyly.

'Well, don't leave it too long,' Zoë cautions. 'When you get back you've only got one more night with him.'

Sasha's face falls. It would seem she's found her groove at Tiger Tiger and, judging from her expression, the thought of going back to how she was before terrifies her.

Helen takes her hand. 'Trust The California Club,' she soothes. 'By the end of the week your wish will come true.'

Sasha looks confused. 'But I've already got my wish, I mean, I found somewhere where looks don't matter.'

'Your real wish,' Helen whispers.

Sasha looks at her, wide-eyed. At the same time my heart dips. Can The California Club read the invisible ink behind what we wrote down on our slips of paper?

'You mean the wish they grant isn't necessarily what we wrote down?' I have to be clear on this. Is there still a chance for me and Elliot?

Helen smiles enigmatically. 'What you wrote is just the starting point.'

'Come on, Gypsy Rose Lee – spill!' Zoë heckles.

Helen takes a seat beside Zoë, lays a hand on her cheek, closes her eyes and says, 'I see a man with a large penis in your recent past . . .'

'Who told you?' Zoë leaps back.

'Guilty!' I raise my hand. I was dying to tell someone and the others were all busy when I tried calling them *en route* to Union Station.

'Something I should know?' Sasha raises an eyebrow.

When Zoë's done telling the Eddie Powers story, Sasha asks me for a Joel update. After my near-miss with Elliot I want to run to Joel's consoling arms all the more but explain that I've let him slip away. I'm just about to get paranoid that he deliberately vanished without trace, never having any intention of seeing me again, when Zoë turns our attention to Helen's sex life.

'So where's Reuben tonight?'

'Oh he's um, home or out, I'm not sure. Surfing, probably. Who knows where!' She gives a strange unnatural laugh.

'So which is better, surfing or sex?' Zoë probes.

'Reuben says that if you reckon surfing's better than sex then you're not doing it right!'

'But what do you say?'

'Sex with a surfer is the best!' she laughs.

'Really?' It's the one species Zoë hasn't tried and she's obviously concerned she's missing out.

'Well, not just any surfer. With Reuben.' Her eyes shine bright. 'He's The One, for sure.'

We all give a 'dreams-really-can-come-true' sigh then Helen gets to her feet and asks, 'Ready to see your room now?'

'You betcha! Where is it?' I ask, peeling myself off the shiny bedspread.

'Over the other side, three floors up.' Helen motions ahead. 'You're sharing with me, hope that's OK.'

'Of course!' Darn, I won't be able to have a good cry and purge myself of the Elliot disappointment. 'Is there a mini-bar?' I try and sound casual.

We follow Helen up a spiral staircase lined with bright green carpet for that essential astro-turf look without the hazardous grazing possibilities.

'Up again!' she calls as Zoë and I pause for breath on the second floor.

Another spiral twirl and she steps back to let me insert the key.

'Carin,' I read the hand-painted driftwood plaque.

'Apparently it's a Swiss word of endearment,' Helen tells me.

I open the door.

Just as the Tack Room was an assault in red, this is like dreaming in bubblegum – I've never seen so much pink! I look up at the vaulted ceiling where painted wooden beams fan out tent-like from a central peak and find a hefty burnished gold Cupid holding a seven-stick candelabra dangling from a brass chain.

'Imagine if the hook gave way – you'd be crushed in your bed!' Zoë shudders.

'But what a way to go!' I run my hand over the bedspread – layer upon layer of beautiful roses. Crossing the berry carpet I slot into one of the two high-backed leather chairs the colour of pink sugared almonds to get a different perspective. Everywhere I look there's mirrors surrounded by swirling serifs of dark gold and more and more pink – pink velvet curtains (blush fading where the sun has seared them) and even a pink leather ice-bucket. Hello . . .

'The champagne!' Sasha remembers. There's a sloshing sound as she pulls out the bottle. 'All the ice has melted . . .'

'I don't care!' I'm right by her side holding glasses at the ready.

'I'll go and get some more.'

'Open it first!' I beg.

Helen takes over to pop the cork and fills four glasses to the brim.

'To Lara, on her birthday! May this be the start of a year filled with many wonderful surprises!'

'To Lara!' they chorus.

We take a slug, wincing at the lukewarm taste.

'I'm getting ice.' Sasha heads for the door.

'I'll come with you, I need to get a Coke from the machine,' Helen joins her.

'So do you like the room?' Zoë twirls around like a little girl in her best party dress.

'I love it!' I really do. My only complaint is that it doesn't come with a Romeo type in velvet and brocade, spouting poetry.

'We all took a vote and decided this was the most you – it's that quirky thing you like but by far the most romantic.'

I raise an eyebrow. I'd hardly call my current situation romantic. I feel like I've lost Elliot all over again. As self-pity tickles my tear ducts my survivor instinct urges me to 'Step away from the Cupid!'

'Is that another balcony?' I ask, making a dash for it. I already noted that the first overlooks the freeway. The second offers a panoramic view of a construction site with dozens of diggers nestled at the bottom of the sloping mountains. Not exactly picturesque but the fantasy is within.

'That's the balcony they were hiding on,' Zoë tells me. 'When I came in they all jumped out at me thinking it was you! And all the while you were . . .'

I take a hearty breath of fresh air.

Zoë reaches for the champagne and clumsily tops up my glass.

Lowering her voice she asks, 'Did you think, for a moment, that he was in bed waiting for you?'

She searches my face for the truth.

'Just for a moment,' I confess, unable to look her in the eye.

'I've wished so hard for him to fall in love with you!' Zoë agonizes.

'I know,' I smile, touched by her campaigning but determined not to feel sorry for myself again tonight. How can I complain when I've got my own calamine castle to play in?

But then Zoë slips a comforting arm around me and leans her cheek on my shoulder and I crumble.

'Why can't I let go?' I sigh. 'Even after getting it on with Joel who is entirely divine?'

'Because you love him. Next question.'

I smile for a second then sigh. '*Should* I let go? Is it time?'

'Not yet. At least give it to the end of the week. You heard what Helen said to Sasha – secret wishes can come true too.'

'Do you really think there's a chance? I mean honestly, realistically?'

'There's definitely something wrong between him and Elise and maybe when he figures out what it is, he'll finally see the light.'

'You think they're on shaky ground?' Finally someone who sees things my way!

'There were cracks showing at La Jolla beach, you said he seemed a bit iffy in Yosemite and after tonight, trust me, those cracks will develop into fissures.'

'What?!' I choke at Zoë's metaphor follow-through.

'Is that the wrong word?' she frowns. 'Fissures?'

'No, it's the right one, that's what's so shocking.'

Zoë looks proud of herself, despite my dig, then continues with her take on the situation: 'I think being with us all again is making Elliot realize how far off the mark he is with Elise.'

'Maybe . . .' I concede.

'Look, even if you don't have 100 per cent faith in The California Club, you've got to believe in the power of the Madonna Inn! This place *is* you, you're on home turf here, whereas everything about it is rankling with the crowned princess of Marks & Spencer so she's at a disadvantage.' Zoë gives me a minxy look. 'And you're here with all your friends.'

'And it's my birthday!' I join in the fun.

'Exactly. You can't lose. Progress will be made tonight, I promise.'

'How can you be so sure?' I try for one last wobble.

Zoë reaches back into the room and lugs over a book the size and weight of a paving stone.

'What's this?' I groan.

'Your birthday present! It's a coffee table book about the Madonna Inn.'

'Where's the concrete coffee table that goes with it?'

Zoë ignores me. 'It's from all of us. I haven't had a chance to sign it yet but Elliot has. Read!'

Hey Beautiful Birthday Girl! HAPPY 30th!

I'd tell you to make a wish but I guess we've already done that!!

Actually, La, make as many wishes as you like – one for every cupid in this crazy place! You deserve to have all your dreams come true this year – that's what I'm wishing for you! (And with two of us at it, how can the universe resist?)

Love you, Elliot.

I look up at Zoë. It's lovely – very encouraging and supportive – but I need her to translate the sure-thing aspect to me.

'Love you.' She jabs the page.

'That's just casual, matey...'

'Look at it another way – all that's missing is the I!'

I raise an eyebrow.

'One lousy letter,' Zoë insists.

I start laughing. I'm going to enjoy tonight, whatever happens.

30

The Madonna Inn really comes into its own at night. A million fairy lights wink at you through the stained glass windows, the rockpool fountains are transformed into liquid fireworks by coloured underwater lights and the band lulls you into a retro reverie with dreamy leisure lounge tunes like *Fly Me to the Moon*. My heart aches with 'coming home' satisfaction.

'Wait for us!' Zoë clatters up behind me and Helen with Sasha in tow. Both look amazing – Zoë in her shiny pink dress, Sasha in a backless white halter-neck with one of Zoë's diamanté clips prettying up her newly tufty hair.

'Are the others already inside?'

'Shall we find out?' asks Helen, ceremoniously pushing open the carved wooden doors.

We step into a fantasy of pink and gold even more vibrant and intense than my room. One side of the restaurant follows the curve of a sweeping staircase, the other has booths that look to me like a fleet of Cinderella carriages and in the middle a twisting tree stretches its vines of gold across the ceiling.

We breathe an awed, 'Wow!'

'Welcome to Barbara Cartland Land!' Elliot comes to greet us, giving me a kiss on the cheek and whispering, 'You look lovely!'

I smooth down my devoré dress with renewed pride as he leads us over to a booth of ruched pink leather sporting a perky Happy Birthday balloon. It's one of twelve such balloons strung around the room. I wonder if you have to have at least one birthday or anniversary per party to get a reservation – Restaurant Policy: we aim to maintain a high level of special occasion-ness!

'Isn't this beautiful?' I sigh, ducking under a Tiffany lightshade as I slide in next to Elliot.

Elise pulls a face and titters. 'Am I the only one who finds this grotesque?'

'I think that's the point,' Helen reasons, as the band switches to an Acker Bilk style clarinet rendition of *Edelweiss*.

The way Elise snuffles and shakes her head is so patronizing I want to smack her but Zoë saves me the trouble by jumping in with, 'Don't worry, Elise – when it's your birthday we'll go to a Holiday Inn.'

Before Elise can retort, the waiter comes to the table. His sales pitch on the hand-cut, oak-pit-barbecued steaks tempts even veggie Sasha. And when Zoë learns that Mr Madonna struck up his cattle ranching business with none other than John Wayne she gets giddy and orders a 14-ounce filet mignon.

'Anyone for an olive?' I offer around the platter.

'Don't mind if I do.' Elliot reaches for a fat green one.

'You told me you didn't like olives!' Elise looks aghast.

'I don't, but then again I haven't eaten one in years. I just wanted to make sure I wasn't missing out.'

'Are you trying to make a point?' Elise's eyes narrow.

'With an olive?' Elliot sounds exasperated.

The rest of us reach for the carrot sticks and crunch noisily. Those self-help classes are obviously paying off. Elise is the epitome of peace and harmony tonight.

Drrrrrrinnnnnnng!

What? I can't believe someone has brought their mobile phone to dinner! It continues to ring. I look around for the culprit, eager to give them a dirty look.

'Lara, I think that's you!' Helen nudges me.

'It can't be – you're all here.'

I scramble in my bag. The number is not identified on the screen. I flip open the phone and say a tentative 'Hello?'

'HAPPY BIRTHDAY, DARLING!'

'Mum!' I gasp. 'What are you doing? It's got to be 4.30 in the morning there!'

'I had to speak to you on your special day!'

'Hold on.' I shuffle out of the booth and hurry to the lobby, head down, face as puce as the napkins. 'Are you OK?'

'Of course! Never better!' she cheers. 'But I want to know how you are!'

'Oh Mum, you should see this place.' I sink into a chair beside the flagstone fireplace. 'It's given me so many ideas for the B&B, I was thinking—'

'Lara.'

'What?'

'We've had an offer.'

My heart freezes.

'Have you said yes?'

'That's one of the reasons I'm calling. I thought it would be a wonderful birthday surprise but if you're not sure . . .'

I go to speak but I don't know what to say.

'They want an answer by the end of play today. They're offering the full asking price.'

I feel as though a huge bully is bearing down on me, blocking out all the sun in my world. The worst part is that he's here at my invitation – I told Mum to put the B&B on the market. I thought it was the only way. I didn't expect to feel like this. The more ideas I've had for the B&B the less I've believed I would lose it. I told myself it was history but I didn't really believe it – how can such a big part of my life be removed just like that? I even secretly started to hope that The California Club might come up with a solution for me.

'Lara?' Mum is still waiting for a response.

As I try and formulate a sentence I watch a family come through the main doors and take in their surroundings with a look with absolute joy and wonder. Suddenly I want that more than anything – to create a place that gives such pleasure, and yet happens to be my home.

'You were so keen to sell before.' Poor Mum sounds deflated.

'I know. I know,' I sigh. I find myself thinking of

The Ahwahnee and the Beverly Hills Hotel, The Del in Coronado, the villa at La Valencia and my pink paradise here. Somehow I felt connected to them all because I was 'in the business'. Am I about to end that?

I take a breath and in my quietest voice instruct: 'Do it. Say yes.'

'Oh Lara!' Now Mum sounds in a quandary. 'What if I try and stall them? Give you a bit more time to think.'

'There's no point. I can't afford it.' I have to be practical. And yet it feels so wrong, as if I'm letting my dream slip away without a fight.

'Lara! Food's here!' Helen leans around the corner and beckons me back to the dining room.

'I've got to go,' I mutter, feeling dazed.

Mum sighs, then peps up. 'You have a wonderful evening, darling, don't let this spoil your fun. I'll put them off for one more day, we'll talk tomorrow.'

'There's no point,' I complain.

'Lara Richards, I've known you since you were in my tummy, do you think I can't tell from your voice what you're really thinking?'

'Oh Mum!' I wail, tears springing to my eyes. 'I want it so much! Ever since I've been out here I've been bombarded with ideas to make our B&B the most welcoming and original place in all Brighton! The thought of losing it . . .'

'Hush now. You go and enjoy your dinner. Don't give it another thought. Just send my love to everyone.'

I steady my breathing. There's still a chance. I'll do as she says. I'll hush.

'How did you know we were all here?' I frown, the thought just occurring to me.

'Helen.'

Of course.

'I love you, Mum.'

'I love you too. Don't worry about the B&B.'

I flip the phone closed but I can't move straight away. What's it going to be?

'Excuse me, do you work here?' A young wife leans over me.

'No,' I look up and shake my head. 'I'm just a guest.'

The words hang in there to taunt me. I pray they're not an omen. No. Think positive. Don't let on to the others. Act normal. Drink more.

'Do you know Courtney Cox and David Arquette have stayed here!' Zoë greets me as I approach the table.

'Figures – have you seen how that man dresses?' Elise tuts.

'And Dolly Parton and her family are regulars!'

'That just about says it all,' Elliot chuckles. 'Before you get back in, La, I just need to . . .' Elliot escapes from the booth, putting his hands on my hips as he slides past me, front on. I'm fairly certain he's never touched me there before. At least, it never felt like this before. So intimate. So personal.

'Where are you going?' Elise barks.

'To the toilet, if that's all right with you, my angel!' Elliot rolls his eyes and trots on his way.

'Ooh! Ooh! Fissure!' Zoë hisses in my ear as I slide in beside her.

I don't know what's going on but I feel as though the world is starting to change around me. Maybe it's the booze or the fact that it's my birthday but I'm getting tingles of possibility. Who knows, maybe I will get to keep the B&B, I don't know *how* but maybe there's a way. And maybe Elliot will kiss me again. I thought I'd stopped wanting that but I haven't. I just need a sign from him. Any sign. I watch for his return and try to catch his eye. Just a little aside is all I need.

His first words are not quite what I had in mind.

'I just peed into a waterfall!'

'What?'

'Instead of urinals they've got this water gushing down the rocks and you just—'

'Thank you, Elliot, I think that's enough information!' Elise cuts him short.

'You know, Mr Madonna once took a baby elephant into the men's toilets,' I announce, eager to show I've begun reading my birthday book.

'What?' is the incredulous response.

'It belonged to a zookeeper friend of his.'

'Can you imagine weeing alongside an elephant?' Elliot winces. 'Now that would give you an inferiority complex!'

Everyone cracks up. Except Elise. No change there.

'You know what else?' Sasha looks unusually perky. 'There used to be a lion called the Duchess living here in the grounds. A busboy from the café used to feed him and take him for walks in the mountains out back.'

'I never had you pegged as an animal lover, Sash,' Elliot looks intrigued.

'I know! Things have really changed this week.' Sasha smiles appreciatively at Helen.

'I would have thought either you liked animals or you didn't,' Elise shrugs.

Sasha takes a deep breath, as if she's psyching herself up to make a revelation.

'This is going to sound so silly, and I wouldn't even say it if the wine hadn't gone straight to my head, but ever since I was a girl I thought animals didn't like me!'

'Really?' I frown. 'Why?'

'Well, when I was ten my dad bought me and my sister a cat and it just took an instant aversion to me – it would always hiss and wriggle away if I tried to pick it up – I had all these scratches on my arms – but when Sonia did the same it would purr and nuzzle her and everyone used to say, "Oh that cat just adores you, Sonia!" and I always felt so rejected, like it could see right inside of me and didn't like what it saw. I was always so nervous of people putting two and two together and realizing that I was a fraud because the cat knew what I was really like.'

So that was what was creating all the panic as we approached Tiger Tiger!

'When I found out I was going to be around lions and such I thought I might be in serious danger.'

Helen reaches across the table to take Sasha's hand but is hampered by Elise lunging for the wine. She's certainly slugging it back tonight, shame it makes her stroppy rather than mellow – she's getting scratchier with every gulp. I think Zoë's probably right – the body language and sniping between her and Elliot seem to indicate an unresolved argument. Oh dear.

'But to be honest,' Sasha continues, oblivious, 'Ty was way scarier than the cats and after holding Theo—'

'A cub,' I chip in.

'And he didn't bite me or try to get away, it was just such a wonderful feeling, like being truly accepted!'

'Going back to your sister,' Elise begins. 'It's interesting that you begrudged her even a taste of the attention you were used to – one house pet responding positively to her when you had the entire population fawning over you. Did you want it all for yourself?'

'Elise!' Elliot admonishes her.

'It wasn't like that!' Sasha protests.

Great, trample all over her newfound happiness, why dontcha?

'I'm not saying it was, that's just what they'd say at Breathe.' Elise denies all responsibility for her attack.

'Maybe the reason it was so upsetting for you, was that the response from the animal was what you valued the most,' Helen comes up with a different take on the situation.

'Yes!' Sasha's eyes brighten. 'I can't tell you what it feels like to have an animal trust you. It's given me such a boost.'

'Shame nature boy here doesn't share your enthu-siasm!' Helen teases. 'Danced with any more racoons lately?'

'I don't want to talk about it.' Elliot fills his mouth with steak so further questioning is in vain.

*

410

As the chatter continues and my sour cream melts into my baked potato, I find my attention drifting off towards the dance floor. There's barely a non-grey hair to be found but the double hip-replacement brigade are tinkering around the floor with such obvious delight it warms my heart. I watch a man rise from the table, turn to his lady companion and hold out an open palm to her. It's such an elegant gesture. For a moment I pretend it's my hand he's taking.

'Lara?' Elliot calls me back. 'What are you so transfixed by?'

I heave a sigh. 'I was just thinking how I want to be eighty and still be taken dancing by my hunched-over husband! It must be lovely to have someone to hold on to.'

'When *was* the last time you went out with someone?' Elise asks, blunt as ever.

'It's been a while,' I admit. I don't want to put an actual year count on it so I distract them with a tale of a one-night stand with a Ukrainian cruise ship percussionist.

'I didn't know about this!' Elliot complains.

'It was just after you moved to Manchester – during our absent friend period,' I explain, cryptically referring to the spell when Elliot was in the first flushes of love with Elise.

'Do you know I met Elliot just two days after he arrived – it was as if he moved there to meet me!' Elise crows.

I don't know what Elliot did in his previous lives but he must have been a bad, bad boy.

'Tell us all, sparing no details!' Zoë begs me.

None of them know about the Ukrainian because it was over before it began. We met in a bar in Southampton where I'd gone for an antiques fair and I was so excited to fancy someone I got completely carried away with the fantasy that we would sail away together and kiss away the language barrier. The reality was that I bought a plane ticket to Nice to visit him on an overnight and two days before I flew I rang to check our meeting details and another woman answered the phone in his cabin. Could've been a friend or a work colleague, right? That's what I thought till I heard his voice in the background, telling her to put down the phone. I rang back but he didn't answer. So that was that. Back on dry land with a bump.

Four of my dining companions make sympathetic noises while Elise diagnoses fear of commitment. 'I mean, look at the odds of it working – you couldn't have had more factors stacked against you – he barely spoke English, he was away at sea 90 per cent of the year, if you wanted to call him on board there was a £5-a-minute shore-to-ship charge and the rest of the time he lived in the Ukraine!' She takes another sip of wine. 'I mean Lara, did he really have anything going for him?'

I think for a moment. 'His hair smelt really good. And one afternoon he called me from Sorrento and said the sweetest things – "I play for you!" and "Honey, I miss!"' I smile to myself, remembering the good bits. 'One of the nicest things was his response of total incredulity when he discovered I wasn't married!' I laugh. 'Like I should have been snapped up long ago.'

'I feel the same way about you,' Helen insists. 'I just wish you could be with someone who loves you as much as we do.'

'I think the problem is that there's no one out there good enough for you,' Elliot decides.

'I think you're right,' Zoë agrees. 'I mean there's only a handful of quality men in this world – Elliot you're obviously one but you're taken, Victoria Beckham got the other good one and well, I can't think of any more. No offence to Ty and Reuben but I haven't met them so I don't know for sure that they are members of the elite.'

'I'm hardly the perfect boyfriend,' Elliot looks shifty.

'No, but we're working on it.' Elise gives him a schoolmarmish look.

How romantic.

'You know I'm lucky, I don't like the good ones, they're of no use to me,' Zoë shrugs.

'What a thing to say!' Elise exclaims.

'I mean it. I don't want to settle down. I'm happy as I am.'

'What about you, Lara?' Again Elise turns her beady eye on me. 'Are you happy as you are?'

'Um . . .' I falter.

'Would you say you're close to your family?'

I feel like I'm a reluctant guest on *Kilroy* – enough with the analysis! 'These lot are really my family . . .' I say.

'Oh La!' Everyone except Elise falls into a drink-spilling hug-fest.

'And yet you haven't all been together in over a year.'

What is she trying to say?

'We're together now!' I defy her.

'Yes, *for now* . . .' She gives me a pitying look. 'But who have you got to go home to?'

I've got a steak knife and I'm not afraid to use it.

'I think you've had enough.' Elliot tries to stop Elise from pouring herself more wine but she shrugs him off and sloshes the bottle regardless.

'I'm not unhappy,' I reason. 'Just not ecstatic all the time. But I tell you something, until we got on to this subject, this night was more than making up for any down periods!'

'Too right!' Zoë is more than ready to move on from the soul-searching. 'I say we forget discussing how happy we are and get on to the important questions in life – like what we're having for dessert!'

31

Pink champagne, toffee crunch, lemon coconut, raspberry delight, black forest and banana nut. Six cake options. Six of us at the table. It seems only right that we get one of each.

'My boss told me I had to try them so this is actually work for me!' Helen gets ready to gorge.

All the girls go to pink champagne first – topped with curls of pink chocolate that look like they've been set on rollers, it's a butter-creamy, fluffy sponge yumfest. Elliot digs into toffee crunch, which is covered in smashed pieces of honeycomb. He doesn't have a particularly sweet tooth but we can see that we need to get in quick if we want a taste. All too soon there's nothing left but a few flakes of coconut and the stem of a glacé cherry.

Helen is impressed. The rest of us just feel sick.

'Shall we go through to the bar?' Elliot groans. 'I think I need a digestif!'

'Sod that, I'm having a liqueur!' Zoë grunts as she gets to her feet.

We waddle through to the Silver Bar, taking a table

in full view of the dance floor. Elliot orders the drinks and Sasha brings over a book of all the rooms for us to peruse while we're waiting for the sugar rush to pass. We're all quite tipsy so the images are a little blurry, but we get the general idea.

'Who chose the Jungle Room anyway?' Zoë asks, reacquainting herself with Elise and Elliot's den.

'I did,' Helen affirms. 'I thought it was the most masculine for Elliot.'

He chinks glasses with Helen knowing he could have easily ended up in some floral Valentine.

Elise says she would have chosen the Austrian Suite. Talk about delusions of grandeur – it's the poshest of all, 76 feet long, all mock Louis XIV and regal blue.

'I think the rock ones are the sexiest,' I decide. 'Look at Caveman!'

'Oh no!' Elise shudders. 'I already feel like Wilma Flintstone as it is.'

'Oh I'd love it,' I continue. 'It's so primitive – all tousled hair and animal passion!'

'Tarzan and Jane!' Elliot enthuses.

'Makes you want to tussle and play-fight,' I growl.

'And drag each other by the hair!' he grins, staring straight at me.

'And get all mussed up and sweaty and whooping!' I'm drunker than I realized.

'And then cool off in the shower . . .' Elliot's voice drops.

'Water trickling down those raggedy rocks . . .' I gaze at him.

416

'But you might clip your elbow or slip and concuss yourself!' Elise is horrified at the thought.

Talk about ruining the mood! Perhaps they should install one of those old lady shower chairs for her.

'Look, there's one called Yosemite Falls – home from home!' Elliot laughs. 'You know, it's so weird – I've been surrounded by the real thing for the past three days and it does nothing for me and yet when you throw in a carpet and a TV I think it's the biggest turn-on!'

'Could've fooled me,' Elise mutters into her brandy.

Zoë looks fit to burst – see! See! Fissure! He's turned on and he still didn't shag her!

I wonder if that's true. You'd think after time apart they'd be raring to go.

Sasha traces her finger over the leopardprint bed-spread in the picture. 'I can't believe I've only got one more night with him.'

'If it's meant to be, you've got all the time in the world,' Elise mutters.

We look at her, startled. Which orifice did the romantic in her spring from?

'That's not my personal opinion, I'm quoting Martha,' she tells us.

'What *is* your personal opinion?' Helen probes.

Elise pulls a face. 'Act fast, don't give him time to think himself out of it.'

Now that's telling.

'That's all I was saying earlier.' Zoë leans forward to make her point. 'You miss that window of opportunity to get a snog and it's all too easy to start reasoning yourself out of it – doubting your compatibility and all

417

that twaddle. That's why I always get in there early. Who wants to end up as just friends?'

As soon as the sentence is out of her mouth she gives me a regretful look and mouths, 'Sorry!'

I take a gulp of throat-ravaging Sambucca. This is all too close to the bone for me.

'Of course it can work the other way.' Helen has her say: 'Sometimes pining for someone while taking time to get to know them can really build up the desire and excitement.'

'But beware!' I slur. 'You can go too far with that!'

'How do you mean?' Elise wants to know.

'Oh you know, one day, after ten years of longing and frustration you'll simply spontaneously combust!'

The others look concerned. I've got to get a grip.

'Anyway, there's no set rules. You just do what you instinctively feel is right,' Helen soothes.

'That's all very well if you are in touch with your instincts,' Elise has to have the final word. 'There are women on my course who are so riddled with bad past experiences they don't trust their own judgement any more. Whenever a new relationship possibility comes along, it immediately triggers some hellish memory and they feel vulnerable and out of their depth and so they panic and behave in such a way that they push the other person away.'

Elise has obviously been paying a lot more attention in class than she'd care to admit.

'So what's the solution?' Helen asks.

'We haven't got to that bit yet.'

Great.

We all sup our drinks. When I look up I find Elliot staring at me. And Elise staring at Elliot staring at me. She swiftly clamps her hand on his arm. 'Elliot, I've got a headache coming on. I think I might go to bed.'

We all know what that means – I'm ready to leave and you're coming with me whether you like it or not.

'OK, I'll be along shortly.'

'But—' she begins.

'Probably best you have a head-start getting to sleep so I don't keep you awake with my snoring,' he continues.

That's it, Elliot – stand strong!

Elise looks put out. 'Well, all right then, I'll stay for just one more drink!' she says, as if we're beseeching her.

Suddenly Zoë bursts out laughing. She's been flicking through the room pictures and something about the Matterhorn suite has triggered a memory: 'Did I ever tell you about the guy I shagged on this ski trip?' she asks. 'We did it in the snow! We were mid *you know*, totally naked and we heard these people coming up the path so we fluffed all the snow over us – it was so deep and powdery it only took a couple of seconds. We just lay there like two people on the beach buried in sand. It was hysterical!'

'Weren't you freezing?' Elise winces.

'Couldn't feel a thing – we were so tanked on grappa we didn't even notice we were shivering until our teeth were rattling together when we kissed!' Zoë takes a slug of Baileys then nods at Helen. 'Your turn!'

'What?'

'Best sex story!'

'That's easy, it was two weeks ago – Reuben took me up to Big Bear and we got this cabin by the lakeside, it was all rugs and lanterns and hot chocolate . . . We went skinny-dipping at midnight and then ran back to our cabin and lay by the fire . . .'

'Sounds heavenly!' I sigh. And exactly what Joel was proposing.

'Drinks!' Elliot gets to his feet. 'Anyone? Everyone?'

Considering we're already sitting at strange tilted angles this is probably a bad idea but we all say yes.

'Sasha?' Zoë tags her. 'Best sex!'

'Masked ball in Venice. He never even saw my face. That's all I'm saying!'

'Fantastic!' Zoë raves. 'Your turn, Elise!'

I immediately picture Elise dressed as a dominatrix in black PVC, punishing someone. And then I get a worse thought – her story is going to be about Elliot. It's perfectly possible I might throw up.

When I dare to look at her she seems a million miles away. Her face has taken on a look of enchantment and she seems ten years younger, verging on attractive. She goes to speak and then hesitates, as if she'll spoil the memory if she says it out loud. Checking that Elliot is engrossed at the bar, she leans in and begins in a slurring husk: 'There's this little coastal town with these sweet boutiques and pristine tree-lined streets and everything is so neat. There's no litter, no chewing gum, no McDonald's. None of this tackiness,' she says waving her hand at the red leather bar. 'It's all tasteful and groomed.'

Is anyone having any fun, there? I want to ask. It sounds utterly soulless.

'It just feels so safe,' Elise whispers, hugging herself.

I would never have thought someone so gruff would find twee-dom so appealing.

'Everyone is dressed nicely, there's no scuffed shoes or low-slung jeans or bellybutton piercings,' she adds.

Zoë was right – she is the queen of conservatism!

'We used to get a picnic from the deli and go cycling along the coastal path and every weekend we'd play golf and then one day—'

'Oh my God, did you do it in a bunker?' Zoë's eager to get to the sex bit.

'Imagine the golf balls flying overhead and people shouting "FORE-play!"' Helen teases.

'No we did not do it in a bunker!' Elise humphs, swatting the air. 'We made love back at his apartment on white sheets with the windows open and the softest breeze coming in. It felt so clean, so right. And in the sunlight we could really see each other. We didn't have to hide. Nobody was judging us.'

'Who'd be judging you?' I frown, confused. This isn't in keeping with the pushy Elise we love to hate. I've never once got the impression that she cared for other people's opinions. And then I remember her urgency to get to the Hawaiian No-hope-o class where she planned to heal hurtful memories – could there be a connection?

Elise sighs. 'You can't live somewhere so perfect – "in polite society" – with a secret like that.'

Then there is a secret! I knew she was hiding something. But what?

'I wanted to belong but the community knew and people gossiped and they pointed,' she continues in a trance.

'Why?' I ask softly, hoping to lull her into a confession. I can't bear the suspense!

'What?' Elise blinks, looking troubled.

'You just said people were gossiping and pointing—'

'No I didn't!' she cries.

I hesitate. I don't think she meant to say that last bit out loud. Frankly I think she's losing her marbles so I daren't probe further. I'm not ready for an Elise-style meltdown.

'Do places like that really exist?' Sasha asks, letting her off the hook. 'It sounds like *The Truman Show*.'

'Sounds like Carmel to me,' Helen notes.

'It was,' Elise confirms. 'Carmel-by-the-Sea.'

'Where's that?' Zoë wants to know.

'About 150 miles up the coast from here,' Helen replies, eyes still on Elise.

That's just a few hours' drive from here, closer still to Breathe. The proximity alone must have brought all those memories – good and bad – flooding back. Was this all part of The California Club's plan, getting Elise to confront her past, whatever it might be? I still find it strange to think Elise had a whole other life before Elliot. One she could go back to, I think to myself. I wonder if her mystery man is still there? And whether the big taboo still applies? Could it be the reason why she's such a bitch?

'How long were you in Carmel for?' Zoë asks, taking a more casual line of questioning.

'A couple of months.'

'Months? How did you get the time off work?'

'I left my job,' she says, looking blurry again.

'Were you expecting to stay out here?'

Elliot returns with the drinks. 'Sorry I took so long, I got chatting to the barman. What did I miss?'

'Nothing,' Elise clips, darting warning looks around the table. The subject is clearly closed. Darn! I'm left hoping that there'll be a corrupt hypnotist at Breathe that I can bribe to get Elise to spill. Drink alone isn't enough – she's had three times as much as the rest of us and she's still guarding her secret with snarly teeth.

'Let's do fantasies now!' Zoë continues on her former tack. 'Describe what your absolute dream scenario would be. Lara, you go first.'

On cue, the band strikes up *Begin the Béguine*. 'Isn't this one of your favourites?' Elliot remembers.

I nod.

Elliot sets down the last drink, does a little bow and then extends an open palm to me.

I gasp.

'Well?'

'Please don't embarrass me,' Elise cringes.

Ignoring her, I take his hand and follow him to the dance floor.

'I apologize in advance to your toes,' I smile as we take our position.

Elliot gathers me up in his arms and then holds the

pose, waiting for an appropriate moment to butt into the song. I notice his foot tap twice and then we're off. I'm expecting a shuffling clutter of missteps but within seconds we're gliding. There's no way Patrick Swayze could accuse Elliot of having 'spaghetti arms' – he's created a perfect framework and all I have to do is hold on tight and enjoy the ride.

'How come . . .?' I falter, thrown by his prowess.

'How *Come Dancing*, you mean?' Elliot chuckles.

I nod, intrigued.

'My gran made me take ballroom dancing classes when I was seven.'

'I never knew.'

'It doesn't often come up, mercifully.'

'How long did you do it for?'

'Six years.'

'Six years!' I exclaim.

'I don't remember much—'

'You might not but your feet do.' I nod downwards.

Elliot looks bemused by his own deft strides as though someone else has control of his feet.

The music changes and his body instinctively responds.

'Are we cha-cha-cha-ing?'

'I think we might be.'

His hips begin to swivel and rock in time to the music. 'It's spreading up my body!'

Again the music changes and the twirls begin. I was dizzy before just having his hand on my waist, heaven help me now!

'So what's your name, pretty lady?' Elliot grins,

clutching me to him after a giddying three-in-a row.

'Tammy-Sue, pleased to meet you!' I play along.

'Likewise. I'm Buck.'

'Hey you!' I beam. I couldn't be any happier if he dropped down on one knee and proposed. (After unproposing to Elise, of course.)

And then a saxed-up, punchy version of *Bad, Bad Leroy Brown* starts up and we're swinging.

'You're so good you're making me look good!' I marvel.

'Well, you always were quite a little mover.'

'This is all about you,' I insist, feeling a flirt coming on. 'My strong leading man!'

'Don't let your feminist buddies hear you say that,' Elliot reprimands me.

I laugh. 'You know what they'd say?'

'What's that?'

'Ginger Rogers did everything Fred Astaire did, but backwards and in high heels!'

Elliot laughs. 'They're right!'

As the song comes to an end the band announces a break. Elliot and I return to the table exhausted but exhilarated.

'You never told me you could dance!' Elise adopts her favourite accusatory tone.

'Is that what that was?' Elliot shrugs.

'I'm stunned!' Helen applauds Elliot.

'Any other dark secrets I should know about?' Elise continues sniping.

'I don't think it gets any darker than ballroom dancing.' Elliot takes a swig of his vodka.

'Lara – you never did tell us your fantasy,' Zoë prompts.

I think for a moment. Dare I tell the truth? Or at least a version of it?

'That was it, right there on the dance floor,' I admit. I can still see us together in my mind.

'That's it? Dancing?' Elise isn't convinced.

I nod. 'Well, it's *one* of my fantasies.'

'Tell us another,' Zoë urges. 'One with sex in.'

'Hold on. Who with?' Elise bores into me.

'What?'

'In your fantasy, who are you dancing with?'

My mind is blank. I can't summon one sexy celeb to fill Elliot's shoes. I look to Zoë for help but she's busy deflecting a proposition from one of the band members.

'Owen Wilson,' Sasha saves me. 'You love him.'

'I do! Yes, him. He's divine!'

'Who's divine?' Zoë rejoins the conversation.

'Owen Wilson.'

'Are you telling them about the première? That guy always reminds me of Elliot, especially in *Shanghai Noon*.'

Oh no.

'It's the hair!' Helen and Sasha chorus.

'Just the hair!' I confirm.

In the silence that follows Sasha, Zoë, Helen and myself try and will the cat back into the bag.

Elise gets a feisty look in her eye. 'You know, I'm surprised none of you girls have ever got it together with Elliot!'

Oh my God! SHE KNOWS! *SHE KNOWS!*

426

A few tinkles of nervous laughter. This is even awkward for the people *not* in love with him.

'None of this lot would have me!' Elliot tries to make a joke.

'I wouldn't be so sure,' Elise says, darkly.

My heart is pounding. I feel on the verge of being exposed.

'Surely there must have been one occasion . . .' she probes further.

I swear I see the tiniest smile flash across Elliot's face but he immediately blanks it out.

'Maybe when you first met?'

'Other than that monster five-in-a-bed orgy, there's been nothing, really,' Zoë wades in.

We all laugh. Me to the point that I get hiccups. Then an old lady who looks just like Sofia from *The Golden Girls* saves the day by begging Elliot to take her for a spin on the dance floor.

It's a sight to behold. She barely comes up to his waist.

'You know, there's a bedroom here called Tall & Short.' Sasha flicks to the appropriate page. 'Says it's for tall husbands with short wives, or vice versa – the bed is custom-made so it's five foot long on one side and six foot on the other!'

'I hope you're not suggesting they sleep together!' Elise grumps.

Visualizing the pairing, all of us fall about.

Even, eventually, Elise.

The sensation of real laughter is clearly such a shock to her system that five minutes later she announces she's going to bed. And this time she doesn't even attempt to engage Elliot.

'To sleep,' she sighs, lurching up from the table while he's still on the dance floor. 'Perchance to dream . . .'

And with that she's gone.

Where does she go in her dreams, I wonder? It's funny, after spending the whole week dreading visiting Elise at Breathe I am now curious enough to be looking forward to our trip there tomorrow and the chance to put another piece of the puzzle together.

'Ready to go again?' Elliot returns granny-free and looks at me expectantly.

I wonder if he knows the truth.

'I don't know if I've got any energy left,' I fret, limp of limb.

'Oh go on!' Helen, Sasha and Zoë hoist me up into his arms.

'Come on, old lady.' Elliot puts a supportive arm around my waist and leads me to the dance floor. 'I'll be your Zimmer.'

Slowly the thrill of being held revives me. He takes my hands and we begin to gently sway to *I'll String Along With You*. Then, just when I think we're going to get away with a lilting melody, a jive sets in. For three consecutive songs. I can't remember having a more vigorous workout. The old folk don't seem to be breaking a sweat but I'm on fire. Finally the band slide into a slowie.

'Thank God! I'm beat!' I pant, ready to return to the table. But Elliot pulls me back into his arms. Close to his hot body.

'Stay for one more,' he breathes.

I relax into his chest. I can feel every contour beneath his shirt. I wonder if he can feel me just as well through the fabric of my dress.

'Are you having a good birthday?' he asks, sounding as if he really cares.

I look up at him and beam a Yes.

'It's so brilliant that your mum called.'

My face falls, remembering our conversation.

'What is it?' Elliot frowns, looking concerned. 'She's OK, isn't she?'

'She found a buyer for the B&B,' I blurt.

'Oh Lara!'

I bite my lip.

'You don't really want to sell do you?'

I shake my head. I know I can't speak without getting quavery so I say nothing.

'Ever since you told us at La Valencia it's been playing on my mind. I haven't said anything because I know you didn't want to talk about it but you can't let it go, you just can't. We have to find a way.'

We. He said we. There is hope!

Elliot pulls me back against his chest and gently rests his chin a-top my head, laying a comforting hand around the back of my neck. And then I feel him kiss my hair, just once in that, 'It's going to be OK, I'll make it OK' way.

I close my eyes and surrender to the moment. I

429

don't want to worry about the B&B now. I just want to dance.

For two more songs I remain pressed to his body, moving in perfect unison, feeling closer than ever. Wanting him more than ever. From my fingertips to my toes I tell him so, without saying a word. He pulls me closer still. He can hear me. At last he can hear me, I just know it.

Suddenly I feel the floorboards give way to carpet, then paving, then gravel.

Tentatively I open my eyes and look around me. We're outside, sheltering under a magnolia tree. At first I think the waxy blooms have been laced with fairy lights but then I realize it's the stars peeking through. We've entered our own magic kingdom.

'You danced us right off the dance floor!' I smile, inhaling the sweet perfume.

'Yes I did,' Elliot says solemnly.

I take in the new look on his face. 'Why?' I say huskily.

He looks straight into my eyes. 'I wanted to see how it would feel if it was just you and me.'

My heart pounds and I feel light-headed. I take a breath. 'And how does it feel?' I venture.

He answers with a kiss – his mouth meeting mine in the most tender, rapturous, generous caress. As I respond he clasps me to him with such a passion I'm catapulted to a place of blissful abandon. I want to kiss him for ever. My fingers tangle with his hair and he emits the gentlest murmur of pleasure, sending me spiralling in a whirlpool of desire and adoration.

430

And yet something pulls me back, gulping for air. 'What about Elise?' I gasp, summoning all my restraint to lean away from his beautiful mouth.

Elliot freezes for a moment. 'Elise?' he repeats, as if he doesn't know who I mean. Then he hangs his head and pinches his brow, expelling a desperate moan.

'I can't do this while she . . . if you're . . .' I stumble.

Where are these words coming from? Why is it me summoning her up? Me, spoiling the most exquisite interplay?

Elliot lifts his head. 'You're right.'

Am I? I feel sick, suddenly terrified that I've cut short the kiss too soon, before he could really feel all that he could feel for me.

'OK.' He puffs, straightening up and seemingly steeling himself. 'Here I go!'

Then he turns and runs up the hill, on a direct path for Jungle Rock.

I blink in disbelief. *Here I go?* I look around me wondering what just happened. *Here I go back to my fiancée* or *Here I go to break off the engagement so I can be with you?* Which is it?

'Elliot!' I call into the night but there's no reply.

Why did I speak and ruin the moment?

Because I don't want to be a kiss on the side. Because with me it's all or nothing. Because just me is enough. That's why.

I listen for sounds of Elise hurling artefacts around the room or trying to flatten Elliot with a boulder. Nothing. I can't see her getting dumped quietly. This

431

doesn't bode well. Maybe he can't wake her up. Maybe he's just pressing a pillow over her face.

'There you are!' Helen appears by my side, along with a worse-for-wear Zoë and Sasha. 'We thought you and Elliot might have snuck off for a snog – you were so melded together on the dance floor!'

Before my face can give the game away Zoë asks, 'Where is he, anyway?'

I wave my arm towards his room.

'Is he coming back?'

'I don't know.'

'Lara, you're looking weird, I think we'd better get you to bed,' Helen asserts.

'I've just been sick,' Zoë confides.

'I feel fine,' Sasha shrugs. 'I might stay for one more.' She goes to turn back but promptly trips down a ditch running alongside the paddock.

Helen hoiks her out, dusts her off and issues the following instruction: 'Bed. Now. All of you!'

'To sleep,' I mutter to myself as we mount the spiral staircase. 'Perchance to lie awake all night wondering whether the morning will bring a dream come true or just a near miss . . .'

32

The digital clock glows red numerals at me in the blackness: 4.30 a.m.

Too early to get a verdict from Elliot. My thoughts flip to the B&B – 12.30 p.m. in England now. I wonder if Mum's signed anything yet. Not going to think about it. Go back to sleep.

Thirsty. Need a drink.

Returning from the bathroom, glass in one hand, I feel my way around the bed with the other.

'Sorry!' I whisper to Helen as I thwack my leg on the bed frame and then jiggle the wooden headboard as I climb in.

No reply.

I prop myself up, sipping my water and wondering how long it's going to take me get back to sleep. Gradually my eyes adjust to the darkness. I look over at Helen, or at least where Helen was when I last saw her. Unless she's been run over by a steamroller in the night, she's no longer in bed with me.

Feeling for the bedside lamp, I spike myself on the gold thorns twisting around its stem. And then there was light! Yup, definitely a vacancy in this bed. I throw back the covers and inspect every nook, drawer and balcony. She's nowhere to be found. I'm not quite sure what to do next – with all the spiral staircases and hidden rock corridors this is not the place to go sleepwalking. There must be some other explanation. I suppose she could have gone for a walk. Maybe she couldn't sleep. Maybe she's taken up smoking. Maybe this is all a dream? Perhaps if I turn off the light and close my eyes the universe will realign itself and she'll reappear.

I settle back down and switch off the light. The next thing I know it's 6.57 a.m. Slowly I extend my leg and feel for Helen with my foot. When I reach the other edge of the mattress encountering no obstacles I know the situation hasn't changed. She's still gone. It's three hours until we're due to meet for breakfast but I know I'm not going to get back to sleep now. And then it dawns on me – she's probably gone surfing: 4.30 a.m. seems kind of early to set off but that's the kind of dedication you need, I presume.

Glugging back the remains of my water, I go for a refill. Until now, I hadn't noticed that the flowers on the bathroom wallpaper are actual embroidery. I run a finger along the stitching, then catch sight of myself in the mirror. My dishevelled, black-eyed face is the last thing you'd expect to see framed by pretty pink enamel dog roses and lovebirds. Something must be done.

After a quick shower and spruce (including dis-covering that Helen's orange hooded top gives my

skin a much-needed reflective glow) my stomach
suggests breakfast. I remind it that we're having a big
pig-out with everyone at 10 a.m. but it's insistent, so we
come to a compromise on a slice of peach pie and a
Cinnamon Spice tea. See how I'm not freaking out
about Elliot? I'm thirty now. A grown woman. If I just
concentrate on the pie, I'll be fine. Besides, what harm
can befall me in a place with Heidi waitresses?

The Copper Café is abustle with young girls in white
puff sleeves smiling beatifically and pouring piping
hot coffee. When they offer a splash of milk I have no
doubt they're getting it from the cows with their own
fair hands. I decide to forgo the dainty chairs with
metal backs twisted in the shape of hearts in favour of
a sturdy stool at the horseshoe bar. A cutesy waitress
called Amoret takes my order and fills my glass goblet
with iced water. I notice that every place-setting
around me has a different coloured goblet – amber,
aquamarine, ruby, baby pink, crystal clear and what
can only be described as urine yellow.

'These are beautiful,' I comment when Amoret
returns with my pie.

'We sell 'em in the gift shop. My mom's got the
whole set – says they look like jewels when the light
shines through 'em.'

I smile. This place is so magical and cosy. I feel
like I'm inside the Gingerbread house. This is how I
want our breakfast room to feel. I close my eyes, say
a little prayer and take out the mobile phone.
Pressing each digit with care, I dial my mother and

wait for her to answer, feeling as if I'm about to leap from a trapeze.

'Lara?'

'H-how did you know?' I gasp.

'I just got a feeling,' Mum says, obviously on edge herself. 'Now listen. I've spoken to the buyers and told them we need the weekend to decide—'

'You gem!' I cut in. 'Did they agree?'

'Reluctantly. They think I'm playing them off against someone else.'

'You are – me!' I laugh, feeling giddy at the prospect of having more time to come up with a solution even if I have no idea what that might be. Hell, I'll even try the ancient Hawaiian art of problem-solving if that's what it takes.

'Darling, I've got to go – I'm getting a second opinion on the rewiring cost – but call me at the weekend.'

'I will! Mum, I love you, thank you so much!'

'Anything for you, darling! Have a good day!'

I snap the phone closed. That's one bit of good news. I pray I'm on a roll. Still, if Elliot doesn't come through for me at least I'm going to be surrounded by counsellors for the rest of the day.

'Anything else I can get you?' Amoret presents me with the bill.

'No thanks – actually, there is one thing . . . you haven't seen a girl about my height with wavy, streaked hair down to here, probably in a yellow hooded top . . .'

'Surfer girl?'

I nod.

'If it's the one I think you mean, she left with the rest of them about twenty minutes ago.'

'The rest of . . .'

'. . . the surfers,' she confirms.

If they're only just leaving for the beach now that doesn't account for Helen's disappearance from the room in the middle of the night – unless her surf buddies are staying here at the Madonna Inn and she knew that ahead of time and went to crash in with them. Funny she didn't mention it. And that she didn't leave a note. I wonder if it's secret California Club business they're up to?

'Do you know where they were going?' I ask. 'I mean, obviously the beach . . .'

'Most of them go to Pismo, there's good pier breaks there.'

'Is it far?'

''Bout ten miles.'

I look at my watch. I've got plenty of time. It would be great to go for a paddle and exfoliate my feet on the sand. Maybe I could even try a few Surf Diva moves. I've got a sneaking suspicion that Helen's boyfriend will be among the pack and I'm extremely curious to meet him. I take one last sip of tea and go in search of a taxi.

Twenty minutes later I'm at the pier.

There they are, weaving dangerously close to the girders. I walk along the weathered beams of wood to the best vantage point and lean over the railing, spotting Helen almost straight away. Wow! She's got moves! Swimming back out to sea, she exchanges

437

smiles and banter with various surfers and then blows a kiss to one. They make some kind of signal to each other and paddle like crazy, catch a wave, surfing exactly parallel then suddenly Helen jumps from her board on to his and they ride up to the shore with their arms around each other. Once he's retrieved her board, she grabs a towel and starts rumpling dry his hair. He leans down and kisses her. Even from this distance it looks a great kiss. I wonder if it was him she snuck out to in the night. But why wouldn't she say?

All at once I feel shifty, like I'm spying on one of my best friends, and decide to go over and say hello. After all, it's perfectly reasonable that I should come down to the pier like any good tourist.

As I clomp down the wooden steps and lollop across the sand towards them, I watch him peel off his wetsuit – there on his calf is a Maori tribal tattoo. A-ha! So the guy at La Jolla was indeed her boyfriend. As I get closer, something else looks familiar – his face. I stop mid-step. It's Alex, president of The California Club.

I don't get it. If Alex is her boyfriend, who's Reuben? Is she cheating on him? Or maybe he doesn't exist – it's funny that we've never met him. Hmmm. No wonder she could swing us temporary membership. A beach ball rolls across my feet. I kick it back to the kids playing nearby. Now I'm in a quandary. She obviously doesn't want us to know the truth: maybe she feared it would undermine his credibility or get us thinking she had been blinded by love into joining some cult. Either way, I feel I've seen something I shouldn't.

As they turn in my direction I drop down into the sand and lie as if I'm sunbathing, only fully clothed. I sneak a peek in their direction. They're sitting down now, legs interlaced, swigging Snapples, obviously in no hurry to leave. I have to make my move before they do. I'm tempted to shuffle forward on my elbows like a soldier advancing on the enemy but instead decide to make full use of the hood on Helen's zippy top.

The cab takes twenty minutes to arrive, by which time I'm panicking that I'm not going to beat them back to the Madonna Inn. I get the driver to take me up the driveway, right to the door (well, not up the spiral staircase, obviously) to save me vital minutes. I'm only just inside when I hear a key in the lock. Desperate to look like I've barely left the bed I grab my birthday book and flip to the section on ranching.

'Howdy!' Helen grins as she enters.

I don't want to ask her directly where she's been in case she lies and thus freaks me out so I settle for: 'You were up early!'

'Yeah, I went for a surf. It was beautiful out there this morning.'

'Did it rip?'

'Yeah!'

See anyone you know? I'm dying to ask. Instead I say, 'Were there many people in the water?'

'Yeah – total surfer soup but I still managed to get a few good breaks.'

'Do they mind non-locals cluttering up their waves here?' I feel as if I'm interviewing her.

'No, it's cool.'

She's definitely not going to mention him. Or her other friends. What *is* going on?

'Is that my top?' she asks.

'Oh yeah!' I blush. I forgot about that.

'Keep it, it looks good on you.'

'Thanks!' I watch Helen start packing her bag, then – trying to sound as casual as I can – ask: 'Have you spoken to Reuben today?'

She looks startled. 'No, why should I?'

'I don't know, yesterday you sounded a bit vague about where he was, I was just wondering if everything was OK.'

'Everything's fine. Really. He's great.'

'Oh good.'

'Has Alex got a girlfriend?'

'What?' Again she looks caught out.

'You know, Alex from The California Club.'

Keeping her eyes firmly on her bag she replies: 'Yeah, I think he has, actually. You don't fancy him, do you?'

There's no easy answer to that so instead I go straight to: 'What's she like, his girlfriend?'

'Oh, I don't really know her.'

'Pretty?'

'Nothing special. But he's more about the person than looks. Anyway, I'd better jump in the shower. Are you hungry?'

'Always,' I call after her then roll over on to my back to contemplate the pink-beamed ceiling one last time.

What the hell is going on?

33

Copper Café – the sequel. Only this time we're in one of the booths featuring a mural of bearded fellas and wagons at harvest time. My girls are all present, if a little hunched and heavy-lidded, but Elliot and Elise have yet to arrive. I feel sick with anticipation. I wonder if he's breaking it to her now. And she's breaking down . . .

'I'm ravenous!' Zoë scans the breakfast menu. 'I think I'm going to have a starter and a main course.'

I'm way ahead of you, I think to myself.

'Are we going to wait to order?' Sasha asks our leader, Helen.

'I think we may as well go ahead – hold on! Here they are now!'

As the Es walk towards us, my eyes scrabble over them looking for clues. They both look rough, but then we all do. Elise's eyes are red-rim free. Bad sign. And she's still wearing her engagement ring. That says it all. My heart plummets. Nothing has changed. It was just a moment of drunken madness – a birthday kiss that went awry. As I sink into a dungeon of disappointment I'm aware that there's a waitress by my side but due to the rushing in my ears I can't hear what she's saying. I feel her hand on my shoulder and look up. It's Amoret.

'I was just asking: Did you find them all right?' she repeats, filling my coffee cup.

Uh-oh. 'Yes! Yes, I did! Thank you!' I gabble, praying she doesn't follow up with any giveaway surf comments. That's all I need.

'Oop, that's me done!' Her last trickle of coffee drips into Sasha's cup. 'Excuse me a moment while I get a refill.'

Please let that be the end of the conversation.

'What were you looking for?' Elise asks.

She would, wouldn't she?

'Um, I just wanted to get a couple of these goblets to take home.' I chink my glass with my ring. 'She directed me to the gift shop.'

'Oooh! Shopping!' Zoë perks up. 'I haven't been yet, what sort of things have they got?'

I dodge her question with a suggestion: 'Why don't we take a quick look now?' I have to get away from the table. Away from Elliot.

'Can you give her our order?' Zoë checks with Helen.

'Tell me what you want.' Helen is a mistress of efficiency even with sand between her toes. She whips out a pen.

'I'd like the Roman beauty apple, the Swiss sausage frittata and a hot cocoa.'

'Flavour?'

442

Zoë checks her options. 'Chocolate mint. With cream.'

A collective. 'Ewwww!'

'What?' Zoë is indignant.

'Lara?' Helen's pen is poised.

I can't possibly eat a thing – my stomach is in knots but I don't want to cause a scene by saying 'nothing, thanks!' so I mutter, 'I'll have the breakfast sundae—'

'What's that?' Elise barks, obviously concerned I might be getting something better than her.

'Fresh fruit, vanilla yogurt and granola,' I read, aware that Elliot is trying to catch my eye. I can't look. 'And a glass of buttermilk!' I blurt, as if coming over all *Little House on the Prairie* will make everything all right.

'Got it!' Helen nods.

Once outside the restaurant I quickly divert Zoë to the front door and gasp at the fresh air.

'Lara, you all right?'

'I'm just having a wave,' I clutch my throat.

'Bastard hangovers. You know we'll soon be at that age where you daren't drink for fear of the morning after. Take another breath.'

I wish I could tell Zoë what's really going on but I can't risk her storming in and punching Elliot. She'd be so mad at him for not following through. Maybe he's discovered Elise is dying. Or maybe he decided to hold off until The California Club week is complete. I get a sudden surge of hope. It's possible, isn't it? If he'd terminated their engagement this morning she surely would have stormed off, maybe even flown

443

straight back to Manchester and that would have blown it for everyone . . . Maybe he's just biding his time.

'Feeling any better?' Zoë asks.

'Much.' I nod. 'Let's go in.'

I'm not giving up on him yet. I've come this far. Gotta have faith.

'Appliquéd jumpers!' Zoë whoops as we enter the gift shop/boutique. 'Oh, look at this one with the dachshunds on!'

I join her fondling of the chenille.

'I like this one with the satin ballet shoes!' Oddly I really do. It's so easy to mock people that wear these themed, seasonal sweaters but I can't help thinking that someone who can wear a jumper decorated with sequined reindeer probably has a better sense of humour than we realize.

We move on to the T-shirts, where a design featuring a gold lamé bucket and spade puts me in mind of this morning's beach mystery . . . I decide to casually throw a question Zoë's way.

'You know before we got here, did Helen tell you much about her fella?'

Zoë thinks for a moment. 'Not really. I think it was a case of "You'll see for yourself soon enough!"'

'So nothing about his job, for example?'

'I'm sure she said he was a bit of an entrepreneur but I don't remember her saying anything specific.' Zoë moves on to the blouses and two-pieces. 'Little Sofia from the dance floor would feel right at home here, it's like the wardrobe from *The Golden Girls!*' she chuckles at the shoulder pads and drapey co-ordinates.

'Have you ever seen a picture of him?' I continue.

'Reuben? No. I imagine he's pretty sexy. And lean. Surfers don't tend to be blubbery, do they? Oh look – here're the glasses!' She leads me round the corner. 'Which ones are you getting?'

I opt for the amber and a periwinkle blue.

'How can you not get pink?' Zoë tuts, picking the pale rose and one with an oil-slick shimmer effect.

We clink over to the till, where I add a pack of pink golfballs for my Mum. While they wrap our wares, Zoë flicks through the counter copy of my Madonna Inn book, pausing on the wedding page.

'Would you get married here?' she asks.

'In a heartbeat.'

'It looks like it would be worth it for the cake alone,' Zoë coos. 'I'm so hungry!'

'Do you think Helen's going to marry her guy?' I try to bring up the subject one last time.

'I wouldn't be surprised. She does sound head-over-heels.'

'Don't you think it's funny that we haven't been introduced to him yet?'

'Not really,' Zoë shrugs. 'We were only in San Diego for one night. I'm sure when we get back there we'll meet him.'

I'm dying to tell Zoë that I think we already have, and reveal what I saw at Pismo, but don't want to go causing trouble or unsettling anyone until I find out a bit more about what is going on. But how am I going to do that from Big Sur? I heave a sigh. I'll burst if I have to keep one more secret!

With very little conversation to interrupt our eating, breakfast takes just a matter of minutes. It'll soon be time to leave. I wonder how I can engineer a moment alone with Elliot before we go our separate ways? The old panic rises up in me again. If I don't speak to him now, get some kind of gauge on how he's feeling, then the whole incident could be forgotten. I can't risk that. Think, Lara!

'Last chance for a wee before we hit the road!' Helen – a.k.a. Brown Owl – announces as we throw down our napkins.

Go, Elise – wee! But only Sasha and Zoë take her up on the offer, leaving me to wander out to the carpark with the Es.

'One more night and we can be properly together again.' Elise gives Elliot the most claustrophobic of cuddles. 'I'm not going to let you out of my sight for a single second!'

Almost immediately he untangles himself from her arms.

'Um Elise, do you mind? I need a word with Lara alone.'

She looks like she's been slapped. I'm pretty shocked myself – I didn't expect such a direct approach from either of us.

'We'll just be two minutes,' he urges.

Glowering at me as if it's my fault, Elise stalks off.

When she's out of view, Elliot gingerly looks into my eyes and asks,

'How are you feeling?'

I don't know if he's enquiring after my hangover or checking to see if our starlit passion is still a viable commodity the morning after, so I begin with caution.

'OK,' I smile, trying to convey that another kiss would be more than welcome. 'You?'

He smiles back. 'That was quite a dance last night.'

'Mmmm,' I concur, still waiting for some clarity. I daren't go first. It's up to him to state his intentions. He's the one with a dangling fiancée.

'Listen, I've been thinking about the B&B,' he begins.

The B&B? What about me? What about us? Still, I'm listening.

'Maybe I do have the money to help you.'

'What?' I laugh. 'Did you win the lottery overnight?'

'No.' He shakes his head and takes a nervous breath. 'But if I didn't buy this house with Elise . . .'

'You would be short one marital home,' I finish his sentence for him.

'What if I didn't need one?' He looks intensely at me. 'What if I didn't get married? Not to Elise, anyway.'

My heart does a loop-the-loop then everything goes black. For a split-second I think I've fainted but then I realize someone has their hands over my eyes. The prickly kiss on the neck is the giveaway.

'Joel!' I gasp.

Before I can even turn around he's swept me up into a body-compressing hug.

'Let me look at you now you're thirty!' he sets me down and then holds my face in his hands.

'Where'd you come from?' I splutter. I can't believe his timing – wait till I tell him about Elliot, he'll be delighted! Mission accomplished!

'How did you know we were here?' I ask, still dizzy.

'Zoë,' he explains. 'When you left us at the diner we had a little chat. I wanted to get here last night but I had a business dinner I couldn't get out of.'

'But we're just leaving.' I look around, the others are on their way over.

'Well you know how I live to chauffeur you,' he twinkles.

'You're coming to Breathe?' Oh joy! I don't have to travel alone with Elise. 'Where's your car?' I look around for his black jeep.

'We're not driving.'

'I'm not jogging!' I warn him. 'It's got to be 100 miles.'

'We're flying! Friend of mine's a pilot. He's got this great little four-seater Cessna. He can set us down within a few metres of the entrance.'

I shake my head in amazement. 'You blow my mind!'

'Elise won't fly in something that size,' Elliot cautions, looking surly.

'Hey man, didn't see you there!' Joel reaches across and shakes his hand. 'What's going on?'

'Nothing much!' Elliot glowers. His whole countenance has changed. The tentative, hopeful look he had just minutes ago has clouded over into something moody and dark. Handshake over, he goes to turn away, only to find Elise stomping towards him.

'Is it all right for me to come back now?' She gives Elliot a withering look.

Elliot holds up his hands as if to say: I'm done here – do as you please.

'Elise, this is Joel,' I introduce them. 'Remember you spoke to him in Yosemite?'

Elliot turns back, looking perturbed. Why does he always act so weird around Joel? He can't be jealous, not after last night. It's blatantly obvious who my heart has chosen, *surely?*

'Oh yeah.' Elise eyes Joel from spiky head to Nike toe. 'Hi!'

'He's going to fly us to Big Sur. It's a small plane but really safe,' I assure her.

Elise immediately backs up. 'No way.'

Elliot gives a 'told you' shrug and folds his arms.

I open my mouth to try again but Joel lays a 'I'll handle this' hand on me.

'Well, it's entirely up to you but we're talking a smooth glide – the weather conditions are perfect, totally clear sky and we'll fly good and low so you can practically dip your pretty little toes in the sea.'

The toes bit has got to be too far. Oddly, Elise doesn't squawk an objection so Joel continues. 'By the sound of it you haven't had too much free time to explore Big Sur. This way you'd see it in all its rugged beauty.'

Elise seems mesmerized by him. 'Well, if you're sure . . .'

'Would I lie to you?' Joel charms her.

Elliot and I lock eyes. Our song. For a moment I feel

like we're raised above the other two, connecting again. Then Joel pulls me back into his arms.

'It's so good to see you!'

I want to hug him back for a good ten minutes but Elliot looks so raw I keep it to a minimal squeeze, then prise myself away and wave over the others to join us. They all chatter busily with Joel (who naturally forms the centre of attention) and I take the chance to beckon Elliot off to one side.

'What you were saying before . . .' I begin, eager to get back to the bit about him becoming co-owner of the B&B and better yet, the bit that sounded for all the world like a proposal!

'Forget it!' he snaps.

'Forget it?' I repeat, stunned.

'I don't know what I was thinking.' He angrily scuffs at the turf with his trainer.

'You're taking back the offer?' I want to be clear before my emotions bust through the dam that's barely holding them back.

'You didn't accept it,' he growls, avoiding eye contact.

'I didn't have the chance,' I reason, trying to keep calm.

'I wonder why.' Elliot scowls at Joel as if he'd like to deck him.

'So that's it, is it?' I can't believe this.

Elliot shrugs.

He's behaving like a child and I can feel the frustration bubbling up inside me. 'Is there something bothering you?' I decide to ask him straight.

450

'Like what?' he pouts.

'Like Joel,' I prompt, exasperated.

Elliot snorts and looks away.

'What?' I grab his lapel, frowning into his face.

'Nothing!' Elliot grunts, pulling away. 'If you want to make a fool of yourself . . .'

'Excuse me?' I laugh, utterly outraged. 'What do you mean by that?'

'Falling for all his "my friend's a pilot" nonsense!' Elliot sneers.

'Oh I suppose the plane is imaginary, is it?' I scoff.

'Forget it!' Elliot tries to walk away.

'Don't do that!' I block his exit. 'If you've got something to say, say it,' I hiss, trying not to cause a noticeable scene. Fortunately we're no match for Joel and Zoë in full flow.

Elliot runs his tongue along his teeth then glares at me. 'I don't like him.'

'I don't like Elise,' I counter.

'I just told you I'm not marrying her!' Elliot blurts then hushes himself and looks guiltily in her direction.

'Does she know that?' I ask.

'Not yet.'

'We're leaving in five minutes. When were you planning on saying something?'

'It's not that simple,' Elliot says quietly.

'Well I wouldn't rush into it,' I ooze sarcasm. 'You might find you change your mind five minutes later.'

I can't believe we're at each other's throats like this, especially after our most blissful magnolia-scented

451

night. How is it possible for things to sour so quickly? Does this mean we were never meant to be? We experience the merest hint of togetherness and then instantly self-destruct!

'I'm sure Joel can give you the money for the B&B,' Elliot taunts, angling to have the last jibe.

'Oh yeah, I know for a fact that it's his dream to own a clapped-out townhouse in a country that rains nine months of the year,' I spit. 'I bet he's never even seen a pebble!'

'You two coming?' Helen calls over.

Elliot and I trip over each other trying to get to her first.

I am *seething*! I've never seen Elliot like this before. What an arse! It just goes to show – you think you know someone . . . Well, Elise is welcome to him. Not that he wants her any more. I should be over-the-moon but I don't care. I hope he stays miserably single for a very long time. I can't believe he'd give me false hope like that. He knows how I feel about the B&B, never mind about him. What a bastard!

'Joel!' I call.

'What, my darling?'

'Piggyback!' I jump on board and laugh maniacally as we hurtle past Elliot and Elise. You want to see me look foolish – you've got it! I squeal as Joel offloads me on to the top bar of the paddock fence and then swiftly turns round to face me, keeping me balanced by placing his hands on my thighs.

'Glad to see you're not getting any more mature with age,' Joel puffs.

452

I grin back at him. He couldn't have said anything better. I lean forward and cup his face.

'I'm so glad you're here!' I say, before planting a firm kiss on his lips.

Did you see that, Elliot? That's me bouncing back. You think I'm crushed? I'm not. I'm not. I'm not.

34

I'm still trying to quell my irritation as we pull up at the airfield. I've never once argued with Elliot in the ten years I've known him and consequently I found myself distracted as I said goodbye to the others. I realize now that I meant to get more of the lowdown on Sasha's fundraiser plans – all I know is that she wants us at Tiger Tiger by 6 p.m. tomorrow evening. I hope it's a success. If it is, maybe she and Zoë could think about arranging a fundraiser for me and the B&B . . . Another flare of indignation sparks within me. I hope Elliot gets his bottom chewed off by a bear.

'This is Richard, our fly guy.' Joel introduces us to the pilot. We shake hands with the smiler in the check shirt and take our position in the plane – me alongside Richard for the privileged front-seat vantage point, Joel in the back with Elise so he can use his big muscles to restrain her in case she gets hysterical and tries to strangle the pilot or throw herself out the window. Now there's an idea. Disappointingly, I don't get nearly as much satisfaction as I normally do conjuring *Ways to Zap Elise*.

'Up we go!' Richard seems to be willing the plane to part with the tarmac as we trundle and whirr down the runway. For a moment it seems a physical impossibility that the four of us and a hunk of metal could get airborne but he levers us upwards and miraculously we don't bump straight back down.

'Don't forget to breathe!' Joel leans forward to remind me as we climb on invisible rails, up into the sky.

How did he know I've been holding my breath since take-off? I also haven't moved so much as an eyebrow hair for fear of unbalancing the plane. I consciously try to relax my body, lowering my shoulders a millimetre at a time. I can't believe I'm up here, hovering above where the verdant land of California cuts haphazardly into the sea, creating one of the most raw and refreshing coastlines in the world. Joel's done it again – sent my spirits soaring against all odds.

We stop for a drink just a mile or two from Breathe, perched at cliffside tables in the sun, watching the surf thrash and spray. Even the usually drag-me-down presence of Elise can't touch me. I'm overwhelmed with feelings of well-being. No wonder this place is such a mecca for those seeking spiritual enlightenment – the scenery does half the work for you.

'I suppose we ought to be getting on,' Elise says, looking at her watch. I suck down the last of my pink lemonade. If I didn't know better I'd say she was actually keen to return to Breathe. Joel is good enough to escort me to the room I'll be sharing with Elise, just to make sure I'm not going to be painted orange and offered up as some sacrifice to the sun. As it turns out, long robes and daisy-chained hippie hair are conspicuous by their absence.

'I think you're going to be OK,' Joel assures me. 'But if there's any naked bongo drumming make sure you call me,' he adds with his trademark saucy smile.

'Elise!' A group of three middle-aged female students hurry over to embrace their clanswoman.

'How are you feeling?' The first gives her a sincere arm rub.

'You were so brave the other night,' the second coos. 'I just know you're about to have a break-through!'

'You're just in time to come to Family Circle with us,' the third chimes in.

'Lara,' Elise turns to me. 'You'll join us, won't you?'

Four heads tilt in enquiry. This is spooky. I reach for Joel.

'Sorry babe, I gotta fly,' he shrugs. 'You go have fun!'

'Just give me a minute,' I tell Elise, pulling Joel off to one side.

'Take me with you,' I beg him.

Joels laughs and shakes his head. 'Come on, just one more night and you'll be a California Club graduate. Think of that beach-house!'

I wheeze a resigned breath and ask, 'Are you coming to the Tiger Tiger fundraiser tomorrow night?'

'You bet – Sasha told me all about it while you were off colluding with Elliot in the Madonna Inn carpark. What was going on there?'

'Don't ask,' I groan, refusing to relive the vexation.

'I told her I'd bring along a few richie friends of mine,' Joel continues. 'See if we can get them drunk enough to make a donation.'

'Lara!' Elise calls over, tapping her watch.

I propel myself into Joel's arms, grabbing the chance of one more empowering hug. He squeezes me till my head is about to pop off then releases me.

'Go!' he encourages. 'I'll see you tomorrow.'

'Bye!' I wave him off and then turn towards Elise. Here I go, then, about to get in the Family way.

After an initial meditation where I very nearly drop off to sleep, all the women in the group are instructed to hold hands and form a large circle around the cluster of men. The men are then asked to pair up, one taking the role of father, the other the son. Apparently our role is to provide a protective circle of female energy around them so they feel safe. Fine, so far. Then we are all asked to sit down. Better still. The lights dim. Maybe I will get that nap after all. But then I hear what they are asking the men to do – the 'father' takes the 'son' in his arms and rocks him and tells him that he loves and is proud of him, that he will always be there for him no matter what. The sight of one grown man cradling another like an infant is quite bizarre. At first I feel uncomfortable to be watching, embarrassed for the toddlers especially but then I see how much they all seem to need to do this, how perhaps only a handful of these guys ever heard what they really needed to from their fathers, and my heart goes out to them.

'Now the women in the centre . . .' The group leader instructs.

Oh no! I can't partner Elise. I look to my left for an alternative but the skinny redhead has already been snapped up. Surely Elise will refuse to participate. This is everything she claims to despise.

'Obviously this is completely ridiculous,' she hisses at me under her breath, 'I just play along to keep them happy.'

'Right!' I nod, stepping forward with a sense of dread.

'Mother or daughter?' Elise asks.

I'm torn – on the one hand being the daughter just requires being cuddled and cooed over but at the same time I don't want to hear Elise's voice replace my own mother's, not even for a minute.

'Mother,' I decide.

'OK. You sit down first.'

I sit cross-legged on the floor and wait for Elise to climb into my lap. Other than our perfunctory kisses hello and goodbye I've never really touched her before so it feels odd to have her lean so deliberately on me, and weirder still for me to be placing my arms about her like I cherish her. I pray to Julianne Moore for some acting skills to get me through this. The group leader waits for us all to settle into position then nods for us to begin. Voices instantly start cooing and encouraging around me. The old devil in me would be tempted to lean close to Elise's ear and curse, 'I always wanted a boy!' but the mood in the room seems strangely sacred. Besides, I'd get lynched by the ring of masculine energy. Instead I close my eyes and pretend I am returning the favour to my own mother.

'You are a unique and special gift to me,' I begin, wondering where the words are coming from. 'Wherever you go, please know that I am always loving you, always watching over you in my heart, wishing the very best for you.' Wow. I'm good. I'm a mom! 'I watch everything you do with pride.' I pause, I wonder if Elise's mum knew about her dalliance in Carmel and if she did, did she judge her along with everyone else? Dare I speak the words she may most need to hear? 'I will never judge you, darling. Whatever you do, whoever you choose to love I will support you.' I sneak an eye open expecting to find a sneer on Elise's face but instead I see a tear slide down her cheek. Oh my God. My own eyes well up with compassion. She is human, after all. What do I do now? I look imploringly at the group leader as she passes by. She gives me a 'keep going' nod. I squeeze my eyes closed again.

'You'll always be my little girl, Elise.' I surprise myself by saying her name. 'And I'll always be your mum. Your happiness is my priority. Just be happy and you'll make me happy.'

Elise's body starts chugging with sobs in my arms. I've gone too far!

'There, there!' I soothe. Oh bloody hell! I look frantically around me but I'm not the only one getting a sodden lap. Girls who've never heard their mums say I Love You surround me. I squeeze Elise tighter and she grips me like a vice. I feel my loathing of her morph into pity. What has she been through to end up like this? I think of my own mother, always so easy-going about my choices. I never felt an ounce of pressure from her. Fleetingly I wonder if I should rustle up a quick abandonment complex on account of her moving to Spain but realize it's entirely unnecessary. I know I'm loved, she could move to another solar system and I'd still feel that. Elise suddenly sits upright and wipes her face. 'They're just not content unless you blub here!' she sniffs crossly as the lights come up.

'Are you OK?' I ask.

'Of course! This isn't for real!' She gets to her feet, avoiding eye contact. 'I've got to make a phone call, I'll see you later.'

I watch her hurry out of the room, head down. She's going to call her mum, I'll bet you anything. I look at my watch. She better be a party animal – it's 1 a.m. in the UK. Hope she doesn't shout at her while she's feeling so vulnerable. I know my mum would just take it in her stride but I don't want to disturb her sleep. I'll call her tomorrow – still 24 hours for a B&B miracle to occur. No worries.

I stroll out and assess the chart for the evening classes to see if there's anything that might prove inspirational, while sneaking a sideways glance at the students around me – who else can I turn into a blubbering wreck?

'I'm going for the White Lotus Poetry Workshop,' a shrimpy fella informs me. I decide to leave him be. Too much of an easy target.

Think Like an Ocean. That sounds groovy. *Returning to the Simplicity of Life*. Great in theory but I have a feeling the reality means living in a shack. *Inner Goddess*. Love it – there's got to be glitter involved. *Self-Betrayal*. Bet that's a good 'un – high cry potential. Ooh, I like this life maps one – you do a chart of your life so far to see how you got to where you are today and then use that information to plot your most creative future. The teacher – Ann Sayre Wiseman – looks nice enough. I reach for the pen to add my name and in doing so see Elise has put herself down for the *Radical Honesty* workshop running at the same time. That's tempting. She might blurt everything out and save me the trouble of hiring that private detective. I suppose I could always try and catch her directly after . . . Then I spot my name in Elise's handwriting under the heading *Banish Body Hang-Ups*! The cheek of it! I wonder if she's trying to get me back? All the same, it's a class anyone blessed with cellulite would be keen to attend. What harm could it do? I'll pop along right after dinner.

With just ten of us (including three men) in the group I thought this might be the chance to make some real progress regarding my bulging calves. And, you know, if the nudity hadn't been compulsory I might have even stayed for longer than sixty seconds.

I shudder as I get back into the open air. What now? I've missed the start of the life map class so that's no good. The *Ritualistic Dance* involved covering yourself in clay, as I recall. I could press my ear up against the

461

Radical Honesty workshop. Or maybe I'll just tiptoe back to the room for a sneaky kip – I only had five hours' sleep last night and it's taking its toll.

There's a man (I think) doing a headstand in the corridor and in trying to avoid him I walk straight into a large pair of cushiony breasts.

'That's it – reach out and touch another human being!' Their owner embraces me. 'If you want to be hugged, just reach out!' She squashes me close to her for far too long. She's not wearing a bra.

'Thank you!' I puff, finally extracting myself.

'Any time!' She wobbles on her way.

I shake my head and open the bedroom door, inadvertently bursting in on a couple snogging.

'Oop, sorry! Wrong room!' I scuttle backwards and close the door. Then I pause. Hold on. Room 33. It is the right room. And one of those snoggers looked extremely familiar. I open the door again and find the two bodies now perched either end of the bed looking the picture of innocence. Did I just imagine it? I look at Elise. She holds my gaze shamelessly. I look at the man. Handsome. Grey hair. He must be at least fifty.

Suddenly I have no idea what I'm doing there.

'Um – I just needed my jacket. Going for a walk. Here it is.' I grab it off the back of the chair then scarper.

Unbe-freakin-liveable! No wonder Elise has stuck the week out – she's been getting it on with one of the students! Outrageous! I wonder if that's why she needed to talk to me in Yosemite? Was she going to ask me for Elliot's definition of infidelity? Snogs abroad don't count etc. Wow. Talk about fissures – Elliot wants to call off the wedding and Elise is snogging other men. I'd be apoplectic on Elliot's behalf were it not for the fact that she's actually doing him a favour. I wonder if I should tell him – it would certainly make the break-up easier on him guilt-wise. Then again, after his behaviour at the Madonna Inn . . . I swivel around trying to wriggle free of my tangled emotions – I wish I could deduce how I really feel but everything is so knotted and confused I can't think straight. Does this make Elliot a free man? And if so, how does that affect me? I'm still furious with him for rescinding his offer – how could I ever trust him again? Hmmm. Does that mean I'm willing to try? Am I really still hoping he'll come through for me?

'Lara! Wait!'

It's Elise. This should be good. Bring it on, sista! (She's no daughter of mine!)

'It's not what you think!' she says as she hurries up to me.

Nul points for originality on the opening gambit.

I turn to face her and coolly tell her: 'You don't know what I'm thinking.' For once I have the upper hand.

She stands with her hands on her hips, ready for a confrontation.

'Go on then,' I goad her. 'Tell me that was just a one-on-one healing session with a fellow student!'

'He's not a student,' she asserts.

'Teacher? Ooh nice!' I roll my eyes.

'He's not a teacher.'

'Guru, spirit guide whatever . . .' I wave dismissively. 'He's my ex.'

I think for a moment, then check: 'The one from Carmel?'

She nods.

He's older, yes, but not exactly Anna Nicole Smith fodder – why would everyone be whispering and pointing? I wonder if he's a known crim—

'He came to say goodbye,' she says, wistfully.

'Where's he going?'

'Nowhere,' Elise tuts. 'Goodbye to our past. Martha said I needed some closure—'

'Is that what they're calling it these days!' I can't help but snipe.

Elise takes a deep breath. 'I promised my mother I would never see him again but tonight I realized I have to do what's right for me.'

Oh gawd, that'll be my fault with all the 'if you're happy, I'm happy' roleplay. I should never have got involved.

'In order to give myself fully to Elliot, I had to find a way to let go.' Elise continues.

'Of what, your inhibitions?' I can't stop myself, I've waited too long to bitch back at her and now she's given me a prime excuse.

'Yes I kissed him but that's it, the end.' Elise implores me to believe her.

I am utterly unconvinced. 'Is it? What happens when he needs closure on your closure?'

'If you're going to be—'

'What?' I snort. 'Vaguely suspicious when I walk in

464

on my best friend's fiancée snogging some other bloke?'

Elise looks down at the ground. For a moment I see the forlorn little girl that was crying in my arms. Oh what's the point in yelling at her? Elliot doesn't want her anyway – at least that's what he says – she can do what she likes. It's nothing to do with me.

'I'll see you later.' I turn to walk away.

'If you knew what Elliot and I have planned, you wouldn't be so quick to judge.'

There's only one thing that would make sense of her summoning up the love of her life shortly before her marriage to another man. 'Polygamy?' I suggest.

'Oh bollocks to you!' she spits, turning on her heel.

'Always a pleasure, Elise!' I call after her. Then add, *'Elsie!'*

But she doesn't hear.

I stand alone in the darkness. 'What Elliot and I have planned . . .' she said. Then it's not done. Apparently they both get to kiss other people but they still have plans together. Plans that don't include me. I know what I'm feeling now – bitter disappointment, like I've lost my best friend and my ability to hope all in one go.

I wonder if there's a class called *How To Cope When You Discover That Nothing In Your Life Is What It Seemed* that I could pop along to.

35

What a trip this has turned out to be. I knew I'd clash
with Elise eventually but there is no way I could have
predicted these circumstances. I expel a long breath
and then find a bench away from chanters and people
trying to rearrange their body parts into a Picasso
painting. I sit down and stare gormlessly into space,
but then I hear a rustle as though someone is coming
my way, so swiftly I yank my legs into a lotus position
and close my eyes – they'll think I'm meditating.

Drinnnnng!

I forgot the first rule of inner peace – turn off all
mobile phones. Ah well, seeing as I'm faking, I flip it
open.

'Lara?'

'Sasha!' I instantly cheer up.

'You'll never guess where I am.'

'Give me a clue!'

There's a strange moaning grunt in the background.

'Was that an elephant?' I query.

'Yes!'

'Are you in Africa?'

466

'No!' she laughs. 'But it's the next best thing. Ty's brought me to Shambala!'

'Really?' Should that mean something to me?

'It's this amazing animal sanctuary over in the Santa Clarita mountains run by Tippi Hedren.'

'Melanie Griffiths's mum?'

'The very same! We just had dinner with her.'

'You're kidding!'

'It's one of the things they do to raise money for the Roar Foundation. Ty said I needed a break before the big day and he just spirited me here!'

That boy has really come through in a big way. 'So, what's it like?' I ask.

'Lovely – so many more trees and space than Tiger Tiger and a big river . . .' Sasha sighs. 'We're staying overnight in this safari tent – absolutely everything is leopard print – it's just like Jungle Rock but without the walls!' Sasha laughs.

'Where's Ty?'

'He's just gone for a wee.'

'So you can talk?'

'I can whisper.'

'Well?'

'Oh La, when I got back from the Madonna Inn he just walked straight up to me and kissed me!'

'What did you do?' I gasp, feeling a little fluttery myself, imagining the impact of his affection.

'I couldn't stop crying.'

'In a good way?' I check.

'Oh yes! It felt like this massive relief – to be with him. I don't think I've ever been so happy.'

467

My heart feels weirdly tugged in two directions: exhilaration for her and pure envy.

'Enjoy every second,' I urge her.

'Oh I will! What are you doing now?'

I don't want to tell her that I'm sitting by myself, staring out at a black sea so I say, 'Just about to take a moonlight yoga class.'

'Oh. Well, have fun. Don't get stuck in any compromising positions!'

'I won't,' I laugh. 'Say hi to Ty for me.'

'Hold on, he's here.'

'Lara?' There's that familiar rumble.

'Hi!' I smile. 'I hear things are going well!'

'They really are. And it's all because of you – what you said to me that day.'

'Don't be silly,' I shush him. 'You two would have worked it out in your own time. You're meant to be together.'

'Well, I'll agree with that last bit,' he concedes. 'But thank you anyway. We're seeing you at the fundraiser, right?'

'Yes, definitely.'

'Good. Sleep well, honey.'

'Night!' Sasha calls in the background.

I flip the phone closed.

For the next hour I just sit and stare out to sea. The quieter I am, the more aware I become of the rush and slap of the water below me. If I listen closely it's almost as if I can hear my own name.

'Lara . . .'

There it is again. Louder this time. I look around me. No one there. Great. Now I'm hearing voices.

'Over here!'

Staying rooted to the bench, I lean forward and peer into the darkness. Still nothing. Then over to my left a bush parts and a lone figure emerges.

'Elliot! What are you doing here?' I scramble to my feet.

'I had to come.'

I go to hug him, then I remember I hate him.

'Elise is—' What do I say? I don't want him walking in on them, that's just cruel. 'Doing a late class, I think.'

'It's you I've come to see.'

I get a flicker of hope – an apology and a promise to be my dance partner for all eternity would just about do the trick right now. Instead he sits at the edge of the bench looking like a condemned man.

Finally he speaks, his voice a mere croak. 'Do you love him?'

I raise my eyebrows. 'Joel?'

'Yes Joel,' he says impatiently.

'What if I did?' I challenge him. I won't be bullied.

He hangs his head, looking beaten.

I soften my voice. 'What if I don't?'

My heart beats loudly in my ears as I take a step closer to him. I've never felt so near the verge – will he catch me if I fall?

Elliot looks up at me with tortured eyes. 'All these years, Lara, it was always you I thought I'd marry.'

I try not to lose my footing and plunge in the ocean.

What?! When did he think that? How could I have missed that vital sentiment?

I daren't speak for fear of waking from the dream I must be in.

'When I first met you I just thought, I'm gonna get all my crappy relationship stuff out of the way and then I'm gonna fall at your feet and beg you to marry me.'

I open my mouth and then close it again. Our ten-year past has just taken on a different hue. I don't know where to begin. Eventually I manage to form a question.

'When did you change your mind?' I ask in a small voice.

Elliot looks confused. 'What do you mean?'

'You proposed to Elise, not me.' I can't say it any plainer than that.

Elliot frowns, looking as if he's having some kind of revelation. 'She proposed to me,' he mutters.

He doesn't get off the hook that easy. 'But you said yes.'

'Yes, I did. At the time, having just lost Mum – I'm not making excuses, but I don't think I was really *present*.' He swallows, looking mournful. 'Now I feel like I've taken you for granted for so long. Until this week I've never had to see you with another man . . .' his fists clench ' . . . in that way.'

He really is jealous. For real.

'At least not with anyone you might actually have a future with.' He looks bleaker than ever. 'I suppose he would be considered quite a catch, Joel.'

If he didn't look so tormented I'd smile. All my anger has dispelled and I feel my heart melt. Look at that crumpled face – what have I done to him? I long to take him in my arms and tell him that he's the only one for me but I daren't. I'm still not sure what he's saying. I don't think he is either. But this might help . . .

'Joel and I are just friends. Anything else that was there, is done.'

'So you're not . . .' Elliot looks hopeful.

'I'll see him again. He's coming to the fundraiser. But just as a friend.'

Elliot blinks, trying to process the information.

'As far as Elise goes, that's your decision.'

Elliot stares off at the black sea and shakes his head, 'I've always found it so hard to say no to her.'

A cloak shields my heart again. Don't fail me now, Elliot!

'So what now?' I try to remain neutral and in control of my emotions – there's jagged edges all around this love, I must beware.

He looks imploringly at me, as though he wants me to tell him what to do.

I stand quietly, keeping my distance though it's killing me. I know Joel would tell me that it has to come from Elliot. And I can trust only his actions. And yet his words weave around my head – 'It was always you I thought I'd marry.' It's not too late. The pact isn't broken. Not yet . . . Be strong. Choose me!

'Elliot, you came!'

Suddenly Elise is running towards him.

I want to scream, *No!* and wrestle her to the ground,

but still she advances. I look at Elliot but I can't read his reaction. What's going on? She's obviously expecting him. They must have had an arrangement. Maybe this is part of the plan she was referring to. So he lied – this wasn't about me at all. The earth seems to shift and I stumble forward, steadying myself on the bench. I feel sick, as though my heart has been poisoned.

'The minister is here.' Elise notifies him. 'He's all ready.'

Minister? It can't be! Are they getting married *now*? Is that the plan? My mind speeds out of control – maybe the man from Carmel is a minister. That would certainly explain the scandal. But why introduce them to each other? Maybe it's one of Martha's more abstract suggestions. In this place anything is possible: they'd probably see it as the perfect handing over – old love for new love. Only the old love is looking pretty sprightly and the new love is on shaky ground.

Elliot looks helpless. He doesn't want to marry her, he said that. Apparently that doesn't mean he won't. Suddenly I despise him for being so weak. Is he going to go along with her wishes without a fight? I'd fight! I'd fight right now if only I could be sure I wasn't fighting alone.

As Elise pulls him away towards the main building, he turns back and pleads, 'Wait here.'

Then he's gone.

I've never felt so cold.

What just happened? I feel as if I'm having a series of hallucinations. I can't tell what's real. I don't know

472

what or who to believe. *Wait here!* he says. *Won't be a mo – just getting married.* He didn't even give me his jumper this time. I shiver and try to get a grip. Of course he's not getting married. He can't be. I've got it all wrong. He's just . . . I heave a sigh. As hard as I try, I can't come up with an alternative theory. Then I realize I shouldn't have to. Why didn't he just tell me what's going on? Why did he run when she called?

I feel heat burning up from my stomach. I'm angry. Beyond angry. Incensed! Watch out – I'm summoning my inner goddess! Here she comes now.

'You know what?' I say out loud. 'I've waited ten years for you, Elliot. I'm not waiting any more.'

36

I didn't want to break The California Club rules this late in the game but when I double-checked the small print the only condition of my visiting Elise was that I stay overnight. It didn't say where. I chose the car. And 4 a.m. is morning, right? I turned on the ignition at the first hint of daylight and drove like the clappers to Tiger Tiger. And I didn't cry. Not once.

My biggest wobble came when I switched to the 10 freeway and saw signs for the airport. *I just want to go home!* my body yearned. But I told myself that comfort was closer to hand – ninety minutes more and I'll have my girls around me. Then I can collapse. But until then I have to hold it together. I overtake a white Ford Focus and move into the fast lane. Before now I've felt timid driving on the freeways, today I dare anyone to cross me. That's the one liberating thing about feeling like this – I've got nothing to lose any more.

And yet my mind keeps going over everything Elliot said. He was so nearly there. It felt like a ten-year courtship was about to come to fruition – ten years of conversations on every topic, seeing each other at our best and worst, laughing and crying together, then finally, if a little belatedly, there was slow-dancing and even a kiss. We've come so far and yet there's always something missing, he's never said *I love you* to me. He talked his way around it, hinted at it, written two out of the three words in my birthday book, but he's never once been direct. I'm wondering if his sudden reservations about Elise could be put down to pure wedding nerves. In the absence of a stripper for him to have a last minute mistake with, he chose me. Other than the fine looking raccoons there wasn't a lot of choice. I sigh. At the end of the day, he went with her. How much more of a blunt message do I need?

But why should they get married without their ready-made congregation – me, Sasha, Zoë and Helen? Does she really have enough power over him to make him turn his back on all of us?

Enough. Think about something else. Anything. I flick on the radio. OK. I'll be needing a lyric-free station, can't take these wailings about the love I lost. Jazz FM. Perfect. For two minutes. All too soon the free-form tinkerings make me feel I'm going insane so I settle instead for the chirpy trumpets of a local Mexican station.

Finally, Tiger Tiger. Oh, the roar of the cats and the smell of the sun-baked poo. The first face I see is that of Ryan and my heart fair explodes. He understands, I know he does.

'Lara!' Sasha staggers around the corner. 'You're so early!'

'Need a hand?' I help her with the outsize floodlight

she's manoeuvring. It's one of about ten dotted around the pens.

'Where did you get all this stuff?' I ask.

'Local movie suppliers – a couple of them remembered Ty from way back, they've been really generous.'

'They've loaned it all for nothing?'

'Well, Tiger Beer are sponsoring the event so they're going to come along tonight and get tanked.'

'Fair enough.'

'You know who's been amazing?' Sasha shows me where to set down the light. 'Boris!'

'What's he been up to?' I smile.

'You'll see. I don't want to spoil the surprise.' Sasha dusts off her hands.

'Is Zoë here?'

'She'll be here for lunch. And Helen. They said they couldn't get hold of you but I guess you got their message?'

'No.' I shake my head. I turned off the phone last night and haven't switched it on since.

'There's some kind of passing out ceremony for The California Club.' Sasha wipes her face, leaving a streak of dirt across her cheek.

'What does that involve?' I ask, smudging it away for her.

'I'm presuming just a speech and handing over the keys for Marilyn's Beach House. Maybe they give us a certificate!'

God knows what mine would say. *Failed – wish incomplete. Try again next year.*

'It was supposed to be at The Del but Helen rearranged it cos of the fundraiser. I was just going to set up some chairs out on the porch, what do you reckon?'

I can't quite picture Alex in his immaculate suit sitting on a rocker but then again, who knows?

'Where's Ty?'

'He's just gone into town to get the rest of the equipment. Carrie should be back this afternoon. Right now it's just you and me.'

It's the perfect cue to pour my heart out, but then I find myself locking eyes with Ryan again. My plight counts as nothing compared to him and his compadres.

'How's Oliver?' I ask.

'Getting better every day. Ty is so good with him, I just leave them to it.' Sasha leads me to the kitchen and hands me a glass of water.

'Everything OK with you? How was Elise – nightmare?'

'You can't imagine!' I take a big gulp of water to force down the swell of wretched emotion.

'Ah well, it's over now, isn't it?'

I nod, setting my glass down on the side. All over. I want to crumple and sob but this is Sasha's big day – a *good* day, not a poor me day.

I clap my hands together hard, hoping the sting will revive me. 'Tell me what I can do to help.'

Though Sasha won't give me the details, I'm beginning to get an idea of what she has planned. The cats will be floodlit by huge black lamps on stands, a vast screen is to be stretched across the backlot for some kind of projection, and judging by the number of ice chests that Ty is now unloading, there's going to be an awful lot of beer drunk. He looks great, gives me a big hug and a whispered, *I love that girl of yours!* when he sees me. We work in companionable silence doing last minute cage-cleaning duties until The California Club is called to order in the early afternoon.

Having become something of a perfectionist sprucing Ryan's cage, I'm last to arrive. Everyone else is already assembled on the porch. Quite a contrast to the Salon at La Valencia but that's just as well – I wouldn't be able to rock up there with straw in my hair. I smile at Helen, who barely manages a mouth-twitch back. I'm guessing she's peeved that there are two notable absences.

'Where's Elliot?' Zoë hisses at me as I lower myself into the worn out rocking chair.

'No idea,' I shrug. He could be on his honeymoon by now, for all I know.

'But you were just with Elise, weren't you?'

'I haven't seen either of them since last night.'

'OK!' Alex calls an end to our whispering. 'Welcome to the concluding meeting of The California Club!'

We shuffle excitedly in our seats. We did it! Against all odds we got through the week! I flash back to the day we all set off and it seems like a lifetime ago. So many memories, so many emotions . . .

'Now obviously not all of you are present today because, well, *we've had a surprise wedding*!'

478

Zoë and Sasha gasp, looking aghast as they whip round to face me.

Then it's true. He did marry her. And now he's too ashamed to show his face. I can't keep the demons at bay any longer – I feel as if I'm being buried alive.

Alex rattles on regardless. 'I've just sent out for a bottle of champagne so we'll have a toast just as soon as that arrives. In the meantime we have a selection of awards we would like to present.'

'Hold on!' Zoë gets to her feet. 'The wedding?'

I grab Zoë's arm and try and pull her back down to her seat. 'Just leave it, please,' I implore her.

'But—' Zoë protests, then, seeing the desperation on my face, caves in with a muttered: 'I don't believe it. Why would they do it behind our backs? I mean—' she throws her hands up in exasperation.

Sasha shakes her head, still in a state of disbelief.

Helen doesn't look her normal radiant self as she steps forward with a collection of carved Coke and Tango cans.

'Um. Obviously the news is quite a shock to us all but I don't want to let it spoil our celebration here. So I'm just going to . . .' she trails off. Alex gives a little cough hoping to set her back on track.

'Sorry,' she says fighting to regain her composure. 'Each of you has excelled in some way and we would like to honour that by presenting you with the following awards.' She speaks with forced enthusiasm. For such an all-knowing being she looks knocked for six. I realize then that it's not just me the wedding has devastated, it's all of us. Somehow that helps to share the load. Once again I feel Zoë take my hand, as Sasha takes the other.

'*Most Miles on the Clock*: Lara!'

'Hey, watch it!' I try and join in the fun.

'We've estimated that you've travelled a total of 1300 miles in the past seven days,' Alex adds. 'You're definitely road chick of the week.'

I accept my customized can with a little bow. Road chick – that's better.

'The *Turn That Frown Upside Down* award goes to . . . Sasha.'

She flushes hot pink.

'To see you go from lost to found has been a real triumph and inspiration.' Helen beams with pride.

Sasha accepts her award and with a trembling voice says, 'I just want to thank The California Club and Helen in particular for—'

'Hey this isn't the Oscars!' Zoë heckles. 'What do I win for?'

'Actually you and Lara are joint-winners of the *Best-Dressed* award – for your *Gentlemen Prefer Blondes* outfits.' Alex holds up a picture.

'I thought you'd lost the camera!' Zoë gasps, grabbing my arm.

'So did I,' I frown. 'I couldn't find it after the Madonna Inn.'

'I took it!' Helen confesses.

Ooh she's a cunning one, always a step ahead.

'*Worst-Dressed*,' Helen continues apace.

My hiking outfit must be a definite contender but I'm spared the final honour – Alex holds up a photograph of Elise in a flesh-coloured leotard doing 'downward dog' in a yoga class.

'Eww!' we reel back. 'Who took that?'

'We have our contacts,' Alex smirks.

'Is Martha one?' I ask. She definitely seemed in league at times.

'Maybe.' Helen smiles, then announces a tie for *Hottest Romance*.

'Literally a tie!' she giggles. 'Ty and Sasha with Lara and Joel!'

'What about me and Boris?' Zoë complains.

I turn to her and gawp, 'You didn't!'

'No,' Zoë chuckles. 'But I very nearly would!'

'And finally,' Alex concludes the ceremony, '*Fish out of Water*: Elliot.'

Silence.

'He never really took to the wilderness, did he?' Helen sighs as our mood loses its momentary frivolity.

'Oh I don't know,' I beg to differ, thinking of him grinning like a fool on horseback, nuzzling my neck at the bear talk and, best of all, lying by the big log fire at the wedding reception – I'd never seen him looking so content.

'I can see what you had in mind for the rest of us,' Sasha frowns, 'but what was the thinking behind sending him there?'

'What you just said – thinking,' Helen explains. 'Elliot is always so busy distracting himself with work or TV or computer games, there's never any quiet time to listen to himself. When he wants a thrill he just plugs in or rattles his bones on a rollercoaster. We wanted him to get some natural highs, to feel good just from being alive.'

'And we thought if he had the chance to really think about some of the decisions he was about to make, um . . .' Alex falters, realizing this bit didn't quite pan out.

I stare at the dusty wooden floorboards. It so nearly worked. I wonder what happened to send him back to her? What hold does she have over him?

Sasha's not done. 'I have one more question. I understand how The California Club knows all about us because you could tell them, Helen,' she ponders out loud. 'But what happens when you get a new member you know nothing about?'

Helen turns to Alex. 'Is it time?' she asks him.

'I guess so!' he grins, holding her gaze.

'Everyone!' Helen gets our attention. 'I want you to meet Reuben, my boyfriend.'

Sasha and Zoë turn around to look for him. I stare straight at Alex.

'And the award for *Most Duplicitous Couple* goes to . . .'

'I thought you were beginning to suspect,' Helen acknowledges my dig.

'Hold on!' Zoë sits up straight. 'Alex is Reuben?'

He steps forward and shakes each of our hands. 'Nice to meet you all again!'

'Why did you lie?' Sasha frowns, looking hurt.

Helen pulls a face. 'I thought things would sound more convincing coming from a stranger in a suit.'

'Can I take it off now?' Reuben wriggles in his jacket.

'Go ahead,' Helen nods.

He liberates himself quicker than Houdini and rumples his overly prepared hair. 'That's better!'

The truth is slowly dawning. It's not just Alex that doesn't exist.

'The California Club?' my voice quavers. 'Is it real?' I don't know if I want to hear the answer.

'Of course!' Helen laughs.

'Wow!' Zoë breathes, relieved. 'For a minute there I thought you were going to—'

'But you're the only members.'

Silence while the information is processed.

'Helen, what's going on?' Sasha looks uneasy.

'I invented it.' Helen shrugs.

'But why?' I protest. 'I don't understand.'

Helen takes a breath and then begins: 'In the year since I left, you've all been drifting away from each other. In fact you've just been drifting, full stop. And complaining. Every time I'd want to tell you about my beautiful new life I stopped myself because I thought it would just seem like gloating – you were all so down. Sasha, you tried to cover it up but you know you're the world's worst liar. It was breaking my heart to feel you slipping away, I knew I had to do something drastic to reach you.'

Sasha blinks back at her.

'Zoë, I know you'll always land on your feet but it sounded to me like you were wishing your life away, looking at celebrity magazines and feeling incomplete because you'd never been papped coming out of a restaurant on the arm of a footballer. You've got so much to offer and it was frustrating me that all your energy was being put into empty dreams. I remember wishing I could give you all your dreams so that then you'd realize how much value your normal life had. And how much further you could go with it.'

Zoë sits back in her seat, stunned.

'Lara,' Helen smiles. 'When everyone else moved away you stayed put and you've been waiting for us all to come back ever since. I told Reuben that if I had a wish for you it would be that you would get the chance to travel and then maybe you'd understand what pulls people away, and that it's not always personal. And it's certainly not a rejection of you.'

She sighs.

'And then there's Elliot. Which is really half of you, I always think.' She looks straight at me. 'I honestly thought he was about to make the worst decision of his life. Everything he told me about Elise, I kept thinking *WRONG! WRONG!* You know we'd all love to see you and him end up together but even if that was a wish too far I at least wanted him to have a small break from her. They moved in together too soon, he never had the chance to think . . .'

We're back full circle to the thinking.

'Then one day Reuben got sick of me saying what I wished would happen for you all and suggested I do something about it.'

Reuben wraps his arms around Helen, looking proud to be a part of the scam.

'I can't believe it!' Zoë mutters.

'You can't have known what we were going to write, that first night on the beach.' Sasha narrows her eyes.

'I've known you guys for ten years,' Helen reminds us. 'None of you were out of character.'

I think for a moment. She's right. 'But what about Elise?'

'She was the wild card. I couldn't predict her wish but oh the joy when I saw what she wrote!' Helen gets a mischievous twinkle.

'What if she'd said she wanted to go paragliding!' Zoë plucks a random alternative.

'It could have been arranged. Reuben's lived here his whole life, he has a lot of friends.'

I think *faulty harness* but it's too late for that now.

'Did you know Ty already?' Sasha wants to know.

'Just enough to know that he isn't as gruff as he might appear. It crossed my mind that there might be an attraction but there was no major matchmaking intended.'

'What about Joel?' My stomach flips. 'Was he one of yours? A plant or a stooge or whatever you call it?'

'Now he was pure heaven-sent!' Helen laughs.

I'm relieved at that at least. I'd hate to think he'd just been doing a job.

A young girl creaks on to the porch chinking a bottle of champagne and six glasses.

'This is my cousin Beth,' Reuben introduces us. 'She helped us with the logistics.'

'Just how big an operation was it?' I ask, imagining a whole team with high-tech headsets standing before a flashing map of California.

Helen laughs as she hands out the fizz. 'Big.'

'God I need this!' Zoë takes a pre-toast gulp.

I'd do the same but I fear I might choke on it.

'Everyone got a glass?' Helen asks. 'OK then, let's raise them to—' She goes to make the toast but the words seem to stick in her throat. 'Reuben, could you?' she asks.

He puts his arm around her. 'To Elise and Elliot.'

'To Elise and Elliot,' the rest of us mumble, turning what should be an exultation into a dirge.

Beth looks confused and tugs at Reuben's sleeve.

'What?' He turns to her.

'It's Elise and Andrew,' she corrects him.

'Elliot,' Reuben assures her. 'Elise and Elliot. Sickening, really.'

'No.' She stands firm. 'She married Andrew.'

'Beth, what are you saying?'

'Martha said Andrew, definitely Andrew,' she insists, getting impatient that no one seems to believe her. 'She said they made a cute couple even though he's old enough to be her father. Elliot's your age, right?'

'Who the hell is Andrew?' Zoë yelps, looking ready to keel over with confusion.

'I think he might be a minister,' I offer in a daze.

'Andrew is her ex-boyfriend, the one from Carmel,' Helen asserts.

Sasha grips my hand, pressing home the realization that Elliot is still a free man. I don't know whether to laugh, cry or faint but Helen looks like she might beat me to it.

'Helen are you all right?' Reuben steadies her. 'This is exactly what you hoped would happen!'

486

'I know, I know.' Helen sits down, still looking shell-shocked. 'I really thought she'd married Elliot. I'm just so relieved . . .'

She's relieved?! There are no words to describe what I'm feeling right now. Hot tears of joy sting my eyes, though I still don't understand the hows and whys. And I'm not the only one.

'Why do I always feel like I'm missing something?' Zoë frowns. 'Can someone please tell me what's going on?'

'You remember Elise telling us about the guy in Carmel?' Helen begins.

We all nod.

'The one where there was some scandal,' I prompt.

'He's her uncle.' Helen reveals the secret at last.

We gasp.

'Oh my God!'

'Is that legal?' Sasha frets.

'They're not blood. He was married to her mum's sister. They'd never even met before she went to stay with him a few years ago.'

'And they fell in love, just like that?'

'He was having problems with his marriage, she – the aunt – was back in England on a visit and yes, they fell in love. Unfortunately for Elise, the aunt was very popular in the village and everyone knew the niece was coming to stay and so when they found out . . .'

'*Scandal!*' Zoë coos.

'Elise couldn't bear the shame. She's a conservative girl at heart and so she left him, came back to England and latched on to Elliot – the right age, right job, no skeletons in his closet. He was her chance for a normal life.'

'How do you know all this?' I marvel.

'She told me.'

'When?'

'We've been emailing since they met. I mentioned to Elliot one time that I'd heard Doris Day had a hotel in California and he remembered Elise talking about it because it's quite a feature in Carmel – one of the only hotels that allows cats and dogs.'

'So he put you two in contact.'

'Exactly.'

'And slowly you wheedled her life story . . .'

'You know me!' Helen shrugs, cheerily. 'I like to know everything about everything.'

'Why didn't you tell us?' Zoë humphs.

Helen gives me an enigmatic look. 'I had my reasons.'

I shake my head. 'I feel like I'm peeking behind the curtains at *The Wizard of Oz*. Who are you?'

'I'm your friend Helen. The one who wants the best for all of you. The one that wants to see you all as happy as I am,' she says and squeezes our hands. 'Or an interfering old cow, depending on how you look at it.'

We laugh and hug her.

'Any more questions?'

'Thousands!' I laugh.

But number one would be: 'Where's Elliot?'

37

'Sasha, I just saw a coach pull into the parking lot –
please tell me you haven't hijacked a group of tourists
to make up numbers?' I raise an eyebrow at her.

'Don't be silly!' she chuckles, continuing to unload
beer on to a trestle table staffed by Reuben and cousin
Beth (even though she's under age).

'What then?' I persist.

'Come and see for yourself.' She sets down the final
bottles with a clunk and takes my arm.

As we head down the driveway, a bizarre hotch-
potch of humanity begins to file past. A blonde in a
skimpy white dress, a man in a gorilla outfit, a couple
looking like they're going on safari, even one chap
with a stethoscope round his neck.

'I didn't know there was a fancy dress theme,' I
frown. 'Hey that guy looks like Paul Hogan – see, he's
got the full *Crocodile Dundee* clobber.'

'Remember the Reel Awards?' Zoë appears behind
me.

I spin around. 'You booked the lookalikes?'

'A select number – I got Ty and Boris to help me put

together a list of all the famous people that have starred alongside animals in movies and then I called to see if I could find a match – that's King Kong and Fay Wray.'

Of course.

'Dr Dolittle . . .'

It's all beginning to make sense.

'Meryl Streep and Robert Redford . . .'

'Don't tell me! *Out of Africa*? They look so convincing.'

'Boris and Holy Mary did the make-up,' Zoë grins. 'They're even bringing along some old movie memorabilia for us to auction later.'

'This one's a toughie . . .' Sasha nods over to a beefcake in a loincloth.

'Tarzan!' I hoot. 'Wow, he's a big fella, isn't he?' The ground fairly thuds as he passes.

'Jane'll be along later, she missed the coach,' Zoë tells Sasha.

'I thought Cheetah was a chimp,' I frown as the next chap to pass us hoiks a toy orang-utan into his arms.

'He was, that's Clint Eastwood for *Any Which Way But Loose*. Which reminds me – I'd better go and set up the film clips.' Sasha bows out.

'We're having a kind of Animal Oscars,' Zoë explains. 'Ty's put together a montage of all the moments where the animals out-acted the actors.'

'Hm?' I'm distracted as a dashing couple pass us. 'Is that . . .?'

'Katharine Hepburn and Cary Grant.'

'For *Bringing Up Baby*?' I gasp. 'I thought you slept

all through that!' I laugh, recalling the Sunday I rented it.

'Most of it,' Zoë concedes. 'But I remembered the bit with the leopard – we're going to team them up with Stella later.'

'Zoë, this is amazing! Look at you!'

She's radiant.

'I forgot the last reel!' Sasha yells as she hares past us.

'And Sasha!' I laugh 'I've never seen her move so fast!'

'I know – she never used to get this psyched about her modelling jobs, did she?'

I shake my head, thrilled that she's found a passion.

'She's worked so hard,' Zoë acknowledges.

'What about you? You've been slogging your mules off in a diner all week and yet you've pulled together the most perfect theme for the party – it's inspired!'

Zoë can't help but puff with pride. 'It's funny, isn't it? I worked for a charity for four years and it never once occurred to me to try and come up with any fundraising ideas because that wasn't my job. I was all about the paperwork. Now I think I might have missed my calling!'

'It's not too late,' I remind her.

'I know!' she gives me a radiant smile. 'The Dyspraxia Foundation aren't going to know what's hit them when I get back!'

'Then you're staying with them?' My heart boings with joy.

'I'll leave when I feel I've really achieved

something,' Zoë tells me, looking uncharacteristically virtuous. 'I haven't given them all I have to give yet.'

'Oh, Zoë,' I cheer.

'Don't, I'll cry and we've got a special guest of honour coming, I don't want to mess up my make-up!'

'Not Eddie Powers?' I gawk.

'Noooo!' Zoë tuts. 'Although maybe I should've got him along to do a tune – he could have sung *Wild Thing* every time someone made a donation . . .'

'It should really be Tom Jones singing *What's New Pussycat?*' I joke.

'Or better yet, the Stray Cats!' Zoë counters.

'What about the Super Furry Animals?' I hoot.

Zoë's creativity is contagious. Maybe if I brainstorm long enough I'll come up with a solution for the B&B. Just a few hours to go before I have to call Mum. I am *so* in denial.

'Zoë! Can you find Ty and get him to turn on the floodlights – people are starting to arrive!' Sasha swirls past, again at 100m.p.h.

'What can I do?' I grab Zoë before she tears off.

'See if you can get any of the guests to adopt a cat – they'd get full visitation rights and get to feed them the food that they purchase!'

'Will do!'

'Get Helen to help you!' Zoë calls back.

I take a moment to get my head around the evening's event. It's a much bigger deal than I imagined. I think I was just expecting a handful of potential sponsors, like Carrie's contacts from San Francisco –

492

apparently they're here somewhere . . . Carrie herself is over at the makeshift photo booth setting up the backdrop so people can get a Polaroid with Theo or Maxine in return for a $10 donation. I'm definitely getting one of those myself. Maybe I'll get it framed and label it 'The California *Cub*'! I sigh. I wish I could feel I'd made more of a contribution. Still the night is young and judging by the people streaming through the gates there's a good many guests to accost. I'll get a donation out of them even if I have to pick their pockets.

In amongst the strangers I recognize the odd face – particularly odd in the case of the neighbours from Zoë's building in Korea Town. Then there's Todd and Betty from the diner, Sunset sheathed in tiger-striped sequins and – my heart does a quick loop-the-loop – Joel.

'Lara,' he purrs. 'How's my little sex kitten?'

'I'm fabulous!' I'm surprised to hear myself say. I could have sworn I was miserable.

'Nice outfit!' He eyes the pair of pawprints *faux*-tattooed just above my cleavage in homage to rapper Eve.

'You like?' I peer down at them. 'I used real tiger paws to make the print.'

'Oh really? How about we use my real hands on your—' He goes to grab my bum.

'Joel!' I stop him with a hearty shove.

He grabs me into a hug. 'So tell me, did the cat get the cream?'

My face falls. 'If you mean Elliot, no, she didn't.'

He heaves a dissatisfied sigh. 'That's no good. I'm going to have to have a word. Where is he?'

'No idea. Nobody knows.'

'Really? I can't believe I was wrong about him – about the two of you. I'm never wrong—'

'Joel!' Three waxy-faced guys with baseball hats, beards and beer bellies bowl up. Judging from the assortment of movie logos they're sporting they're Hollywood bigshots. (Just as well they're wearing the logos or the diner starlets wouldn't know to fawn over them.)

'These are my friends,' Joel seems to be using inverted commas around the word friends. I suspect he means: These are the richest guys I know.

I shake hands with them all. One of them says, 'Nice tats!'

I force a smile. 'The bar is over to the right,' I usher them through.

'Sorry about that,' says Joel, hanging back. 'I'm gonna see if I can get them to part with some major moolah – you don't happen to have a casino hidden out back, do you?'

'Sorry,' I shake my head. 'But I'd be more than willing to mug them a bit later . . .'

'I'll bear that in mind,' Joel winks.

Gosh it's good to see him. Every time we part I think it's going to be for the last time. And every time it's not just feels such a bonus.

There's a small cough in my ear. 'Ms Russell?'

I recognize that Russian rumble – Boris!

'Hello, honey!' he greets me with raised arms as if

about to do a jig. 'Please, I want you to meet my daughter Natasha . . .'

'Hello,' I smile at the striking woman beside him. 'Thank you so much for coming.'

She smiles warmly back. 'I am so pleased to be here!'

'And this is little Cory, my grandson.'

'Are you Zoë?' he gawps up at me.

'No, I'm her friend Lara,' I tell him. 'Do you want to say hello to her?' I beckon Zoë over: she's looking kid-friendly as ever with a bottle of beer in each hand.

'Are you Cory?' she asks, homing straight in on him.

He nods back wide-eyed, instantly as smitten at his grandfather.

'So you two are brothers, right?' she teases, pointing between Cory and Boris.

'Noooooo!' he gurgles.

'Oh! So you must be his dad!' Zoë addresses Cory.

'Noooo! I'm his grandson!' Cory asserts.

'Ohhh! My mistake. You look very grown up for your age, how old are you again?'

'Seven!' he states proudly.

'Same age as me!' Zoë whoops.

'No you're not!' Cory protests, twisting around in delight.

'OK, maybe I'm a little bit older but not much. Do you wanna get your picture taken with a tiger cub?'

Cory looks to Boris for approval.

'Of course. Yes! Yes!' Boris encourages him.

'Where is it?' Cory claps excitedly.

'Over here. Shall I lead the way?'

'Will you get one too?' Cory needs to know.

495

'I will if you'll be in it with me,' Zoë tells him. 'I'm a bit scared of tigers. Are you?'

'Don't be silly – they're just baby ones!' he reprimands her.

'Oh OK. If you say it's going to be fine, I'll do it.'

'OK!' he chirrups.

An hour later Zoë returns, beaming. 'I'm in love with Cory!'

'I think the feeling's mutual!' I smile.

'He's got the best manners, that kid – how often can you say that these days?'

'Almost never,' I admit.

'And he's so smart. Boris said he's been asking a million questions about tigers and now he's got it all down pat, like a mini Rainman! Apparently he's like that about basketball – knows everything there is to know.' Zoë takes a swig of beer and looks contemplative. 'It breaks my heart that kids like that get ridiculed for being different.'

'Lucky he's got such a great family,' I note.

Zoë nods. 'Shame he's an only child – I know this boy back in England, William, he was diagnosed with dyspraxia really young and he has an older brother Alistair who must be twelve now and he's just so bright and reads and reads but at the same time has all this energy and you know what boys that age are normally like about having to hang out with their younger siblings, but not Alistair. He totally embraces William. Apparently his dad, who dotes on the pair of them, made an agreement with him – he'd

496

cut him some slack provided he watches out for William. And he does. You know that no matter what, he has William's back. No fuss, no complaints, it's just second nature to him because it's his brother.' Zoë's voice quavers. 'You should see them together!'

'I'd like to,' I say. I mean it. 'Zoë, we've got to see more of each other when we get back.'

'I was just thinking that!' she nods vigorously.

'How about once a month you come to me, once a month I come to you?' I suggest.

'Sounds great,' Zoë approves, then nudges me. 'Sister!'

I smile and hug her tight. We're back in each other's lives! Not that we were ever really gone but all the same, I wouldn't want to keep drifting as we had been – on the rare occasion we would meet up we'd spend all our time reminiscing. Now we have so much new stuff to discuss.

Suddenly I frown. 'I didn't realize Josh Hartnett had made any animal movies,' I muse over Zoë's shoulder as an extremely convincing lookalike loafs past.

'He hasn't. But as co-organizer I get a few perks,' Zoë winks.

'He's good, that guy – got the hair mussed up just right, same poetic purity in his eyes . . .'

'That's cos he's the real thing.'

I look at her.

'He's the guest of honour I mentioned.'

I blink in disbelief.

497

'Boris knew the make-up artist working with him on *Hollywood Homicide* – you know that Harrison Ford movie?' Zoë prompts.

'You're saying that's the real Josh Hartnett?' She's got to be kidding.

'*Yes!* Shola asked him along and he said, Why not! Thought it was a good cause.'

'You sound so blasé!' I reel. 'How come you're not dangling from his neck, trying to get him to do his amazing shy-boy smile?'

Zoë shrugs. 'He's cool but I prefer his lookalike . . .' On cue, she waves across at Josh number two, currently opening a bottle of beer with his teeth.

'His name's Chip,' she sighs as he gives an extended burp.

'Oh my God, he's like white trash Josh!' I gawp. 'You chose that doofus over the real thing?'

'He's too clever.'

'Who's too clever?' I bleat.

'The real Josh – too deep, too wise, old head on young shoulders – all that stuff.'

'Really?'

'If you spoke to him, you'd know what I mean. He's not got that "it's all about me" thing going that movie stars are supposed to have. He's all questing and thoughtful and was talking about writers I've never heard of.'

'And that's a bad thing?'

'It is for me. It makes me feel unread and unworthy. I mean I like a doofus but I don't want to be one!'

I burst out laughing. 'Zoë you're crazy!'

'It's all about what's right for you, not what everybody else wants,' she asserts.

'How much have you had to drink?'

'Not enough! Watch this – Honey, can you open a beer for me?' she calls over to Chip.

I can't bear to watch. I go in search of Sasha.

'I can't believe no one has adopted Ryan,' she sighs, leaning against my favourite guy's cage.

'You're kidding? I thought he'd be the number one choice – he's a liger after all!' I look at Ryan with ever-loving respect – he's so regal and yet so magnificently moth-eaten, like a once moneyed lord fallen on hard times.

'Maybe because I made him a star attraction people assume he's already snapped up.'

'Oh no!' I wail. 'Listen if I do have to sell the B&B he'll be my first beneficiary.'

'It's OK, I mean the main thing at this point is raising enough money for Paradise Park. He can be my next project.'

'Next?' I query. As of tonight, Sasha doesn't officially work at Tiger Tiger any more.

'I think I'm going to hang out for a bit, you know, after our week in San Diego. There's nothing for me to hurry back to.'

'And everything to stay for,' I smile.

Sasha nods, then looks earnestly at me: 'So it's still up in the air is it, the B&B?'

'I'm just waiting for a small miracle to occur – any minute now!' I look around, searching for a sign. 'Hey, isn't that the director from the Hotel Del?' I'd recognize those fleshy lobes anywhere.

'Yes it is,' Sasha confirms with a wince.

He's currently being crowded by lookalikes Val Kilmer and Michael Douglas (*The Ghost & The Darkness*) but his eyes are straying to a statuesque blonde in a rabbit-skin bikini.

'I don't know why I bothered, he hasn't contributed a penny,' Sasha grumbles.

'Not yet,' I decide. 'Try charging him $1,000 for Sheena Queen of the Jungle's phone number – that should work!'

'Good idea.' Sasha takes me at my word.

I chuckle. There is no stopping that woman now. How nice that I'll have two best friends to visit when I next come to California. Three, if you count Joel . . .

'You're not going to believe what he just did!' Zoë comes romping up to me.

'Who?'

'Joel!' she shrieks. 'He told me he was writing out a cheque for $10,000 just to make his buddies cough up and then when I went to tot up the box of donations his cheque was in there along with all the others! Can you believe that guy?' Zoë skips on her way.

I look over to where he's chatting easily to Todd and Tarzan's Jane. I never cease to be amazed how beautifully he has fitted into my life. Well, my Californian life, anyway . . .

Catching me looking at him, he smiles and excuses himself, holding my gaze as he saunters over.

'What are you up to, minx?' he asks, chipping my chin with his finger.

'Nothing!' I grin. 'Just feeling grateful for knowing you.'

'I'm grateful I got to know you too.'

I replay his words in my head then ask, 'Do I detect an element of finality in that sentence?'

He bites his lip then nods. 'I'm doing it! I know it sounds kind of extreme but I always wanted to go climbing in the Himalayas.'

'My God, Joel!' I gasp.

'Well,' he shrugs, peering at me through his blue-black lashes. 'I've seen all you guys chasing down your dreams and I've decided to go after mine.'

'Does that mean you're giving up your job and everything here?'

'For now. I've kinda done LA.' He takes a breath. 'The way I see it is I can keep climbing the same mountains or I can try something new.'

'Wow. Well if you ever get sick of going upwards you can visit me in Brighton – we've got a famous crevasse called Devil's Dyke you could drop down into.' As soon as I've said it I realize it's all wrong. 'But then you're really more of an "up" guy, aren't you?'

He laughs. 'I guess so.'

'Joel?'

'Yes?'

'I just want to say thank you . . .' I say softly.

'For what?' He tilts his head.

Can he really not know?

'All you've shown me, all you've shared.' A smile plays on my lips. 'Not to mention . . .'

'Aha!' He grins. 'That was fun.'

'You've got a magic touch!' I laugh.

'Not everyone brings out the best in me like you do.' He sounds serious.

'Really?'

'Really. I like myself when I'm with you. I can't always say that.'

I'm touched. It's nice to think that maybe I gave a little something back after all the good he gave me.

'Are you going to visit us at the Beach House?'

He shakes his head. 'I leave tomorrow.'

'God! I don't want to say goodbye to you!' I heave a sigh.

'Then don't. Just say good luck, and I'll say the same to you.'

He leans forward and kisses me on the forehead, letting his lips rest there for a full minute. It's strange but if I never see him again I'll still feel that we had a complete experience with each other. That doesn't stop the first tear streaking my cheek, however. I reach out and pull myself into his chest one last time, letting a little run of tears sink into his shirt. River deep, mountain high. That's how I'll always think of Joel. To the max!

I listen a while to the soothing beat of his heart then slowly release my grasp. Keeping my eyes tightly closed, I count to a hundred. When I open them again he's gone.

38

The party is over. It's time to wend our way to what will be our home for the next week.

I find Sasha lying in a contented heap on Ty's chest. In turn she has a conked-out Theo nestled in the crook of her arm.

I kneel down beside her and whisper so as not to disturb her new family. 'Are you coming?'

She lifts her head and looks imploringly at me. 'Would you mind if I stayed? There's so much to clear up and I just want to revel in it all a bit longer.'

'No rush, come tomorrow when you're ready.' I lean over and kiss her forehead, then Ty's, then rumple Theo goodbye.

Sasha pulls me back. 'Zoë's going with you, isn't she?'

'I'm just going to get her now,' I tell her.

Last time I saw her she was snogging Joshalike over by the cubs' paddling pool. Ah yes. They're still at it.

I cough a little as I approach.

They continue oblivious.

I cough more. In the direct vicinity of Zoë's ear. She looks up, practically cross-eyed with lust.

'Huh?'

'Ready to make a move?' I ask her.

She looks uncertain

'You can bring him,' I suggest.

'She's coming back to mine,' Joshalike croaks.

'He's got an audition at 8 a.m. tomorrow morning – it makes more sense—'

'OK!' I concede. 'I'll see you later.'

'You'll be with Sasha?' Zoë checks.

'Actually she's staying, but obviously Helen's going back so—'

'Give us a hug!' Zoë reaches for my hand.

I lean over and embrace her, inadvertently inhaling Joshalike. He smells divine. Little wonder she feels compelled to go with him.

'You two be good!' I pull away, quickly refilling my nostrils for the road.

'I'm always good!' Zoë winks.

God, they're dropping like flies. At this rate it's just going to be me and the ghost of Kate Morgan.

Helen and Reuben, however, are already in the carpark, raring to go.

'Lara!' Helen beckons me over. 'We just heard there's this great break going off in Mexico, if we drive down there now we should make it by sunrise.'

'Do you wanna come with us?' Reuben asks.

'Um,' I hesitate, not quite sure what to say.

'Don't be silly – they're all gagging to get to the Beach House,' Helen dismisses his invitation on my behalf.

'Yeah!' I *faux*-cheer.

'I bet Elliot'll be there waiting when you get there.'

I look up. I can't believe I'm still hoping. 'Do you really think so?'

'Where else is he going to go?' Helen reasons.

Not quite the romantic encouragement I was hoping for.

'You don't think it's weird that he didn't show up here?' I worry.

'Not really, none of us expected the party to go on so long,' Helen shrugs. 'I told him before that we'd probably be back in San Diego by 10 p.m.'

I look at my watch. It's now 2 a.m.

'We should get going,' Reuben says and places a hand on Helen's back.

She leans forward and gives me a big hug. 'I'll be back by lunchtime tomorrow. Make sure Zoë doesn't trash the place!'

Even after they're gone, I continue to stand there in the carpark. Just me and a million stars.

I feel oddly peaceful. Everyone has gone their own way, once again. Maybe this is how it's meant to be. Maybe I'm supposed to be alone. Maybe it's my turn to have some time to think.

I reach for the car keys and walk over to my latest rental. My only regret is that Helen has put the idea in my head that Elliot might be there. Waiting for me. I added that last bit myself. Why? Why am I setting myself up for another fall? Why do I keep hoping? What would it take to get me to let go? Maybe this is the closure I need. The final kick in the teeth. I surely can't take any more than this. If he's not there, that's well and truly it. There'll never be another night like tonight.

Once I'm on the road, the strange sense of calmness returns to me. I think it's the surrealness of driving on near-empty roads at night – I can't see further than the tarmac lit by my headlamps – I could be anywhere. For nearly two hours there's no voices, no music, just the hum of the engine.

Then comes the Coronado Bay Bridge, suspending me high in the darkness between two sets of sparkling city lights. I get tingles and I have to concentrate to steady my breathing. I'm nearly there.

Gold lightbulbs trail an outline of the hotel's turrets, luring me closer, into the carpark. There's a space for me right beside the bungalow. The key is in my hand. I approach the pergola-gate. And then I stop. I can't do it. I can't stop wanting. If he's not there, I don't know if I can take it. And if he is and he doesn't want me . . . As long as I stand here it could still happen. I'm staying here.

For five full minutes I stand perfectly still, paralysed by my fears. Then I swallow and force out a breath. *You can take it*. I tell myself. *You're stronger than you think. Whatever happens, you will survive*.

I reach out and slowly insert the key in the slot. The light flicks to green and there's a click as the latch is released. I pull open the gate and move towards the front door. Again the key. Green light. Go. I gently push down the handle and enter.

There's one low lamp on and the TV is playing its

welcome music. No obvious signs of life. No jackets on chairbacks, no scuffed-off shoes, no minibar empties or room service trollies. I slide my hand along the pine of the dining room table and walk into the lounge area. I was expecting soft powderpuff pinks but the décor is more sunny country cottage in feel. All of the bright floral sofa cushions are plumped and indent-free so I move slowly into the first bedroom, almost as if I'm trying to leave no trace myself. Two quilted beds. Unscrumpled. I try the next. The master bedroom. Empty. The bathroom. Empty. The walk-in wardrobe – what am I doing? I'm going to be checking the cutlery drawer next. He's not here. I catch the sinking feeling before it hits my knees, hauling it up, up over my head and then casting it aside. It's just me and it's OK.

Returning to the lounge I fold back the louvred panels of the patio door and step out on to the decking. There's a cool breeze from the sea but it feels good. Reviving. I walk down into the neat garden area and find myself drawn to the canvas hammock. There's a blanket draped over it, and I use it to cocoon myself snugly into place. Normally I'd cry now. Or pace wildly. But I think of Kate Morgan and how the waiting and disappointment led to her death. Then I think of Marilyn. You could say she too died for love. How many cautionary tales do I need?

I wonder what those women would do if they got a second chance, a new beginning? I know what I want. The B&B – something I can put my heart and soul into. Some way I can welcome new people into my life. Somewhere for old friends to gather.

But there's still the problem of the money. Not something that most of the guests at this Beach House would be caught saying. $2,300 a night, I coo to myself. Still, if there were six of you sharing . . .

Suddenly I sit bolt upright which, let me tell you, in a hammock is no mean feat. Six sharing – six rooms at the B&B. What if I took the idea of adopting a tiger and applied it to the B&B – six sponsors, one room each. I could go to my clients, they're all pretty wealthy. Give them a choice of room, consult them on the design, make them feel it's their own. But how would we tie the looks together? We'd need a theme. Oh my God! Ideas start rushing through my brain so fast they create a mental twister. I throw myself out of the hammock and scramble up the stairs. Paper! Pen! There's got to be – I yank at the drawers and find headed notepaper. I can't write fast enough for my thoughts – six rooms, one for each of my friends, one for me . . . I said I wanted a memory with each of them to last a lifetime. Now I've had the adventures, here's my chance to immortalize them:

Room 1: Elliot/Yosemite. I'd create a mountain hideaway with a log bed and real fire with heaped cushions and rugs (but definitely no bearskins) on the floor and a blue-black ceiling studded with twinkles so that it would be like sleeping under the stars at night. I'd do the bathroom with Native American tiling as a tribute to the Ahwahneechee and instead of room service we'd offer special bedroom picnics.

I grab the next sheet of paper. *Room 2*. Elise. Well, she was part of the experience and there's nothing wrong with a bit of spiritual enlightenment. I could go Bollywood with gold shrines and hot pinks or what about hues of Buddhist orange? No, I know – pure white: white floors, walls, bedspreads . . . with tranquillity candles and fresh orchids and in the bathroom a Jacuzzi surrounded by inspirational thoughts like *Learn to listen – opportunity sometimes knocks very softly* stencilled in silver on the walls.

Room 3. Helen. Surf's Up! Blue walls with a glittering wave motif, surfboard as a bedhead, fishtank running the length of the bath and a tube of complimentary sunblock on the sink. As the *pièce de la résistance*, I'd swap the wrought iron table and chairs currently on the balcony for a free-standing hammock, like the one I was just cocooned in!

This is too exciting. I want to squeal and ring my mum but there's still three to go.

Room 4. Zoë: this would have to be the suite, done up in full 1930s Hollywood glamour – pinks and silvers and fanned art deco mirrors. Ruched satin on the wall heading the bed, carpet you sink knee deep into, movie star portraits in the bathroom and vintage perfume bottles on the dresser. DVD player with a stack of black & white classics. Glass of champagne on arrival and maybe even a personalized mini Oscar statuette as a memento on departure? (And the award for our Best Guest goes to . . .)

Room 5. Sasha. Obviously animal print but to avoid looking too Bet Lynch on Safari I'd do the walls in an enlarged print – hand-painted leopard rosettes the size of my hand on two and then big broad tiger stripes

509

on the opposing walls. That would give it a more contemporary feel. I'd frame a huge blown-up photograph of my favourite liger and drape muslin around the four-poster like Sasha had at Shambala. And instead of leaving a single chocolate on the pillow I'd put a whole Lion Bar! Then it hits me – what if half the profits from the room went to adopting Ryan? My feet do a little tap-dance under the table.

One more – my room. I think of all my travels. What would best represent that? I know – the Road Trip Room! Set a kingsize mattress in an old Cadillac and you're away! Imagine having a real milometer on the bed?! The minibar would be stocked with root beer and Dr Pepper and crisps and jelly beans and all the classic junk food you eat while cruising. I could even do the bathroom as a retro gas station with old Americana tin signs and a showerhead on the end of the gas pump! Mr & Mrs Madonna would be proud of me!

I take a deep breath and a fresh sheet of paper.

And the name of the place . . . I'm shaking – THE HOTEL CALIFORNIA!

'Bloody brilliant!' I hoot out loud.

In response I hear a skidding-squeak followed by a splash. I look over at the sink in the kitchen area. Not a drip.

Strange.

Then I notice the music centre and stack of CDs in the corner. I feel like dancing! Philharmonic – no, chillout – no . . . Fantastic – they've got Pink!

'*Get This Party Started*!' I sing along, and then swing

510

round to find a man staring at me. He's wearing just a towel and a bewildered look. And he's very wet.

I leap back.

'Elliot! Where did you come from?'

'Bathroom,' he states the obvious.

'But!' I look behind me – I already looked in there.

'There's two,' he replies groggily. 'I must have fallen asleep in the tub – what time is it?'

'Four a.m.,' I tell him, trying not to stare at the trickles of water working their way down his bare chest.

'No wonder the water was so cold,' he shudders. 'Jeez I must have been in there hours!' He rubs his arms, then pulls a face. 'Which would explain why I have the skin of a seventy-two-year-old man.'

I stifle a smile.

'Where are the others?'

'They'll be here tomorrow,' I tell him. 'Tonight it's just me.'

My last four words create a strange tension in the room.

Daring myself to break it, I say: 'We heard about Elise . . .'

'Isn't it great?' He looks genuinely happy. 'That was a truly fortuitous sequence of events!'

'Was it?'

'Well, not all of it, obviously.' He looks regretful. 'I came back for you and you were gone.'

I shrug carelessly. 'So what happened?' I need to know.

Elliot sighs, seemingly taking a moment to decide

where to begin. 'She told me at the Madonna Inn that she'd met this great minister and she wanted me to meet him before I went back to Yosemite.'

'So you were visiting her, not me?'

'Not at all. I came to see you, to apologize and—' he stops.

'Yes?'

'Let me just explain about Elise first, so you understand.'

I nod for him to continue, holding myself in check.

'I don't know if Helen told you but our original plan was actually to get hitched out here.'

I shake my head. I did not know that. But I know one thing – the Secret Service needs to recruit Helen ASAP.

'That's why it was pressing down on my head so much. Helen had already helped us sort the paperwork so we were all legal and ready to go.'

'And you were going to get married without any of us there?' I still can't believe it.

'No, it was always going to be at the end of the second week – a kind of grand finale to the trip – but I started to have doubts, as you know, and meanwhile Martha's encouraging Elise to confront her past.'

I can't help but smile at this: good ole Martha.

'She held off contacting Andrew until that very last day and then persuaded him to stick around to meet me because she wanted his blessing. I came to see you, she pounced –' Elliot winces. 'But as soon as I saw them together . . . there was no mistaking it, it was meant to be.'

'And you told her that?'

'Yup.'

'What did she say?'

'She just broke down and cried – hard to believe, I know,' Elliot shrugs. 'Elise never cries.'

'No, I believe you,' I say under my breath.

'She was at it for a good hour. I guess she'd been keeping a lot in. Once she knew she was free from me and there were no recriminations they couldn't wait another second to be together. It was just approaching midnight and it seemed kind of romantic, I suppose – they decided to get married right there and then.'

'In front of you?'

'She said they would never have got back together if it hadn't been for me and she asked me to give her away.'

'You're kidding?'

'No! Actually it felt good – knowing she was going to a good home and, er,' Elliot gives a wry smile, 'being certain that she was gone.'

I raise an eyebrow.

'She was a piece of work, wasn't she?' he asks.

'Yes she was,' I understate.

Elliot suddenly looks serious. 'When I found you'd gone, I felt like I'd lost you. Really lost you. I tried to imagine how I'd feel if I never saw you again because right then I felt I didn't deserve to. But I couldn't bear it.' His voice quavers and he hangs his head.

'Why didn't you come to the fundraiser?' If he wanted to see me so much . . .

'Honestly? I couldn't face seeing you with Joel.'

'Really?'

Elliot nods, looking thwarted. 'I can't explain the effect that guy has on me. It's like Superman and Kryptonite – I just become this cowed, weak onlooker when he's around. And the more foolishly I behave, the brighter he glows.'

'But deep down you're Superman?' I tease.

'OK, bad analogy,' Elliot cringes. 'If anything I should be the green thing – I mean it, I've never experienced jealousy like that, *ever*! I felt sick to my stomach every time he touched you.' Elliot swallows hard, as if the memory alone is making him nauseous. 'I was desperate to see you, to explain everything, but I couldn't risk messing up again like I did at the Madonna Inn.'

Now it's as if Elliot experiences a chill. 'Where is he, by the way?' His eyes are scanning for a giveaway trace of Joel.

'Gone,' I say simply.

'Gone gone?'

I nod.

Elliot begins with a smile that almost instantly becomes a grin. 'I don't mean to look so happy!' he apologizes, looking like he might do a back flip then twirl me round like a cheerleader's baton to celebrate. Instead he takes a tentative step towards me and though he doesn't actually brush the table, all my scribbled pages flurry to the floor. Almost as if a ghost swept them there.

'What's all this?' As he bends down to gather them up his towel separates at the thigh.

Why is every bit of him so irresistible to me? I want to go to him but I know I have to hold back a little longer.

'My future!' I hold my head high.

'The Hotel California . . .' he reads. 'Hey, I like it!'

I babble my plan to him, nineteen to the dozen. He looks impressed, nodding, and with his face brightening throughout the descriptions of what I'd do to the rooms.

'Are you still looking for a partner?' he asks when I'm done.

'Maybe.'

'Would you consider me?'

'Depends what you'd have to offer.'

'£45,000 for starters. If we need more we can remortgage and split the payments – equal partners.'

'That's just money,' I shrug. I want more.

'I could set up a great website for the hotel with 360-degree room tours and an interactive reservation system—'

'That's just technology,' I cut in.

Elliot thinks for a moment. 'I'd do all the late night check-ins?'

'Better . . .' I concede.

'And every Saturday night I'd create a different martini for you and serve it on the terrace at sunset.'

'Even in the rain?' I ask.

'Even in the rain,' he confirms. 'In fact rainwater may become a featured ingredient, along with a seaweed twist!'

I chuckle approval, remembering my snowflake

margarita, then steal some extra oxygen as he steps closer, his damp skin raised with goosebumps, his soapy-clean smell surrounding me.

'Give me the deal clincher!' I challenge him.

He takes my hands and looks me directly in the eyes. 'Lara, I swear, every day I will find a new way to love you more.'

My eyes sheen with tears.

'I can't breathe without you.' He leans in and sighs into my hair.

As I go weak he clasps me to him and his mouth merges with mine – warm to wet, soft to strong – then he pulls away and explores my eyes with his.

'Lara, do you love me?'

I can't believe he needs to ask.

'I've told you so every single day since I met you,' I smile. 'Just not out loud.'

'Tell me now,' he urges.

Ten years I've waited for this moment, dreamed of it.

'Elliot,' I say his name, loving that I can say it in the way I've always wanted to. 'Elliot, I love you!'

My heart has a fiesta with streamers, whistles and glitter bombs – the works! I said it!

'I love you!' I say again, laughing at how good it feels.

'I love you, Lara! Truly.' He says it to me, caressing my face. 'I always have. I just needed The California Club to show me that.'

I start to tell him that it was all just a fantasy but then change my mind – turns out I got my wish after all.

'Helen's right,' I sigh. 'There is magic in the air here.'

Suddenly the lights flicker and fizz until the only illumination comes from the moon. Elliot's arms close tighter around me. And then, though I have both hands entwined in his damp hair, his towel tugs loose and falls to the floor.

'What the—?' he laughs.

I smile as my hands slip down each silk-covered nugget of his spine, down to the muscular curve of his beautiful bottom. Sneaking a look around me I whisper to Marilyn and Kate Morgan: *Thanks, girls – I think I've got it from here . . .*

Win a fly-drive holiday to California!

with ebookers.com

ebookers.com is offering one lucky reader the chance
to win a fantastic fly-drive holiday to California.

There can be few places in the world as suited to a fly-drive as West Coast
America. Choose between arrivals in either Los Angeles or San Francisco
and then plan your route accordingly. Whichever option you choose, you'll
have the freedom to see exactly what you want, when you want. Jump into
your car and explore one of Americas most varied, sun-drenched regions
– California really is the epitome of the American Dream.
The prize includes 2 x return flights with British Airways into Los Angeles
or San Francisco, 7 days 2 door economy fully inclusive car hire.

To enter, answer the questions, complete the tie-breaker in no more than 15 words.
Complete this entry form and send to California Club Competition, c/o Marketing
Dept, 32 Haymarket, London, SW1Y 4TP. Closing date 30 November 2003.
QUESTIONS:

1. Who does Sasha cut her hair for? _____

2. When Zoe dresses up as Marylin Monroe, who is Lara transformed into?

Tiebreaker: (complete in no more than 15 words) *My California Club dream would be...*

_____

_____

Name _____

Address _____

_____

Daytime contact No _____ E-mail address _____